Innocence Lo[st]

The Spirit Callers [Series]

By

OJ Lowe

Text copyright © 2018 OJ Lowe

All Rights Reserved

The events and characters depicted within this book are all works of fiction. Any similarity between any person living or dead is coincidental.

First Published 2018 as Innocence Lost.

Contents.

Contents..3
Chapter One. The Wedding of Meredith Coppinger...............5
Chapter Two. Vazara is Burning. 20
Chapter Three. The Reformation. 34
Chapter Four. The Recruits. 48
Chapter Five. The Mission..62
Chapter Six. Sore Points. 75
Chapter Seven. Back to the Battlefields.........................88
Chapter Eight. Scorpions and Sand. 102
Chapter Nine. Doors Not Closed. 116
Chapter Ten. Process of Elimination. 132
Chapter Eleven. Rocastle's Secret...............................146
Chapter Twelve. Creating the Unstoppable.....................160
Chapter Thirteen. Into the Green. 173
Chapter Fourteen. The Harshest Lesson. 193
Chapter Fifteen. Running Blind. 213
Chapter Sixteen. The Trove.....................................226
Chapter Seventeen. A Prelude to a Hunt........................240
Chapter Eighteen. The River Runs Deep. 259
Chapter Nineteen. Campfire Tales...............................271
Chapter Twenty. Last Rites. 283
Chapter Twenty-One. Jungles and Dragons.....................294
Chapter Twenty-Two. King of the Plants. 307
Chapter Twenty-Three. Cradle to the Grave....................323
Chapter Twenty-Four. Shock Above the Sands.................337

A Note from the Author..350
Also, by the Author. 351
About the Author. 352

Chapter One. The Wedding of Meredith Coppinger.

"I understand, Agent Caldwell, that you do not wish to be a part of this raid. I really do. I understand that it doesn't sit right with you that we are going to disturb your nieces wedding. I also understand that we have a chance to capture Coppinger here and now. We cannot turn that down. And although you might not be there, a familiar face might be good. It might help calm a tense situation. You have the interests of all parties at heart here. That makes you the perfect candidate to lead it."

Edict from Brendan King to Agent Connor Caldwell, aka Collison Coppinger ahead of raid on the Dupree/Coppinger wedding celebration.

It should have been the happiest day of Meredith Coppinger's life. The day that she married the love of her life, the moment they declared their feelings for each other in front of friends and family, an elaborate ceremony to show their dedication to one another and their desire to spend their life together. That had been the plan.

There should not have been uniformed men and women with blasters currently breaking up her reception, forcing their guests to the wall to be searched. One of those men should not have been her Uncle Collison, big and beefy with the Unisco vest covering his ample midsection, a recognisable figure amidst the chaos. He'd been the one to approach her with the warrant, had slapped it into her chest without even a hint of decorum. He was lucky she hadn't tried to hit him with something. Lydia, her beloved, looked furious about the whole thing and had since stormed off, leaving just the two of them alone.

"My sincerest apologies," he said. "We're looking for your mother."

"And you thought she'd be here?" Meredith couldn't quite keep the contempt out of her voice.

"Her only daughter's wedding? It is the sort of crazy thing she'd do."

"My mother's not crazy!"

"She's responsible for the deaths of dozens of people. Minimum. She did it in front of the kingdoms for an ill-defined reason. She murdered Ronald Ritellia for Divines sake!"

"Nobody's going to miss him."

"Perhaps not, but there were plenty of people there who will be missed. People had families and your mother broke them up with what she did!"

"Hey, my mother wasn't the one who broke this family up though!" Anger rushed into her voice. "You're the one who left this family behind, Uncle Coll, didn't want to be a part of it. Or is it Connor now? I'm sorry, that never made much sense to me."

"It seemed like a good idea at the time." Collison rubbed the back of his head ruefully. "You look pretty, by the way Meredith. I'm sorry it had to be like this."

"You didn't go out of your way to stop it though, did you Unc?"

"Can't. Kingdoms come first." The level of arrogance in his voice was astonishing, the very idea that he'd picked Unisco over his own damn family made her want to puke over her radiant new wedding dress. "Your mother is the most wanted woman in the kingdoms right now. The sooner she's locked up, the better. Things can go back to normal when that happens."

"You didn't rush to get her locked up though, did you? How long were you enjoying her hospitality before you turned on her?"

"Oh, you have spoken to her then?" His voice was savage, he gripped the back of the chair, his knuckles going white. "It's not what you think, Meredith. You weren't there. You know nothing, niece!"

"I know more than you think! And don't call me niece! You lost that right long ago."

"Meredith…" He was struggling now, she could tell, her words had hurt him, but she could see the hurt was genuine, the regret held no fakery in it. "It's not like that at all. It's never been like that."

Her mother wasn't there. Not now. Though earlier in the day, she had made her presence felt, Meredith had been placing her veil over her face and there she'd been, stood towards the back of the room with Domis at her side. She'd long since gotten used to seeing him wherever her mother went. Small woman. Large shadow.

She turned, not quite able to hide her grin. Their relationship had never been terribly close. In truth, she'd gotten the impression that her mother didn't like her too much. If she looked closely, she could see the disappointment on her pointed features sometimes. It wasn't her fault that Claudia Coppinger had wanted an heir to take over the company rather than fulfil her own dreams and live her own life. Shouldn't she have been proud of her daughter regardless, rather than constantly make her feel like she was failing to live up to expectations? Meredith wondered if she was being hopelessly naïve, although if to want a mother's love was naïve, she didn't know what to think.

She'd come though, strode into the room like she owned it, took her daughter up into her arms and hugged her tight. Domis did his best not to acknowledge it, stayed staring impassively into space. He never showed much emotion where she was concerned. She got the feeling he didn't like her yet had too much respect for her mother to do much about it. Good. The help should know their place. She often felt like her mother let Domis have free reign and that wasn't right. It wasn't even like he made the place look pretty. Granted, he was good in a fight. There'd been an attempt on her mother's life some years earlier, the memories of what Domis had done to the assassin had never faded from memory. She hadn't let it.

She'd never actually seen a human being broken in two before and it was the sort of memory that stuck with you. The sort of thought that lingered deep in the recesses of the mind, threatened to spill out when least you expected it. Every time she saw him, she saw him with the assassin's neck in one hand, legs in the other. His weapon had dropped, he couldn't have fought back if he'd wanted to. Her mother certainly wasn't in any danger. In any sort of sense, there was no need for what had happened next. She could remember the look of concentration on Domis' face as his muscles tensed and the assassin's body went taut. Then the screams started, choked out through Domis' grasp but recognisable as sounds of pure terror. He hadn't let up; the sounds hadn't abated. Her mother hadn't even moved to stop him. Why would she though? Her mother didn't care. It had been a long time since she'd given anything close to resembling a fuck about anything that wasn't the company.

Every time she thought back to that memory, she wished she'd closed her eyes. It wouldn't have cut out the sound though. Wouldn't have silenced the sounds of a spinal cord being torn to pieces, tendons and ligaments snapping, joints splintered to pieces. She wished she'd stayed home that day. Too many regrets. There hadn't been many more trips out for a while after that, not while her mother had been engaged in a business war with Matthew Prince.

Meredith thought that'd surprise her mother if she knew her daughter knew that name. She'd always underestimated her. Never given her the credit. Maybe she thought her slow and stupid. A terrible view to have about your own offspring. Just because she wouldn't didn't mean that she couldn't. Maybe she was being naïve again but there was more to life than flogging some monolithic company that was too big to fail. She didn't want that to be her life. Never had. Never would.

Maybe with an attitude like this, it was a touch hypocritical for her to show up on what should be the happiest day of her life like nothing had ever gone wrong between them. Then again, what more could she expect? Expect nothing in this life, Meredith dear, and you'll never be disappointed. Life won't give you anything except a kicking when you're down and it's all about how you react. What sort of thing was that to say to a seven-year-old? Not one of her best memories and that was quite a competition to be found victorious in.

"Mother," she said as they broke apart from each other. Meredith Coppinger could count on the fingers of her left hand the number of times she'd called her mum 'mother' in her entire life. It felt like as good a time as any. She saw her mum raise an eyebrow in bemusement. She hadn't expected it. Amazingly, the smart comment hadn't come her way. Mum always thought she was cleverer than everyone else in the room. It was probably that sort of thinking that had led to her becoming the most wanted woman in the five kingdoms.

"Meredith." She could feel the eyes examining her, taking in every inch of her from her diamond-encrusted shoes, to her wedding dress, to the crystal bands that bound up her hair. All of this had been paid for before the troubles had started, thankfully. They couldn't take it away from her. Not now. "You look very nice."

She couldn't even fake the emotion. Couldn't do that for her own daughter on her wedding day. If she hadn't spent all that time on her makeup, she might have shed a tear. As it was, she closed it all away. Stared at her with cool detachment. Mum could do it. Meredith could as well. They weren't so different after all, as much as neither of them would ever want to admit it. Same DNA. Same basic molecular level. Older. Younger. Both stubborn as the hells.

"Thank you," she said. "I didn't think you'd come."

"Oh Merry." She hadn't called her that for years, she realised with a jolt of surprise. Not since she was a little girl. The moment she'd reached her tenth birthday, it had stopped. A lot of the affection had ceased then. Probably about the time when she'd realised her daughter wasn't ever going to be what she wanted her to be. "I wouldn't have missed this."

"Even though you don't like Lydia?"

"I've never said that I don't like Lydia."

You've never needed to, Meredith thought. It's been plain to see on your face. The look of disgust whenever she's close to me. You think I don't see it, but I do. I see more than you give me credit for, mum. You only see what you want to see, and you always have. It's been your failing for as long as I can remember.

Instead she smiled. "I didn't think you'd come though. Because of... Well, stuff."

There it was, that curl of the mouth, a flicker of dismay that she'd come to recognise more than a smile. A smile would be just too nice of a gesture.

"Oh that," she said, waved a hand dismissively. "Don't worry about that. It's all in order."

"Mum, you murdered a bunch of people. We saw you on the viewing screen!"

"Yes," she said. "And what's your point?"

What's your point? She wanted to scream, bit her tongue to keep it from crawling out. Not on what should be the happiest day of her life. Her mum wasn't going to ruin it. She wouldn't ruin it. She'd call Unisco herself first, get them out here to throw her in jail. Maybe they'd toss away the key. She deserved to rot away where the sun didn't shine.

It wasn't worth disturbing the wedding. Domis would almost certainly defend her to the death. Probably theirs. She didn't want another unsettling memory to add to the collection where her mother was concerned. Better just for her to leave as soon as possible. That'd satisfy everyone. Nobody needed die. Nobody needed disturb the proceedings. Things would be calm, it'd be a happy day and life would go on.

If I need to explain to you what my point is, you're not going to get it so why should I bother? The words were on her lips, she let them die away. She wouldn't waste her breath on the subject.

"Aren't you worried about what's going to happen if they find out you're here?" That was about as diplomatic as she could be. "You could be arrested, or killed…"

"Yes, yes, I'm aware and that'd ruin your day so no doubt you wouldn't want that to happen." Mean, callous humour filled her voice, never mind that it was true, she wondered if it had been that obvious what she'd been thinking. Mum always had been able to read her too well. She didn't like it, she'd tried to develop a better face for hiding it. Apparently, those efforts had been well wasted. Maybe Unisco would kill her and remove one massive problem from her life. She could live quite nicely off the credits left behind, well enough to forget the legacy of hate that would be left behind. "We might never see each other again after today, Meredith."

Good! Here's hoping. She set her face into a look she hoped came across sorrowful. She doubted it'd fool her for an instant, but she had to try and look sad, if nothing else. She owed that to herself.

Sometimes she wondered why she bothered making the effort. Part of her remembered the credits due to her on her mum's death. That was part of the reason. The other reason, she figured, was she didn't want to wind up like her. Cold. Emotionless. Cut off from those that she should love. A contrasting view, one that might have caused anyone to look at her with horror, but they'd never spent any amount of time with Claudia Coppinger and played her games. The one good thing all those deaths on Carcaradis Island would accomplish was telling the kingdoms that her mother was a bad woman, that she'd always been bad and now that evil had come to light. Vindication was the sweetest drug of them all. There'd been times, she'd wondered if it wasn't her mother, it was her. Was she the bad one? A disappointment of a daughter? The words themselves had never been uttered, but the expression on mum's face told no lies.

"I hope that isn't the case," she said. Voice neutral. Face neutral. Display absolutely no hint of emotion that will betray you. Domis still loomed. It wouldn't take a lot to imagine him grabbing her up by the throat, squeezing and squeezing until her bones crumbled into dust. That'd dampen the day. She could be flippant about it, she didn't feel that it was a true danger. Not now, not ever. Her mother might be capable of many things, but would she harm her own daughter? She found she didn't want to know the answer. Ignorance covered a lot of sins and they were right when they said it was bliss.

Mum's lips curled into a smirk. "Liar," she said. Meredith didn't blink. Let her think that she knew that. She was wrong in this instance. She very much did hope that she saw her mum again. Maybe when she went to trial. She'd be the first to volunteer a character statement against her. As her daughter, she felt her voice would ring the loudest in a courtroom.

"You're wrong," she said quietly. "Couldn't be more wrong."

As recent conversations between them went, this was one of the more civil ones, she found. How upsetting would that revelation be to someone who hadn't grown up with the relationship the two of them had shared?

"I'll let you believe that, but you're only fooling yourself, Meredith." She drew herself up to her full height, eye-level with Meredith. A poisonous smile replaced the smirk. There was nothing in the eyes that she recognised, no love or affection, just bitter contempt. "I always had so high hopes for you and here we are."

"I'd have thought you'd have been happy for me," she said. "I'm making my own path.

"On my credits. That's going now," her mother said. "Your inheritance, it took a bit of a hit when the Senate seized Reims. This wedding…" She threw out a dismissive hand. "It's the last thing you ever get from me. Sorry, sweetheart but this is the way it must be now. When I die, you get nothing."

The apology sounded hollow, triumphantly pleased in the echo of the dressing room, dangerous satisfaction in the words. It might have been the roar of blood in her ears, ripping through her veins like a magrail.

"I wouldn't say that," she said eventually. "I wouldn't say I get nothing. I'll definitely get something I always wanted when you die."

For the first time in ages, her mother looked curious by something she'd said. "And what's that, daughter mine?"

"I'll be free of you."

The look on her face was priceless, Claudia Coppinger wasn't a woman ever accustomed to looking like she'd been slapped. Some sights were worth waiting for. Hearing her shocked into silence was perhaps the greatest achievement of her life. Domis tensed up, a man ready to fight if ordered to. That single sight told her that maybe she'd overreached, taken it too far. She'd not known that was possible. Under normal circumstances, her mother had a composure of iron. Then again, these circumstances weren't normal. Not even close. Things had changed too much in recent days.

"You're an ungrateful little bitch!" There was the venom in her voice, the sort only reserved for special occasions. She'd heard it when her mother had forced her to work off her debts in the past, forced her to work fourteen-hour days in whatever pissing little jobs she could find at her company, anything to break her spirit, get her used to the monotonousness of a crappy life she'd never asked for and had never wanted. She'd wanted freedom, not a glorious prison cell. "After all I've done for you, after all I've turned a blind eye to... Hells, after all I've given you, this is how you repay me!"

"Scorn and contempt go a long way, Mum. It inevitably breeds threefold. You can only put so much in before you start to reap what you have sown. And you have sown so damn much over the years. You know why I went out and spent your credits like they were going out of fashion? I didn't have to be at home and talk to you! I can see why Uncle Coll walked out on the family because I don't want to live like this."

"Your uncle betrayed the family. He didn't believe. He sided with the enemy! He nearly killed me."

"And a shame he didn't succeed!" All of it was coming out now, years of anger and resentment leaking out. And with it came the tears billowing for her eyes, she knew she probably looked horrible for it, but she didn't care. This... The chance to tell her mum exactly what she thought of her was perhaps the best wedding present she could have asked for and one that she didn't expect to have fallen into her lap. Someone up there loved her. Mentally she thanked Gilgarus for the opportunity. "If Uncle Coll wanted to kill you, he probably had the right idea. I get the feeling things would have been better if he'd succeeded."

Her laugh was bitter with resentment. "Meredith, you're a silly little bitch. Things wouldn't have been better if your uncle had killed me. They would have stayed exactly the fucking same. Nothing would have changed. People with only the faintest hint of authority would have carried on telling us what to do with only a fleeting knowledge of the consequences of what they preach. I always tried to teach you that. Every action has a consequence. One day, you're going to regret what happened here."

"And one day, you're going to regret how you treated me my entire fucking life! I hope it's a really pointed way, like involving me having to make the choice to switch off your life support! I'm not sure what'll take up the other fifty-nine seconds I'd have to make that decision!"

"That hurts me." She didn't look very upset. Even now she was trying to go for the guilt, fondle switches that had grown rusty from a lack of turning. "Regret has a funny way of sneaking up on you. If that's the way you feel, then I'll leave. Enjoy your day."

"Don't let the door hit you on the way out." She turned back to her vanity, half expected to feel Domis grab her up. How long since anyone had spoken to Claudia Coppinger like that? She felt, well alive. Equal parts exhilarated and terrified, her entire body aflame with glee and shock. Had she just done that? Emancipated herself from her past? Set herself royally up for the future? She'd burned the bridges at long last. She'd never walk across them again, why not make sure she couldn't.

Part of the reason she always wondered if her mother hadn't liked Lydia was because of her irrational fixation on the idea that someone would only marry her for the credits. They loved each other. The proposal had been mutual. Lydia had always insisted the credits didn't matter. Wasn't like she was a pauper to start with. Lydia Dupree was a talented spirit dancer, not quite top bracket like a Selena Stanton wherever she may be or a Mia Arnholt or even a Harvey Rocastle, as much as a pariah as he was these days, but definitely the next level down. It was where they'd met, after all.

"There you have it, Uncle Coll," Meredith said. "She was here, but not now. I doubt I'll ever see her again. I hope I don't."

He surprised her at that point, reached out and hugged her tight. His vest felt scratchy against her face, the logo pressed against her cheek. "Sorry, Merry. I know you and Claudia always had a tricky relationship."

"You know the sun's quite hot as well, don't you? If we're making understatements about our relations with her."

Uncle Coll grinned at her, the sum total of the expression leading to more affection shown in four seconds than her mother had in the last fifteen years. "True, very true. I never was entirely happy with the idea of her bringing a child into the world. But, your mother, if nothing else always was quite stubborn."

"You keep making these understatements, Unc."

"I walked away from the family, because I didn't want to be sucked into it. I didn't want to be a cog in a giant machine, I wanted to be my own man. I always understood you felt the same way. She didn't like that, in part it's probably my fault as much as hers. Probably thought you'd make the same choices I did. I'm sorry for that."

He reached up to his earpiece. "Everyone, she's not here. Stand down. Make sure you make your apologies to the guests. This is a wedding after all." His attention was back on her. "I am very sorry about this, Merry. We got a tip she was here…"

Meredith snorted. "It was probably her that called it in, one final shot at me. She'd love doing this, a chance to disrupt my day."

Uncle Coll shrugged. "To that, I cannot comment. It's a very brave thing you did, finally standing up to your mother. If it took the threat of the credits being withdrawn to make you rise onto your own two feet, then we should have declared war on her long ago. Take it from me, Merry, credits aren't everything. Wealth brings its own problems, insolvency brings its own freedoms."

"I haven't told her yet," Meredith admitted. "Lydia. Unc, I just got married and became broke on the same day…"

"No different from most other weddings in my experience there." The grin on his face as he said it made her smile, despite the situation. "But I know what you mean, Merry. If she loves you, it'll not matter. If she was just marrying you for the credits, now's probably the best time to find out."

"You sound like my mother."

"Your mother's a very cynical woman. Unreasonably so sometimes whereas I like to believe the best in people and I want to tell you that every little thing is going to be okay." He hesitated, smiled at her. "I know I wasn't invited, but I'd like to meet her. I know we've not really had much to do with each other. Most of my encounters with you were when you're a child." She must have looked surprised at that for he smiled at her. "I walked away from the family business, I always wanted to keep in touch with your mother. She is my sister after all. I didn't agree with her having you, I think despite everything you're a sensible young woman. You know what you want, and you stuck to it.

You didn't get sucked into being what she wanted to be. Mothers being disappointed in daughters is the oldest story in the world. We're Coppingers, we took it to the next level naturally."

He tilted his head, fiddled with his earpiece. "Excuse me one moment." He toyed some more, authority filled his voice. "I said stand down and withdraw! I'll meet back up with you later, for my report. I'm going to interview the bride… What do you mean, which one? Coppinger's daughter, you wanker! Dupree's not important to the investigation!"

"Won't you get into trouble for this?" she asked. The comment didn't bother her. Ever since she'd come out, it hadn't been the worst thing ever said to her. She'd just always known that she'd liked girls. Never really had to think too hard about it. She knew what she liked, and she went for it. "Isn't it a dereliction of duty?"

Uncle Coll smiled at her. "At the moment, I'm in a pretty strong bargaining position. They're wanting me to build a psychological profile of your mother. Can't see them getting too upset with me. Besides, in their eyes this constitutes an interview."

"And in your eyes."

"It's a reunion with a niece I wish I'd gotten the chance to know more over the years. Merry, I know that I can't change the past, but if you or your new wife ever need anything, I want to tell you that you can come to me and I'll do my best to help you." He tapped the Unisco logo on his vest. "I've got some friends in high places as you can see. If she ever gets back in touch with you, give me a call. Wouldn't you like to be the one responsible for her arrest?"

It was on the tip of her lips to say she'd love to be the one responsible for her being killed resisting arrest. That might not have gone down too well. Whatever else she might be, her mother was still his sister. Interests had to be conflicted at the very least.

"Merry Coppinger, right?"

She looked up, heard the voice and was drawn to it. So alluringly musical, it hinted at a synchronicity of naughtiness and innocence. The face that the lips belonged to wasn't harsh to look at either, she could have stared at it all day. Given the chance, she might do, although drooling might not be the best thing this early on.

"Huh?"

Inwardly, she congratulated herself. Way to make a first impression, knobhead. Embarrass yourself in front of the stunner. Want to drool over yourself while you're at it.

"Sorry, is it Merry or Mary?"

She didn't compete under Meredith. Too formal. Only her mother called her that now. Everyone else. Merry. The name had stuck. Besides, it was unusual. Although this divine creature wasn't the first to ask her if it really was Mary. Lots of spirit dancers had unusual stage names. Merry wasn't so unusual.

"Merry on stage," she said, before giving her a smile she hoped was somewhat alluring. Not that she was holding out much hope. Not a chance a woman who looked like her was... Well, single for a start, never mind interested in her. "Meredith to, well, my mum." Why are you talking about your mother to her? She wanted to shake her own head, run off and curl up into a ball, moaning to herself at her complete failure at charm.

That spotlight behind her didn't help with the effect, lighting her profile up like she was a gift from the Divines. Brown-blonde hair cut short against caramel coloured skin, a nose so button like she wanted to feel it go through one of her holes, preferably while her tongue was going to work on the other one. Those lips looked so wicked, hinted at so much and she'd loved to have taken said hint.

"Let me guess," she said, unable to stop herself in time. "You're here to tempt me, aren't you?"

She cocked that wonderful face to the side, Meredith allowed herself that chance to break the gaze, inadvertently trailing her eyes down that body. Everything she knew she wanted to handle and more. A little moan escaped her, she felt her cheeks burning with embarrassment. Not a chance this vision hadn't noticed what she was doing. Whether she had, or she hadn't, she was too polite to mention it and for that Meredith was relieved. Maybe she hadn't noticed it. A girl could dream, right? Aspirations of not being completely humiliated in front of your newest crush were the sort of goals that always sounded attainable, yet she always came up so short on.

"Tempt you?" She sounded surprised. "Maybe you have me mixed for someone else."

"Dear Divines, there's someone else walking around who looks like you? And here I thought my legs were about to give way as it was." Shut up, shut up, shut up! You can't flirt to save your life. If her cheeks had burned before, they were scalding now. Someone somewhere was going to be able to cook eggs on her face. Felt like everyone else in the changing room was stopping to look at the two of them. They wanted to see her make a complete and utter arse of herself. She knew it was ridiculous. That was how it felt. There were too many people in here, all of them had better things to do than look at one of the newbies. They had their own problems to deal with.

Yet, as she brought herself to meet the vision's eyes, she could see more than a hint of red underneath them. Terrific. She wasn't only embarrassing herself, she was making the first person to give her a friendly word since she'd gotten here uncomfortable. A friendly face was hard to find in the world of spirit dancing, people were out for themselves. Most of them would stab you in the back for a few extra points from the judges.

"As much as I'd like to follow that up with a clever comment," she said, offering her a hand. "I'd have started by saying hello. Lydia Dupree."

Meredith shook the offered hand, tried to keep her face in some semblance of neutrality. If she kept her mouth shut as much as possible, she couldn't put a high heeled foot in it. Somewhere at the other end of the room, she could hear the fat man in the green jacket laughing like a probed hyaena. He was one of the favourites for the competition, her opponent in the first round and to say the confidence was leaking out of her with every passing second. He'd already fired the first verbal volley at her as she'd walked in, found a few weak spots and hammered away at her with delight.

"Hi, Lydia Dupree," she eventually managed. "What can I do for you? Other than make you feel massively uncomfortable?" Her foot was edging dangerously close to her mouth again. The sound of laughter slipping from her was a little reassuring. Good, make her laugh. She can't walk off in disgust if she's laughing like that. Divines, I hope that's joy.

"Just wanted to offer you something."

She was up on the edge of her seat immediately, she hadn't known her body could unconsciously react that quickly. "Yes?"

"Advice. Rocastle. Ignore him. If you let him get to you, you've already lost. He's the master of finding a tiny thread in your psyche and pulling it until you fall apart. His game only looks good because he has a habit of making his opponents crack under the mind-games." She smiled at her. She'd known then that she was in love. "In short. Ignore the giant bullying prick and give him a kick in the balls! Best thing you can do to deal with him."

"Thanks," she'd said. "I guess. But, why are you telling me this?" It seemed like a reasonable question to ask.

Lydia winked at her, she felt her legs threaten to give again, the warmth flooding through her.

"Well," she said, the smile only growing. "You're not the worst looking woman ever to walk in here. And we could all use a friendly voice in our corner sometimes. We come into this world alone, doesn't mean we have to walk through it that way."

"Do you ever regret it? Leaving the family and changing your name?"

He looked at her with bemusement, before slowly shaking his head. "Some things I regret. That I don't. Anyway, I never changed my name. Not officially. I just competed under the name Connor Caldwell. I didn't want to be associated with the name Coppinger on a professional level. I was always him, just when I stepped onto the battlefield, I wanted to be someone else for a while. Anyway, like anything, if people start to know you under a certain name, then that name sticks after a while. I mean, someone asked me why I started to affect a Southern Premesoir accent for a bit…"

"Didn't you spend a lot of time around there?"

"Hells, I always wanted to do that. Work down there, wrangle cows and bulls and other sort of livestock. Always thought it looked like a great life. You pick the accent up after a while. It was eye-opening. Loved every second of it. Eventually, I got picked up by a local Unisco recruiter, asked if I was interested."

"I bet Mum was surprised when you pulled the blaster on her and announced that."

Uncle Coll laughed. "Merry, if looks could kill, it's unlikely that I would be here talking to you. I graduated as a specialist in undercover operations and covert intelligence. Not an easy path. I was always okay at the hand-to-hand stuff, I mean after wrangling a one-tonne bull, what's someone who weighs a fraction of that realistically going to do to me? Never enjoyed the violent stuff though. When your mother got back in touch and showed me everything she'd done, my first instinct was to report everything immediately. I held back, not out of any great love that I had for her, but out of necessity. Revealing my hand early could have been disastrous."

She smiled at him. "Are you really allowed to tell me all this?" It wasn't what she'd wanted to hear, but she found it fascinating. "Isn't it classified."

"Merry, my dear, nothing about what your mother has done is going to remain classified for very long. If she wins, she'll be shouting her own version of history from the rooftops. If we win, the story will come out, so we can prove our own superiority. You might as well hear the truth before someone else decides what that means."

He held the door for her, she could see her bride across the other side of the room, Lydia never looked so beautiful as when she was angry and now she was furious.

"Besides, Mrs Dupree," Uncle Coll said with an almost fatherly grin. "I have a feeling you're not going to be wanting to play up your relationship with your mother for the times ahead. You made the right choice I feel there, taking her name."

"I didn't do it for that," Meredith said. "Despite what Mum always thought, I don't tailor my life to go out and spite her."

"She always was self-absorbed like that," Uncle Coll smiled. "Don't spend your life trying to please others, Merry Dupree. Make yourself happy and if it's meant to be, that happiness will extend to others."

"Merry Dupree, huh?" She tried it out in her mind, said it aloud and smiled at the thought. "Think I like that, Uncle Coll."

He gripped her hand as they approached her bride. Her new wife. The ceremony had been everything that she'd ever wanted, an extravaganza best described as the forte of the disgustingly wealthy. If you had it, you might as well flaunt it. That was the attitude of most spirit dancers she'd ever met, the sort that she wanted to be. The wealth wasn't hers, never had been and it never would be again. That thought might have been something that horrified her in the past, chilled her to the very bone at the idea of everything she'd ever known being cut away from her.

She didn't feel that way seeing Lydia's smile, everything felt like it was meant to be right. If she'd known a feeling like this existed before, she'd never experienced it. Elation was a natural wedding day experience, right?

Even the look Lydia gave Uncle Coll wasn't enough to sour it. Fury and beauty. Without one, the other could not flourish. They'd worn similar dresses, off-white cream with scarlet sashes from right shoulder to waist, the other shoulder bare, the skirts long and flowing, down to the ankles. To complement her dress, she'd added a white lace choker around her neck, thoughts already in her mind about what would be happening once they went upstairs to consummate their union.

"And what the hells do you want now?" Lydia asked, rounding on Uncle Coll. "Haven't you people done enough damn damage here already without disturbing us even more? Her bitch mother isn't here and…"

"Lyds," Meredith said, taking her hand. "This is my uncle, Collison. Just let him speak, please, babes."

"Mrs Dupree," Uncle Coll said. "My deepest congratulations on your nuptials here, my niece is a wonderful woman and I hope you'll both be very happy together." He clasped both hands in front of his chest, gave her an uneasy grin that he managed to make look roguish. "And I hope you can accept my deepest apologies on behalf of Unisco for what happened here today. Your new mother-in-law is a woman in deep demand, there are law enforcement agencies across the five kingdoms who would very much like to speak to her. We had a tip that she was here, and as distressing as that might have been for you, we had to respond to it. She's a dangerous woman and we believed very firmly that her presence would have been toxic for your happy day. We all have our duties in life."

He could speak well, she gave him that, and Lydia could too by the way she looked mollified. She cocked her head to the side with a smile before offering him a hand which he shook.

"Pleasant to meet you, Collison. I can't say that I'm happy about it, but I appreciate you've got your job to do. And I'm glad someone is at least looking for her."

"We'll find her, ma'am. Don't you worry about that."

Meredith had never seen Lydia grin so widely. "I'm not worried. I already found the only Coppinger I ever want to spend my life with."

Aww! Meredith blushed under her makeup, not caring if anyone noticed. Uncle Coll and Lydia were chatting, she'd offered him wine and he'd accepted. Already they were getting on better than her mother and Lydia ever had when they'd met. Things were looking up, the first day of the rest of her life. She meant to start it as she intended to continue. To love and to cherish. For better or for worse. For richer or poorer. This was who she was now. Meredith Adele Dupree. Wife of Lydia. Niece of Collison Coppinger.

Disowned daughter of a madwoman and a man she'd never known. Heir to whatever legacy her mother inflicted upon the five kingdoms, a burden she'd just have to bear. A new start, a rosy future.

What more had she ever wanted?

Chapter Two. Vazara is Burning.

"The conception of war always brings the birth of opportunists, of cheats, bad men, liars and cowards. Those who would grow up to furnish the fields of discontent. In a world where courage is rapidly becoming as scarce as diamonds, it takes a special kind of man to do what needs be done. As long as I draw breath from my body, Vazara will not fall. Not to the Vazaran Suns and not to Coppinger!"
Leonard Nwakili speaking on the evening of invasion.

Tripoli was on fire, the skies alight with the smell of smoke and thick with laser fire as fresh off-the-line Coppinger designed Razr aerofighters and Vazaran Sun Corsairs swept through their native sky, their weapons pummelling what little was left of the Vazaran navy with all their might. They'd been fighting through the night and most of the day, their numbers greater than Nwakili could have anticipated. His spies had failed him when he'd needed them the most. Even had his information been accurate, it wouldn't have been enough. Not even close. Most of their capital ships had been knocked out already, the remnants of one dreadnought still burning in the sand outside the city. Already the capital city had despatched drone fighters up into the fray to try and turn the tide, but it was too little too late. The small, man-sized figures might have had the manoeuvrability in conjunction with the heavier firepower that aerofighters might have offered but alone it would only be a matter of time until they were picked off one by one. Speed and agility meant little when heavily outnumbered.

Even with the aid of anti-aircraft blaster cannons, they wouldn't last much longer. The oncoming army tore through the cannons mounted throughout the city with all the savagery of fire ants through flesh, the deafening blasts silencing under a dozen simultaneously smaller ones, each gun dying in a blaze of scarlet fire. Still there were men on the ground but they couldn't help with the problems in the sky. Surface to air munitions were all but depleted, used up in the first waves of attack. The ground invasion would come soon, once large pockets of resistance had been knocked out by the forces in the air. Out in the distance, they were massing, ready to swarm. The moment their boots met the streets of his city, that would be the start of the end.

Nwakili watched on a monitor, his heart heavy with the force of anger and the tugging lull of regret. In truth, he couldn't pinpoint an exact moment when this had come to reality. He'd known it was coming, he'd prepared as best he could but by the same token he hadn't expected the resistance to them on their way north to Tripoli to be so… lacking. Perhaps his own fault. Perhaps he'd taken it for granted that all these rumours of his own people being welcoming to Coppinger ideals would be just that. Rumours. He didn't entirely believe her claim that she'd brought the Green to Vazara. Nor entirely was he convinced it was a natural phenomenon. Deserts didn't just become covered in fauna overnight. He'd been reliably informed that the ecosystem had been drastically altered. Indigenous Vazaran creatures who needed the heat and the dryness to survive were now struggling, most of his efforts before this war had come dangerously close to his home had been to ensure that as many of them were put into the proper habitats as possible. Some of these creatures were rare and beautiful, they wouldn't be around forever. He had a duty to preserve some of the great treasures of Vazara for the future generations.

Maybe that had been a mistake. She'd used that against him. Now that it rained every other day, people were no longer going thirsty. A long time ago, Coppinger had sat in this very palace and discussed with him the possibilities of water purifying planets in Vazara, building at least one per city. Because after all, she'd said, nobody should ever have to go without water, especially not in a kingdom like this. He'd granted her that permission, they were going into overdrive now, supplying free water to everyone who wanted it, she'd won their hearts through their stomachs. The crafty bitch. To say he was impressed at her cunning might be an understatement, he just wished he hadn't been the victim of it. Normally Nwakili didn't wish, he didn't like to dwell on what could have been.

Most of his navy was done for. When he'd heard they were coming, he'd gone to the Senate for help, demanding a five kingdoms task force to help protect his kingdom. They'd dragged their heels over a larger force, sending scant numbers as token gestures, ships and men that had been past their best years ago, men who had no interest in fighting for Vazara. Their efforts had been made, they'd fought gamely but they'd died very quickly. Perhaps that had been the start of the end for him. Those who he'd considered his allies hadn't even lifted their fat fingers to help him, instead choosing to ignore the problem he faced. Because, he could already imagine them saying, while the Coppinger is focused on Vazara, it gives us a chance to shore up the other four kingdoms, make sure she can't do the same there.

If he made it out of here alive, he would have to seriously consider where Vazara stood in relation to the Senate. Considering cessation of membership would be the only problem he'd truly like to have right now, rather than face the imminent death and destruction of everything he'd looked to build over his years as ruler of the kingdom. It put things into perspective, he knew that much.

He sat in the central room of his palace, the most fortified room available and continued to watch on the row of monitors, more and more of them losing their feed by the minute as videocams went down across the city. Soon he'd be completely blind from here. Still, he had plans. He wouldn't go down without a fight. Rumour had it that Coppinger had despatched one of her top lieutenants to help take the city and he intended to take the bastard with him. His own personal guard, the D'Han had already planned to ensure the first who entered the palace gained a swift and dangerous welcoming. The first through the door wouldn't live to enjoy the glory. Out on the streets, the ground battle was starting, his own forces were firing at the invaders, blaster rifles chattering, as they prepared to lay down their lives in the name of the one true Premier and it filled his heart with warmth that even despite the hopeless situation, they still believed in him.

The feeling didn't last long. As noble as their acts were, it was only a stopgap, a necessary sacrifice to ensure that they slowed up the enemy. They were prepared to give their lives, he was prepared to spend them to maximum effect, all in the name of granting the rest of the city enough time to prepare. Coppinger forces… He'd heard that some of them were clones from somewhere, that dossier had come out a long time ago, courtesy of his old contacts at Unisco. Terrence Arnholt, the director hadn't been in the best of shape recently and stuff was growing a little lax where the organisation was concerned. Brendan King, despite what he might have thought about himself, didn't have the chops for the role. He was too proud, too stiff necked and he lacked the diplomacy Arnholt could bring to any sort of discussion. He didn't inspire loyalty the way the stricken director did. Still rumours of Arnholt's recovery grew stronger every day. He'd been badly injured six months ago in that fiasco at Carcaradis Island. He really could have done with Unisco backup right now. All that time he'd devoted to serving them and this was how it ended. He'd liked to think that Arnholt would have moved to help him, even if others in the agency had not. Terrence damn Arnholt. One of the best men he'd ever known. If he'd had a glass, he'd have raised in memory of the man he was likely never to see again. Nwakili knew he wasn't getting out of this building alive.

Coppinger tanks were entering the city, hovering behemoths that skittered lazily above the surface of the streets, their high-powered weapons opening up on any moving target that caught their gunners' eye. The first one through the space where the city walls had been earlier received an explosive blast, shook it off and kept on coming. More rained down, covering the armour with fire and Nwakili grimaced angrily at the little effect it was having. That armour had to be thick.

He'd insisted on a rooftop contingent of explosives experts near each gate in the city, each of them bearing explosive launchers for this situation. No good, no avail. There probably wasn't enough firepower left in the entire city to deal with them all. And if they'd been banged up by the resistance on their way up north, it didn't show.

Ukara, Adedeji, Bala-Bala, Tomasberg, Nelkendi... All of these cities should have been between him and the invasion force, all of them should have had to have fallen before this happened. He idly wondered what had happened, communication with them had been lost a long time since. Knocked out by force? Or surrendered willingly? He didn't know, didn't want to either. If he'd been betrayed, at a time like this he'd prefer to be ignorant about it until it didn't matter one way or another. Nothing short of a miracle was going to save him or his city.

He stood up, gave the monitors one final look before closing them down. The tanks were cutting a swathe through his city, not even following the roads, some of them were blasting buildings of out of their way and moving through the rubble, forcing their way through the debris like demonic metal children emerging from a ruined womb of brick and stone. In the short space of time that he'd been sat here, they'd cut their way through half the city, they'd halved the distance between them and the palace. They'd be here soon. Tanks on his doorstep would not be a good sign.

Just for a moment, he thought about surrender. Maybe they'd let him live if he promised them that he'd let them have it. And then he violently rejected that notion in the space of a heartbeat. Whatever else might be said about him, let it never be said that Leonard Nwakili went down without a fight. He'd won the Premiership of Vazara through every bit of skill and guile he'd had, it had been gruelling and more than once he'd felt like throwing the entire thing in for something easier. But he hadn't. He'd fought his way up to the top and he'd been there ever since. Barring some unpleasant misunderstandings with Coppinger, and he wasn't the only one who'd been fooled by her, he felt he'd done good in his time in charge. He felt he'd been a good Premier. Better than most. He'd done a lot for the kingdom, at least he'd tried to.

Of course, being fooled by Coppinger meant for a lot less when a lot of the other main parties who'd dealt with her weren't actually alive any more. Ritellia for instance. And unlike that poor excuse for a man, Nwakili couldn't actually claim to be corrupt, at least he didn't think he was. When she'd made all these overtures, he'd asked questions. Questions beyond 'how much?' Questions she'd been able to answer satisfactorily, and he'd gone away secure in the knowledge that there wasn't anything untoward going on with either her or her attentions. He'd been pleased with the way things were at the time, but it didn't do him a whole lot of good now, did it? If he'd known what he knew now...

He didn't hold much with wishes. Hindsight was always perfect vision. In the recent months, a lot of people would have done things differently if they'd have known what the consequences were going to be.

The moment the tanks entered the grounds of the palace, they caught the first surprise that had been left behind for them by the D'Han. The first two hovered over the line of motion mines that had been carefully planted just below the surface of the flowerbeds, their presence triggered the sensors in the devices and they screamed straight up out of the ground and punched ragged holes underneath the tanks before exploding. The business edges of the mines were lined with lukonium for added penetrative force to their boom, rumoured to be the hardest metal in existence. If anything existed that was harder, it hadn't been discovered yet. Whatever the tanks were made of, it didn't hold up against the force, the explosion imminent after. The first two went straight down and exploded in a cloud of deeply satisfying fireballs. Those straight behind them crashed straight through the wreckage, emerging out the other side with dents and burns pockmarking their shells

More came, more followed and Nwakili watched them trace their way of destruction over the gardens that had once been tended to by his wife. When he'd heard they were coming, he'd sent her away who knew where. His wife and his daughters wouldn't be any sort of chip to be used against him in the coming slaughter. If he didn't know where they were, he couldn't tell the enemy. He'd made sure they had enough credits to start over, had emptied the last few dregs of the Vazaran treasury out. If he was going down, he might as well make sure that those he left behind were provided for. His first corrupt act, he'd agonised over it after they'd left and yet ultimately had decided he couldn't give a damn. Things were about to go bad, he wasn't going to be held responsible for his actions. The way this invasion had turned out, it was just about likely that Coppinger might seek out to punish him even after he'd gone to the grave by exacting retribution on what was left of his family. He was doing everything to ensure that didn't happen. His sons... He didn't know. They'd gone to fight, to lead armies in his name and never come back. He hadn't seen anything of them on the monitors before he'd left them behind. He suspected they were dead; the anguish was locking him up inside, carving at his insides with unceasing abandon. Dwelling on that right now would be fatal. He couldn't allow any distractions. If he made it through the night, he'd mourn them. Their deaths would have meaning. If he were to fall, then it would be for nothing.

The second wave of tanks hit the pulse emitters, almost solid waves of sound ripped out across the gardens, tore the fountain to pieces and the scattered stones bent huge dints into the outer shells of the incoming forces, bending cannons out of shape into disuse. Then came the flames, dozens of them roaring out the burning grass and across the battered hunks of metal. His predecessor as Premier had been a man very prone to believing he would be invaded at any given time and he'd set out to employ as many possible countermeasures as he could. Nwakili had never imagined cause would ever come to use them for himself. If he listened, he could imagine hearing the screeches of men roasting inside them. It wasn't satisfying, he took no pleasure in admitting that it was their own fault. They'd picked this fight and they'd paid the price. That they were only clones meant very little to him. Flesh was flesh after all. If he had a huge clone army with the means to grow more, he'd be throwing them away as cannon fodder as well. Some tactics never go out of fashion. Better them than men and women who had lives outside of their military duty.

More tanks were coming but they were fewer and further away now, he hoped that they were running low on their numbers. War was an expensive business. More to the point, the wreckage of those that had come before were blocking them away from making easy headway up to the front door. Nwakili smiled, watched as the clones, all clad in uniform battledress of sand colour armour broke from behind the last tank, two battalions of them and started to make their way across the gardens. The slight distortion about each of them suggested they were all wearing personal shields as well. Of course, they were! Standard procedure as well would be that they'd be packaged in overlap shields. Stand them close enough together and each shield reinforces one another. Twenty of them stood in a group would look like an easy target, yet in reality they would be probably the safest on the battlefield. They moved like they were trying to keep their defences up, weapons raised and going in lines of four across the deadly ground. They were anticipating more traps.

His predecessor had burnished a name on these gardens and only yesterday they'd been beautiful, alight with the colour and life that the light of his life had worked to give them. However, that they'd once been known as the Killing Ground didn't escape him. As they made their way across, several of the D'Han rose up out of hiding, each of them packing BRO-70 rifles in one hand, spirit summoners in the other. All of them were outfitted with a czernikian lion, a magnificent crimson furred feline beast with a shaggy black mane and twin tails, the symbol of his administration. When he'd formed up the D'Han to be his own personal guard, he'd written it up as a decree that everyone who entered the order would be granted one of the spirits as the sign of their authority. The creatures were protected; he'd seen to that. Only he could authorise the release of one from their reservation where they were allowed to breed in peace.

Those two groups of clones never saw it coming, taking attacks from a dozen different angles, not just from rifle fire but also from uniblasts courtesy of the lions. As strong as those shields might be, they weren't impenetrable, concentrated fire would get through eventually. All it would take was time and they'd fall. This wasn't the main force, just an advance guard to weaken resistance so the rest of them could move in. Nwakili knew their priority was to minimise casualties while ensuring complete elimination of the enemy as quickly as they were available to. Eventually, they'd get through.

Eventually wasn't soon enough.

Something… Someone moved in on the D'Han almost faster than his eye could follow and one of his elites was down with his neck at an odd angle before he could even react. Credit to them, their attention didn't immediately deviate from the assault on the battalion but as another went down under the huge bulk of a figure who'd broken into the fray from out of nowhere, their focus started to turn. Nwakili watched through a scope, saw the remaining D'Han open fire into the big man's bulk, saw him stagger back a few feet, throw his head back but didn't fall. He couldn't hear anything, no sound but were his shoulders shaking…

Fuck!

He'd read the reports from what had happened many months ago, heard all the stuff about what had gone down between Coppinger's forces and Unisco, not just at the calamity that the Quin-C final had become but what had taken place on her bloody airbase. Rumours of a man who had been able to shake off being shot…

Fuck!

He was supposed to be dead. The big man moved, scooped up a D'Han, one in each hand and squeezed hard, breaking bone under the sheer force of his fingers before throwing them down, laser fire cutting away at his body. His clothes came off worse in it all, the skin and muscle beneath them burning away and reforming several inches at a time. The lions went for him as well, those brought more problems for him, he went down under the sheer weight of six huge cats and Nwakili saw the ground run scarlet underneath him, claws and teeth ripping away through fabric and flesh, straight down almost to the bone. He felt hope fill him up, however momentarily it might be. This could be the turning point.

With the lions in the process of ripping the troublesome man to pieces, the D'Han went back to face the battalion, turned just in time to take faces-full of laser fire themselves, torn to pieces in seconds by the relentless assault. As their callers went down, the lions ceased attacking the big man and went for the clones. All but one of them bounded for the shielded clones, intent on doing to them what they'd just done to the brave men and women who'd brought them into existence.

That final one tried to move, found it couldn't as Domis… Nwakili thought that was his name. David Wilsin's report had been scant in places… grabbed it by the tail and tugged it back towards him, determination etched on his face as he slammed an elbow down into its spine, the roar of pain drowning out every other possible sound as the lion's legs buckled down behind it. With his face etched in concentration, Domis lunged forward, wrapped those huge arms around its upper body and held it in a chokehold, his face contorted with concentration as he cradled it almost lovingly as if he wished to bury his face in the fur before twisting violently.

It didn't take long for them to get to the front door after that, Nwakili noted with a feel of grim fascination. They were certainly an effective unit, he'd had to concede that. If what he'd heard was true, and he had little reason to doubt that it was, then they'd been bred to do just that. Their jobs were simple. He'd liked to have fought with soldiers like those at his back. As highly skilled as fellow agents had been at Unisco, it had always been worth remembering that they were as much a group of individuals as much as anything else. These guys moved as a team. Already they were laying charges around the doors, determined to get in before too much more time had passed. They'd breach soon, he was sure of that. There might be a few of the D'Han left but their numbers too scant to make a difference.

Nwakili leaned down, picked up the BRO-60 and ran it over with skilled, practiced hands, running every check he knew to guarantee it was in working order. He'd tried to keep it as much of a secret as possible that he'd been part of Unisco though as with any open secret, the knowledge had slipped out. Some people, when they retired and entered public service, did let it be known. They were under the impression that it'd garner them cheap publicity points. Identities were kept secret while with the organisation for privacy purposes, to avoid reprisals. After though, the records were sealed, and nobody could link you to any given mission bar the director himself. He wasn't as young as he once had been, but he still did his best to stay in shape.

Still lean. Still trained against the D'Han on a regular basis. No better way to test your bodyguards were up to muster.

When first he'd done it, he'd beaten them down easily, suspected that they were holding back against him. His response to that had been to brutally beat the next one he'd fought, proclaiming that this would happen if they held back while in his service. He knew what he was doing, and he'd know if they were doing it as well. As much as it had hurt him to do it, he'd also promised them that should he suspect they were holding back, they'd be dismissed from service and, this had been a particular stroke of genius, would find it hard to find work again in Vazara. He'd noticed a marked improvement in them ever since then. He'd even managed to learn a few new tricks. Past a certain point, the only way to improve was to teach, because through critique of others, you learned new things about yourself.

After all, he'd since pointed out to them that their purpose was to protect him. What better way than to ensure he was in the best possible shape to ensure that he could protect himself just as well, should they all be killed in duty.

The weapon was in good shape, fully loaded and ready to be used. He put it back down, pulled on an impact vest and adjusted it across his body. This model had been reinforced, heavier than normal but still manageable and infinitely preferable to the alternative. Quickly he added various other bits to the ensemble, lukonium spikes strapped to both knees and elbows, even to the tips of his boots. The last thing he added was a special bit of kit that he'd had designed especially for a situation like this, a pair of reinforced gauntlets that came back almost halfway up his forearms, a trio of lukonium spikes protruding across the knuckles, a set of almost invisible wires linking back up to a miniature thumb scanner across the underside of the wrist. If the rumours about Domis Di Carmine were true, and every bit of ocular evidence he'd gathered so far said they were, it might save his life. He'd intended the device to be used against armoured opponents, but it might yet serve purpose here. The man was a monster, a fearsome foe in a fair fight. Good thing he intended to cheat as much as possible.

The doors blew in, the first few clones through the door ran straight into the automated guns, laser fire spitting rapidly out in their direction to shred them into tiny pieces in short order. Grenades came in on them, the explosions boomed, and the guns fired no more, torn apart by the explosive force directed against them. From the shadows, Nwakili cursed. He'd hoped that they'd thin out the ranks more than they had. He knew the palace better than anyone currently living, he'd made a point to ensure that was the case for circumstances just like this. It might save his life one day.

Maybe he should just hide out in there, let things blow over. It'd nice to be naïve enough to believe that'd be the case. If they searched the palace and couldn't find him, maybe they'd give up. Maybe. Or if he was being realistic, they'd probably just blow the place to pieces with their superior firepower and make sure they took him out that way. They could do it. And he couldn't think of a less satisfying way to die. If he was going to go down, he wanted to see it coming. He wouldn't be wiped out like a rat, hiding in the dark. He hefted the Broxtie, looked down the sight at those scurrying around below him. The shadows were his friends, always the first lesson he'd learned about stealth back in the Unisco academy. They didn't look like they had thermal capability as part of their equipment. They couldn't have planned that far ahead, surely. They couldn't have predicted they'd be facing him in an environment like this.

Silently, he followed them from the floor above, always looking down on them. They advanced towards the stairs at the end of the entrance hall, they'd be in the throne room in a matter of seconds. What would they do when they found out he was nowhere to be seen? Right here, right now it would be a struggle for him to deal with them. He was outnumbered as long as they were grouped together this tightly and their shields were running hot and linked together. Maybe he should outwait them. Those shields could only hold up for so long before they ran out of power. Combining them together did share the burden but still there was a limit to their batteries. When it went down, they'd be vulnerable. Easy to scythe down with laser fire from here, they'd be dead before they knew what was happening. Classic ambush tactics, attack when they're vulnerable and don't expect it.

Before he could consider it too much, the last of the D'Han struck from the shadows like crocodiles from a river, the three F's. Fast. Furious. Fearsome. He'd taught them that move, after all, used those exact words. Three of them broke out, swept from the murk and he heard the sound of breaking bones in the otherwise silence of the palace. Outside the war might be raging but in here, his home was quiet. Even the boots of the invaders felt muted in the vast below

Until they weren't. He saw the shadow cast by the big man long before he actually entered, watched him stride past the burning remains of the shattered doors and Domis threw his head back, sniffed the air like a dog for a heartbeat. His clothes were ruined from laser fire and lion attacks, yet he showed no sign of discomfort. Nwakili stiffened, wondered if the man's senses were as keen as he was making them out to be. What did it mean for him if the big bastard could tell where he was? He didn't know. He didn't want to know. He held his breath, lined up the sights with Domis' head. Any hint of a threat and it'd be all over. If he was certain it'd make a difference, he'd already have pulled the trigger. The great shaved head turned slowly until finally they were lined up with what Nwakili could see through the scope.

One eye winked and Nwakili was ashamed to say he felt his nerve go in that moment, his finger tightened, squeezed the trigger, sent a three-point burst straight through Domis' skull. The big man went down with a roar, clutching his face and Nwakili went quickly over the balcony, firing the Broxtie into him as he fell, the blasts ripping fresh wounds into the naked skin of his back. Nwakili caught the odour of burning flesh, powerful up close, put it out of his mind as he failed to hold back on the shots, emptying the power pack into Domis. It was overkill, a part of his mind was screaming, nobody human could survive this sort of punishment and yet Domis still twitched, his wounds healing over before his very eyes, old ones recovering even as new ones were borne. Another part of Nwakili's mind was screaming that he might have made some sort of horrible mistake. Should have run while he had the chance.

Too late now! He'd made his decision now he'd live with it. Stand and fight, for that was the only way this was ever going to end.

He swung out with the butt of the assault rifle, caught him on the jaw with a resounding crack and brought the weapon back to strike again. Domis caught it with one of his shovel-sized hands, twisted it out of his grasp and hurled it away into some far corner of the hall. Behind him, the D'Han were still grappling with the clones, he didn't have much time. He pivoted, drove the spiked tip of his boot into Domis' throat, felt warm blood spatter across his arms and face. The smug look on the big man's face fell away as he grasped at his wound, scarlet flowing hard around his grip.

Nwakili threw out an elbow next, drove it down towards one water-coloured eye, felt it puncture with a satisfying splutter, he knew he'd found his target and it felt good. He left the spike in, felt it break away. Every opponent has a weakness, just a matter of finding it wherever it may be. He went for the other eye, Domis might be strong, might have a freaky ability to deal with whatever damage was being thrown at him but if he was blind then it wouldn't mean too much. The big man twisted away from his blow, rose like a salmon and hit him square in the chest with a punch that would have made a mule envious. His vest absorbed most of it, regardless the force from the strike threw him back and he was suddenly struggling for oxygen, gasping hard for it. He'd never been hit that hard before. Never. Already Domis was up on his feet, the spike still protruding from his eye. Blood gushed down around it, his face ugly with fury.

Both of them raised their fists, went for each other, Nwakili ducking under the first blow, an almost clumsy punch that sailed high over his head. Maybe he'd fucked his opponent's depth perception and he didn't know where he was. That'd be nice. He hit him hard in the abdomen with both hands, left two more spikes lodged in the solid flesh. It was like punching a side of beef, hard and unyielding. The wound on his tattooed neck had all but closed up now. Nwakili couldn't believe something could bleed that much and fail to die but bleed Domis continued to do as he danced around him, left another spike embedded in the base of his back. Not quite on the spine but close enough. The big man roared, almost stumbled to his knees. How he was still standing, Nwakili didn't know but he took the moment to drive a fourth knuckle spike into the side of his head, straight through the ear. A bellow of pain and the big man was suddenly pawing at his ear to try and pull it out. One in through the eye and one in through the ear, anyone else would have been dead from brain trauma by now.

Nwakili had held this suspicion and was privately amused to have it proved. He wasn't that good with pain after all. He healed quickly enough to avoid being overwhelmed by it. A laser blast burned flesh, damaged it, tore through it but didn't leave anything in the wound that couldn't be fixed in time. These spikes remained in, their edges jagged. He wouldn't be pulling them out any time soon. That would be excruciating for him. He smirked at his own cleverness, drove his other spiked elbow down into Domis' shoulder, he was on the ground now and struggling to function, cradled into the foetal position, whimpering like an infant.

Nwakili had felt nothing but contempt for him throughout. If there was any pity in him, it was too faint for him to acknowledge. His people were dying, his city was burning, and this fucker had been in part responsible.

"You want mercy, see the Divines," he said, kicking out hard, two, three, four times to the face and Domis was on his back, whimpering in pain. Last two knuckle spikes were driven in hard and Nwakili stepped back to survey his handiwork. He picked up the Broxtie, slammed in a fresh power pack before moving his finger to the thumb pad on the inside of his wrist. "Because you'll see them soon enough. Tell them I sent you. Nobody fucks with Vazara!"

Lukonium might be hard but by the same token it could be hollowed out, just as those spikes had been, unknown to Domis. Anything could be placed inside them as long as it fit. Like say, highly concentrated explosives? He shielded his eyes as each of the spikes exploded one after the other, taking Domis with them. He'd put the poor bastard out of his misery, more than he deserved, that was for sure. Dead. Sometimes, it took an expert touch to deal with a freak like that.

Up ahead of him, the D'Han and the clones had ceased their fighting for a moment, the explosion startling them into inactivity. Nwakili raised the weapon, fired several times and the clones went down hard.

"Vazara will never fall," he said softly. "It always has been and always will be. Fall back, people. It's time to…"

Before he could give the order to retreat, he was cut off by a tremendous snap and crack and suddenly he could no longer stand up, the sound beat the sensations as white-hot pain ruptured through him. His leg couldn't hold him any longer, his ankle twisted at an awkward angle, bone tearing out through muscle and flesh around the iron-hard grip locked around his limb. Fresh agony hit him as Domis tipped him down to the ground, burns healing all over his body even as the big man rose. Half his face was little more than bone, the muscle was knitting back over it as Nwakili could only watch in horror, the eye reshaping in the socket, flesh covering the taut red muscles in a matter of seconds.

"But you will," Domis said with a rasping voice slowly becoming smoother over the course of his words. "You will fall. Always is not forever." He bent down, scooped Nwakili up off the ground one handed. There was something almost pleased in his expression, like a father praising a pet who'd performed better than expected. "You came close. You fought well, I expected less from a politician. Good. Good. I won't forget this day."

Nwakili spat in his face, not the most dignified thing he'd ever do but by the same token, it'd probably be one of the last, so it didn't matter. Domis smirked. "I was hoping for at least one of these Vedo I hear so much about, but I was granted a good workout by the grace of my Mistress. This will be a noble death. Fear not, Premier, the five kingdoms will move on. They're about to be saved, starting with your cesspit of a kingdom. Your friends in the Senate have abandoned you." He smiled coldly. "Swear fealty to her and I'll let you live. She might even let you keep all this. She loves life, she will never abandon you in your time of need."

Could he do that? Sudden panic gripped at his heart. Nwakili hadn't even considered that an option. Surrender. Bend. He might not have to die after all.

But what sort of life would it be? At the beck and call of a madwoman, always having to watch out for fresh new assassins who'd be out for his blood because he'd betrayed the other four kingdoms. It'd mean turning his back on everything he'd believed in, everything he'd based his life on. The Senate might have betrayed him, but it didn't mean his own loyalty to them had been shattered. He'd sworn an oath, he'd meant it. Even his imminent death wasn't going to change that. Leonard Nwakili knew he didn't have much left, but he did have his integrity and he'd take it to the grave with him.

He couldn't do it. The moment the words came out of his mouth telling Domis to go and engage in a depraved act with a goat, the big man reacted, grasped him by the neck and the ankles before smashing him down hard face first into the ground. Not just once, not just twice but repeatedly, over and over. Even if Nwakili had been able to fight back, any resistance would have been knocked out of him by the first blow. Gratefully he lapsed into unconsciousness, the pain the last thing he felt as a living man. Soon there was very little left to distinguish him as a human being, never mind who he'd once been.

Several days later, an announcement was made on the steps outside the very same palace following a frantic effort to clean up the gardens and restore peace to the city, that Phillipe Mazoud had been named the new Premier of Vazara. Mazoud was there, making efforts to look what he probably considered to be regal, while Claudia Coppinger herself placed the crown on his head and took his oath to serve her in her new world and to renounce the cruel and self-serving Senate of the Five Kingdoms.

"Because," Mazoud said, looking at the videocam with a pleased expression burned into his features. "The Senate did not come to Vazara's aid when my predecessor asked for it. Vazara will not ask again. Vazara will not offer it. For all intents and purposes, five has just become four for the time being. But fear not, other kingdoms. One day, we will be reunited under a new banner. The Age of Unification has passed. The Age of Coppinger has begun."

Chapter Three. The Reformation.

"To change is to survive. To adapt is to thrive. Sometimes in order to raise up the new, the old needs to be displaced. There will be those that don't like that. They fear change in the same way they fear inevitability. The kingdoms have changed too many times already for the fear of change to paralyse us with its poison. If we do not do something, gentlemen, we may face greater change than simply Unisco."

Opening statement in the argument for Unisco reform in the Senate.

They'd swept through the plans for new Unisco reformations just a few scant hours after the attack on Carcaradis Island. The Senate had acted, and nobody had been able to stop them. With Terrence Arnholt on his deathbed, Brendan King had been stepped up to the role of temporary director until they knew for sure what would happen. With their leader out of action, they'd done the best they could to keep on going, but everyone knew Brendan's authority to only be temporary. It made it hard to take him seriously. The changes had kept coming and coming despite protests from him becoming increasingly feeble. Either he'd given up or chosen not to oppose them. Fervour had been ramped up in recent days, the need for suspected Coppinger sympathisers were to be rounded up as quickly as possible, apprehended and interrogated was present across every agent, even if they weren't sure where to look.

Meanwhile, Arnholt was recovering slowly from his wounds. When the memo had gone around the building he'd be returning, there'd been a collective sigh of relief. Even the true director might not have been able to resist the changes that had been imposed on them by the Senate, but many felt he'd have done a better job of compromise than Brendan had. Too many suspected he wanted the job full-time to try and fight with the powerbrokers on a decision like this. The Senate had a big hand in appointing the director of Unisco after all, rumour had it that they'd not been entirely happy with Arnholt's wilful ways after granting him the job.

It even hadn't escaped the outside world with several political commentators remarking on how unsavoury it was to be reshaping and restructuring Unisco at a time when national securities across the five kingdoms were about to be tested. They'd either been ignored or marginalised. Everyone had been surprised when Arnholt had endorsed the changes, speaking passionately about the decision to reform a previously oversized unwieldy organisation into thirteen separate departments under the same banner. He'd spoken minimally about

34

them but with great passion, chosen to go along with any hope for change, citing the importance of dealing with Claudia Coppinger as quickly as possible.

Outside, a storm was brewing, lightning striking the sky at intermittent intervals, thunder threatening to rip through the rain with its omniscient boom. And shielded from it all, the heads of the thirteen departments found themselves meeting on Arnholt's first day back on the job, along with an aide of their choice. The director was the first to arrive, still walking stiffly following his shooting, but otherwise feeling in good health. He entered the room and took in the view for himself, running an absentminded hand across the back of his seat to check for dust. He did it for another, still deep in thought. In the pit of his stomach, he wasn't as happy as had been made out by the changes thrust upon the organisation in his absence, he definitely wasn't happy with Brendan King for facilitating it. The relationship between the two of them had been fading for many months now, they'd once been close friends, now they could barely tolerate each other. Like it as not, he was King's boss and as he'd told him on more than one occasion, if he didn't like it, he knew where the door was.

Whether he was happy or not was irrelevant to this whole situation, the sad fact remained that it had happened. Leave the blame at the door and see that it works. His only option was the same as the one he'd offered King. If he didn't like it, he knew where the door was. And he wasn't about to walk out amidst a crisis like this. That'd be irresponsible, he'd be failing in his duty of care to the kingdoms. When the Coppinger situation was defused, then there would be words with the people who'd set about making these unwanted changes. He'd at least recovered in time to have final say on the choices for the department heads, he wasn't about to leave that in the hands of Brendan King. He didn't want to have twelve people sympathetic to probably his biggest rival to the position sat around him. It could make things very difficult indeed, although he held no doubts as to the integrity of those who worked here, he didn't believe in taking undue chances.

Predictably, King was the first man through the door, along with his chosen aide, Nicholas Roper. Arnholt wasn't surprised by the choice, Roper had been quietly going about Unisco business more and more over the past six months according to the records, completing every assignment laid to him with the same ruthless efficiency as he employed on the calling battlefield. He'd completed more assignments in the past six months than he had in the two years before it, more than that, he was actually volunteering every time one linked to the Coppingers came up. He looked fantastic, like he'd really been putting the time and effort in at the gym, he looked as deadly now as Arnholt had ever seen an agent ever.

It didn't take a genius to see that he'd made it personal. Given Rocastle had pretty much admitted to the death of his future wife and Rocastle's ties to the Coppingers, Roper had cut himself off from the life he'd led, leading a terrifying one-man stream of vengeance. Rumour had it that Brendan King was on the verge of making him his second in command in the operations department. Not only had he been completing assignments himself, he'd been running command for others, a less dangerous position but one no less stressful. The operations department was in as good a pair of pair of hands it'd likely ever be in. He might have doubts about the way King had run the entire organisation, but he'd been in charge of ops for over thirty years before and he knew what he was doing there. And Roper, well, Arnholt had a great sense of personal gratitude to the man. He'd saved his daughter's life after all.

Through the door next came the new deputy director, Walter Swelph and the head of the Management department, the day-to-day stuff that Arnholt himself didn't have the time to deal with. Swelph was a new appointment to the post, another Arnholt wasn't entirely pleased with, he'd been a joint Brendan King-slash-Senate appointment and while he hadn't done anything out of character, he was looking for an excuse to step him back down. Swelph was a bald man prone to paunchiness with an impressive moustache that hid most of his mouth. His aide followed him in, a petite redhead in a severely cut suit of midnight blue, Arnholt didn't know her name.

More and more were coming in next, Liam Caulker, the head of Intelligence, Rosemary Dyer of Records and Allison Crumley of Public Relations all in conversation until they stepped through the door, he caught some of it. Nothing beyond what he'd have expected of them. William Okocha and Ross Navarro of Surveillance and Equipment respectively came in next. Navarro had undergone something of a meteoric rise in the organisation recently, he'd not long since been a pilot and engineer but following the Carcaradis Island event where he'd held out under Coppinger capture, he'd taken to the organisation with a new lease of life. Not, Arnholt had noted, unlike Roper. Possibly the hardest decision he'd made in regards of the roles, he had to admit. Six months ago, Alvin Noorland would have been nailed on for it. Unfortunately, that was no longer an option. They all missed Noorland.

The Espionage head, Parley Khan, mother of Prideaux, strode in alone, no aide with her. That surprised him, or it would have had he not known her as well as it did. She didn't do things by halves. That included responsibility. Her daughter was the same, he had a lot of respect for the both of them. Tod Brumley, now responsible for Recruitment and the academy came in on her heels. Brumley looked tired, like he was yearning for simpler days. Nobody had had any responsibility foisted on them that they were deemed incapable of dealing with, yet some carried it better than others. Tobias Ojo, head of Logistics walked in with Daniel Kearns, in charge of the Liaison department and Othella Carpenter, the Property manager for the organisation. It was her duty to discover suitable locations for safehouses and field offices, a prestigious position.

That left, by his count, just one more department. Silently he cursed them as he looked at the timepiece on his wrist. They'd best not be late for this meeting. Already they were viewed as a less than credible way for credits to be spent during the current crisis, and given the way things were, he couldn't afford for them to come off as a bit of a joke department. It just wouldn't do. He felt it had been a good idea at the time, he just hoped that he wasn't going to be proved wrong.

The door opened, and he breathed a silent sigh of relief. Vassily Derenko, the newly minted head of the Department of Mysteries, along with Ruud Baxter at his side, walked in like they owned the place. Arnholt was privately just glad that they'd shown up. Neither of them looked unduly bothered by being the last to arrive, they sat down at the back of the room, the only seats left in the room. Nobody else met their eyes.

    That particular department was a new addition and one he had personally invested the effort into, though he was aware that there were those who bore scepticism towards its inception. That those same individuals doubtless didn't know the true purpose behind the department made him care very little about their opinions. He'd needed something like this. He had Baxter's people running around as part of the organisation, Baxter had initially wanted to be in charge of the department himself. Not a way in seven hot hells was Arnholt going to let that happen, before the atrocity on Carcaradis Island, Ruud Baxter hadn't been a Unisco agent for a good five years. He'd left on good terms. Even passed his majeur de ceperacion, the last such time it had been implemented. But the Vedo… They brought plenty to the table. He just didn't want them self-governing. Hence his appointment of Derenko to the role to ensure they were overseen correctly. Derenko had brought in a dozen or so major crime bosses from across the five kingdoms on that Eye of Claudia mission, he'd earned a promotion. And, Arnholt had been pleased with this idea, he'd seen the work ethic from Derenko many, many times to make him think this the right idea. More than that, he was strong-willed enough to resist Baxter's particular brand of suggestion if it came down to it. The most important trait of them all.

This department, if it was going to get off the ground, needed someone like that in charge. Someone who would make it work. He still wasn't keen on the name, but it was possibly the least important facet of the entire process. They dealt in the unknown, a department slowly increasing its personnel. Baxter had tested many of the Unisco agents for an uncanny ability to touch the Kjarn and he was building up the ranks of those he was training. In six months, the number of Vedo had exploded from a handful to more than fifty in training. Hence the reason he was surprised Baxter was present. Those who he'd already trained had gone on missions. None had been killed. Every commanding officer he'd read reports from had praised them as important assets that had made the difference, had spoken about their ability to fit into the makeup of the team, of their professionalism in the field under fire.

So far, he felt justified. However, he would have felt a lot more confident in the program if he'd been certain that across the other side of the board, Wim Carson wasn't doing the same thing. On that front, they remained ignorant and it rankled. Considering that had been Baxter's entire offer, to hunt the rogue Vedo down, it felt like the Vedo were getting more out of this offer than Unisco were for the time being. If the arrangement was to continue, that might have to change in the future. Successful skirmishes were one thing. The big battles were where the wars were won.

The time for introspection was over. He cleared his throat, banged his fist on the table and spoke aloud. His first speech since returning to active duty

"Welcome," he said. "We all know why we're here. It's good to see you all for the first time in your new roles. I know none of us are happy about the way this has been forced upon us…" He lingered his gaze on Brendan for a moment, the man's craggy features set in a decidedly neutral expression. If he didn't appreciate the comment, he didn't show it. "… But there's nothing much we could have done about it. What we need to do is ensure that we get up to speed as quickly as possible. We can't afford to screw around with the task at hand here and now. The Coppingers…" He wasn't comfortable referring to the group under that moniker, but it had stuck. They followed Claudia Coppinger's insane leadership, they'd been party to what she'd done at the Quin-C final. It summed them up. They were what they were and nothing more. "… They're not going to go away. You each know what you're meant to do. Do it. It's been six months. We all know what we're good at. We all know what needs to be done. The swifter we resolve internally, the faster we can get back to where the true work is."

There was a huge elephant in the room, he didn't want to bring it up, but he had no choice. "First things first... Vazara."

If anything, the silence in the room became even more potent. They'd all seen the signs. The news footage. They'd heard the stories about how Nwakili had demanded more protection from the Senate to shore up his own rapidly depleting army and he'd been let down. It was something that had cost them a kingdom. The silence wasn't for that. Leonard Nwakili had been a Unisco agent once. The loss was profound, to say the minimum. When one of their own died, they felt it.

"We all know what the Senate did. We cannot change that. What we can do is remember Leonard Nwakili and everything that he did while he was alive. He was a good man..." He hadn't been really, but to be pedantic about him now that he was dead just felt churlish. "... and he played his part in the security of the five kingdoms when he was with this organisation. Vazara has lost a leader who you always knew where you stood with. I will miss dealing with him."

He knew what to expect with Phillipe Mazoud as well, but it wasn't really anything he looked forward to. "He was my friend. He epitomised the spirit that Unisco needs to utilise in order to conquer this challenge." He cleared his throat again, saw everyone had their heads bowed. Deep within the centre of each Unisco building, there was a wall with the name of every Unisco agent, past and present who had been killed in action. Though Nwakili had long left them, his name was being added to it even as they spoke. The way he had acquitted himself in his final moments, he deserved that honour.

"Vazara. It has fallen. Phillipe Mazoud has declared himself Premier under the blessing of Claudia Coppinger. We have lost an ally; they have gained a foothold. More and more people from that kingdom feel she's got the right idea. The word from our intelligence sources tell us how they feel she gave them something nobody else has been able to do, ever in their history. She gave them their kingdom back, she stripped away the harsh deserts and gave them fertile land and more water than they can ever drink. She built the factories to purify the water, she invested in the kingdom and there are no longer people starving there. They're getting basic human rights we take for granted over here, and for that, she has their undying love. She's won a major victory, as far as that kingdom is concerned."

Okocha scowled, Arnholt tried not to look at him. Hard to tell what was going through the minds of the Vazaran Unisco agents at a time like this. There had to be some sort of conflict within them. He didn't doubt the professionalism of any of them.

"Premier Mazoud's first declaration was to split away from the rest of the five kingdoms. He made his point that Unisco are no longer welcome there, our jurisdiction is no longer recognise. Any Unisco agents of Vazaran descent who wish to return and work for him will be forgiven for their betrayal of the kingdom and will be permitted to use their talents to increase the Vazaran advancement."

"Great," Liam Caulker said. "Unbalanced. So far nobody has taken him up on it. His word means about as much as you'd expect it to."

"Chief Caulker how do gauge the situation in Vazara at the moment regarding Mazoud," Derenko asked. "Because as we've just been informed, they love Coppinger. Mazoud though, is someone who has always been tolerated, rather than loved as I understand it. Even when he was in charge of the Suns…"

"That about sums it up. Tolerated. He's doing a job whipping up pro-Vazaran fervour, appealing to the national identity and a brave new future. Some are buying it but not everyone. Because that was the one thing you could say about Nwakili, he did have a lot of support. As damn close to unanimous as Vazaran politics has ever had. He didn't have to shout a mass of nationalistic drivel to get his point across, he knew that sometimes you have to do the unpopular thing. Mazoud hasn't had to do anything like that yet. My analysts tell me he'll put it off until he absolutely can't."

"And the thing about making the unpopular decision," Okocha said. "Sometimes it's necessary. That's Mazoud all over. A vanity project wrapped up in a self-absorbed package. He won't do it until it's too late."

"We can't let him carry on until he shoots himself in the foot," Brendan said. "He could do untold damage until them. He's a maniac in charge of a group of maniacs and it will spell the end of us all if we aren't careful."

"Unfortunately, we cannot deal with him until we're further along on Coppinger. He has her backing," Caulker said. "Analysis of the situation suggests she wouldn't take kindly to it. There would be reprisals. We cannot ignore what sort of credible threat this might impose. Anything from trade sanctions…"

"Which might already be cut off," Tobias Ojo cut in. "Mazoud has already said he doesn't want to send anything out of the kingdom."

"Good," Okocha said dryly. "See how long that lasts him. Vazara doesn't produce that much of its own food, or it didn't. Killing the desert isn't going to change that overnight." He laughed out loud. "Hells, we were the sort of kingdom that'd export our gold to import our food. No wonder it went bad so quickly." Another laugh and he turned to Caulker. "Liam, do you think Coppinger will hold him up if he fails?"

"Hard to say. Our most credible intelligence source on Claudia Coppinger was less than complimentary about her tolerance of failure. Based on what Agent Caldwell gave us, that would suggest she'd cut him loose if need be. On the other hand, you cannot run a kingdom like you would a business. Too much chopping and changing might destroy any goodwill she's built up under the people if she backs a failing ruler and then removes him again and again. Some people can only be pushed so far."

"I already have people in place in most major Vazaran cities fermenting anti-Coppinger dissent," Parley Khan said, forming a triangle with the length of her fingers. "A slow process to be sure but it can't be rushed. The Vazaran Suns have taken control of the security of the kingdom, both internal and external. Mandatory service periods as well. They've increased their numbers a dozen times over in the past few months. They don't want any Senate influences in there. They certainly don't want us. Any Unisco personnel found inside the kingdom will be treated as enemies of the state. Death penalty."

Brendan made an unsettled sound, Arnholt stroked his chin thoughtfully. Something didn't sit right about that. Not in conjunction with the look on his face. The ops chief looked troubled, pensive even.

"Then we leave Mazoud in place for the time being?" Tod Brumley asked. "Seems like it could be risky."

"We do not have a termination order for him," Arnholt said emphatically. "Unfortunately. He has not been added to the kill list, as distasteful as that might sound. The Senate wants to negotiate with him if they can." He didn't add that he thought it a waste of time, instead carried on with the facts as he had them. "There's no hard evidence to suggest that he was involved in the displacement of Nwakili. Anything beyond circumstantial. We've all seen the footage of Domis Di Carmine terminating Nwakili." He grimaced as he said the words. He thought he'd seen it all in his life. Yet there had been something about the savagely dispassionate way in which Domis had gone about the job. "He was placed in the position. It looks unfortunate for him, but the Senate is reluctant to sanction a hit on the head of one of our former kingdoms."

"Is that what we are now then?" Tobias Ojo asked. He had a surprisingly high voice despite his stocky build. "Four kingdoms rather than five? We've been broken by this bitch?"

"It would appear so for the time being," Arnholt said. "Can't do anything about it. Reunification is something that the senate wishes to strive for. As long as Coppinger is alive and at large though, I can't see it happening."

"Our profiles of her says that it won't," Rosemary Dyer said. "We looked into her past, every speech she's ever made, every business decision, every aspect of her personal life we have on file. Her father was one of the largest critics of the original unification. Her uncles fought in the Unifications Wars for Canterage. Both of them were killed in the battle of Sangar To. Just two more names on the remembrance wall."

"If her family fought for Canterage in the Unification," Brendan King said. "Then why is she doing this for Vazara? They were the enemy."

"Your guess is as good as mine." Dyer said. "She has a lot of empathy for the kingdom. If we had to guess at where she's hiding, that is where she'd be. Used to go there a lot as a child and then more and more in her later life. Before Reims was seized, they put a lot of credits into the kingdom. How long she's had this planned, we don't know. But it looks like there was a lot of thought in it."

"She knows the region, yeah?" Daniel Kearns spoke up. "You're always strongest on your home turf, yeah? You know where you're strongest, where you have the advantage in a fight, yeah? You go where you can reinforce, where you can build, where you can set a marker in the sand, yeah?" He had that tendency to add the question inflection to every statement he made, it was something that made Arnholt want to punch him in the face. On the other hand, Kearns wasn't to be underestimated. He had a devious mind, he knew exactly what he was doing, and he was glad that he was on their side in this fight. "Vazara was pretty unregulated by five kingdom standards before, yeah? If I was going to do what she was going to do, Vazara is where I'd do it, yeah? She's got the popularity, she's got the resources, yeah? Put it together, she has a power base, yeah? I mean add in the fact they're a pretty superstitious lot and that trick with growing the rainforest…"

"I want to talk about that in a few moments," Brendan cut in. "Apologies, Daniel."

Kearns glared at him before carrying on as if he hadn't spoken. "It certainly looks like there's an element of divinity in the whole thing, yeah? It's a neat effect. I don't know how she did it, I've spoken to several scientists who should be in the know and they can't explain it either. They stopped just short of using the word miracle to describe it."

"Miraculous is right," Brendan said. "My sources say the same as those of Chief Kearns. No explanation. No sort of logic or reason as to how or why. It seems to have formed out of her whim. But I think

Daniel has a point. The reasoning is sound. If I were to enable an operation undertaking what she has done, I wouldn't have done much differently. That worries me. Not quite as much as another problem." He cleared his throat. "This ban on Unisco agents has come at an awkward time. Following the emergence of this green phenomenon, I despatched a team to seek out the source of it all, for intelligence purposes. We need to know how it started and why. Recently I lost contact with them."

"I see," Arnholt said. "Did they find anything? Forward any findings to us before they vanished"

"Not to my knowledge?" Brendan said. "I would send another team after them but…" He let it hang. "However, I do have an alternate solution to the problem."

Why, Arnholt mused, did he feel he wasn't going to like what the statement was going to be?

"In my other capacity as an expert on history and the distant past…" Brendan started to say with unflinching pride. Arnholt saw Baxter roll his eyes. He knew the feeling. "I was recently asked to join an expedition into the heart of this new Vazaran forest to examine their effect on some ancient temples. Due to the nature of my work here, I naturally declined at the time."

"And you want to send someone along as part of the party to discover exactly what happened to your team?" Crumley asked sharply. "Are you aware of the possible repercussions of an act like that?"

Brendan said nothing for a moment. "I was not proposing to send someone along, Ms Crumley…" Arnholt saw Allison flinch a little at the condescension in his voice. Sometimes he got the impression Brendan wasn't always the fastest on the uptake when it came to remember Crumley was on the same level as him now. "I was proposing to go along myself. Sending random Unisco agents would be an unacceptable risk and very few of them bear my knowledge in this field."

It was Arnholt's turn to say nothing. He didn't want Brendan out of the office taking stupid risks. If the fool got killed in the line of duty by the Vazaran Suns, then it'd be a massive pain having to appoint a replacement for him. On the other hand, though…

"I'll consider it," he said. "Allison, what sort of effect is what Unisco doing having on the public moral? No danger of it shifting towards Coppinger and her group across the other four kingdoms is there?"

"Potentially," Crumley said. "The longer any sort of conflict stalemates, the more attractive the underdog looks. Especially given the underdog has given us a bloody nose with Vazara. We lose another kingdom; the people will lose faith in us. Once they start to support the Coppinger cause as they have done in Vazara, her ranks will swell."

"It's true," Okocha spoke up. "My department has been sifting through any sort of footage we can find of her and she's started to refer to them as her believers, she regularly walks through throngs of them in Vazara, just appears out of nowhere, no prior warning and just vanishes after a brief appearance. We can't lock her down, if we could…" He mimed the shooting of a blaster with his fingers. "It's probably the only thing that's going to resolve this conflict as swiftly as possible."

"I don't disagree with you there," Khan said. "Removing Claudia Coppinger has to be as much of a priority as possible. Six months since they posted the bounty on her and nobody has even got close to her. If any of her inner circle tried to hit her, we've not heard about it."

"In six months, we haven't even gotten a hit on any of her lieutenants either," Caulker added. "Rocastle hasn't been seen in that time, we know all about Domis and how he was supposed to have been killed…"

That had been one of the few supposed victories out of the Carcaradis Island fiasco, Arnholt noted, that David Wilsin had claimed to have killed Domis in mortal combat. When there'd been evidence to prove otherwise, he'd been apparently incandescent with rage.

"And as for Wim Carson…" Caulker was one of the biggest vocal opponents of the Department of Mysteries and he wasn't shy in letting his feelings be known about it. He shot Derenko and Baxter a glance. Baxter grinned sweetly at him.

"Wim Carson is likely holed up along with Coppinger and Rocastle and anyone else you'd care to think of in the Coppinger hierarchy," Baxter said. "If you've been as of yet unlucky enough to find them, we're having the same lack of luck in that department."

"Can't you divine them?" Ojo asked. There was more than a hint of sarcasm in his voice. "Or something like that? You've got powers. Use them."

Baxter fixed him with a cool stare. "If it could be done, do you not think it would have been? It's a big set of kingdoms. Sometimes you need to know where to start looking. So far, we've been able to ascertain one hundred percent where they aren't. Which is a good start. I have Vedo crawling all known former Vedo refuges but so far it has yielded nothing." He said the last part in a tone of voice that suggested he thought the act was a massive waste of time. He'd already stated as much, Derenko had mentioned it in inter-departmental reports. "Given the limited numbers we currently have, it's a tremendous drain on our resources, but those are the orders."

"Welcome to Unisco," Swelph remarked. "Making do with what you're given."

Baxter said nothing, just stared at the man with his miscoloured eyes and smiled. "Of course," he said. "And generosity is an underrated trait. We have no problem following orders, as has been shown many times already. How many lives have we saved? Can your bureaucracy put a number on that, Walter?" His voice took that tone on, the one which was almost impossible to ignore. It wasn't loud, more intense, a deep sense of warning buried deep within it. It was like the threatening buzz of a hundred thousand bees, the menace a solemn implication.

"Nobody is understating the contribution of the Vedo to Unisco," Arnholt quickly interjected before it turned nasty. Baxter was blessed with an abnormal amount of self-control but the last thing he wanted was Swelph to push something in that he'd regret. "It has been mutually beneficial for both groups to conjoin in this partnership. I'm sure they'll get their man sooner or later. Hopefully sooner."

Every department was allocated its share of funding. Some were larger than others, carried more manpower and therefore their budgets were larger than others. The Department of Mysteries as currently the newest and still the smallest department despite swelling its ranks in recent months, was bequeathed the lowest number. It really was a true test for Derenko. Yet the results had been encouraging so far. "It is an arrangement that I'm sure we can continue for a long period of time, beyond the extent of this current crisis."

"That's assuming any of us are around after the end of this crisis," Carpenter, ever the optimist, remarked. "We might lose."

"With talk like that, we will," Tod Brumley said. "Director, Chiefs, we're still doing well at the academy. We talk about how people are wanting to join the Coppinger movement, because they believe in Claudia Coppinger. Well we're getting many more applicants now, people actively seeking us out." It did used to be the other way around, Arnholt noted to himself. Unisco agents from the Recruitment department would seek out the most promising, candidates from the new spirit callers around the kingdoms and see if they could be spirited into the academy. "We've been all working around the day to vet applicants, we have many potential new agents all in the works. But it's still not enough. For each one who makes the grade, there are a dozen who don't."

"Is that the fault of the instructors or the candidates?" Navarro interjected. "Sorry, Tod, but sometimes you can make a beautiful piece out of a shoddy material but not with a substandard tool."

"Yes, and sometimes flawed material is flawed material," Brumley said. "Don't bandy metaphors with me, Navarro. I was doing this when you were still up to your elbows in engine oil."

"That might have been but at least I remember what it's like to be doing the job on the ground floor," Navarro shot back. "You seem to forget what it's like to be walking through that door. Part of the Unisco training is to prepare them for what's out there…"

"And we don't do that by coddling them! We've got a war on. We need them fighting fit."

"Which they won't do if they're out the door because one of your heavy-handed instructors decided that…"

"Enough!"

His warning voice wasn't anywhere near as potent as Baxter's, but it had the same effect. Both Navarro and Brumley shut up at that as Arnholt looked around the table and sighed. "Okay, I think we made good progress today with these discussions. I want plans of action, people, I want three ways that your department is going to implement to try and win this damn war by the time we meet next." In this time of crisis, he felt it was best to get them together twice a week minimum. Some of them had complained, however briefly but he'd made sure they'd understood his point of view in the end. "I don't care how ridiculous they sound on the surface, if you can make a good argument for them, then we need new ideas. We need new strategies. We can't afford to cede anymore ground to them. If they gain another foothold, they'll climb even higher. Brendan, see me afterwards." He banged his fist on the desk. "I'll see you all in three days' time. Dismissed!"

Eventually just he and Brendan remained in the room with the departure of Nick Roper, Vassily Derenko and Ruud Baxter bringing up the rear. Arnholt stretched his arms before moving to sit down across the table from his operations chief.

"So, you're wanting to go to Vazara," he said. "Where, I might remind you, Unisco agents specifically aren't permitted to operate anymore?"

"We've all done stuff we're not permitted to," Brendan said. "You've sanctioned things that would make the Senate sit up and rub their eyes."

"Yes, and it was the right thing to do at the time. This… This seems a little unnecessary."

"Director, we won't be going in as Unisco agents. We'll be going in as archaeologists. I don't want to abandon the fight here, but I think this is important."

"Oh undoubtedly," Arnholt said. "You thought it was important enough to send a team out there in the first place! What were you thinking?!"

"I was thinking we need intelligence on something that for all intents and purposes, coincided with the greatest threat to the five kingdoms making an announcement of divinity to a watching audience of billions of people. Given that seems to have authenticated her claim somewhat amongst some people, I think it's important that we find out exactly what happened, so we can refute her claim. We're not going to win this war unless we utilise every weapon we have, and the truth has always been the greatest weapon one side can bring to bear against another."

"I don't want you going there alone," Arnholt said. When it was put like that, Brendan did have a point. Anything that potentially weakened Claudia Coppinger could be helpful. "Take at least one agent with you as bodyguard. And I want you to take one of the Vedo as well. You're travelling in hostile territory and I don't want to risk you falling into enemy hands if we can help it."

"So, said agent is to eliminate me if we're captured?" Brendan King almost said it with a grin. Arnholt only shrugged. Too much had passed between them for the exchange to be friendly. Both knew where they stood with the other. Cold hard truth. That was all that remained between them.

"Hey, you said it. Not me."

Chapter Four. The Recruits.

"Our academies have long been our pride and joy. In the past, the program has been a long one, a careful one that we've carefully tailored to the most suitable candidates to advance in whichever field best suits their talents. Today however, the kingdoms have changed. We need Unisco agents out in the field and we need them now. The two-year training period is no longer feasible. In two years, we might all be dead and living in a madwoman's fantasy. It's not a pleasant remit, but my goal is to see that the training is compressed down to as short a space of time as reasonably possible."

Tod Brumley's first remit as Head of Recruitment and Development under the newly reformed Unisco.

Six months ago.

It had been common knowledge for years now that the great grey facility sat outside the Canterage town of Torlis was the Unisco academy. People who lived in Torlis had long been greeted with the comment 'oh, where the academy is,' and for the most part had gotten used to it. The media often referred to it with great affection whenever the need came up, a blight on the landscape in truth, a speck of ugly grey amidst the endless green. Torlis had once been in danger of going out of existence until the academy had been built and now it was surviving, if not thriving. Always there were cadets with spare credits to spend in the town when they got a free pass from the facility, the night life had the potential to be a lot more interesting than it once been and stores that peddled in small luxuries that couldn't be found on the site did a meagre but profitable trade. Cut off from mostly anywhere, they could and did charge whatever outrageous mark-up they chose on supplies. Although their names weren't known in the context of what they did, such luminaries of the spirit calling world had passed through the doors of the Torlis academy such as Nicholas Roper, David Wilsin and Wade Wallerington in the most recent famous examples, going all the way back to the old guard, Brendan King and Terrence Arnholt as well as the late Leonard Nwakili, all of them had trained here and all had gone on to make their own indelible marks on the five kingdoms.

However, outside the organisation, very few knew that the Torlis academy had long since ceased to be used for actual training of new recruits. Instead it had been converted out as a storage facility, enough staff rotated there to keep the ruse going for as long as it needed to be kept active. Since the fame of the grand old academy had reached notorious levels, the executive decision had been made to open several much smaller facilities across the five kingdoms. Secret ones. Ones that wouldn't be a massive target. Being sent to Torlis these days was a sure sign that your career at Unisco wasn't going anywhere fast, even with the threat of the Coppingers.

Amidst the reformation of the organisation, there had even been talk of shutting the place down completely and diverting the manpower and funds to more important areas. Arnholt wasn't entirely in favour of it. One big useless target was infinitely more inviting than several small hidden and useful ones and he'd found that it was a good smokescreen. If the Coppingers wanted to make a strike at Unisco, then Torlis would be as good a place as any. Unfortunately, they hadn't yet taken him up on that invitation and he wasn't sure how much longer he could keep dangling it there. Pressure had been mounting on him to cut the place loose, ultimately there would come a point when he needed to.

For the time being, it was irrelevant. Torlis continued to hold bits of useless supplies that they didn't want to dispose of completely and was manned by staff who had sinned grievously in their duty. Whenever a Senate official wished to examine a Unisco training facility, events that were becoming rarer these days, Torlis was the one they were taken to. For all intents and purposes to everyone outside the Unisco high command, Torlis continued to thrive, turn out agent after agent year after year. The future was bright, and they were all made in Canterage.

The truth of course was something rather different.

Theobald Jameson remembered that first day distinctly, even months later. He doubted he'd forget it. He'd arrived at Torlis not entirely what to expect. He hadn't been ready for the aeroship sat in the background, nor the men in the black masks who'd broken into the crowd of new recruits, felt the pricks of needles in their arms and the sudden deep embrace of unconsciousness. There'd been two teams of them, maybe twenty a side. Some of them had been wearing red armbands, some of them blue. He'd not understood why at the time, the reason or the logic behind it, just worn his red band with pride. He was doing this, for the first time ever in his life, it felt like he was doing something to make things better. He hated the Coppingers, he hated them almost as much as he hated his father. There was a fine dividing line between them, his father had ruined his early life, the Coppingers had ruined what potentially could have been the finest day of his life when their crazy bitch leader had attacked the Quin-C final when he'd been about to claim victory. She'd shown up and things had turned to shit. Literally.

People had died, he'd been lucky not to be amongst their number. And so, it had been Anne who'd suggested this. Anne who'd trained him when things had looked their darkest, become the closest thing he'd ever had to a friend, not quite a partner but something could gestate there. He didn't know if he wanted it. His heart had remained closed off to other people for so long, opening it up hurt more than he'd ever imagined. For some reason, she seemed to like him, so he couldn't complain too much. Friendship was something he'd once thought to be beyond him, but she'd disproved that. She'd taken him to her heart and he'd tried to reciprocate as best he could.

Those were his thoughts as unconsciousness had taken him, the first to assault him as he'd woken to bitter winds swiping cruelly at his face. His eyes had slid open to the unwelcome sight of the ground charging towards him, thousands of feet away, unfamiliar weight across his back. He'd scrabbled at it, a cape billowing in the wind. The summoner wasn't around his neck, the next thing he'd gone for. He could see a big temple or something far below, he was going to hit it, he flapped his arms like a great big bird, already desperate to avoid hitting it. It didn't do much good, hit the church or hit the ground, it wasn't going to be pleasant. Somewhere amidst the roar of the winds in his ears, he was aware he was screaming and shouting, throwing curses out at those who'd done this to him and he ran hands over his body, looking for something, anything to get him out of this. They couldn't be about to let him die like this, surely, the absolute bastards…

His fingers closed on a thin metal loop protruding from his cape and with no better option at hand, he tugged on it hard. Behind him, the cape stiffened hard, slowing his descent and jerking him back firmly as the material froze solid, catching the winds in its voluminous folds and for a moment, he was hovering like a giant kite. A strange sound echoed through the winds, he thought he was laughing and then the sensation faded and once more he was falling. Maybe a hundred feet from the ground, he found the loop again and tugged frantically, same sensation, same pressure on his back and same intense feeling of relief. Bloody air loops. He'd never worn one before, he was lucky that he'd not panicked beyond reason. Theo didn't want to think about what might have happened if he had.

In the grounds of the temple, a big white ring had been painted into the grass, and with his cape still stiff, he jerked his body clumsily towards it. It wasn't anything approaching graceful, he felt like he was wallowing through it. At least now his fall had slowed to a glide, the terror he'd felt earlier rushing away from him. When he hit the ground face first, he'd never been so grateful to feel the pain of a bust his nose. Blood streamed down his face, he wasn't ashamed to admit he was relieved. Very relieved. He couldn't stop shaking; his hands were trembling as he lay there on the grass for a few long moments. His breath came out in deep ragged gasps, he might be close to tears, but he wasn't about to break yet. It had come as a shock to the system, the anger was boiling up inside him. He blinked several times, wiped his busted nose with a sleeve and grimaced as the sting rupturing through his face. It wasn't the first time he'd suffered that injury, wasn't even the most debilitating instance. His eyes watered, blinking hurt, but considering he'd just been thrown out of an aeroship…

Bastards…

He made a fist, punched the ground hard. The soft earth gave under his fist, he sat there for a moment before pushing himself to his feet. He could see the temple properly now, was more like some sort of monastery now he considered it. Looked too grand to be a church, least not the ones he was used to. It was more ornamental, a work of art as well as a place of worship. That idea filled him with distaste, he didn't hold much truck with religion. Some part of him wanted to believe, the part of him that didn't want to take any chances. Theo stood, saw the speeders coming in fast. Three of them. He tensed up, jerked his head back and forth, cursed that he didn't know what was going on. Stupid, stupid! Getting exposed out in the open like this was a rookie mistake.

Except that's exactly what he was here. A rookie. He hadn't even started training yet and already he'd been thrown into it.

Okay, Unisco. You want to play this game!

When the speeders arrived at his landing site, he'd made it a point to be somewhere else. The sun was high in the sky, he was at least grateful they hadn't made him skydive at night because that might have been more than his nerves could deal with but concealing himself would have been easier if there was some sort of cover. He'd hurled himself into a nearby bush, wriggled across the ground on his belly when he was sure they'd passed by. He caught a glimpse through a gap in the branches, saw the men on the speeders… well most of them were men. There was a woman as well, all in black uniforms… were all carrying blaster rifles. He didn't want to get into confrontation with them, he still wasn't sure if this was some sort of induction or training. It could be, it might not be. If they were throwing him in at the deep end like this, then maybe they were a lot more desperate that he'd thought. He continued to worm his way across the grass, only drawing shallow breaths. Ahead, he could see the monastery looming high against the skyline, a dozen little black dots moving around the perimeter of it in various patterns.

He didn't want to go there. Not if they were in the same company as the people on the speeders. That said, it was the only building for miles around. He'd been dropped here for a reason. He craned his head back around, saw the group on the speeders stood examining the crash site. They were too far to hear, he didn't know how long he had. Crucially, all of them were facing away from him, just for that moment. Looking at his surroundings, a good five hundred feet of open grassland between him and the monastery. He didn't stand a chance of going in through the front door, they'd spot him long before he got anywhere near it. So, what now?

He was a decent runner; he'd admit that. He wasn't prepared to say that he could sprint five hundred yards before some unknown people with blasters turned their heads. And however fast he might be, it was a fool's errand to think he could outrun a speeder. The clue was in the name.

Theo continued to crawl his way across the grass until he'd heard the shout and the first shot and then any hint of being subtle, any logical thought about how he was going to approach this went out the window. The earth kicked up beside him and his nerves went, he was straight onto his feet and running as fast as he could. He'd never realised the power of motivation in being shot at to beat any personal best sprit records.

In a way, it had been a good thing for then. He'd later realised it might not be much good for an actual operation given they knew now of his presence, but at the time it had been a relief. He'd stumbled, thought he'd been hit for a moment before spotting the opening in the earth, half covered by some bushes. They were shooting at him now, blasts of laser coming his way, some of them even had spirits out and were launching streams of fire and uniblasts towards him. He'd not hesitated, knew he needed to get out of the line of fire and he'd thrown himself through the thorns, shredding his hands and face despite his best efforts. He swore angrily at the pain, although better to be cut than shot, he'd continued to push his way through the tunnel, relieved it was wide enough not to risk suffocation. It looked like it grew deeper the further he went, hopefully high enough to stand. Pushing himself along on his ass wasn't a good way to do it but he'd had to take what he was given right now. As shafts in the ground went, it wasn't too bad. The soil wasn't damp beneath his fingers, although he could feel it intermingling with the sweat and the bloody cuts on his palms. With every movement, he felt the terror beneath his skin threaten to erupt again, sure more shots were going to come his way and he was going to feel the burn of blaster fire scorching into his skin. If he died down here, they wouldn't even need to bury him. He'd be nothing but a memory. That thought spurred him, managing to squeeze to his haunches and push on in a squat half-walk, half crawl position that was uncomfortable but definitely faster. Soon the soil was replaced by bricks and mortar, thick with the smell of aged wine and old dust amidst a thousand other things that he couldn't place.

He'd been surprised to discover it came out here in what was clearly a cellar of sorts. That shock had only intensified to see the little man sat waiting for him, a bemused smile on his face as he rested a giant blaster pistol on the bench besides him.

"Good afternoon," he said pleasantly. He had plastered dark hair close cropped to his skull, wore glasses and had a faint hint of Burykian about him. "Let me guess… Jameson? Theobald Jameson… Theobald Cyris by birth."

"Don't!" he almost snapped. "Don't call me that."

"Apologies. But you must have known that wasn't going to remain secret for very long. Not to us. There were those that wanted not to admit you on those grounds." His smile grew in length, if not pleasantness. It looked like a scar cut into his lips. "But the sins of the father should never be held upon the son. Your father is a nasty piece of work."

"That's putting it delicately," Theo replied, resting his fingers in the loops on his waistband. The little man was right. He had been expecting it. Just not yet. He'd thought it'd be a while before anyone brought that up. "If he dropped dead, I'd go dance on his grave the first chance I got."

"And hence, the reason you have been allowed to enlist here. Those who vouched for you were very persuasive in their arguments, they called long and hard in your favour. We have a process here; I think you'll find. Unisco, we vet our candidates in as firm a manner as possible. Can't let just anyone in. The good Agent Sullivan was very vocal in her protestations about the relationship between you and your father."

"Is she here?" Theo asked. "She never mentioned what I'd be walking into."

The little man smiled, this time just a hint of warmth in it. "They frequently never do. In fact, they're encouraged not to. We like to test a number of things before we even offer you a place. Adaptability. Planning on the fly. Reactions under pressure. Changing circumstances. Even facing the unknown."

"All this's been a test?" He'd guessed as much, but hearing it confirmed was a bit of a shock to the system.

"Naturally."

He swallowed down some of the anger inside him threatening to boil over, flexed his fingers hard against his side. It took a few moments before finding the composure to answer. "And did I pass?"

"Well you managed to avoid being shot, you discovered the way down here... Every scenario is different. You didn't avoid detection, so it wasn't a flawless pass, but it was far from a failure. You show promise, Theobald. If you're willing to commit, then we are willing to take you. But before you do, you should know that these next few months of your life in our care will be absolute hells for you. And even then, it doesn't get easier. The days of your life being easy, the days of them being your own, they will go forever. You will be ours. If that doesn't sound like something you can commit to, nobody will think anything less of you." He leaned forward in his seat, rested his elbows on his knees and continued to smile. It felt like his eyes were threatening to drill into Theo's skull and he cleared his throat loudly.

"Ah what the hells," Theo said, shrugging. "Not like I've got anything better to do." He tried to make it sound nonchalant, rubbed the back of his neck uneasily and managed a small smile. Backing up felt like a good idea given the way the small man was fixating on him. "I mean, if you'll take me, I want to give something back. I can do that. This, even. I can do this. Do your worst."

"You know, you may have cause to regret those words sometime soon," the little man said, the amusement in his voice, if not his smile. "Plenty do. But I like your spirit, Jameson. We'll see if your body is as defiant. It's very much a compressed training course, used to take two years but we're trying to half it at least. It'll be rough. Very rough. You're at least a competent spirit caller so we can skip most of that part of the training with you. All of it with you will be the physical and mental stuff. Now you are soft, but we will make you hard. We will make you a living weapon. That is what you are getting yourself in for. You may go now."

He'd gestured to a door behind him, and with the feeling of relief a weight from his shoulders, Theo had made to go through it. At least until he'd stopped up short, the relief turning into bitter bile.

"Ah... Do I have to call you Sir?"

"If you wish," the little man said. "You have a question."

"The way I got here, with the air loop and the falling..."

"You want to know what would have happened if you hadn't figured it out before hitting the ground?"

Theo hesitated only for a fraction of a second before nodding.

"Everyone does, but not everyone chooses to ask. Some are happier not knowing. If you really want to know..."

"Would you really have let a recruit die?" He was surprised by the sudden urgency in his voice. "Really?"

"Theobald... No. We wouldn't. We'd be castigated if it got out someone had died like that. Those were safety loops. If you hadn't worked it out by two hundred feet, the automatic current would have kicked in and you'd have floated gently to the ground. Granted we wouldn't have taken you in, but at least you'd be alive. You think you're one of the lucky ones because you worked it out?" A chuckle broke into his words. "Maybe in the end, you'll start to consider those who were sent home the lucky ones."

Over the next months, the little man... Director Kinpatso Takamishi of the Unisco training facility in Iaku, to give him his full title... had been proved right. It had been an utter bastard of a time. The nights where he hadn't gone to bed with his body aching horribly could have been counted on the fingers of his right foot. If it wasn't the hours of just endless running and obstacle courses or the gruelling sessions of unarmed combat, it had been the mental fatigue of spending time in classrooms, running through various exercises intended to help boost deductive skills, environmental awareness, memory, languages, field skills... Even the damn rules, there were more of them than first he'd thought there would, and they were required to recall them all in an instant. Sometimes he went to bed so tired he couldn't even remember his name, only to be awoken a few hours later with some sort of crazy training drill.

He didn't regret it though. He thought he'd been in decent shape before. Now, he was becoming a weapon, no part of his body didn't feel solid with muscle. He could do a push up one handed. And in a strange way, he was happy. Not an ecstatic kind of happy, the sort that would probably have candy-fried his brain before long but the sort that came with a deep sense of satisfaction that he was improving himself. Satisfaction beat ecstasy any day of the week in his mind.

That sense of contentment had turned into a deep burn of dissatisfaction when he'd discovered who else was thriving at the same facility. It had taken him days to discover his presence but to say there'd been a complete sense of unease at the appearance of Peter Jacobs at the academy was an understatement. So much for anonymity. He might have all this new training inside his head, but the old demons remained. He still didn't like people on the whole. Their capacity to be wholeheartedly, unintentionally or not, desiring towards being liked by every individual who they crossed paths with, he considered a weakness. Jacobs was no different. He knew of the man, knew that he'd extricated himself into a partnership with Scott Taylor to gravitate towards his star.

Strangely enough, when he thought of Taylor, Theo found himself admitting a sense of grudging respect for the man who had been his opponent. He'd given as good as he'd gotten and there'd been several moments during that bout in the final, Theo had been worried about defeat. Granted it hadn't been a victory but considering the circumstances of that day, he was perhaps justified in considering being alive to be a victory. Jacobs had approached him not long after, the two of them had been in different teams in their initiation, hence the reason it had taken him so long to recognise him. That, and the paralysis with a lack of caring.

That was then, now would have been different. One of the classes here at the academy had consisted of dealing with facial recognition.

"So, you're here," Jacobs said, and Theo had given him a cool thousand yards stare while debating whether to call him on his choice in stating the absolute obvious.

"That's right," he said. "Nothing much gets past you, does it?"

Uneasy grin, had he touched a nerve? He hoped so. Already he was feeling uncomfortable with the way this conversation might go. Being as brusque as possible might end it sooner rather than later and that would be a good thing. It never failed.

"It was suggested to me that this would be a good career path for me," Jacobs said, shrugging. "Thought I'd come along, see what it was like. So far…" He tensed up and let out a little grimace. "So far… Hurts a lot. You feel it."

"I'm doing the same tasks you are, I'd assume, so yes," Theo replied. Something gave inside him and he cleared his throat. Somehow proffering information came out as harder than holding it in. Nothing new there. "You do that obstacle course yet? The one with the laser grid? Stings, doesn't it?"

Jacobs grimaced again, more blatantly obvious this time. "Oh yeah. Must have hit that thing like six times. Got a rash on my back where I nearly fell on it."

Theo chuckled softly. "Graceful, huh?"

"We're all learning," Jacobs said nonchalantly. "I'd be worried if I could do all this stuff already. It's not an achievement if you don't work for it."

Well that much was true, Theo had to agree with. Granted it was nice when stuff came easily your way, but on the whole, after all this effort and pain, it'd be awesome when he graduated, and he could legally carry a blaster and a badge. Some had dropped out already, the dorm room where he was sleeping was a few beds lighter than it had been when he'd arrived. Sooner or later they'd be filled again, he guessed but for now he was enjoying the slight dip in the noise and the commotion. Whether they'd left voluntarily or been told they weren't going to be up to muster was something he couldn't say. He didn't know which'd unsettle him more if he was in that position.

"Taylor isn't here, is he?" Theo asked. He hadn't seen his former opponent around, yet that didn't mean he wasn't somewhere on the premises. The building felt like it went on forever and the two teams had been kept separate for the most part, though there were rumours they'd be put together when the groups had been thinned down to the last men standing.

Jacobs shook his head. "Nah, last I heard, he was in Premesoir with his girlfriend, enjoying some relaxation after the Quin-C." He narrowed his eyes at Theo as if expecting some sort of comeback. Theo didn't oblige him. The past was the past. And that was one thing he was getting out of this if nothing else. The stuff on the spirit calling side. Already there'd even been some of that snuck into the training. Because after all, when the people you were up against were capable of weaponizing their own spirits, it made for those who were better to challenge them. Thanks to the history lessons they insisted on forcing him to sit through, he knew the details on that, as much as he might consider it unnecessary.

"Well it's okay for some," Theo said sniffily. "I didn't expect him to actually be doing something that matters."

"That's Scott for you," Jacobs remarked. "Always seeing things in a different way to everyone else. I love the guy like a brother but..." He shrugged. "Sometimes you get to criticise brothers, right?"

Theo who had no siblings that he knew of and Jacobs whose sister had been killed recently felt that neither had of them had the right to pass comment on that particular thought.

"So why did you sign up?" Jacobs asked, Theo just fixed his eyes on him in a hard fashion in lieu of saying anything. He tried to imagine the guy hurtling out of an aeroship and scrambling for an air loop. Somehow, he just couldn't see it.

"I'd ask you the same question but I'm sure you'd tell me," he said dismissively. "I've got to go. Got safe cracking one oh one in a few minutes and I really don't want to miss that."

"I'm sure it'll really open doors for you that one," Jacobs said before killing himself laughing in a fashion Theo found more than unsettling. He allowed himself a smirk more at the reaction than the comment. It had been witty, but the reaction had been more than unsettling.

"Yes, perhaps."

Jacobs clapped him on the arm, Theo fought the urge to give him a venom-filled stare and then they were going their separate ways, much to his relief. Still amidst all this chaos and this hardship, all this new stuff that was being crowbarred into his head, it was nice to see a familiar face. Even if it was one that you hadn't cared for in the past.

That hadn't been the only strange part about the previous months in the Iaku academy, one other incident came to mind that had drawn confusion. He'd been dragged out of an unarmed combat class that day, something he hadn't been enjoying even before he'd been clocked on the jaw by a girl whose name he thought was Tamale. He knew it was going to bruise as well. She had one hells of a swing on her, that girl.

"Theobald Jameson! Report to the medical wing."

Before that, he hadn't even known that there was a medical wing. He'd supposed that there must have been, much in the same way that he supposed there was a whole section of support staff who made it a point of never being seen by those that were being trained. More than once he'd wondered if they had stealth training as well. The more he thought about it, the more he swore it started to make sense.

He'd gone there in the presence of Bruno Hans, one of the burly instructors who taught unarmed combat. At least Hans looked like he knew how to fight, unlike the slim Burykian, Naka, who'd just been teaching them shang-chiy. All white haired and bearded, he looked more like a monk than a combat expect, an impression quickly thrown away when he sprang into action.

Theo hadn't been expecting what he found in the medical wing, a small sterile room filled with empty beds. He supposed that was a relief. As tough as the training might be here, it wasn't verging on the point of dangerous. It seemed like they did know where the breaking point was for their recruits and although he was being pushed close to his, he hadn't actually gone past it yet.

Out in the middle of the room, he saw a table had been set up and the man behind it wasn't who Theo had been expecting. A slender woman was stood behind him and his heart did a little leap as he saw her. Unconsciously he smiled at her and she returned the expression.

"Hey," he said, more to Anne Sullivan than Ruud Baxter. A year back, he might have been excited about meeting Baxter. Now, not so much. Just another spirit caller. He'd met plenty of them. He'd fought plenty of them. "Fancy seeing you here."

"Cadet Jameson," Baxter broke in with a voice that demanded attention, it tugged his thoughts away from Anne and towards the man with the mismatched eyes. "Sit, please!" It was the sort of command that left no room for interpretation and Theo found himself sitting down across the table from him. "Doubtless you wonder why you've been called away from your training."

"The thought had crossed my mind," Theo said uneasily. He'd had no idea Ruud Baxter was involved with Unisco before the whole Coppinger crisis. He'd thought the man was dead. A lot of people had until he'd reappeared months earlier and footage had emerged at the Quin-C final of his people running around with glowing laser swords not unlike the one Anne had clipped to her belt. Sword hilt on one hip, blaster pistol on the other.

Huh… It was a very unusual look for her in his experiences of her. For the longest time, he'd thought she was just a sweet young woman who lacked better judgement than to try and change him. Now though, he had to wonder.

"Nothing too tragic," Baxter smiled. "We just require some blood from you, Cadet. Nothing more. When you've given it, we'll let you get back to your training."

Anne looked like she wanted to say something to him, instead chose to remain silent. He found her presence looming behind Baxter reassuring, even if the silence wasn't.

"Blood?"

Baxter had produced a giant needle and nodded in agreement. "That's correct. Roll back your sleeve."

He didn't like needles and he got the impression both of them knew that. Anne finally broke her silence, spoke to him as the needle went in, drew the blood and he found himself listening to the reassurance in her words, even if he couldn't make most of them out. He smiled weakly at her and she returned the gesture. It was hands down the sweetest thing he'd seen since being thrown out of that aeroship.

"What exactly do you need blood from me for?" he asked, not moving to roll back his sleeve.

"Just some minor tests. Under Unisco directive forty-two alpha six," Baxter said. "Which is…?"

"An executive order," Theo said. "I know; I've had the training." That had been a particularly boring day in which the various directives had been gone through by a particularly thin and sour-looking instructor named Christophe. He'd done his best to pay attention but even with the break from being punched, it was still one of the hardest days he'd suffered through here. "I understand that."

"It won't hurt," Anne offered. He almost shot her a sour look of his own.

"I wasn't worried about that. I'm just... I don't know what you want my blood for. And I don't know why you'd have an executive order for it."

"It's not just your blood, Cadet," Baxter said. "We're testing all Unisco personnel for..." He paused for a moment, considered his words. Theo found it more unsettling. "We're testing it for a tiny concentration of particles. In some people, this concentration is larger than others. A lot larger. Mine, for example. Agent Sullivan's. It's a big job, we'd have done you sooner if we could. Trust me..." His voice took on a silken tone and despite any better judgement he'd had telling him otherwise, Theo found himself listening a little closer. Anne rolled her eyes. "... We won't use it for any nefarious purposes. We just wish to test your suitability."

"Theo," Anne said. "Trust him. As people go, he's not a bad guy."

He'd given them the blood. Not that it felt like he'd ever had any choice. An executive order couldn't be refused, not without serious ramifications. They were infrequent, even if they'd been told every Unisco regional head got a blank one to use every year for emergencies. In short, more trouble than it was worth to refuse it. He didn't want to be in that sort of trouble already.

Still Anne's words had reassured him, even if Baxter's manner hadn't. There'd been something more than creepy about him and it wasn't just the mismatched eyes. He had a quiet intensity about him, a hint at something disturbing beneath the surface. It told him that there was a dangerous man, he didn't even have to hide it. Some Unisco agents, you could see it on them without even trying. Others did well to conceal it.

Anne had come after him, cornering him in the hallway outside, much to his surprise. She'd felt... Distant in there. Like a different person, somebody that he used to know but didn't any longer.

"So, how's it going here?" she'd asked, looking around the sterile corridor. It lacked the personal touch, he had to admit. Now he knew there was a medical wing here, he'd never consider it the same way again.

"Good. Good. Thanks for recommending me," he said. "It's been a bit tricky so far in places but nothing I can't handle."

She smiled at him, reached out and took his hand. Her hand might have been smaller, but she packed some hells of a squeeze into it. She was warm. "I know you can do it," she said. "And I know you'll make a damn good agent. I was right about you. I'm sorry about the blood..."

"What is it about the blood?"

Her smile faded into apology. "I can't tell you, I really can't. I'm sorry." He knew she was lying in an instant, they'd been taught a little about body language and she was displaying many of the symptoms of untruths. Unable to meet his eyes. Quiet, rushed voice. Arms folded in front of her, a defensive stance.

His own smile faded, taking his good feeling with it. "I see."

"Don't be like that," she pleaded. "We won't do anything nefarious with it. Promise. If you can't trust me, who can you trust?"

A very good question indeed. And one to this day that he still didn't have an answer to.

Chapter Five. The Mission.

"Your presence across our expedition would be most appreciated. I'm glad you changed your mind. Your name helps open doors that might otherwise be closed to us. I'm aware that the political situation in Vazara is a little testy at the moment, but all our approvals have been signed off, our visas approved. We'll meet you at the following date at the following location."
Message from Doctor Alex Fazarn to Brendan King regarding expedition to Vazara.

Recovering hurt.
To go from being broken to being whole again was a harder job than he'd expected, nor was it a pleasant one. Six months of fixing himself following his last mission and he believed he was ready. He couldn't argue with the doctors who'd said he wasn't before. The job was a hard one and going out unfit was suicidal.

Boredom was the greatest enemy though. Six months without an active mission and he was ready to climb the walls in frustration. David Wilsin's body still ached in places. Chances were, he'd been warned on more than one occasion by multiple doctors, that they would likely continue indefinitely. Fixing bones wasn't that much of an issue these days. It could be done in hours if need be. Wearing them in, on the other hand, wasn't entirely pleasant. Six months he'd been waiting for it to wear off and slowly it was happening. The drugs had helped but he'd been weaning himself off them, trying to manage the pain. He'd tried telling himself that he didn't need them. Some days he even felt normal. He'd broken a lot of bones, enough for the non-Unisco doctors who'd first examined him to question how it had happened and he'd not entirely had an immediate answer through the pain.

He hadn't been able to tell them the truth, for obvious reasons. Couldn't mention his fight with the hulking man mountain... Couldn't tell them the truth about how they'd gone toe to toe and he'd thrown everything at his unstoppable opponent and been shrugged off completely... Couldn't tell them about Agent Harper and how she'd died. He'd told them he'd fallen down some stairs, it'd been about the best he could come up with in the moment.

They hadn't believed him. It was the story he'd given them and stuck to it, even babbling under painkillers. Truth be told, he'd been impressed with the resolve he'd shown in himself. Eventually they'd come to accept it, not as the truth, but as the only truth they were going to get. He'd been transferred to a Unisco medical facility the first chance he'd gotten, had had his injuries fixed with impunity. He just wished that the process of healing would speed up, that the aches and twinges of pain would leave him. A reminder that nature couldn't be denied what she wanted.

All thoughts he put out of his mind as he raised the X7 in a two-handed grip, tried to ignore the tremors rippling through his arms and stared down the sight at the target. Twenty yards away, visibility good. Not too long ago, an easy shot. Unisco training meant even an average agent could make a shot like that with no difficulty. Those that couldn't were drummed out pretty quickly, moved away from the field. Perfection, or as damned near close to, was needed. It was not a cruel act, rather a means to survive.

He fired, aimed at the sweet spot in the centre of the composite target and frowned as he saw the burn mark present itself a good few inches up and left of where he'd pointed. Not satisfactory. Acceptable perhaps, would probably be a kill shot on a living enemy, it'd definitely disable them unless they wore armour or a shield, but for his own personal standards, then it wasn't good enough. He squeezed off more shots, emptying the power pack before pausing to survey his handiwork. Only one landed where he'd intended to put it, some of the shots hadn't even brushed the standard of acceptable.

He couldn't take much more of desk duty. They hadn't even given him as much sick leave as he'd wanted, granting him two months to recover, the following period of his time at Unisco consisting of office work. He'd spent his time compiling intelligence reports, examining various information coming in from the field, basically everything he'd suspected they'd done before but now had confirmation. Working in what was now Liam Caulker's Intelligence department wasn't entirely as bad as it could have been. Nobody had shot at him since the mission aboard the Eye of Claudia. That was almost worth it all on its own. Still in the time he'd spent sat at the desk, he'd started to realise the ugly truth about himself.

He wanted it back. He wanted to be back out there where the action was. More than that, it felt like he needed to be. As much as he might have tried to convince himself in the past that he wasn't a trigger-happy asshole like some of the people that worked out in the field for Unisco, he definitely missed it. He missed that shot of adrenaline rushing through his veins when the action kicked in, the feeling of cold metal in his hands, the exchange of shots no matter how terrifying it might be. It was always set to be a brief but exhilarating life; he'd had that proven to him already.

The whole Harper thing had proved that. Melanie Harper had been a Unisco field agent like him, part of the team who'd entered the

Eye of Claudia with the sole intention of capturing Claudia Coppinger and bringing Nick Roper out of his undercover role. The latter a stint so secret that only the director and Will Okocha had known about it beforehand. They'd gone in, they'd achieved the mission and Harper had been the only casualty. She'd been killed in close proximity to him, life snuffed out of her by the big man. Domis di Carmine. He was the one who'd damned near maimed Wilsin in the process. Beaten him down and killed Harper. Wilsin had fought back, continued to fight and fight until he'd taken an opening and he'd thought he'd killed Domis. At least he'd avenged Harper. She'd been a friendly enough woman, married to one of the training instructors in the Banga academy. Soon as he could, Wilsin had sent Dirk Harper his condolences. She didn't deserve what had happened to her. And to just rub salt into his wounds further, Domis wasn't even dead. He'd been the one who'd killed Nwakili and a part of David Wilsin had died all over again when he'd seen him stood parading the premier's corpse around like some sort of grisly trophy.

You never knew what you had until it was gone. His old life felt so very far away right now, going back to it felt almost impossible. Things had changed. They'd changed a lot. The re-shuffle of Unisco might not be good for him, they'd set up thirteen new departments to replace what came before. He had only seen Arnholt in passing in recent months, sightings of him around the buildings were becoming less and less. Between the Senate's investigation of the ICCC and their connection to Claudia Coppinger and the same organisation determined to appoint their new leader to walk straight into a crisis, it felt like he might be getting stuck in a rut. New agents were coming through all the time, the training facilities had been working overtime, those that had nearly been there had been fast tracked, those that had started within the last year were almost there. Tod Brumley, now in charge of recruitment, was rumoured to be close to breakdown over the sheer amount of numbers that were passing through now. When new people got into your old position, the chances of you getting it back felt slimmer and slimmer.

He'd fired another power pack off at the target, wiping it clean with each fresh load. Training rounds were different to the regular loads they used out in the field, they carried a lower power yield. He had to do this. He couldn't spend another year like this. He wanted back out there, he'd been pushing himself to get back into fighting shape for weeks now. Pain be damned, he was doing this. Slowly his blaster eye was coming back in, he could even take to the mats and deal out as much as he took in unarmed combat. Some of the staff ran refresher courses across the week and he'd gone back through the basics, reworking his knowledge and his technique. That had been going on a lot longer than the shooting. His doctors had told him that he needed to. The more he worked at it, the sooner the bones would start to feel natural again.

David Wilsin was being watched, he could feel the gaze on the back of his neck and he did his best to ignore it as he continued to work through the six power packs he'd brought to shooting practice. He couldn't say for sure who was watching him, but using the clues that were available to him, he could hazard a guess. The breathing was heavy, a decent sized man then, going to seed, maybe a bit of a gut. He'd walked the stairs up here and now he was panting. Probably not a field agent, maybe someone in management. He could smell them as well, a faint hint of earth and clay hidden heavily beneath a potent aftershave. Only one man wore that combination of scents.

When the last pack ran dry, he cleared his throat and removed his soundproof headgear. "Chief," he said warmly, turning and firing off a salute with his non-blaster hand. His visitor looked older than he had the last time Wilsin had seen him on Carcaradis Island. Those days felt too long ago. What had gone on there had changed everything, expecting the people who had lived through it not to have was a fallacy. His face was more lined, his eyes weary and he'd packed a few pounds on around the waist. Yet he still didn't look like the sort of man you'd mess with. He'd always had that way about him. Once his hair had only been greying but now there were definitely some hints of white in it. Being stripped of command didn't look like it had suited him, he looked sullen and tired.

"At ease, Agent Wilsin," Brendan King said, and he duly dropped the hand, popping the pack out of his weapon before sliding it into the holster at his waist. "Heard you were down here."

"And you thought you'd stop by to see me? I'm touched."

"Yes well," King looked uncomfortable, enough to set Wilsin's warning senses jangling. Of all the possible reasons he could have for walking in here, very few struck him as being good "When the needs must." He inclined his head towards the door. "Walk with me, David. It's time that we had a talk."

Wilsin nodded, loaded up a fresh power pack into his weapon and closed up his jacket, buttoning it at the front. He'd been waiting for this day for a while. King led, he followed, the two of them striding in silence until they reached an office. King pushed the door open, didn't even knock and moved to sit behind the desk.

"Please, sit," he said. This wasn't his regular office, but he treated it like it was. It didn't look like it belonged to anyone, Wilsin noted, there was a distinct lack of personal effects ongoing in the room. It had the strange sterile empty effect going on with it that felt so familiar to anyone that had ever attended a Unisco training academy. Torlis had been like this. He had a feeling the one at Iaku was as well. For a few moments he hesitated before sliding into the empty seat.

"How have you been?" King eventually asked. "You suffered some bad injuries, I've read your medical reports and it's good to see you back on your feet."

Wilsin considered the question, weighed up his answers, wondered what he could possibly say. It felt like his situation had been wholly summed up in just those few short sentences.

"Recovering," he replied. "Still some discomfort but that's not to be unexpected, they tell me."

"Only natural," King said. "I hear you want to return to the field soon."

"That's correct," Wilsin said stoically. "I've been out of the game and I want to get back in it. I want…" He caught himself before he said something stupid. Admitting he still wanted revenge wouldn't be a good thing. Might bring up all sorts of questions whose answers wouldn't reflect well on him. "… I want this to be over and I want a part of it. We need everyone available."

"Liam Caulker speaks well of you," King said, as if he hadn't spoken. "Says you've shown a sort of dedication that he hadn't expected of someone in your position. I also hear you've been learning Vazaran."

"Just the prime language and a few key phrases in local dialects," Wilsin said. Every Unisco agent was required to know at least two of the prime languages across the five kingdoms to the point of fluency. Each kingdom since the five of them had become united, had set about to ensure that they had one main language exclusive to their region, as well as the universal tongue that kept everyone talking no matter where they came from. But some local dialects still survived. People could be insular when they wanted to be. "It seems like that's where we've got the most trouble lately…"

"Actually, Vazara is no longer our problem technically," King said. "They've broken from the rest of the kingdoms, they're on their own. Their people come into our jurisdiction and break our laws, we can lock them up. But any sort of operation on Vazaran soil is not something we can go about lightly these days. Which is why I'm here."

"Do you think they'll remain apart forever?" Wilsin asked. "I mean, if we remove Claudia Coppinger from the board, do you think Mazoud will…"

"I do not know Mazoud as well as the director does. He was once one of us, you know, a very long time ago and not for very long, but do not assume him to be our enemy. Our true enemy in all of this, as you have said is Coppinger. With her out of the picture, we can start to rebuild some semblance of normalcy. With her still active, it is a futile gesture. She has Mazoud under her thumb and isn't going to let him go. His success is tied to hers. Without her, he might not survive what happens next. She is immensely popular in Vazara. She did what nobody else ever did. She's given them hope. She has given them what they believe to be a future. That sort of gesture builds fanaticism."

"The whole stuff with the Green? Did anyone ever manage to explain that away?" Wilsin felt he already knew the answer to this question, something confirmed as Brendan King shook his head.

"No. Never. If we could…"

He didn't have to finish that thought. If they could prove that the sudden rush of fertility and forest that had rushed through Vazara wasn't a divine act of generosity from Claudia Coppinger, then it might rob her of some of her followers. It might show her up as a fraud. It might do a lot of things.

What King said next startled him out of his thoughts. "Not quite yet anyway. There might be something…"

Usually there always was a potential something. He didn't know why he'd doubted otherwise. That Brendan King had a plan wasn't something he shouldn't be surprised by. Wilsin couldn't even bring himself to hide his relief.

"Only a small chance, mind," King said, almost more to himself than Wilsin. "But we're not really presented with a lot of other options. The Coppingers have dispersed, they're hiding in plain sight." He looked exasperated by the notion and Wilsin couldn't blame him really. After all it was the same tactic that Unisco agents had been employing for years and they'd had pretty good success with it. "The only time we can hunt them down in great numbers is when they want to be found. Every one of them that we take off the board, two more replace them. It is a war of attrition that threatens to grind us down unless we can change the rules of the game quickly."

"I didn't realise it was that bad," Wilsin admitted. "I mean we've had some losses recently…" He was thinking of the shooting of Unisco agent Baleric Tong in Burykia while he'd sat down for a meal. The Coppingers had taken credit. They'd cited it a blow against the cruel enforcement of the laws of decadence by a bloated government. "But…"

"You don't have a but, do you Agent Wilsin," King said. "You've been in Caulker's department; you've seen some of what comes through. We can't go on like this. They use clones as well, you know. Automatic training schemes go through their minds while they're being grown, they can produce new soldiers, pilots, spies faster than we can. We're looking for their facilities, but intelligence is slim on that part."

"You're not wrong," Wilsin said. "So, what's your something? A location for one of their key bases?"

King shook his head. "Nothing so prosaic. Nothing useful really. Get our people into one of them, we might be able to strike back. No, what I have in mind is... Different. Several months ago, I dispatched a research team into the Green in Vazara, I wanted definitive answers and I don't trust what our supposed allies in that bloody kingdom are telling us. I sent them right to the heart, get to Ground Zero and see what they could pull up for me. Maybe there's something that can prove things one way or another what happened. Unfortunately, I lost contact with them. We can't find them with our satellites, anything across that area is hard to pin down. I have been granted permission to send a second team in, a much smaller one and I intend to lead them." He smiled wearily. "If you feel up for it, I want you on it."

Wilsin couldn't hide his surprise. "Me, sir?"

"Yes. If you feel up to it. I saw what you did on Carcaradis Island, I've read your reports. You've acquitted yourself admirably ever since you became an agent, I believe firmly in your capabilities. You're exactly the sort of person that I wish to have watching my back on this jaunt."

"Sir, if you'll have me, I'll be there," Wilsin said immediately. "I needed this, thanks."

"David." King's voice took on a more personable friendly tone, the sort that Wilsin had very rarely heard from him before. "Agent Harper... It wasn't your fault, you know. You didn't get her killed."

"I know I didn't," Wilsin said, blinking. He hadn't expected those words and it felt strange that they'd been brought up. "I know that."

"What you're feeling over her death, it's natural. When someone dies around us, on our side, and we live through it to regret, it's hard. Guilt is the most natural thing imaginable in all this. I'd be worried if you weren't feeling some sort of sorrow over it. I saw you at her funeral. You looked like you were taking it badly. She knew the risks. We all do. Dirk Harper doesn't blame you. Nobody else does either. If you're feeling conflicted over it, direct it at those that are truly to blame."

"The whole Domis thing pisses me off," he said before he could stop himself. "I mean, I killed him. I thought I had. Shot him in the head and kicked him out of that thing. He should have died. Nobody should come back from that."

"From our reports, it appears that like his boss, conventional means are not going to be enough to destroy him," King remarked. "He's an unusual figure. Most of what we have centres on what he can do, not who he is. You couldn't have known, you know. Better that you survived to tell the tale than dying with Harper."

When it was put like that, it stung a little. Wilsin cleared his throat. He didn't want to go through this conversation much longer. Brendan King being friendly and comforting, he didn't want any evidence of the world going to hells more than he already had.

"Nothing about this whole Coppinger thing is really in our remit, is it sir?" he asked thoughtfully. "We're all operating out of our comfort zones."

"Just a little, David. Just a little." He said it with a smile rippling across his leathery features. "Of that, we can have no doubt."

"Tell me more about this mission. Any way I can help, I'll do it. Besides, I want to get out of this building."

"Our mission is to travel to Ground Zero for the outbreak of the Green," Brendan King said. In front of him, a hologram showed an outline of Vazara, the parts of it that had been overcome by the green highlighted in the same colour. It was, Wilsin noted, an eye-watering amount now. It had taken a few days to be noticed outside of the kingdom. Now, well over half of it was green, mostly in the middle and spreading outwards. Slowly it was advancing. And what would happen when it overtook the whole kingdom? That was something he'd wondered about whenever he'd seen it mentioned. Nature didn't behave like that, not that quickly anyway. Who was to say it'd even stop the moment it came to a large city. It had swallowed up whole towns and villages so far, the people not heard from since.

And we're about to walk straight into it. It had already claimed one Unisco team and they were about to feed another to it.

This time would be different though, he hoped. For starters, they were forewarned that there was a very real danger there… Or maybe comms just didn't work that far into the Green. Maybe they'd meet the other team on the way… It was good to hope.

"Our objectives are twofold," King continued. "One, we are to investigate the site and discover any possible intelligence in relation to what caused it and how we can stop it. More to the point, the exact nature of the link to Claudia Coppinger. Two, we are to search out any evidence for what happened to our previous team if we can."

The two of them weren't alone for the briefing, a third man had joined them who was also going on the mission, a wiry figure with brown hair and a scar on his cheek who'd introduced himself as Ben Reeves and then sat down to listen to King. Wilsin didn't know who he was, only that it was likely he wasn't a Unisco agent. They carried a certain bearing, he hadn't noticed it until Nwakili had pointed it out to him during a conversation some months ago, but there it was. Just because you didn't notice something didn't mean that it wasn't there. Something worth remembering about the job in general. Anyway, whatever the bearing, Reeves didn't have it.

Wilsin suspected he was a Vedo. Now that he found interesting, not just that King felt the need to bring one on the mission but that he'd been able to coax one into coming along in the first place. There were only a limited number of them working with Unisco, there'd been twelve at the start and a few more had graduated into it. Still to get them trained up to an acceptable level for the higher command to accept them going into the field... It all took time. Granted they all seemed sound people and you'd want them at your back, but something about it didn't just sit right with him.

It wasn't that he didn't trust them. After all Ruud Baxter, their leader, was a legend. If he said they were okay, then chances were that they were okay. It was just... He didn't know. His instincts told him to be worried. He couldn't entirely trust what he couldn't understand. That they commanded a mystical power was something he'd been told before, he hadn't been at the moment when they had revealed themselves. Those who had been in the stadium on Carcaradis Island spoke of them with reverence, of their glowing swords and their superhuman abilities in the same way the public spoke of great spirit callers.

"We are going to enter Vazara as part of a research team that is going in to examine the Green," King said. Wilsin knew he held a position as part-time lecturer at the University of Bacar, managing to balance the two roles in his life. Rumour had it he was spending less time at the university these days what with the Coppinger crisis. He wondered if that was the source of King's newly whitened hair.

"Our third role is to protect the team on their journey through. We cannot reveal our true identities to them. Although we will be armed, we cannot admit ourselves to be linked in any way to Unisco. If we do, we will not be allowed to leave the kingdom. Mazoud has made that very clear. Leave your X7's at home, alternate weapons will be provided. Agent Wilsin, you're joining the team on the proviso that you're looking for spirits in the Green. Mr Reeves, your background in xenobiology gives you an excuse to be there."

Reeves shrugged his shoulders at Wilsin. "Hey, I didn't always wave a sword made of light around. All of us had something before this, y'know."

"Understood," Wilsin said. "Brendan, I'm with you. It's good that someone's pushed for this to happen. I'm worried about that jungle."

"We're all worried about the Green, David. It can't be controlled, and it looks out of control. There's no rhyme or reason to it and that terrifies me almost as much as what might happen if Claudia Coppinger wins this war. Because make no mistake about this whole situation. It is war."

That brought up an uncomfortable silence for a few moments before Reeves broke it with a cough. "No pressure then, wouldn't you say?"

"Sounds simple enough," Wilsin said. "The assignment. Be good to get back out there." He folded his arms and leaned back in his seat. "When do we get underway."

"The Green covers some several hundred miles currently," Reeves said. "Might be a long walk."

"I'm not in a hurry for anything else," Wilsin said, shrugging at him. "Are you?"

"One more thing…"

Ross Navarro entered the room at King's word, a large steel container crate in his arms. He looked like he was wincing under the effort of moving it, the silver box almost the size of his entire upper body and it looked heavy by the way his muscles were taut with the stress.

"Hey, guess what time it is?" he said. "It's new equipment time."

Privately, Wilsin loved this point of the mission. The bit just before when they came around with any sort of equipment that they thought might be needed. Of course, it was the first time he'd experienced it under Navarro. Most of the times he'd gone through it, it had been Alvin Noorland. On the big ones anyway. Navarro was still an unknown quantity to him. He had a good history, a meteoric ascent into his position. Even if there were some who said it had only been a gift from Arnholt because he'd spent weeks in Coppinger captivity, something to placate him.

"Ross," Reeves said amicably. "How's it going."

"Great, thanks Ben. Should see some of the stuff we've got cooking up, it's going to be bloody exceptional. Hey, how's Alex? Not seen her for a while?"

"She's good. Really taking to the training. Master Baxter thinks she has great potential."

"Always knew there was something special about that girl," Navarro said. "Should have seen the way she flew. No fear."

"I've never felt that the absence of fear is a good thing," Wilsin said thoughtfully as Navarro set down the case and started to open it up. "If anything, more the reverse."

Navarro ignored him as he slid the case open and propped the lid up, clearing his throat. "Okay, so since Chief King requested that you leave the X7's at home... They're so associated with us right now that it might not be best to advertise their presence."

"I'm curious about something," Reeves said. "If you take weapons into Vazara, even if you have the proper permits, you're going to attract attention, right? They're going to know you have them. So why not go in with nothing and just buy some when you get there. There's got to be a dozen people selling blasters on the quiet in any Vazaran city. That way they don't know you have them."

"It's not about secrecy," King said. "We want them to know we have them. We're not there for insurrection, rather in the name of science on the surface. Going into the Green, we have a right to be able to protect ourselves. We start buying up blasters on the quiet and they do search us, we can't tell them where we got them and why we have them when we do, it's not going to look particularly good. At least taking them in, we know they know about them."

"Sorry, I've never smuggled weapons into a hostile kingdom before," Reeves said, more than just a hint of sarcasm in his voice. A Unisco agent would never have gotten away with talking to King like that but here he didn't reply.

Wilsin ignored them both, walked around to look over Navarro's shoulder into the case. Inside, it had been split into three sections, one of them lined with blasters of varying sizes. He studied each of them for several seconds, pursing his lips before pulling up a huge blaster pistol with a swing-out power pack.

"Ooh good choice," Navarro said, watching as Wilsin looked down the sight. "Tebbit T6. Very potent. Six shots but it's capable of punching a hole through anything short of a hovertank. Lot of stopping power. A lot heavier than the X7, that, so I'd practice with it first if you want it."

Wilsin hefted its weight in his palm for a few seconds, considering it. He reached into his holster, removed his X7 and replaced it with the Tebbit. He could feel the difference in weight as it tugged at his belt, but it wouldn't be an insurmountable problem.

"You know what, I'll take it," he said. "Take that and ten power packs of charge. Might need it all. Looks like the sort of blaster someone like me might take into a hostile environment. Massive. Over the top. Ostentatious."

Brendan King went next, taking a Featherstone 54SF with fifteen shot pack. It was not a weapon Nick Roper would have approved of, Wilsin noted with a smirk. He famously didn't rate Featherstone products. When he was offered a blaster, Reeves shook his head and tapped the cylinder at his belt.

"I got this," he said. "It's all I need."

"Take a blaster, Mr Reeves," King said. "You start waving that thing around if things get tetchy, it's going to draw a lot of attention down on us. I'd rather you have it and not need it."

Reluctantly, Reeves did, picking out a Bellario-4 and pocketing it, a small blaster pistol and not especially effective over any sort of range but Wilsin knew it'd do the job up close.

"I'll sort you a holster out," Navarro said. "Okay, so as for your other equipment, we've thrown positioning systems into the mix, portable for minimum effort in transport. If you get lost, and there's a good chance of it given it's a jungle out there, it'll keep track. We'll key in your muffler chips as well to ensure that you don't lose track of each other… Ben, I'll sort you something else out."

Since he wasn't technically a Unisco agent, Reeves wouldn't be bearing the chip in his face that made the muffler technology work to obscure identities. We've thrown in three lukonium machetes, should let you get through the toughest terrain. Ropes, medical supplies, even a grappling gun. There's three sets of hand scanners, in the absence of a proper spectrometer…"

"What's our time frame?" Wilsin asked. "I mean, what's a reasonable time to expect getting to the target zone?"

"Hopefully weeks rather than months," King said. "Getting back will be easier."

"It will," Navarro said. "We're putting together a positioning beacon for you. If at any point, you need extraction then activate it. It'll send a signal to us, we'll send an extraction in to pick you up. They'll be with you as quickly as they can. Get in as legally as they can manage, pick you up, get out."

"Well that'll be an experience," Wilsin commented dryly. He couldn't see how this might possibly go wrong. It sounded sarcastic even in his head.

"I'll be in charge of the beacon, Agent Wilsin," King said. "It stays with me."

"Your packs will also contain water purification tablets, a lot of them. That's one thing that you won't have trouble finding in Vazara now." Navarro laughed as he said it. "Ironic really, huh?"

"Looks like things are all in order here," King said. "You've done well, Chief Navarro."

"Hey, it's my job." Still Navarro did sound pleased. Praise from Brendan King was praise indeed. "We'll arrange for food as well to be picked up when you get there. We still do have some contacts in Vazara. People loyal to what was before, rather than what it's become."

"All sounds good to me," Wilsin said. "When do we get this show on the road then?"

Chapter Six. Sore Points.

>*"There'll always be criminals. With great opportunity comes great risk and when we live in a time of prosperity, there'll always be those who put their minds to try and get there a little faster, a lot easier than working for it. There will always be men and women like this, from Regan Community Enterprises to the Montella Family to the assassins, Kenzo Fojila. They'll see an opportunity. They'll find a void and move to fill it. That's what they do. It is their nature. They will always exist. And fortunately, so will we to combat them wherever they may go."*

Unisco Criminology Professor Rita Melane's opening lecture to students at the Iaku academy.

Some months back.

"Again."

Theo grit his teeth and braced himself, dug his feet into the mat and met the eyes of his opponent. This wasn't much of a contest on the efforts of either of them. Neither of them knew enough to truly hurt each other deliberately.

That just left the potential for accidents. He didn't like that idea, although if he didn't want to risk getting hurt, he probably shouldn't be here. He'd never been in fights before this, at least not ones on even footing. The guy they'd pitted him against didn't look much more competent. He'd been told that he'd been at the Quin-C although Theo didn't remember him, which admittedly meant nothing. He didn't remember most of the cannon fodder who'd made up the earlier rounds.

"Today!" Khazeer said abruptly. It was voice of a man who didn't want to have to repeat himself.

Daniel Roberts grinned at him, adjusted his stance slightly, shifted his weight onto the front foot. His eyes betrayed nothing. That grin pissed Theo off. He tried to shove it down. Fighting while angry did nothing for anyone. They'd had a senior Unisco agent in to talk to them about that some weeks earlier, telling them how he'd caught the killer of his fiancé and had beaten him senseless in the most dispassionate way possible. Personally, Theo hadn't believed him. Nobody was that ice cold. People were only human after all. They thirst for revenge and when it was offered to them, they'd try to assuage that thirst.

He nearly missed the punch coming for him, blocked it with his forearm and grimaced with the effort as he felt the blow jar through his arm. Most of Roberts' weight was behind it, he wasn't huge, but he was definitely on the stocky side. What he had, he used well.

"Good!" Khazeer barked, hands on his hips as he stood watching on the side lines, a whistle around his neck and a shocksword in the other. "Now counter! Don't stand there. If you don't hit him, he will hit you."

Really, Theo thought dryly. No shit, boss.

In a way, hearing all of this first-hand was helpful. The first time anyway. The second time it became annoying. The third time tiresome. He'd heard it now more times than he could remember, he wasn't even sure how long they'd been training, how long he'd been stood in this ring with Roberts, but he was tired of it.

"Again!"

Theo lunged backwards, let Roberts fall with him, dragged most of his weight down and sent a knee into his stomach that doubled the stockier opponent over almost into two. He was through playing nice, he'd have dropped an elbow into his spine had Khazeer's whistle not cut through the red mist.

"Good. That was good." Maybe he'd managed to fool Khazeer for the moment. All it needed was a show of force and he'd done it "But you need to keep your temper. Lose it in a fight and you'll lose the fight. And you need to keep your focus as well…"

Roberts rose up suddenly, the top of his skull grazing Theo's nose. He recoiled back in surprise, more shocked than hurt, frantically blinking to clear the spots from his vision, tried to remember where he was. Roberts was on him in that instant, tackling him to the ground with his superior weight. He didn't follow up, just sat there on top of him for a minute or so.

"You know what, that's enough for today," Khazeer said softly. If Theo craned his head, he could see the look of frustration on his face. "Hit the showers, put some cold packs on your bruises, report to your next class."

Unisco training. That session summed it up in its entirety, at least the way Theo had seen it so far. One gruelling ordeal following another, very little chance to rest and recover. Time became confused between it all. Sometimes they'd start when it was dark on runs that were way too long, sometimes they'd not see daylight between classes. It was often late at night again by the time they went to bed, weary bodies threatening to break down crawling into rough sheets that felt like silk against the stresses of the day.

Often it felt like sleep was cut to a minimum. Theo got the impression that his head had barely hit the pillow and he'd closed his eyes before he was being dragged out again and thrown into three hours of unarmed combat with an equally bleary-eyed cadet or shooting practice against targets that to his unpleasant surprise shot back. Nothing lethal but the darts carried a nasty payload of electricity that stung horribly when they landed. Then there were the lectures and the lessons of the stuff that they were expected to know as Unisco agents, the processes and the procedures, the theory behind the practical lessons they engaged in, facts and figures and histories and case studies, more learning than he'd done at any point ever and his brain felt like it was going to burst.

 More than one trainee almost collapsed in a nervous breakdown, taken out of the rooms in a gibbering wreck. Sometimes they returned, sometimes they didn't. It was brutal, more than once Theo had actually considered quitting before reminding himself that to do that would be to let them win. And if they won, then that would be essentially him losing and he wasn't going to give them the satisfaction of beating him. That small thought deep in the recess of his mind was everything that kept him going. He didn't want to lose. Not now. Not ever.

 It was easier if he imagined the instructors as the enemy. They had their purpose, he had his. They were doing their jobs. It was important to take it in, learn from them but at the same point, not to give in to them. He couldn't give in to them, he wouldn't do it but sometimes he felt like he was reaching the end of his rope with them. Much more and… He didn't want to think like that. It'd be his loss if he gave this up. He wouldn't be able to live with himself if they forced him into quitting and that was the memory he plastered across the forefront of his thoughts every time they dragged him out of bed.

 Peter Jacobs was coping as well, surprisingly Theo thought. The stories about Unisco went something along the lines that they only liked new callers who they could mould and shape into something better, along their own terms and lines. Raw material rather than the finished product. They didn't like those who'd already been calling for a period of longer than three years or so, they were set in their ways, they were used to the luxuries and the rewards of their chosen profession and they didn't do well with the change when they were forced to adapt.

 He knew this because they'd been told it their first lecture, how they weren't expected to make it through, but they were open to being proved wrong as a collective. He'd been surprised by Jacobs immensely. He thought he looked like some idiot who'd drop out after a few days, realising that this had been a massive mistake, but the stubbornness was there. He almost looked as determined as Theo himself to ensure that he didn't crash out in disgrace.

Even if he thought he was a bit of an idiot, he could respect blind stubbornness. Not admitting when you were beaten was an admirable skill to Theo. Some gave up at the first sign of a hurdle. They were worthy of wholehearted contempt, they deserved everything they received, which in a perfect world would be very little.

He'd long come to realise that wasn't the way of the kingdoms though. The world wasn't perfect. Those who deserved nothing sometimes thrived and those to whom everything should come often were the recipients of nothing. To describe life as cruel was an understatement but often he'd felt the urge just to get on with it. Bemoaning his lot wouldn't change anything, no matter how much someone hoped it might.

Pete Jacobs and Daniel Roberts had struck up a friendship of sorts. They'd been forced to room close together, sharing the cramped bunk beds in a communal dorm with every other new male cadet that stank of sweat from the previous occupants, sweat and stuff that Pete didn't want to think about. Walking in, he'd seen his bunkmate stood leaning against the beds, an eyebrow raised.

"Hey, it's you," he'd said. "Peter Jacobs. Hoped it'd be you."

"Really?!" Pete had sounded surprised. "Me?"

"Well, yeah?" Roberts had given him a grin. "Don't worry, I'm not crazy. Just... Well I thought it'd be a good thing."

"A good thing?" Already the first day had been long with the orientation they'd made them all sit through, two hours of talking concluded by an instructor with a paintball rifle bursting in and firing into the crowd, just so they could see who'd react fastest in the face of an unexpected crisis. Pete was proud to notice that he'd avoided getting any paint on his jacket. The only stains were from the grass where he'd landed roughly following his arrival on location. He still couldn't believe they'd thrown him out of an aeroship. More than once he'd wondered what might have happened if he hadn't worked out the airloop quickly enough. That had been a bit of a cheap trick in his book.

"Yeah we got something in common. We were both at the Quin-C. Remember me? I got knocked out by Weronika Saarth..."

"Erm..." Not even in the slightest, Pete wanted to say. He remembered Saarth far more if he was honest, a striking redhead who'd royally kicked off after she'd been beaten by his good buddy Scott Taylor in... he thought it was the quarter finals. Funny story for all involved, unless you were her. "Vaguely. I'm not going to wake up and find you staring at me in the dark, am I?"

"Pfft!" Roberts actually snorted at that. "I don't think they'll let us sleep long enough for creepy night time activities. Besides..." He lowered his voice an octave or two. "There's people here I'd rather spy on at night, am I right?" He held up his hand and Pete waited a moment before smacking it with his own. There had been some women at the orientation, but nothing was further from his mind. Not right now. He'd made a choice to do this, he was going to do it damn right. As much as he might like the idea of casual sex, he wasn't going to start chasing it while he was here.

Besides, every story of Unisco agents said that they got plenty as part of the job, seductive enemy agents and alluring allies all were fair game. Use every tool at your disposal, someone had said, and he wondered if he was to take them literally on that.

He said as much to Roberts who'd nodded in agreement. "Oh, hells yeah. I can't... I was at the final. I..." For the first time, his composure broke, and it was Pete's turn to nod. He remembered it too. He'd made it out unscathed. Plenty hadn't. How many lives had been torn apart because of what Coppinger had done? When Nick Roper had mentioned to him that there was always more that could be done, he'd made a plunge into a decision that had led him here. The man could have been his brother-in-law but for Harvey Rocastle and Wim Carson.

Had revenge motivated him to come take this path? He didn't want to think so. Looking at himself in that light wasn't something that he really wanted to do. Pete hadn't ever thought he had a vengeful bone in his body and he didn't want to start now. No, it wasn't the thought of avenging Sharon, though he soon might have the power to do that when he completed all this. There'd been a considerable age gap between them, they'd never been as close as say the Arnholt siblings whom he'd become quite good friends with on the island. They'd not shared a father by blood, though if she failed to love his father because of it, she'd never shown it. John Jacobs had done a lot for her, been there for her when her own father hadn't, and she'd respected him massively for it.

No, he wanted to honour her. He'd found things out after her death he hadn't known about her before, through a combination of her fiancé and her former teacher. Ruud Baxter in particular had been very eager to talk about her. He'd spoken highly of her, told him stuff about her past that had been going on while he'd been just a little kid, too snot-nosed to know better. He'd told Pete of her time training to be a Vedo and he'd been more than a little awed by it. Pete had seen them in action at the Quin-C final and how they'd sprang into action when the Coppingers had attacked. Each one of them had been hailed as heroes.

Baxter had also told him of how her past as a Vedo had ultimately led to her demise. How Carson and Rocastle had come to her with intentions of forcing her hand. She'd fought them, and she'd died for her efforts. Badly. He'd seen her before the funeral and it wasn't a sight he was ever likely to forget. No matter how good a job the undertaker had tried to do, he hadn't quite been able to fake away the trauma to the back of her head where she'd been blasted with a kinetic disperser. They'd hid the bruises where she'd smacked the wall, covered up the great tear in her chest with her clothing but he knew it was there.

The funeral had been a complete farce in the end, but Roper had ultimately explained away why he'd done what he'd done in the aftermath of the carnage of the Quin-C final. He'd explained the need for the greater good, that he'd done it to try and honour her by catching a dangerous person. He could appreciate it, even if he couldn't entirely forgive him for it.

"We've all got reasons we need to be here," Pete said softly as he looked at Roberts. "You want top bunk or bottom one?"

"Top," Roberts said immediately. "They come in here shooting again, they'll probably hit you first." He grinned as he said it and despite everything on his mind, Pete grinned too.

"Yeah but you know what?"

"What?"

"They do that, I'm closer to the door. Be up and gone like a shot. I'd practice your flying dismount from that thing." He inclined his head towards the top bunk. "Lest you land like an idiot."

Silence hung between them for a moment, lost in contemplating the ridiculousness of the conversation they were having. He'd missed this. He hadn't seen Scott for weeks now and this sort of talk was something they'd done from time to time when they'd travelled together. Happy days, even if they felt so long ago now.

"You know what?" Roberts said. "We're not going to get shot at in here, are we?"

"Well I'd bloody hope not," Pete replied with a grin. "But I never expected to get shot at in the first session of orientation either."

"Oh, I know, right? And what the hells was the idea in tossing us out an aeroship to get us here in the first place?"

To that, Pete had no answer he could give.

The two of them had joined Theo in the mess hall one day, surrounded him before he could get up and leave. Something he almost certainly would have done given the chance. He ate alone here, had chosen it as his own section and everything. Today had been different, he didn't want to talk to anyone. He'd heard the whispers about him today and he'd done everything to ignore them. Who the hells were they to talk about him? Like their own pasts were so clean.

"Oh, come on, stay!" Roberts said jovially. At least it was a pleasant preference to the mutters behind his back. He'd nearly gone for at least two people so far over it. "This whole lone wolf thing is getting old, man. You're not fooling anyone."

"Excuse me?"

"You're letting the side down, Theo," Pete said, glancing around the mess hall. The food wasn't much to write home about, but it was passable. It was better than he might have managed out on the open road, but he'd definitely had better. A lot better. It was meat, he knew that much but what sort of meat was rather difficult to say. It had a lot of texture to it, he'd spent minutes chewing at it and the damn thing still wasn't showing any signs of defeat.

Given that his question hadn't had an answer, he didn't find himself rushing to ask another. Instead he chewed thoughtfully, not letting his thoughts be voiced. He continued to work the meat, chewing thoughtfully as he tried to passively ignore the two of them staring at him. The meat couldn't win forever, he finally swallowed it down and looked at them both pointedly. "I wasn't aware there were any sides," he eventually said. He hadn't been either. An interesting choice of phrasing. "I'm on my side."

"Told you," Roberts said. "Not a team player." He sounded more than a little triumphant as he said it, managing to effectively annoy Theo without even trying. "Seriously, dude, can't go in like a one-man army at this. You might have this whole thing going on, but it'll get you killed out there."

"And what do you care about that?" Theo said through gritted teeth. The flavour of his food turned to ash in his mouth, burnt and tasteless charcoal at the back of his throat. Of the days he'd had here, today was turning out to be one of the worst ones so far.

"Well someone has to, right?" Pete said.

His thoughts drifted back to the class earlier, memories swimming back through his mind. He'd been sat towards the back, a data pad in front of him, maybe the whole of the group being trained locked in a room that was only slightly big enough for purpose. The lecturer had been someone he'd not seen around the facility before, a crimson haired woman with a pointed nose and a slight build. When she walked, it was with an uneven gait, like a disabled heron. He'd noticed one of her legs was a little longer than the other. Strange. It was hard to tell how old she was, her skin was free of wrinkles but in her eyes, she looked as if life was finally getting to her. Her voice was hoarse and croaky, or perhaps she'd just spent a lot of years on the tabac leaves. She'd only been introduced as Professor Melane.

Since he'd started training for Unisco, he'd started to notice stuff like this. They insisted on it. Perfect awareness not just of the people he'd meet but of his surroundings. There'd been lessons in it early on, they'd expected the students to hone it as often and as rapidly as possible. One of their favoured tests had been to pull someone out the mess hall after they'd eaten and get them to recite the floor plan, tell them exactly where everyone had been sat. Another was to give certain cadets contraband beforehand and to make the student being tested work out who was carrying it based on the way they moved and acted.

Those who got it right were allowed to eat again that day. Those who got it wrong were given some slight menial task, just enough to remind them that they were being reprimanded. A reminder to work at it harder in the future or there might well not be another chance to get it right. He'd had one reminder and then he'd really taken to it. As things went, it wasn't quite as hard as he'd expected. It wasn't all about constant staring, just trying to remember every detail. That was impossible.

He'd heard about those with photographic memories, he didn't have that. What he'd found was that it was easiest when you relaxed, didn't try to remember everything. Just take in a few key bits and remember those. With those out of the way, the rest soon fell into place. It worked for him, that was all that mattered, and he couldn't complain about it. It was a journey, not a destination. A dozen steps to mastery and you could only take one at a time.

Her subject had been criminology and she'd been pulling out some examples of how the great criminals of the five kingdoms of the past had operated. She'd spoken at length as to how the Montella family had crippled half of Serran and some of Premesoir at one point, how they had their fingers in most of the key enterprises. If they didn't want something getting built, it wouldn't. If they wanted to skim a few thousand spirits off the beginner supply a month, they would do. He'd heard stories in the past about how new callers had gone to pick up a starting spirit and been informed that there were none left despite a mass delivery taking place a day or so earlier.

Then again, his own origins had never quite been the same as those of anyone else. He'd never been to Serran at the time when the Montella family really were their own bosses, last he'd heard all the big names had gone to trial for many counts of criminal activity. There'd been the Regan's in Canterage, typically understated but no less viciously enterprising when it came to the chance of a profit. Their speciality had been fixing spirit bouts and gambling, but they'd proven themselves to be the top dogs in the Canterage underworld when it turned to violence, fighting off every challenger who tried to muscle in on their business interests. They'd recognised the nature of how many credits could be made out of spirit calling early on and they'd gone to take their own chunk of it. Rumours had it they'd been moving into drugs as well before Sammy Regan had been killed earlier in the year and they'd yet to recover ground from it. He'd been the big brain behind it all, had made sure he stayed that way and after his death, they had nobody else of his calibre.

All of them had been interesting to hear about, in their own way. Seeing the way that they'd done things, even now looking at the way that their actions had had repercussions, he could see for the first time, the size of the job at hand. All of them seemed to pale in comparison to what Claudia Coppinger was doing now, wherever she may be, but there was still one other name to come up in the lecture that he'd been praying wouldn't be mentioned, but alas it looked as if he were to be disappointed. Especially as the picture of the sharp featured man flashed up on the wall. He still had hair in the photo, still looked like a friendly uncle when the reality was quite different. Even in the picture, the sheer imposing nature of his presence wasn't lost.

"John Cyris," she'd said, staring out at the class through her pink rimmed glasses. "I'd have hoped all of you have at least heard his name, I'd think that at least some of you might know a little more about him…" He'd wondered if that was a dig at him. It wasn't a warm day, but he'd felt the sweat soaking his forehead. It wasn't what he wanted to discuss right now. "But that's not important. As criminals went, John Cyris went down a route that many of them have tried, but remarkably, he got away with it longer than most of them do. He tried to appear a respectable figure in the community, some of the enormous profits that he made from blackmail, intimidation, trafficking and theft amongst others went straight back into good causes. He considered it a perfect way to launder so many illegal credits."

Thinking back, Theo could certainly remember a lot of what Cyris had said about charity in the past and not a lot of it was complimentary. For fools and the unfortunate, he'd always remarked over dinner. Helping out those who couldn't help themselves. He didn't have time for those. He saw people in two different brackets. Those he could use and those that he couldn't. That was the sort of man that his father had been, and he probably still was. People didn't change in his experience. Barring that solitary meeting many months ago, he'd cut Cyris out of his life completely. No regrets about it either. He'd never been that sort of guy to hold regrets. And he'd never been especially close to the man either. He would have cut him away a long time ago if he'd been able to.

"And he was right. For a long time, Cyris was based in Delhoig, he had a big compound there and ruled his own little kingdom from it. He had a wife and a son..." Theo felt a little stab in the back of his spine at that. He was sure she was narrowing her eyes at him as she said it. Maybe he was being paranoid "He had three acolytes, Jenghis, Silas and Mara who carried out his will..."

Actually, he could remember those three quite well. Jenghis had been his first crush, a tall statuesque woman with huge black-purple hair and the sort of breasts that he'd have loved to have buried his face in. He'd never been that interested in sex and yet he'd always had that urge. Mara had been a polar opposite, smaller and non-descript, olive skinned and more than a hint of danger about them. If Jenghis was the honey, Mara was the trap. And Silas... Theo had always gotten the hint that his father would have preferred Silas to be his son. The two of them had always had a bond that had initially made Theo jealous. Eventually he'd given up trying. Fuck the pair of them had been his sentiments at the time.

"All of which meant that very little could be traced back to him. They operated through layers and layers of operational security, they were very successful at it as well. Cyris made several viewing screen appearances, he came across as a bit of an evangelist, he often voiced his thoughts on the divines and about making the kingdoms a better place. Not entirely..." Melane said, bringing to voice the thoughts that had been bubbling in Theo's mind. "Not entirely unlike Claudia Coppinger is now. He sought out those with little going for them, the uneducated, those teetering on the brink between jail and death and he made their lives better. Not massively better but just enough that they would continue to work and work for him, giving him everything they had in the promise that things could only continue to improve. Often it would cost them their lives. He became like a Divine to them."

She clicked her clicker and it showed the compound, weird seeing your old house like this. The three acolytes, Jenghis looking as fine as he remembered her... Mom...

"Fuck me," he said quietly. Someone heard him and laughed, although they probably didn't get why right away. He didn't have any pictures of his mother. They'd been lost, allegedly, when she'd died and Cyris had been typically unapologetic about the whole thing. Theo had been grief stricken and his father had just carried on like nothing had happened, more than that, like he'd been glad she was gone.

Charlotte Cyris. Memories were one thing. Actual physical evidence was another thing entirely. He'd forgotten... Not the blonde hair but how shiny it was. Not the brown eyes but how soulful they were. She looked... Happy here. He coughed a little, tried to blot out the feeling in the pit of his stomach. He didn't like feeling like this, he always tried to shove down how much he still missed her to this day. If there was any sort of Divine justice, his father would have died, and his mother would have lived. Instead, he'd been condemned to the cruellest twist. One parent who'd died and one who didn't love him at a time when he'd needed them both.

More than once, he'd wondered how the two of them had ended up together. His mother was an angel; his father was a demon. He'd always heard that opposites would attract but that was taking the piss massively. Even Cyris looked happy in the image. The only one who didn't... How old was he there? Ten? Twelve? He couldn't remember. Didn't want to if he was honest. It was painful thinking back to that time. What sort of shit had his dad been up to? Had his mom known? He didn't know. Maybe he should find out but...

He gulped a little. For so many years now, he'd always laboured under the impression his mom hadn't known. She'd been innocent, his father had tricked her like he tricked everyone else. Only Theo had seen through him. He didn't want to believe the worst of her. It'd destroy everything he'd ever thought of her. Now he thought about it, he wondered how she couldn't have known what her husband did. Nobody could have been that blind.

Some of them were looking at the picture, then back at him. That irritation only grew, the idea that they knew forming like a tumour in the back of his mind, itching away at his brain. One guy smirked at him, he didn't know his name, but he was going to find out... No! No, he couldn't do that. Couldn't strike out like that. He'd learned so much here in the academy that he wasn't going to risk getting kicked out over something stupid like this.

"Eventually though he did fall," Melane said. "Cyris and his Freedom Triumphant philosophy, the idea that we're all free from any sort of shackle, that's our right and we should honour it, even the entire organisation he named for himself, Cyria, it all came crashing down around his ears. He was arrested, although not convicted. His reputation however, as someone respectable was destroyed. Close eyes have been kept on him ever since."

It sounded like something his father would do. Slip through the cracks and get away with it, if not smelling of roses but not entirely caked in the shit stink. Something ground in his hand and Theo realised he'd been clenching his fists, cracking his knuckles together hard.

"His wife died," she said. "His son broke away from him, cut all contact." Theo was sure she met his eyes when she said that. He felt the blood flush his face. He wished he was somewhere else right now. There wasn't anything about this that was really bloody awkward. He wished she'd just come out and say it, point him out and advertise to the room that he was sat here. It'd cut out any of the suspicion, any of the mutterings. It'd be out in the open and he wouldn't mind that rather than wait to feel a dozen knives sink into his flesh, opening him up by degrees.

"Jenghis was killed when Cyris was arrested. Silas evaded Unisco personnel. Mara was arrested along with her boss. You might wonder why you're being told all of this," Melane continued. "The short answer is that it matters. To learn for the present, you must look at the past. If something has happened before, it can happen again. Claudia Coppinger has employed some of the techniques that John Cyris employed, techniques that worked so well for him. Like Cyris, she hid behind a façade of respectability, unlike Cyris, her reach has the potential to affect billions. Already she has broken the five kingdoms with the help of the Vazaran Suns, who incidentally, we're going to talk about next in great detail."

"So, is it true then?" Roberts asked, leaning over the table to look at him. Theo gave him such a scornful look that he ducked back in retreat, suddenly apologetic. "Sorry."

"Personal space," Theo growled. "What do you think? More than that, why do you even want to know? It doesn't matter that bloody much!"

"John Cyris, he really your dad?" Roberts asked with a whistle. "Woah!" He sounded more than a little impressed. Theo wasn't sure why. "How did they even let you in here then? Wouldn't you fail a background check?"

"Clearly not," Theo said dryly. "Or I wouldn't be here, would I?" He tried not to think too much about the good words that Anne had put in for him. Already he'd had this thought, he'd guessed that there might be those reluctant to allow him to enrol in the academy because of where he'd come from. "I'm not him and I never will be. You want him; you can have him. He means nothing to me. I've never considered him my father."

He meant it as well, it felt good to get the words out. Like a great pressure had been released off his chest. Weird. He tried not to think about it, gave a relieved smirk to nobody and finished the last of his meat.

"Hey, we all got secrets," Pete said. He looked at the meat on his plate, rolled his eyes. Theo noticed he'd only eaten his vegetables, left the meat behind. Maybe he didn't eat meat. Or he might be reluctant to eat this shit. He couldn't blame him. If there was any better choice, he wouldn't have touched it either. "I don't care your dad was a nutcase... I mean..."

"Are you going somewhere with this?" If he was trying to make a point, Theo wanted him to get it out, rather than suffer through this excruciating little back and forth much longer to try and avoid hurting feelings. Suffering by degrees was worse than one great poke that got to the heart of the matter.

"Just that we're all in this together," Roberts said. "We need someone to partner up with for the next set of exercises. We want you."

Okay, he'd figured they'd wanted something. But that... That was unexpected. He hadn't even heard that. Normally he didn't do teamwork, yet that had been one of the first things Anne had pointed out to him. You join Unisco, you damn well better learn to work as a small piece of a much larger part. If you don't, you'll die. Worse than that, you'll get others killed as well. So far it hadn't come up. But now...

"Why?"

The question looked like it had surprised them both, like neither of them knew how to answer. "Well," Roberts said, shrugging. "We know you've not got anyone else."

"Plus, you're a total badass," Pete added. "I mean, it's not like there's people queuing up to ask you. We're totally getting in there. Look, I'm not saying let's be best friends..."

Good, Theo thought, because there's likely little chance of that happening. If I wanted friends, I'd find better ones than you two jokers.

"... I'm saying let's work together to get through this, let's all graduate together and then take it from there. You get me?"

The really worrying part was, yes. He did get him. Everything he said made perfect sense. There really was very little arguing with it. It did work out for everyone. Him, these two idiots. Unisco. Everyone.

"Well your logic isn't disputable," he said eventually. He offered each of them a hand which they quickly shook one at a time. "Okay. Let's do it."

Nobody could ever say he wasn't a pragmatist when he needed to be.

Chapter Seven. Back to the Battlefields.

"I'm happy to announce that now we've sorted out our internal disputes, professional spirit calling bouts will resume imminently with our sanctions. Although it may yet be weeks before we can set up any ICCC sponsored tournaments, any town with a stadium that wishes to place a bout on can now do so with our blessing. We all have troubles in our lives of late, we face threats that we cannot see, and it is always good to take the time away from that worry to relax and recover."
Words at an ICCC press conference from newly elected president, Adam Evans.

It had been too long since Wade had last been to Burykia. Not that there was a particular reason for it, he'd long since come to realise that there were only so many places he could spend his limited time and neither his personal travels or any professional duties had taken him there. That had changed when Pree Khan had wandered into his office and dropped a portable projector on his desk. He looked at it for several long moments before raising an eyebrow to her.

"Good morning to you too, Prideaux," he said, saw her face twitch. Nobody called her that. Not even her mother and she was a fearsome woman. Rumour had it, Pree had been avoiding her since Parley had been promoted. Family affairs could be tricky. He was glad his cousin wasn't part of the same hierarchy as him.

"Fancy a trip?" she asked, leaning over his desk with a big grin on her face. She looked pleased with herself, like a cat that had managed to snag some cream. "I've got a thing in Burykia and I want someone I can trust as backup."

That should have sent his danger senses jangling. There was something in her attitude that didn't sat right with him. On the surface, she looked calm enough, her face not giving anything away. It might have been easy, might have been difficult. He wasn't getting any gauge of it from her. Pree was a strange woman to judge, she didn't let her emotions control her behaviour.

"That's suitably vague," he said, reaching over for the PorPro and squeezed the activation button. Wade glanced around his office, one he shared with sixteen other agents when he wasn't in the field and felt glad he was alone. This didn't feel like something he wanted to share with others. On his desk, a few casefile discs had been slowly building up across the last weeks to an almost unhealthy pile, a never-ending cycle of work replacing what he'd already dealt with. He might share the office with sixteen others, but he didn't think all sixteen of them had ever been here at the same time.

"It's a suitably vague prospect," Pree said, shrugging. He didn't quite hear her, already busy scanning through the digital file projected up in front of him. "Got a tipoff. Someone wants to talk about Coppinger and her lot. They want someone reliable out there to talk to them. Could be nothing. Could be everything. Absolute fucking A-Squad."

"And there's nobody reliable currently in Burykia?" Wade had asked, leaning back to look up at her. "Nobody a little more anonymous than you or me?"

"It was handed to me," Pree replied. "Don't have to like it but what can you do? They wanted me to go deal with it. It's only a few hours flight from here. I want you to cover my back."

"Why?"

She gave the impression the question had taken her by surprise, even if he didn't entirely buy her act. "Excuse me?"

"Why me?"

"Well, my choices aren't exactly numerous now," she said, casually waving a hand around the office, empty but for the two of them. "And you should see the other offices. You're miles ahead the best of a pretty mediocre bunch."

"Interesting way to describe your co-workers," Wade said, leaning back in his seat while resting his arms behind his head. "Makes me wonder what you say about everyone else when they can't hear you."

She smirked at him, the mischievous grin of her teeth bright against her brown skin. "You really want to stay stuck in the office for a while longer?" Pree gestured at the pile of file discs on his desk, one of them fell from the top with a faint clatter and Wade felt an itching sensation run across the back of his neck. Idly he rubbed at it, caught it with his nails and worked at it. "You really want to work your way through that stuff when everyone else is out having fun?"

"I'm not sure I'd entirely count getting shot at as having fun," Wade said. Unconsciously he reached up and rubbed his eyes. The skin around them still felt rough like the scars might have faded, but they were still there beneath the skin, his eyes still sensitive to harsh light. He remembered that day he'd nearly lost his sight all too well. Going out into the field hadn't quite had the same attraction since the day he'd nearly died.

"But it beats running overview, right?" Pree said, sitting down on the edge of his desk, the toes of her boot resting on the nearest chair as she gave him a grin. "They can get someone else to do that. Screw the small stuff. You're Wade fucking Wallerington. The bad guys see you coming, they run the other way, well they would if they knew who you were."

He shrugged. "What do you want me to say, Pree? I got assigned it, the least I can do is see it through. That's what we do, remember? What we're told to."

Pree smiled at him, reached out and grabbed a handful of the discs. "Tell you what," she said. "Make you a deal. Come with and I'll take half of it off your hands, do the other half on the round trip. It's an easy job." Something about her smile tugged at him, something he couldn't explain. It did sound reasonable. It was nice of her to consider him…

Why would she do that?

He'd said the words out loud, could remember his lips forming the shapes and the sounds coming out of his mouth, even if couldn't remember the conscious decision he'd made to utter them. Her brow furrowed as she studied him with surprise.

"Because I'm nice," she said. "Interesting." She carried on as if she hadn't said that last bit. "Because I want someone deadly as my backup in case the shit hits the fan, Wade. Would you really be able to live with yourself if you sent me off with someone worse and I don't come back?"

That caught him. That was the million-credit question, wasn't it? Being an Agent of Unisco came with an inherent sense of responsibility at the best of time, not just for yourself, but for your fellow agents and those charged with your protection.

More than that, he couldn't actually think of a single reason to claim to her that she was wrong in what she'd said.

At least the flight towards the back end of Burykia had been quick enough for him, he'd not been entirely comfortable with it since the accident. Falling off a dragon could do that to you. Instead, he'd read through Pree's files to try and keep his mind from the roar of the engines outside, the electronic documents telling him they were making a rendezvous with her contact outside a little place called Ryoti. Someone who allegedly wished to spill the beans on the Coppinger operation, just as she'd promised was the case. He had to agree with her in one respect. If this truly was the prize, then they needed to check it out. They couldn't afford not to. Intelligence wasn't so heavy on the ground that they could afford to ignore so tempting a carrot like this. Without intelligence on the enemy, they wouldn't triumph, their hand would weaken, and they'd have to fold before even the thought of victory could blossom in their minds

Now he'd gone through the whole thing, he agreed with the Unisco assessment that they needed the very best people on it and soon.

The transcript of Pree's meeting with her boss had even been included as additional intelligence for reference purposes in the future, they didn't want to use local assets due to the risk involved, just in case the whole thing was a trap to lure out some of the locals. It wasn't a healthy time to be involved with Unisco, Coppinger had seen to that. Therefore, they would bring someone in from outside, nobody that could be traced back to local Unisco operatives. That someone had turned into Pree and himself. A strange turn of events to be sure. It made sense in a strange sort of way. Still it was what it was and here they were on their way towards the meeting. Secrecy was still the name of the game and it was the best disguise they had.

Pree hadn't helped with his growing sense of disquiet, instead she'd sat curled up in one of the seats with her head lolled back and her eyes closed like she didn't have a care in the kingdoms about the situation. She looked so peaceful and it pissed him off more than anything. So much for helping him with the workload. He'd gone through the overviews of several current operations, offered his professional opinion on kinks and weaknesses that could compromise the whole thing. A detached third party with a critical eye. How easily the mighty fell at times. That'd been his job for the last several months. Technically he was still on reduced duties due to his injuries. It'd been a nice slowdown for him, even if he did miss being in the field. When one suffered an injury like his, it made you stop and think things through. He wasn't a young man any longer and privately he was worried it was showing. Another part of him knew that he was being ridiculous. What had happened to him could have happened to anyone…

But it hadn't… It had happened to him and that was the truth that couldn't be denied.

It took him several moments to realise Pree was no longer asleep and studying him with a bemused expression. He slid his eyes up and met hers, regretted it immediately. It was like trying to outstare a pair of diamonds. Something about them cut through him. He'd never noticed it before. Pree was like a chameleon sometimes, he'd thought often. You tended not to notice her unless she wanted you to. No wonder they nicknamed her the Spectre.

Truth be told, he'd never looked that close at her before. He wondered if he should say something. The atmosphere in the back of the transport was devoid of life but for them, just the roar of the engines accompanying them on their way. If he was even more truthful, Prideaux Khan scared him a little. Just a little. There'd always been something a bit off about her. These days, it felt a little more pronounced than it ever had before, she was walking around constantly like she was all too pleased with herself over some unseen triumph.

"Thought you were sleeping," he eventually said.

"Just meditating," she replied. "Should try it. It's good for the soul. Very refreshing. Better than sleep. Sleep rests the body. Meditation rests the mind, the body and the soul."

"You sound like Baxter."

Just for a moment, he thought he saw a little flash of anger pass through those diamond-like eyes and then it was gone. Maybe he'd imagined it. Part of him knew he hadn't though, and he found it unsettling. He should have stayed at home. It'd have been a lot more bearable than this.

"Well the man knows what he's talking about," she said softly. "Sometimes. A lot of the time I think he's full of wind."

The two of them might not be great friends any longer, largely on Wade's part. He had his suspicions about what Baxter had done in recent months and it didn't sit right with him. However, they had been once upon a time, and the urge to rush to his friend's defence hadn't quite faded with the suspicion he held about him.

"He's a great man," he said. "Unisco legend, spirit calling icon and…"

"And those powers," she finished. "The famed powers of the Vedo. You know, I always heard those stories about him. How there was something mysterious about him, how he had a knack of surviving. I guess we know why. Kind of a bit of a kick in the balls wouldn't you say?"

"There's plenty of Unisco agents with a knack of survival," Wade said. "They don't have to have powers for that."

"They also don't walk away when they're needed," she pointed out, a little too harsh for his liking. "They don't hide away for years to train an army."

"Some army," Wade said. "There's not that many of them…"

"That you've seen," Pree interrupted, her voice angry and shrill. "You've seen what Baxter wanted you to see. We all have. Who knows how many we haven't seen."

"You really think that he's lying about what he has behind him?"

"You really think that he isn't?" Pree countered. "I think I'd be more surprised if he was telling the truth. The Quin-C final… You don't throw all your resources into something like that. Not when they should have been badly outnumbered."

"Well he didn't know that something was going to happen," Wade said, even though he didn't believe his own words. Pree let a deep little chuckle out as he said it. She didn't believe him either. Unisco agents were trained to detect untruths after all and he didn't have the energy to spend his time trying to hide it. "He brought them to pay respect to Sharon Arventino, really. That's what he told me. When it all went down, he struck an arrangement with the director."

"You don't believe that," Pree said simply. "Not all of it. You're not simple, Wade. Don't mistake me to be either. It sounds nice and noble and all those other empty words until you really dissect deep into it. Then it falls apart, shows its guts to us all. I know what you truly suspect."

"Believe me, I don't think you do," Wade said. He folded his arm, looked away from her hard stare. Any desire he had to continue this conversation was slowly leaking out of him. It was a lie but not a convincing one. He knew he was afraid of that being the case. In her seat up ahead, she leaned forward and smiled coolly at him.

"You suspect that while he wasn't complicit in the whole thing, he definitely didn't go out of his way to stop it from happening. He had an inkling of what was coming, and he chose to take advantage of it all, to further his own goals rather than make sure the people who died could have had more of a chance. I've had the same feeling as you. Baxter isn't half as good at hiding his own feelings as he'd like to think, I'm afraid to say."

Wade shrugged. "What if he did?" He made it sound casual. He didn't feel that way about it. His feelings on that matter troubled him. He'd known Baxter for a very long time and never before had he suspected him capable of something like that.

"What indeed," Pree said, enjoying his discomfort, it would appear. She took a swing from her water canteen and smiled at him. It was a predator's smile, the sort of expression that made him want to sit with his back to the wall, a blaster in hand. "What do you know of the Vedo preaching, Wade? Anything? Nothing? Something?"

"Just what little bits I can glean," Wade admitted. "You pick up bits here and there. Especially now." Especially since Baxter had brokered his deal, he wanted to add but didn't. He'd met a few of the Vedo that were now attached to Unisco. Fair does to them; they were sound enough in his limited experiences of them. Some of them did like their bizarre little non-sequiturs to throw into conversation when it backed up their point. They were weird folk but in a good way. Weird didn't always have to mean bad, different didn't have to be something to feared. Baxter had been like that, once. When they were both a lot younger. He'd not known why. Not back then. He didn't share his secret with Wade until much later in both their lives.

He didn't feel the need to mention to Pree that after his eyes had been injured, he'd sought his old friend out. They'd become strangers, but Baxter had come in a hurry and with few questions. Time might have separated them, but he'd been there when he didn't have to have been. He'd taught him things he'd only been able to imagine before. Now he could see perfectly. Better than before.

In more ways than one, he might even say. Back then, he'd been a little in awe for some of the things Baxter could do. He hadn't flaunted them, but they'd been there waiting to be unleashed. Part of him had always known there was something different about Ruud Baxter, even before he'd revealed the secrets he'd kept. They'd survived way too much together for him not to catch on. But when he'd learned, wracked with pain and guilt, almost blinded by fire, things had changed. He'd had a moment of realisation that the world was bigger than he'd ever suspected, that anyone ever could have guessed, and just for a moment, it had made him feel so very small.

"Yes, because nothing helps keep the issue in perspective than a few carefully chosen bits of propaganda," Pree said almost scathingly. The ire in her voice startled him, he hadn't expected it and he sat up in surprise. "Sorry. Personal beliefs. It's a long story. They serve a purpose. Doesn't mean that I have to like it."

"We got time," Wade said, glancing at her. "Sounds like an interesting tale."

"Bad experience once upon a time," Pree said. "Don't want to go into it. So, I'm not. It won't make either of us any happier if I do." She let out a little sigh and lolled her head back in her seat. "Hope you understand. We all have demons in our closet we don't want to give the time of day to, I think you'll find."

In a way, he could understand that, could even appreciate it. But it couldn't abate his curiosity. Nor could it silence the feeling in the pit of his stomach, tight like a throbbing flame. He couldn't explain it, the only thing he could even guess at was that it likely wasn't anything good.

"Welcome to Ryoti," Pree murmured as the two of them stepped off the hoverjet and onto the refuelling station platform. From here, they could see out across the town below, easily at the highest point of the surrounding area. It didn't look like much, barring the stadium up in the distance, stood erect like a fist shaking at the sky. "Home of not much and even less."

"You been here before?" Wade asked. She gave him a fish-eyed look of annoyed bemusement, folded her arms and took a deep breath like she was going to get on a soapbox and start a rant.

"What, just because I hail from Burykia, you think I've been to every out of the way town here? Nah, barely heard of it. I'm not from this part. Way back west me, out in the rainless zones. Where all the cool kids hang out, you know."

Ouch, Wade wanted to say. Everyone knew of Burykian geography that the kingdom was largely divided in two by an invisible line only seen on maps, one side prosperous, one side not so. One side was little more than desert and sandy forests for the most part, very few large cities present within them, the other was reminisce of some of the more affluent parts of Canterage or Premesoir. Barring some odd architectural whims, it was hard to tell the difference. A lot of jokes existed about what went on in the rainless zone, the less prosperous part. If Pree came from there, he doubted she'd find any of them funny. It was a rough place. More on a par with some of the worst parts of Vazara than anything else.

"This is the civilised part," she said, baring her teeth in a grin. "Got to say, moderately impressed. Growing up, we used to dream of living in places like this. You know, calm, quiet, low murder rate."

Wade took another look at the stadium out in the distance. He'd seen many since the incident at the Quin-C and the ICCC had almost folded. A fair few of them had fallen into disrepair. This one looked like it had reached better days. Stadiums needed bouts to make income and with them being unable to display any competitive fights, they'd lost a lot of the means to make credits. There were only so many music acts and comedians they could rent out to, only so many stadiums were big enough to warrant attention. A small-town stadium like this, maybe fifteen thousand seats at most if the average was to be believed, probably never full even for final round bouts, he was surprised to see it was in as good a condition as it looked. Workers were all over the structure, scurrying about like ants on a mission, he could see them even from this distance although the nature of their activity remained a mystery.

"Looks like something's going on here," Pree said. She rubbed her hands together, blew on her clasped palms. Her demeanour had changed again, she'd shifted from cold murderess to excited schoolgirl in a matter of moments. "Excellent. That's exactly what we need."

Wade looked at her with a raised eyebrow. "Are you sure? What happened to get in, get the intelligence and get out?"

"I never said we were getting out," she said with a smirk. "Hey, we need an excuse to here. Can't wear the mufflers all the time. Like

I'm going to hide this face from the public." Her smirk grew like she was sharing some private joke with herself. "Come on, let's see what's happening. The exchange isn't right away. And he said he'd meet us at the stadium tonight. Let's scope out the meeting place." She held out both her hands in what she might have meant to be a placating gesture. "Come now, you know it makes sense."

"You sure?"

The two words echoed in the silence as Wade and Pree found themselves looking at each other once more, the unease rising in the back of his mind. Nothing about this sounded like it was going to be simple. Already he was missing the paperwork back at the office, words he never imagined he'd think, never mind say.

"That was my contact," Pree said. "He'd meet whoever here tonight. But this…" She threw out a hand at the big sign ahead of them, set her teeth into a grimace. "You have to admire the audacity if nothing else."

Wade shook his head. "I don't have to do anything. We should cancel right now. Remove ourselves from this entire thing. We can't run a secure op like this. There's too many people…"

"We've done it before."

"Not this many with this few," Wade reminded her. Standard procedure told him that everything about this was a bad idea. If this whole thing was a setup, it had the chance to go badly wrong very quickly and the outcome could be disastrous. "You and I can't run this whole thing… How many people does this thing hold? Fifteen? Twenty? Somewhere in the middle?"

"I don't think…"

"Pree, it's sold out. There will be that many in here. This is reckless. It's…"

"Just a rendezvous with an informant. We're not going to shoot things out. I didn't even bring a weapon, did you?" She grinned as she said it and Wade felt the unease grow. He knew this day wasn't going to get any better. "Oh, lighten up, I'm joking. Of course, I brought a weapon. I don't expect we'll need them though." She gripped her bag a little closer to her. "Come on Wade, you used to have a little more zing than this."

He shook his head. "Pree…"

She turned, studied him without saying a word. He'd almost been expecting an interruption. But none came, she simply waited, face impassive and unreadable. "Pree…"

"You can't keep saying my name. Wade, we can do this. It's only as complicated as we're making it." Pree paused, glanced back and forth, her eyes glittering with cunning. "Besides, I have a plan to blend in with the background. A pretty good one. Believe me, I take no chances with my ops. I had a contingency for this. Part of the reason why I wanted you with me. Trust me on this one."

Wade knew he was going to regret this. Unconsciously he rubbed his eyes. He didn't know why. He knew she was right though. Once upon a time, he would have relished this a lot more than he was. Where his reluctance came from, he couldn't say for sure. He could only guess, and it wasn't a pleasant feeling.

He'd nearly died. He'd nearly been blinded. Both in the line of duty and part of him was struggling to let that go even now. He remembered them all too well and they didn't sit right with him. Not that he'd expect them to. He'd never worked with Prideaux Khan before and it was starting to feel more and more like that was a good thing. He'd never known her to be so wildly reckless, he wondered if he'd been like that before. Gifted with a sense of his own invincibility that had been sorely tested. Everyone suffered that test sooner or later. It was how you came through it that defined you. Ever since then, going back to Baxter showing his true colours, he'd wanted as little of the fight as he could get.

Part of him had already suspected it wasn't worth it. A lot of people were going to die over this Coppinger thing... Screw that, a lot of people had already died over it and more were going to come. And he didn't want his own name to be added to that list. When you started thinking like that, it was time to give up. It took just a split second to register but there it was there. Shame and disgust boiling away inside him.

What was he doing? He was better than this. One setback and he'd let himself retreat from it all like some sort of coward. He knew what it was and yet he hadn't been able to help himself. All the counselling Unisco had offered him and what good had it done him up to this point? His boss had insisted on it; he'd thought it a waste of time but more and more he was suddenly glad that he'd done it. It was like someone had flipped a light switch on in his brain. He was done with it. No more hiding. Only getting stuff done from now on.

"You still there?" Pree inquired politely, waving a hand in front of his face. In the past, he might have recoiled, instead he simply stared at her with cool detachment, let the grin creep across his face. Amazing the effect a few simple words from her could have had on him. He felt whole again. Alive. Anew.

"Yeah, I'm here," he said, all while thinking that was true in more ways than one. "I'm here. Now, tell me about your plan. Let's hear what you got."

"Ladies and gentlemen of Ryoti! Back in action for the first time in months, we have spirit calling live from our stadium! Our brand-new president, Adam Evans said let there be light, and we turned ours back on and we're bringing the bouts here and now, straight to you live! We've got them first and fast!"

Wade heard the announcer on the screen in the locker room and rolled his eyes. That was enthusiasm, he had to admit. He had the right idea. The bouts had been away from the five kingdoms for far too long, no wonder some were happy to get them back. At the same time, part of him wondered with the Coppinger crisis ongoing if it might not be the best idea. Any wannabe terrorist out there who had warm fuzzy feelings about Coppinger might find it a target hard to resist as an opportunity for maximum chaos.

Still at the same time, people needed something to take their mind off the impending terror. Since Vazara had fallen to Coppinger control and Nwakili killed, he'd noticed a marked difference in people when he walked down the street. They were scared. Maybe it was the ICCC's way of defying Coppinger and showing that they weren't afraid of her and what she could do to them. That was a mistake in his opinion. They absolutely should be afraid of her and what she had. She got stronger every day. He'd seen the intelligence reports. It was scary the amounts of weapons she was adding to her arsenal every day. Not just military might but spirits of war as well. He'd seen the one Nick had managed to sneak away from her and had been simultaneously awed and terrified when he'd observed.

He supposed this was why Pree was right. They needed to be here. This afternoon after they'd signed up to enter, he'd gone over everything again that she'd handed to him and he'd decided for himself that it was worth being here. They needed every bit of intelligence they could get their hands on. Just being back in a stadium, feeling the energy of that crowd, it was enough to revitalise him. He'd not felt like this for a bloody long time. For a few moments, he felt just like his old self.

"But we know, folks, this bout is no ordinary bout! For the first time in our humble town, Ryoti is seeing team bouts! All the best locals and even a few internationals are teaming up to give you, the viewer in the stands or at home, the best action around. We've all missed it and. This! Is! Ryoti!"

"Excited?" Pree asked, finishing sliding on her boots over her feet, strapping them up with determined vigour on her fac. She looked nice, Wade had to admit, in her fighting clothes of jeans, boots and a scarlet sleeveless shirt tied up around her midriff to reveal her navel.

Team bouts were different to regular spirit calling bouts. Rather than just one on one, the two of them would fight together at the same time, each use one of their own spirits to counteract their opponents. First team to lose both spirits would be knocked out of the competition. It wouldn't last longer than the night, but the revenue would be massive.

He'd not done this for a while. The two of them had practiced together briefly this afternoon but it was hard to say how it'd go in a competitive environment. About the only thing that they had going for them was that it wasn't a popular form of competition. A lot of others would be in the same situation. They could pull it together. They had to stay in the rounds long enough to be able to slip away and meet the informant. Improvisation wasn't a skill they taught in the academies, he'd always thought that was an oversight on their part. They could do with it sometimes.

Pree had been right, as much as it pained to him admit. If they'd gone in as spectators, it would have been difficult to abate suspicion. There would have been places they couldn't go. This had been the best option. They both were famous enough to be able to enter with few questions asked. The more prestige attached to the tournament, the better for the organisers and the viewing companies if the two of them went far in it. Prestige was the one thing they both could bring. Wade adjusted his cloak about his neck. Might as well give the watching millions a show to remember. He could hear the crowd outside, could hear the cheers and the adrenaline was starting to pump around his body. They were on soon.

"Just a touch," he admitted. "This I have missed." There were two other teams in the room, both a pair of Burykian locals, one team of two men and one consisting of a man and a woman who looked young enough to be his daughter. Maybe she was. They did look sort of alike. Any sensitive information they'd share would have to be on the quiet. Wouldn't do to draw attention to themselves.

The look on Pree's face said it all, that she wondered if he'd missed the other part of the job. He wondered about that himself. Still it did feel good to savour the occasion.

"All of it," he added. "Everything."

It looked enough to placate her. "You seem a bit more settled than you did earlier. Stuff happens, Wade. Nobody goes through their career unscathed. Sometimes we get reminded we're just very breakable. Not just us but those around us. Nobody blames you for what happened. It's about how you move on from it going forward. You let it define you, then you've already lost. You might as well give up. And I'd expect that from some people but not you. You're better than that. I think this whole thing is just what you need." She patted him on the arm, smiled at him and he grinned back.

She was right. No point dwelling on what had happened.

"We have a very special treat for you all here, a pair of late entrants into the competition but by no means any less exceptional, facing off against Nihiro Konba and Tamudai Utsui, our local champions, Wade Wallerington and Burykia's very own Prideaux Khan. Both teams have made their way on the battlefield, and the crowds are going crazy at the sight of our late entrants. Khans' not battled a whole lot in recent years but still an iconic figure from our kingdom for some of her exploits in her younger days..."

Wade smirked at Pree's reaction to what the announcer had just said. Implying she was old definitely wouldn't do him any favours. There wasn't much difference in age between the two of them. Or at least he guessed so anyway. He genuinely didn't know. Actually, he didn't want to know. None of his business really. "Smartass am I right?"

"... And Wade Wallerington, well need I say more. Former favourite at the last Quin-C before having to retire through injury, winner of over fifty competitions, a champion in every sense of the word. What this man does not know about spirit calling isn't worth knowing. We're honoured to have them here. But Utsui and Konba won't see it that way. The bigger they are, they'll just see a target to be knocked down."

"Yeah, right," Pree said under her breath. "Let's put them down quickly. See if we can win this thing before we have that meeting."

They'd briefly run through strategy before the bout, how they'd work together and what possible ways they might combine their spirits. So far, they had a few ideas. Some of them might work, others might not but at least they had something. Things could be worse.

"Remember, teamwork. You cover me, I got you," Wade said softly. "And vice versa."

Konba's spirit was a gorilla, eight feet tall on its hind legs, covered in bronze fur and with fists the size of small boulders. Thick spines broke from the fur across its back while Utsui let out a lesser horned rhino. Even from where he was stood, Wade could see how thick its skin was, armour had never looked so natural. Even minus the horn that some of its genetic cousins bore, it still would be able to pack a punch with its bulk and strength. When it stepped forward, he could feel the ground shake under its feet.

"We got this," Pree said. He got the impression from her voice that she was smiling inside. "This won't be a problem."

Chapter Eight. Scorpions and Sand.

"It happens unfortunately. We can't all be tied to our convictions. The nature of humanity is diluted at times. We want to be more but we're not willing to sacrifice for it. When the going gets tough, some will run. Anyone who betrays me because they don't have the stomach for what must be done? Punish them. Severely. I'll only have those that believe be the ones who follow me into the light."

Claudia Coppinger, regarding the future and the people needed to build it.

Pree went with one of her ghosts, a silver-blue blob of ectoplasm that formed six arms and two legs in quick fashion, four large eyes, two mouths and a protruding caveman brow forming a face. Below the second mouth, Wade noted that it looked like it had a bit of a beard. He chose Thracia, brought the huge sea serpent out to cheers from the crowd, cheers engulfed by the serpent's bellow of challenge to the enemy spirits. The gorilla was dwarfed by his serpent; the rhino staring ahead unblinking at the ghost and the serpent.

Wade inhaled, let the breath go. In. Out. In. Out.

The video referee gave them the signal; he hadn't realised just how much he'd missed that sound and the bout was suddenly in session, he realised that he was smiling for the first time in what felt like months.

This, he could do. This was what he needed to do. Some people were born to do certain things and he knew this was what he was meant to be right now.

No time like the present to test their defences, see what they were up against. Thracia was bigger than Dengu, Pree's spirit, and therefore would most likely be the first target they went for. In team bouts like this, it was a well-known psychological fact. The bigger threat was perceived to be the more dangerous one. Retaliate first, as one of his old instructors had once said. He gave the mental order and Thracia let loose a uniblast of potent golden energy straight towards the two spirits. The gorilla bounded aside, the rhino didn't and took the full force of the blast in the face.

As tests went, only moderately successful. It didn't look fazed by the sheer heat of the energy thrown at it. He'd guessed the skin was pretty much impenetrable and he'd been proved right. Meaning that whatever way they went with in trying to knock the rhino out, it wasn't going to be blasting it head on. Dengu had slipped behind Thracia, away into the shadow of the giant serpent and out of sight. The gorilla and the rhino started to circle Thracia. He knew what they were doing.

If they went for one, the other would attack. Sea serpent scales were tough but at the same time, both opponents looked plenty strong. No point taking unnecessary chances.

"You got this right?" he asked out the corner of his mouth. Pree nodded, a grin playing across her face.

"Just keep them distracted," she said quietly. "Let them focus on you."

He wasn't overtly happy with the plan, but it was the best one they were going to come up with right now. He knew it was the right one, focusing on Thracia gave Dengu an opening to be ignored and when ghosts were ignored on the battlefield, it was often with lethal consequences. Neither of the enemy spirits looked like they'd have too much in the line of elemental attacks which meant there was little they could do to hurt Dengu. Uniblasts didn't really affect ghosts the way they did everything else.

"Come on," he muttered. "Come on." Thracia, do nothing for the moment, he added silently. Just wait until one of them attacks and then...

The gorilla moved in to attack, both fists raised above its head like a pair of giant hammers, muscles tensing up hard as it lumbered forwards on both hind legs.

Go for the other, they won't be expecting it.

He gave his command, the serpent's jaws widened, and a thousand needle sharp blasts of water ripped out the gaping maw. There was a great ooh-ing sound from the crowd as the flurry of needles swept across the grey skin, showing little effect at first. Then slowly, he saw the first drops of blood appear, a dozen and more streams of blood suddenly gushing out the great grey body. He smiled sweetly at his opponents, heard the lesser horned rhino bellow and stamp both front feet into the ground. Dust rose from the impacts, Thracia roared defiantly in response.

There was a charge coming, Wade could see that. The other half of Burykia could see it coming. Meanwhile, the gorilla had continued to move until Dengu appeared in front of the ape, mouths contorted into outlandish grins. The ghost hovered for a moment then burst forward as if fired from a cannon, crashed hard into the gorilla's chest and vanished from sight. Wade watched it stagger back and shake its head, thinking it didn't seem to know where it was.

Wade shot a sideways glance at Pree as if she was going to proffer up an explanation. None came, not least because the rhino had already charged, thunderous footsteps beating into the ground underfoot. It might even have come close to hitting Thracia if the gorilla hadn't leaped into action, powerfully crashed a fist into the side of its head, the blow sending it veering off course. Wade's ears rang from the force of the impact and he winced as the rhino missed Thracia comfortably, smashed straight into the advertising hoardings and went through, unable to quite stop itself from moving in time to crush a dozen seats into useless wreckage.

That's why they never have anyone right in the front rows, Wade thought with a smirk he kept to himself. If there had been, they would likely have been crushed. It was the stadium organisers covering themselves from legal action more than anything else.

Both Konba and Utsui looked confused about what had happened, at least for a few moments. Slowly realisation dawned as the purple glow enveloped the gorilla briefly and then Dengu retreated. Wade had never seen possession like that before, definitely a neat trick. Unfortunately, it wasn't the sort of thing you could repeatedly get away with for sooner or later, the opponent caught on. Sooner if they were any good. Later if they were particularly hapless.

Just as unfortunately for the gorilla, it caught a full-on body smash from Thracia head on while still disorientated. The gorilla might have been big but Thracia was a lot bigger and heavier, all her momentum behind the charge. Just for a brief moment, the gorilla was airborne and hurtling back through the air, arms flailing helplessly. He could see the rhino was back on the field, but it didn't look good. Already Dengu was moving to engage. Both mouths were twisted back into the rictus of a manic grin. Wade got the impression that this was going to hurt.

The rhino bellowed a battle challenge, kept both its small watery eyes on Dengu who circled menacingly, threatening to feint one way or the other before finally it swooped, straight through the rhino's body, Smoky edges whipped back and forth around the hardened grey skin, a dozen insubstantial blades carving away at the armour. Even Pree winced at the sound it made, like air being blasted through meat, blood gushed out the thousand new exit wounds that had been carved across its body. It didn't look so impenetrable anymore. The gorilla landed hard, tried to stand up, might have done had Wade not commanded Thracia to use another uniblast.

The blast hit home hard, put the gorilla down before it could get back up. The ape fell back, hit the ground in an untidy heap, fur burnt into nothing, skin and muscle a horrible raw red colour. Wade could smell the stink of charred meat. It had no eyes left, just empty sockets hollow in its skull staring sightlessly ahead. No way it was getting back up from that. As always, he felt that sense of self-satisfaction when he knocked an opponent out on the battlefield. Not pride, just a professional recognition that the job had been done and it was time to move on. Self-back slapping and congratulations would be a mistake. Nothing had been achieved yet. This wasn't even the main reason they were here. It was just a distraction.

He never would have guessed given his partner's reaction though. Pree looked like she was enjoying it way too much as Dengu responded to her mental commands and dealt the final blow to the rhino, jamming a smoky fist straight into its brain. For a few seconds, it didn't move, the rhino just stood still, stock silent in shock. Wade imagined it wasn't feeling much beyond blinding pain right now. As Dengu withdrew the fist, the rhino collapsed straight through him with a terrific crash that almost shook Wade's teeth. Dengu stood there in the remnants of the rhino's corpse with a bemused look on that twisted face before shrugging. The video referee gave the call, the stadium announcer struggled to make himself heard over the sounds of the crowd going crazy and that was that. One step on the road to the final.

He just wondered what the chance were of them making it there. The competition was still young yet. And even if it was just a local tournament, there was always the chance that one pair of locals could get lucky. That was before their mission was even considered, the spectre of the rendezvous hung over them both.

"You worry too much," Pree said out the corner of her mouth, nudging him in the side. "Just relax. Try to enjoy the moment. Let yourself have this."

"This guy picked one hells of a meeting place," Wade muttered, hands in his pockets as they found themselves stalking the empty halls towards their rendezvous. They'd managed to slip away, they had fifteen minutes before their next bout. Fifteen short minutes before their semi-final. If need be, they'd have to forfeit it. It wouldn't be the first time. Both of them had been with Unisco for a long damn time and they knew the price that sometimes needed to be paid. It had long since been drilled into them in basic training. We'll teach you to win but sometimes you need to know you have to lose. Those had been the words. Back then they'd hurt. Now it felt painfully insignificant compared to the stakes.

Pree said nothing. She hadn't since they'd left the locker room, her jaw set in determination as she pondered some problem she hadn't chosen to voice aloud. From the looks of it, it was a deeply disturbing one. If she didn't want to share it with him then he wasn't going to pry. None of his business. She'd always looked like a woman who had her demons. One simply didn't get into it unless you were prepped for the long haul. There wasn't much he could say to her, he doubted she'd appreciate him trying to get involved.

Between the bouts, they'd done their best to scout out the stadium between them, making notes on where the rendezvous was to go down, keeping a track on where the crowd was in relation to them, just in case. There was always a chance that it could turn violent and neither of them wanted that. Wade had his X7 tucked into a pocket, he didn't know where Pree was hiding hers but despite her earlier joke, she definitely had it on her. He hoped they didn't need them. Things surely couldn't turn that bad. Surely. He regretted thinking that the moment the thought crossed his mind.

They always had the potential to end badly.

The place they were meant to meet didn't have much in the way of distinguishing features, just another bare hallway amidst dozens of them. Only a faded poster of better days remained, a broad Burykian man posing with a giant dog and a trophy remained. The writing had faded and was in native Burykian, Wade couldn't read it, could have asked Pree what it said but he didn't care. A water fountain stood aloof nearby, covered in dust, ignored by the times. They'd already checked with Control to ensure that no remote surveillance caught them, it'd be done in record time.

"Just wait now then," Pree said. The two of them had already activated their mufflers. They weren't getting recognised. Wade nodded. It was the first thing she'd said since leaving the locker room. "See if he shows up."

"You know much about him?" Wade asked. "What to expect?"

She shook her head. "Other than he's male and he sounded terrified."

"Lot of that going around these days," Wade said. "Lot of fear, a lot of uncertainty. It's almost contagious."

"These are dangerous times. I'm sorry if people didn't get the memo," Pree said harshly. "Even before the Coppingers, these kingdoms were never quite as safe as people made out."

Wade raised an eyebrow. "Excuse me?"

"It seems like the further we go, we still take the shortest distance to the grave," Pree said. "That's my opinion. Humanity can make out that it's growing as a species but ultimately, we're just working on ways to kill each other faster. Even now, we're developing weapons at a phenomenal rate to kill others. Probably our young. The keys to our future. All the same while we struggle to keep our elderly and our ailing alive when they likely have little left to contribute."

"Wow..." Wade said dryly. "You're not mincing your words there, are you Pree?"

"I never do. You know where I come from, compassion and weakness are almost the same word."

"I didn't know that, no."

"Just the same as conqueror and saviour. There's no distinguishing between the two of them."

Wade didn't know what to say to that. "Sounds like a language devoid of any sort of complexity."

"Devoid of pretension, perhaps," she said. "You know long ago we were well-known as conquerors, explorers and generals. They had the potential to become the most powerful of the five kingdoms."

"So why didn't they?" Wade hadn't come here expecting a history lesson, but he was interested despite the circumstances.

"In-fighting mainly. The great leaders might have been great, but they were still human. The flesh is fragile, no matter how skilled you might be. And the thing to remember about humans, is we die very easily. It's a sad fact of life but true regardless. And when the great leaders died, those they left behind broke up everything trying to claim it themselves. There's a moral to that story somewhere, I think. No matter how much power you have, it can't survive a dozen people all pulling in opposite directions."

She paused. "Sometimes I think that was where the old order of Vedo went wrong. A dream changes, good intentions don't stand up to the people who try to carry them out."

That made Wade stand up straight. "What?"

"Baxter never told you the full story about what happened to them?" she asked. She sounded surprised. "I thought the two of you were friends."

"He told you?"

"For a long time, they hid away in their hole, the bulk of them cut off from society," she said, not really answering the question. "Dozens upon dozens of Vedo all keeping to themselves. They had knowledge, they had secrets that could have changed the course of the kingdoms if they'd wanted to share. But they didn't. They didn't want to interfere. That was what they said anyway. I always thought it was because they were too afraid of the power. That or they didn't trust the kingdoms with what they had. Or that once they shared their secrets, they wouldn't have anything that made them special anymore. One of those."

"Must have had a reason for it," Wade said. He didn't sound like he believed it. In truth, he didn't know what to think.

"But of course, you can't indoctrinate everyone. Sooner or later someone will start to question the way of things. That person is a negative influence. Your only option is to deal with them or let the insolence grow. There's no middle ground. And you know who the worst of them all was in the old order?"

He had a feeling of the answer, but it was still a surprise to hear the nonchalance with which she said, "It was your old friend Ruud Baxter. He wanted change. I suppose you have to give him kudos for that, if nothing else. He advocated it. The old masters did everything they could to try and bring him round to their way of thinking. Eventually they almost gave up on him, sent him out with an apprentice in truth they didn't want either. She was the daughter of one of the masters, I think."

"What?! They didn't want Arventino?" That he'd known about. In the recent months since Sharon Arventino had been killed, the rumours had abounded that she'd been something special. The way Baxter had mourned her with the rest of the Vedo had been touching. He'd suspected there was something in it. At the time, before he'd known, he'd wondered if it'd been love. Now, he thought otherwise.

"Wasn't that talented all things considered. They thought Baxter would fail with her and then they had an excuse to cast him away." Pree smiled a little, a not wholly pleasant gesture across her face. Again, he wondered how she knew this. Baxter had to have told her, he guessed. "But against all odds, he managed to coax the embers of talent into a roaring fire. Hence the conundrum."

She paused, cocked her head up. "Someone's coming."

Wade silently cursed the oncoming man. He'd been enjoying hearing her speak. All of this stuff had been going on when Baxter and he had been close friends. They'd travelled together, they'd shared a lot of stuff. Apparently one of them had been freer with sharing than the other. It was insight into his friend that unsettled him, worrying that Prideaux Khan whom he'd never suspected knew Baxter that well, knew more than she should have.

The man that approached them looked every inch the uneasy informant, his head bobbing back and forth uneasily in search of an attack that might never come. He was in his forties, the harsh glow of the lights reflecting off his balding head. His paunch wobbled as he lumbered towards them. His eyes were watery, and he looked haggard, his clothes creased and travel-worn, stained with the efforts of his exertions. Whatever else he looked, it wasn't like a native of Burykia.

"You..." He sounded out of breath, his chest pumping, his skin slick with sweat. "... You both Unisco, yeah?"

Premesoiran, Wade would have said if he'd have to guess. Pree stepped forward, all business-like and professional in her demeanour.

"Correct," she said. "And you are...?"

"Davis Teela," he said. "Don't shoot me but I used to work for Claudia Coppinger."

Wade coughed, managed to hide the smile. He'd partly been expecting that. Given the extent of the companies across the five kingdoms, a lot of people had worked for Claudia Coppinger at one point or another in their lives. Most of them hadn't know a damn thing about it. Only now were the extent of her business practices over the last twenty years starting to come out. She'd been infinitely wealthier than any of them had ever imagined. No wonder she'd been able to finance a war.

"Go on," Pree said. "What do you have for us?"

Teela cleared his throat with a squelching hack. He spat it on the ground. "She's got something planned. Look, you got to get me away from her. She's going to kill millions with her new weapon. I want away."

"A new weapon?" That was intriguing. Wade and Pree looked at each other. Though their faces might have been distorted to Teela, they could read each other's expression perfectly. Pree shrugged, just a fraction. Their companion might not have picked up on it, Wade did. "What sort of weapon?"

"Later, later," Teela almost shouted. "Just take me out, get me away from her. I ran but she'll chase me. You don't know what she has!"

"Start with it, Teela," Pree said, her voice steady. There was more than a hint of steel in it. "Who are you and how do you know this?"

"I worked for her in her labs. Helped develop it. Oh Divines, what did I do? Gilgarus forgive me. I made a stupid mistake. Shouldn't have listened to her."

"You know where her labs are?" Wade asked. Even if he was exaggerating the threat, not really something they could discount given what they'd already seen of Coppinger's resources, that information was worth its weight in platinum.

"Some," Teela shrugged. He was starting to regain some composure now. "Not all. Nobody knows all. Except maybe her. And the big guy. Oh Divines, save me from him!" He was starting to panic again, Pree stepped forward, both hands up in reassurance.

"Relax," she said. "We got you. She's not going to get you. Calm down, we'll get out of here, Mr Teela."

"Professor," he added smoothly. The composure as he said that came and went in a heartbeat, drained out of him and suddenly he was a wreck again. He was sincere, some of it might have been false in its sentiments, but Wade didn't doubt he genuinely believed he was in danger.

"Orders are to get him to a safe location as swiftly as possible," Control said. That almost startled him. He didn't know the controller on duty today, the voice genderless and electronic. The days when it might have been Okocha were gone. He'd moved onto bigger and better things. Truth being told, he didn't begrudge Okocha it, but he'd be missed on the other end of the line. There'd been few with the same level of calm and composure in a crisis.

"Copy that," Pree said. "Extracting now." She looked down at Teela. "Come on. Hope you've got it in you to run some more." She held out a hand, he took it and Wade turned towards the exit.

There was someone waiting for them.

He was sure he'd seen her before somewhere, he couldn't place where. All he knew immediately was that she felt wrong. Pree stiffened up like she'd been zapped, Teela let out a yell.

"Oh Divines, not her!" he whimpered. "We're dead. We're all dead."

"Ma'am!" Wade said, one hand dropping to his pocket where the blaster was hidden. "I'm going to have to ask you to move aside. Official Unisco business."

The skin was alabaster white, not a hint of colour beyond the extraordinarily blue eyes, her lips little more than a colourless slash in her face. The hair was the darkest shade of black he'd ever seen, the areas under those eyes dark and gaunt. She wore a thick black coat despite the heat of the Burykian night outside, one where a weapon could easily be concealed.

"Shoot her!" Teela said, almost frantic. "Shootshootshootshoother!"

The woman took a step forward; Wade went for his weapon. Pree was faster, her X7 out and he heard three blasts streak past him, hit the woman in the chest. Part of him knew something bad was going to happen immediately, he was glad that Pree had been the one to pull the trigger not him.

The blasts sizzled against the coat, the material aflame as they scorched through, revealing blackened skin underneath where they'd landed. Beyond that, nothing.

"Oh crap!" Control said. If they'd sounded human, there might have been panic there. As it was, the speaker sounded flatly emotionless. "We've got another Domis!"

This time they both fired, both emptying their weapons into her in the faint hope that it might slow her down. The second Pree's weapon clicked empty, she grabbed Teela's hand again and turned to run, Teela taking rapid steps behind her that belied his great bulk, his breath exploding out of him in ragged gasps. Wade didn't need too much of an invitation to follow.

Behind them, he heard the footsteps. Soon she was going to be running too. He dropped the power pack from his weapon, slid in his spare and hoped like hells that they didn't end up going through the civilian areas. This could turn very bad very quickly.

He hated that he'd been proved right on that count. Normally he might have said so, yet it wasn't the time or the place to crow. Neither Pree nor Teela were lingering, the two of them already well away from him. He needed to catch up. Except...

Wade drew his summoner, slid in a crystal. He hit the activation button, watched as Bakaru appeared between him and the woman. He still couldn't shake the feeling that something was familiar about her. Not that it mattered. If a laser shot didn't slow her down, then it was time to think bigger. A lot bigger.

Normally, he might have wondered if Bakaru unleashing the uniblast against her was overkill. The powerful burst of energy screeched from the dragon's jaws, blazed across the short distance and hit her hard in the chest. Her eyes widened, he saw that just before the force of the blast continued its momentum, pushing her back and back away from him. She opened her mouth to scream, Wade heard no sound over the roar that still filled his ears. The blast faded away, he brought Bakaru back and turned to run. He'd heard the stories about Domis and didn't want to see how much they compared with this woman.

It didn't take long to catch up with Pree and Teela, the heavy man looking like his heart was ready to give out. Wade gave him a reassuring slap on the back.

"She's down," he said. "For how long, I don't know." He took a long look at Teela. "Who or what the hells is she? Talk now and fast!"

Teela straightened himself up, tried to find some composure. "One of Mistress Coppinger's projects. Wanted to see if they could build another Domis." He still trotted along at a decent speed as he spoke. "Think they had moderate success if I'm honest. I wouldn't want to get into a fight with her."

"If she can build one, then they can build more," Pree said thoughtfully. "This isn't good."

"Thanks for that understatement," Wade said. They were approaching the civilian areas now and he slid his blaster under his coat. His summoner still hung around his neck. "Think I lost her. Had to uniblast her."

Pree gave him a scathing look. "Ouch. No such thing as half measures, then?"

"Well we don't know the full measure. A lot's better than a little in this case," he said defensively. "No point taking any… Down!"

She'd came out a side door and was suddenly in front of him, hand shaped into a point as she slashed at Teela. Wade yanked the heavy man back, almost threw out his shoulder under his weight. Pree snapped a kick into the dark-haired woman's side, he heard the thump and saw the look of irritation on her face. If Pree had kicked the broad side of a hunk of meat in a butcher's freezer, the meat might have shown more of a reaction.

"Aww crap!" Pree barely had time to say before the woman grabbed at her, both hands arched into claws, aiming for her throat.

Wade didn't entirely see what happened next, Pree's body blocking his line of sight. All he heard was a violent snap and crackle of electricity, pale blue light bathing the two women for a moment. Pree's hair rose on end and then the woman was recoiling, a deep black burn opened across her front. A look of shock swept across her face before Pree's boot met it square on and staggered her.

She didn't stay to press the advantage, jumped back away from a swinging fist that cracked a fire extinguisher. Vapour started to fill the hallway, hissing angrily out the ruined casing.

"Run!" Pree said calmly. He had to admire her cool under pressure. "We can't win this fight!"

With that, she turned and between them they managed to hustle Teela away through the fog, every footstep sounding thunderous in the quiet hall. Wade was sure he could hear the mysterious woman behind them, hunting them, searching through the vapour. Somehow, she never caught them, though he didn't dare look back. He glanced sideways at Pree, could only see a faint outline. Something about her felt off, like she was bursting with anger at the way things had gone down. Still she didn't say anything, just kept Teela moving on her side. Wade could feel the portly man's heart pounding against his arm.

It hadn't been a great time for any of them. Not a stretch to say that he and Pree could have screwed this one up badly. There was still a chance they could do yet.

Teela's breathing was starting to grow even more laboured, Wade didn't even know where they were at this point. He'd lost track of their position amidst it all, just needed to keep going on and hope for the best. There had to be an exit around here somewhere.

The outside air as they hit a fire door had never felt so sweet, cool air hitting the damp on their skin from the vapour. The alarm trilled out above them, Wade cursed the sound of it, slammed the door shut behind them, cutting it off. The bang as it locked into place reinforced the feeling that maybe they'd just gotten away with it.

They'd parked across the square, as close to the stadium as they could, a rented speeder that had been picked because of its inability to draw attention. It had been a good spot by Pree in the sole lot in Ryoti, Wade had missed it. She hadn't, had declared it perfect for the job, a nice little four-seater just for this circumstance.

"Can't go back," Teela moaned. "She saw me, she knows, I'm a dead man. If I wasn't before, they know what I've done now."

There'd never been any way they were going to let him go. Not if he knew as much as he'd hinted at. Whatever else he might have been, Teela wasn't being subtle. He wanted away from it. He could have played coy and mysterious as much as he wanted, and it might not have gotten him anywhere. If that woman hadn't shown up...

They might not have taken him as seriously. Nothing like a female version of the infamous Domis Di Carmine to raise the severity of a situation.

That sole thought screamed at him, and it was like an iron grip across his chest. He took a step back, suddenly aware of cold sweat across his face, swallowed a lump in his throat he hadn't known was there. He pushed Teela back against the speeder, drew his X7.

"What do you know?" he demanded. "What's going on here? How did she find you so easily?!"

"Wade?!" Pree started to say, just as he pointed the blaster at Teela's face. "What the hells do you...?"

He glared at her, she shut up. "This whole thing stinks! It's too convenient. Talk! Now, or I leave you for her!"

"Okay, okay," Teela said, the colour completely gone from his face. "Okay, I'll do it, I'll talk. It's not as simple as you think. Coppinger hates you all!"

"I'm not hearing anything I don't already know," Wade said angrily. "Come on, or I blow out one of your kneecaps. They can rebuild it, but it hurts like a bitch! Your choice!"

"Wade!" Pree said once again, before her voice took on a hard tone. "If he doesn't talk, hurt him!" He found it hard to say who was more surprised, Teela looking at her with horror, Wade with shock.

"You're right," she added simply. "He knows something. This whole thing feels wrong. Why stop at one kneecap. Blow them both out and leave him for that woman. She'll find him eventually, and we all knock the price of failure, don't we?"

Teela gulped several times, looked like he wanted to let out a few indignant sounds. Nothing came. Wade lowered the blaster, pointed it at his feet. "Don't even try to deny it, Professor Teela. Don't try to lie to me."

"If you do, we'll know," Pree said. She gave Wade a knowing look. "Won't we?" He nodded. "What does Coppinger have planned? What's she up to?"

"Look, like I said, all I know is what I've seen. She's building new weapons. New ways to devastate the kingdoms. More efficient ways. Taking it over the way she did Vazara, she's not sure she'll be able to do that across all five. Sooner or later, you'll all gang up on her and…"

"And her little insurrection is over," Wade said. "Where are her weapons labs? What's she going for? Chemical? More biological weapons?"

"She's going to make the sky shake," Teela said. "The weapon is almost perfected and it's going to be glorious. I designed it all you know. Concept to execution. Nearly finished as well. Even without me, it's a case of when, not if they finish it."

"So why dangle you out here?" Pree said, before the look of comprehension dawned on her. "Ah. Now you're expendable. You built the bomb and she doesn't need you anymore."

Teela looked insulted. "No, no, not at all." He was starting to sweat again, his voice coming out almost in a stammer. "I've got two or three more devastating ideas to wipe this slate clean."

"Yeah but would she go for them?!" Wade asked. "Our intel on Coppinger suggests she doesn't like people knowing too much about how her rebellion is going. I think you upset her. I think she decided to hang you out. Of course, maybe that means…"

He paused, something wasn't right. They reached the speeder, his mind working overtime. Nothing about this situation felt good. Teela had already admitted more or less he wasn't as on the level as they'd initially thought. So…

The sensation was like a punch in the chest, he flung out an arm and shoved Pree away. "Down!"

She hit the ground and rolled, he jumped backwards, just as he heard the tell-tale screech of a missile being launched, almost saw everything in slow motion as the projectile lit up the sky, tore towards their speeder. The explosion threw him back, sent him sprawling across the parking lot. If either of them had been stood closer…

His entire body hurt, he was trying to see through the blood gushing into his eyes but that aside, no serious damage. He tried all four limbs before trying to get up, staggering to his feet.

Teela hadn't made it. No surprise there. It was hard to spot him amidst the burning husk of what had once been an anonymous speeder.

He was there though, if you knew where to look. Pree didn't look in much better condition than him but at least she was alive.

Neither of them hung around. They didn't want to risk whoever had fired at them getting another clean chance to take them both out. Both knew their only chance was to take off at a run and rendezvous later. This mission had officially been a failure. No other way to describe it.

Chapter Nine. Doors Not Closed.

"It is an oft-repeated cliché that all politicians are corrupt. That they're all soulless, credit-grubbing maniacs who would sell their scruples down the river in exchange for a larger house. Some have been proven to be that way. This reporter pursued the late Ronald Ritellia enough for that very thing. What made Ritellia unique though, was that everyone knew he could be bought, often for a lot less than expected, for his financial details were released upon his death. What makes a real corrupt politician is when nobody realises just how inherently dodgy they are, the ones who preach to be paragons of morality only for them to be caught with their trousers in the cash register. Sadly, it becomes more and more common with these dangerous times. Credits buy loyalty and Claudia Coppinger is aware of that more than most, thanks to her dalliances with Ritellia, supplementing both his wallet and his bed..."

Excerpt from a Kate Kinsella article about corruption in politics.

Getting a flight to Vazara in recent days had become harder, David Wilsin had to admit. Nobody wanted to go there and risk flying straight into the middle of a civil war. Most of the aeroports didn't provide it as an option. Of all the vacation destinations out there, it had become a lot less attractive in a very short space of time. Granted, he remembered that some parts of Vazara had always had the same sort of effect on your average tourist that a mincing factory did to a cow. The result usually wasn't that dissimilar either.

He'd met Leonard Nwakili while he was the premier of the kingdom. Regardless of feelings about the man, it was impossible to deny that he'd done an acceptable job of trying to bring some stability to a notoriously fractured kingdom over years gone by. When unification had kicked in and the five kingdoms had joined together, he'd studied his history, Vazara had gotten a much worse deal than the other four. They'd given so much, unwillingly admittedly, and gotten so little back in exchange beyond a history of poverty and disease mixed in with an unhealthy wave of crime. Before Nwakili, the premiers had been an endless array of charlatans, dictators and shysters out to get what they could from the kingdom before people realised their true colours.

Wilsin had read an article by Kate Kinsella a few days earlier, it had made the most salient point about politicians he'd read in a long time. The most corrupt were usually the ones best at hiding it. The two were connected. That had been in an aeroport in Premesoir, it felt too long ago. They'd been travelling non-stop since, flying from Blasington to Munchauzen, Serran which had taken a day, he'd barely managed to sleep over the cough of ill-sounding engines that had hacked their way through the skies. Following the arrival there, they'd caught another flight to Latalya, a port city down by the southern edges of the kingdom cast in the shadows of the Trabazon mountain. From there, you could just about see Vazara, the city of Umdidi, over the Elkan Ocean, on a clear day with a good scope.

With him, Brendan and Ben Reeves touching down in Latalya, Wilsin had been able to sense the mood of the city in a few moments, there was a great deal of tension in the air. The people looked muted and dejected, like they were expecting the worst to happen. He couldn't blame them really. If Mazoud's new regime did decide to expand out and take its control beyond the borders of Vazara, this would likely be the first place it tried to roll over. (Well, there were a few scattered islands between here and there but as far as he knew, they were uninhabited. Nobody knew for sure which kingdom the Tsarco Islands belonged to. It probably wouldn't become an issue until either kingdom wanted to stop the other claiming them.)

The long travel had given them a chance to hone their cover identities, given Unisco wasn't welcome in Vazara any longer. Hence the new weapons and their official ID left at home. The heavy T6 felt unusual holstered on his hip, he wasn't used to walking around with a blaster on display. Brendan insisted on it. They were going into hostile territory, it would be unwise to do otherwise. And, Reeves had pointed out with a dry smirk, it would have made them stand out more walking around Vazara if they weren't carrying weapons. Brendan had glared at him, stopped short of admonishing him. They were using their own names, Brendan had resorted to his doctorate.

Not a lot of people knew that now he was retired as a spirit caller, Brendan King had taken up a lecturer's post at the Blasington Academy of Education for a few years now. The man was a digger, an explorer, an archaeologist at heart and like all great men, he relished the chance to pass it onto the next generation. The way Wilsin had heard it, calling had never been a passion for him, though he'd been outstanding at it, it was never what he'd solely wanted to do with his life. A tough competitor best summed him up, Unisco had required it of him. His ability to create golems had left him a legend, golems both strong and durable. He wasn't the only one out there who could do it, but King's golems were regarded across the kingdoms as the best of the lot.

Without the day-to-day of spirit calling, Wilsin knew Brendan had briefly served as a city champion before giving it up, he'd managed to combine his time between archaeology, endeavours like the expedition they found themselves on now, the classroom and his time with Unisco. He was one of the most senior agents Wilsin knew, he'd been there even longer than the director. Arnholt respected him, even if maybe the stories went that he didn't necessarily like him that much. Rumour had it, he wanted the top job, didn't like that Arnholt had been sworn into it ahead of him. He'd never seen it between the two of them, their relationship had always been best described as coolly professional in his opinion, the way he'd seen it.

"I'm here on a research expedition, joint with Doctor Alex Fazarn of the Tripoli Institute," Brendan had said, laying it all out on the table in front of them, all their documents blown up in projection form; their identification, images of the team they were meeting, their maps, their routes, every list of supplies that they'd need. "Mr Reeves is one of my students from the university…"

Reeves nodded at that. He didn't look perturbed at the idea of the lie. One of the documents that flashed up was his university pass, the word 'student' stamped across it in large blue letters, as well as a faked transcript document, course registry and application, all looking real as far as Wilsin could tell.

"Mr Wilsin…" Not even agent now they were in hostile territory, Wilsin noted, "is under his guise as a spirit caller, interested in exploring this new frontier, to see what has sprung up in the rise of the Green."

"Least I don't have to do much acting," he said dryly. "I am interested in exploring this thing, though I'm not sure I'd call it a new frontier. A little dramatic for my tastes."

It was with an ironic smile, he noted Brendan could hardly call him out for stuff like this now. Not with them, for all intents and purposes, undercover. He could be as cheekily insubordinate as he liked, not that it was in his nature to push it. Brendan well had it in him to make him suffer after the fact.

"But being the first to set foot in there and bring out records of what it's all about? Couldn't pass that up now, could I?" He could feel a little hint of excitement down in the pit of his stomach over there, his heart beating a rapid little crescendo in his chest. The possibilities were endless. Could be nothing. Could be something. Could be everything. Who knew?

There hadn't been much actual information about the Green that had engulfed Vazara since its first appearance, Nwakili's initial tactic with it had been to try and ignore it, movements that had later devolved to trying to stop people from going in. Later that had been bumped down to an invitation list. The edges were being combed daily but still the Green advanced. Scant days passed before the former edges became deeper into the Green. What parts were explored left often contradictory and out of date information. It was perhaps this thought that left a small fleck of unease in the recesses of his mind

To be without bad feeling and unease would be reckless. What if they went in and they were just swallowed up by it all, never to get out. He admonished himself almost immediately, it was the thought of a scared child, not a trained Unisco agent and decorated spirit caller. Danger was supposed to be something he laughed at. When people were of that opinion, he always wondered what sort of lunatic they figured Unisco agents out to be. Nobody ran senselessly into danger, they certainly didn't laugh at it. They took it one step at a time, considered every step, waited for backup… They were trained to believe that rushing in blindly wasn't even an option.

Unlike this mission. Every step looked to have been planned meticulously. Brendan knew what he was doing, he'd been setting up and carrying out operations for years. There'd been well over a fortnight to set it up, that was a lifetime by Unisco standards. Most were rush jobs, thrown together at a minute's notice on hastily verified information. He'd heard about that one involving that Coppinger warehouse as a prime example. He was glad he hadn't been involved in that fiasco, it sounded like nobody involved in its execution had come out of it well. The last he heard, Roper wasn't in a great mood over the way it had panned out. He hadn't been seen for a few days, vanished under the excuse of 'following up a lead', rumour had it he wasn't being put in charge of planning missions anymore and Swelph had placed Davide Icardi in charge of the department while Brendan was away. They needed something, well anything right now. Brendan had told him they'd pinned a lot on Ulikku being able to provide information. Given the mission had gone wrong on his intelligence, they were treating whatever he said with a lot more caution now than they had before.

As much as this mission to Vazara and into the Green sounded like a great experience, he wasn't entirely sure what it had to do with stopping Coppinger. He'd voiced as much to Brendan and Reeves on the flight over. Wilsin wasn't even sure Reeves had taken it in, perched in his seat, legs folded underneath him in quiet meditation and eyes closed. He looked serene, relaxed, like he didn't have a trouble in the world. Wilsin would have killed to have felt like that right now. As it was, Brendan had replied, and he'd gotten the impression he felt much in the same way.

"Coppinger took responsibility for the Green," he said solemnly. "She did this. It's no small thing. Given some of the claims she made in recent months, her aspirations to divinity, we need to see if there's something in this. See if it is man-made or if there's a higher power at work. There's got to be an explanation. Has to be. I'm not entirely sure I'm ready to believe godhood comes to those who are truly willing and able to look for it. I'm not sure I want to believe that."

For someone who researched the past, Wilsin thought, Brendan looked a lot like he didn't want to believe in the future he thought was coming. He wasn't entirely sure he could blame him. The future they were all about to inherit was a very scary and violent place, a place where Claudia Coppinger was about to inflict her madness onto the kingdoms. She had already done her bit in breaking apart fifty years of unity. There was going to be death, plenty of people were going to suffer before she was done. He might not even make it through himself. But if he was going out, he was going to make sure that it mattered.

That was the future that David Wilsin found himself believing in. They had to win. They had to stop her. She'd gone too far. This was the sort of thing Unisco needed to be able to deal with. They always said they were the best, they always said no threat was too large. It was time they backed it up when it mattered. He had to believe that nothing was broken so badly it was beyond repair. The kingdoms might be shattered but maybe one day, they could be back together. Things could be back to normal. Still, before fifty years ago, the norm was that there was no unity, so nothing lasted forever. He knew that.

Peace then. That was the aim. No more Coppinger and her insanity. He'd often wondered about the events that had transpired to set her plan into motion, often he felt that working those out were perhaps the key to, if not stopping her, then reaching some common ground to negotiate. It felt like too many people were just intent on wiping her out without a thought for the consequences. Wilsin wasn't sure that he liked that approach, there had to be a better way. Killing Coppinger might stop the war but it wouldn't stop the madness she'd unleashed. Everything was out of the bottle right now.

It always amazed him that there were those who felt that getting rid of Coppinger would fix everything and it would all go back to normal. He'd heard that view expressed on more than one occasion and it was all he could to avoid shaking his head. Getting rid of Coppinger wasn't going to be the end of their problems, it'd be the start. Stuff couldn't go back to the way it had been before. A lot of bad blood had been shed over the past six months. Vazara had broken away, killed its rightful leader and sought solace in the rule of a maniac and her puppet ruler. The Senate were going to be punishing the kingdom heavily before they even considered letting them back in. They'd feel they had to. They liked their status quo, they wanted to go for anyone who dared to break it. Punishment leads to prevention. Four wasn't going to become five again in the immediate future, but who could say ten years down the line?

With Brendan asleep, he'd said as much to Reeves, voicing aloud thoughts running around his head. Getting them out felt good. And the Vedo was a good listener, he sat serenely, deep in contemplation before nodding.

"You're right, of course," he said. "We know what the Senate will likely do. For an organisation based on democracy, they only like it when it suits them. Remember when half of Serran wanted to secede away?"

Wilsin nodded. He wasn't going to forget that. It was something that had only lasted a few weeks, but it had felt a lifetime, screenshots of voters being beaten as police trying to stop them from voting, Senate-sponsored heavies and sycophants intervening to warn the people wanting to leave what would happen if they did. They spoke of doom and gloom and violence and recession, of dark days to come if they didn't get their way. They didn't care that the people had grown tired of the archaic rules they'd found themselves living under, rules that applied a broad stroke to try and cover sensitive circumstances that couldn't have been dreamed of fifty years ago.

The world had changed. The Senate hadn't changed with it. There were other kingdoms out there, Wilsin was under no illusion that they'd liked to have joined. The Senate wasn't for turning. They had their trough and they were going to ensure they kept it to themselves.

"I sometimes worry for the world we find ourselves moving towards," Reeves said. He slipped back in his seat, unfolded his legs and closed his eyes. "Things used to be so much simpler. And then I met a man with a sword."

He couldn't quite hide the sigh from his voice and that caught Wilsin's attention. The younger man looked tired. He wasn't sure Vedo were supposed to look tired.

"Tell me," he said. "What's the story between you and Baxter. When did you meet him, what made him train you… Never really spent this much time with one of you people before."

Slowly, Reeves opened his eyes, cocked his head at him. "You people?" he asked. At least there was the faintest hint of a grin present. "That doesn't at all sound condescending."

Wilsin didn't know what to say to that, instead shrugged his shoulders. It felt like an empty gesture. "It's true though. Didn't mean it that way."

"Yeah, integration probably hasn't happened as well as they thought it might," Reeves said thoughtfully. "I mean, it's a bit of a change in our game. For the longest time, we kept to ourselves. Then we were thrust into the spotlight."

"Carcaradis Island?" Wilsin asked. He wasn't going to forget the first time the Vedo had been introduced to the kingdoms. How many lives had their appearance saved that horrific day? In future years, they'd probably look back on it and realise it was the single most important day in the recent history of the kingdoms for everything that had spun out of it since.

"Carcaradis Island," Reeves said. "We came for Arventino. To honour her memory and our master. I'd say we didn't know what was coming. I'm not entirely sure that's true. I think Master Baxter had an inkling something was going to happen. Maybe Ancuta did, maybe she saw something that gave her a hint. Nothing much gets past either of them. Suddenly we're working with you, and no offence, David but I wasn't happy at the time."

Wilsin raised an eyebrow. "No?"

"I wasn't a big fan of Unisco. Still probably not. I think you have too much power, too much anonymity and too much scope in how you wield it. I used to think you sacrificed your morals for results."

Wilsin went to open his mouth to argue in disgust, desperate to point out the fallacies in that statement. Some of the criticism stung. Some of it, Reeves might have had a point with. The Vedo didn't give him the chance.

"But!" he said. "And it's a very big but. I grew up. I found Master Baxter. He taught me a lot, not just about being the Kjarn but about developing as a human being. He told me all sorts of stories about the Vedo and about Unisco. How can I criticise Unisco for anonymity when the Vedo were just as bad, if not worse in the past?"

"It's a little different," Wilsin said softly. "As I understand, the Vedo kept their secrets to themselves because they didn't want to share what they knew. We keep our secrets because someone's got to keep the kingdoms safe. Someone needs to stop people like Coppinger. And we need to keep ourselves protected while we do it."

"Exactly. I appreciate that you serve a useful function. Take everything out, I doubt you're a worse option than any other group would be in the same circumstances. That's why I volunteered to be part of the Vedo that came over. I wanted to see it all for myself. I wanted to help. I wanted to make a difference."

"You want a lot," Wilsin said. "I didn't know that was a Vedo trait."

"Everyone has desires, David. It's a case of whether you're in a position to reap the fruits of them or not. Whether you allow them to consume you. Being a Vedo isn't about denying yourself, it's about control and commitment. At least, it is now. I don't know what the old order was like."

"They died, didn't they?"

Reeves nodded. "As far as I'm aware. There are just a few left out there. Arventino was one. My master. Oh, and Wim Carson."

"Bet you thought it was crazy when Ruud approached you, didn't you?" Wilsin said.

Reeves said nothing, tilted his head to the side in consideration and then nodded. "Just a little. This great champion shows up in your town, asks about for a few days and then winds up in front of you. He tells you stuff, hells he goes and shows you stuff." He ran his fingers through his hair awkwardly. He didn't look comfortable.

"What did he show you?" He didn't have to feign interest in this story, he'd been wondering a little about Baxter's methods.

"When you're young," Reeves said. "You hear stories, right? They're always there, you think they can't be true. People who are better than human. Superhuman. That was what the Vedo were to me. I saw Master Baxter summon fire to his hand, I saw him call upon lightning, he had the power of the storm at his fingertips. He jumped from the ground to the roof of my home in a single leap and back again. Sometimes you simply need to accept that you're in the presence of the remarkable. He had all this power, he told me how he wanted to use it. He told me everything, what had happened to the Vedo of old and what he intended to do."

He paused, took a long drag out of his water canteen. It was already getting disgustingly hot, Wilsin had noticed. "When it's put to you like that, how could you turn it down? The chance to make a difference doesn't come to you every day."

No, Wilsin thought.

It certainly doesn't.

He hadn't realised how glad he was to get off that cramped aeroship, stretched out his arms and felt muscles complain with the exertion, even if it akin to stepping from a sweatbox into the fire. The heat clamped around him like a fiery glove, the humidity threatening to overwhelm. It took him a few moments to adjust, shield his eyes from the glare of the sun high above them. Wilsin rummaged in his pocket, found his shades and slipped them on. He looked at Brendan, then at Reeves. Brendan was mopping his face with an oversized handkerchief, he looked like he was already regretting his decision to come out here. Reeves, Wilsin found himself cursing, didn't appear too bothered by the furious temperatures. If there was even a single bead of sweat on his skin, he would be surprised.

"Welcome to Vazara," Brendan said ruefully. He reached into his pack, pulled out a data pad in one swift motion. Some of the rumours about thieves in Vazara, Wilsin thought, it'd need swift hands to stop someone running off with it if Brendan wasn't careful. He thought of the blaster securely hidden in his pack, wished that the time had come where he could wear it openly holstered on his hip, secrecy be damned.

He'd never been the sort of guy who'd shoot first and ask questions later. That had always been more of Nick Roper's forte than his. He didn't believe in drawing his weapon unless he meant to use it. He only meant to use it if his life was in danger. Having things out in the open meant that the deterrent was there. Especially with the size of the weapon that Navarro had given him.

He'd practiced with it before they'd left, just to get used to the weight. It had a kick like a stubborn mule, firing it repeatedly had left his arms throbbing and numb from the kick. He'd never especially considered himself a blaster nut. Didn't revel in the specifications of each individual weapon. How effective it was usually meant the sum of his interest in it. The big blaster was a beast though, Navarro had regaled him with stories of how it'd punch through anything short of an aerofighter hull.

Not that he expected to be facing any aerofighters on this trip. If he ended up doing that, things would really have gone badly wrong. All their weapons had been locked away behind anti-security measures, they were heading into enemy territory now, a place devoid of their authority.

There were people all around them, many but not perhaps as many as there might have been. Small scattered groups waiting in subdued silence for a ship to take them away. Nobody looked happy to be here, they had their luggage and their eyes locked onto the ground as if scared to look up in case they didn't like what they saw. Very few of them looked like tourists. Most of them looked like they wanted to get out as fast as possible and not come back. Wilsin had noted that he, Brendan and Reeves were the only people coming into the kingdom off their flight. That didn't bode well with him.

It all added up to the simple fact that people weren't coming to Vazara. It had always had a reputation as a rough place for those who didn't have the means to protect themselves. Since Nwakili had been killed and the kingdom seceded, that reputation had grown and grown and not in a good way. Stories had been coming out all too often of late and it didn't sit right with Wilsin. People shouldn't have to live in fear like this. Mazoud hadn't taken long to declare it a police state, his operatives were everywhere. Wilsin was sure he could see two of them already, stood leaning against the back wall of the port wearing mirrored shades, trying to keep an eye on everything and everyone.

He said as much to Brendan who shook his head. "That doesn't worry me so much as the ones you don't see. It's an old Vazaran Sun trick that. Have two obvious guys who look like they don't have a bastard clue and have twenty more roaming unseen."

"Can see why they're avoiding eye contact with everyone else then," Reeves said, glancing over at the departure queues. He took a deep breath, sniffed twice and then coughed. "This place stinks of fear. Fear and desperation."

Wilsin said nothing, moved for his own data pad as they moved towards the customs cubicles. Even as they approached, the lines were only handfuls deep, inbound
arrivals numbered in the dozens rather than the hundreds. At least they wouldn't have to wait too long. That was a small blessing. Once through those gates, they'd be in Vazara proper, they'd meet with Fazarn, Brendan's contact and they'd be able to make a start on, well, what they needed to do here.

Security looked a lot more stringent than it had before. Getting into any kingdom had never been an issue in his experience. Normally they were happy to have you. The more people flooding in, the greater the gain to said kingdom. When you stacked it up with the argument that spirit calling was an exceptionally transitory sport, people came and went all the time. If a hundred thousand people go out of Serran in one week, then a hundred thousand people coming in from Premesoir would at the very least keep some sort of balance. People didn't stay in the same place. Wilsin had only recently bought an apartment back in Blasington in Premesoir, his first home. He'd spent two nights there in a month due to work commitments, spirit calling might be in a slump but Unisco was busier than ever.

Being embroiled in a civil war would do that to you. He smirked to himself, stepped into the shortest line. Brendan went to a different one. Always split up in circumstances like this. Be least memorable as possible. People knew who Brendan was. It was likely people might know who he was. Ergo, if they saw the two of them together, they were likely to remember them. That could compromise them going forward. That was a chance that was easy to avoid. Unisco protocol existed for a reason.

Nobody knew who Reeves was, he followed Brendan into his own line. If Reeves was posing as his student, it made sense. They'd be part of the same party. They'd stick together, though it suited Wilsin to be alone. He got the feeling Reeves could handle himself, but he was still an unknown quantity. Too many of the Vedo were, the ones that

Baxter had trained the longest anyway. He knew that Anne Sullivan and Alex Nkolou had joined up and were in the process of being trained and that assuaged some of his worries. They had the training. They could be trusted. Wilsin preferred those around him whose capabilities he could, if not rely on, then at least understand.

He made it to the front of his queue before Brendan and Reeves got to theirs, Wilsin smiled at the stern-faced Vazaran behind the glass. He didn't want to think about what might happen if they were refused entry.

"Good morning," he said, holding his data pad with the relevant documents to the window. The man's expression barely changed. He had more hair on his eyebrows than he did on his head. His eyes listlessly twitched back and forth, examining the screen. He gave every impression he didn't want to be here.

Wilsin didn't blame him. Idly he found himself wondered how long before immigration and border control fell under another wing of Vazaran Sun authority. He'd read all Unisco's files on Mazoud, had drawn conclusions from them that he was the sort of man who if something worked, he wasn't going to give up on it. More than that, Unisco psychological profiles had declared that he'd try and apply it to areas where perhaps it didn't necessarily fit in an attempt to make it run more smoothly. Putting mercenaries in charge of bureaucratic affairs didn't sound like a recipe for success. He was glad they were arriving now and not six months times. Although, depending on how this mission went, six months might be the time they returned. An unhappy thought. Getting out might be even harder than getting in.

They'd have to deal with that when they came to it. Six months was a long time in politics. Things could have easily changed by then. You needed some faith in the world, no matter how bleak things might look like they could get.

The immigration officer was still reading his documents, finally nodded, gestured for him to hold his pad under the scanner on the front of the booth. Wilsin did so, making sure that all the correct tags and codes lined up with the beam.

"Name?"

His accent was thick and gruff, but understandable. Why he needed to give his name when he'd just seen all his documents... Maybe letting the Suns take over wouldn't be the stupidest idea after all.

"David Peter Wilsin," he said, keeping his voice even. Getting into arguments wouldn't be smart. People remembered arguments. It would defeat the point of keeping their presence here low key.

"Purpose of visit?"

"Spirit calling and exploration."

That brought a sad shake of the head from the officer. Wilsin glanced at him through the glass, saw his nametag was faded, discoloured from years of wear. The name had been obscured by dirt on the plastic. That didn't fill him with confidence. He wondered how many people had given that excuse in recent months to come into Vazara. Given the look on his face, he doubted it was many.

"Length of stay?"

A tricky question when it came to buy an immigration visa. Given the expansion of the Green across Vazara, it had more than quadrupled in size since it had first appeared six months ago. Desert had become jungle, none of the cities had been swallowed up yet but if it carried on the way it was… Exploring it could become tricky if you had to travel twice as long to get out as you had going in.

Still, he had the answer Brendan had told him to give. Hopefully one that'd cover them regardless of the circumstances ahead.

"Open-ended year plus," he said, giving him another smile. Wasn't the sort of visa that most arriving spirit callers went for. They were expensive, more than three times the price of normal visas. Yet what made them so handy was that they included the rest of the current year and all the next. That'd give them more than enough time, he hoped.

The officer slid another data pad over to him, a thumb reader on its screen. Wilsin didn't hesitate, pressed his thumb to it and watched the screen go green. It didn't take long, just long enough for his print to go white under the pressure.

"Okay, that'll be three thousand credits," the officer said. On the screen, Wilsin's picture flashed up, his identity confirmed as well as all his relevant information. Strange seeing your life boiled down into a few lines. Three thousand credits, in his opinion, was absolute extortion, though it wasn't him that was paying it. That softened the blow. The credits had come from a Unisco operation fund set up for incidents like this. Their use had been authorised, they'd been transferred into his account and he slid that credit card across to the reader.

It was with a strange realisation of irony he noticed this was the swiftest part of the whole process, the taking of the credits in the first place. Barely three seconds passed between scanning and accepting. With that out the way, all that remained was the transfer of documents from immigration to his data pad wirelessly, he waited twenty seconds as it went underway, then put his pad away as it completed. He gave the guy another smile, this one not as enthusiastic.

"Thanks," he said. "Maybe I'll see you on the way out."

"If you're lucky," the immigration officer said without a hint of jest in his voice. Deadpan, Wilsin thought, heavy emphasis on the word dead, "You'll manage to get out at all."

Wow…

Wilsin's feelings about this entire mission took a downward spiral. He didn't want to think about what he might have meant. Maybe things were worse than they'd all thought they were. He didn't want to think about how much worse that could be.

He'd had to wait a few more minutes from Brendan and Reeves to make their way through to him on the other side, the three of them heading through to arrivals. Even out here, they were probably the largest party. Most of the arrivals looked like they'd come back on their own, most of them of similar demographic. Young, tough-looking Vazarans in their twenties, all giving the impression they were up for a fight. He wondered if they'd come back to join the Suns.

They still had to put their bags through a security scanner, Wilsin noted, the queues coming to a bottleneck ahead. He couldn't help but feel that it was a strange way of doing things, having this last. Other kingdoms made you go through this before you spent credits on your visa. Not here. Other kingdoms didn't search you as you came out, they left it to the kingdom you'd left to check you hadn't taken any contraband on the aeroship. He wasn't worried about the security scanner as he approached it. Navarro had given them special packs to fool the x-ray machines, they were lined with a photo-reflective lead which showed them what they'd expect to see in a pack that would pass muster. Clothes, spirit calling equipment, his data pad.

He did have to admit the closer he got though, Navarro was no Alvin Noorland. He was competent, but he hadn't earned instant faith status yet, he still had a lot to prove. If Noorland had come up with the stuff, he'd have been more confident. Noorland had been a genius, he was still heavily missed by those who'd known him.

Ten people ahead of him. Nine. The machine pushed through their packs, didn't show any sign of registering any contraband. Eight people, then seven, then six. Smuggling it in was stupid. If you wanted to bring a weapon in, they weren't hard to get hold of in any major Vazaran city. Five people. They should have done that. Procured weapons on site. Four people ahead of him. The only downside to that being with that many illegal weapons floating around, you had no idea what they'd been used for previously. Three people. Too many weapons with crimes attached to them. If they were caught with a blaster that had killed forty people, they wouldn't be getting out alive. Two ahead of them. He could smell the sweat of the security officers who were manning the machine. It was too bloody hot here, not a hint of air conditioning anywhere. Any other kingdom, they wouldn't have allowed it. Too many regulations. He was going to be the next one through. If his bag set off the scanners, he counted at least six security officers who'd be ready to jump on him. He couldn't fight off six, not when they all had blasters and probably wouldn't hesitate to shoot a foreigner who'd already paid for his visa. Brendan wouldn't help him. Reeves might want to, he'd follow Brendan's lead though, Wilsin was sure of it, just as he was sure he'd be on his own if it went bad.

He put his pack on the belt, took a deep breath and stepped forward through the body scanner. He didn't have anything about his person that would set it off, he'd made sure of that. Wilsin wanted to walk through unencumbered, he wanted to grab his bag and walk off again. Even so, he found his fists balling up as he stepped forward, some part of him quietly ready for action. Just in case.

Nothing. Nothing on him and no alarm towards his pack. He picked it up off the belt, silently thanked the Divines above and carried on forward out of the immediate area. Reeves joined him seconds later, Brendan a minute after. None of them said anything to each other. Wilsin would have liked to think that was the hard part over. He was deluding himself if that was the case, he thought. The hard part was only just starting.

Brendan knew where he was going, he took the lead and cut through the crowds with a sense of purpose, Wilsin and Reeves following in his wake. More than once, a hand snaked out towards them, determined to try and pick a pocket. One went for Wilsin, he grabbed it faster than they could pull away and yanked one of the fingers back hard. The snap felt painfully loud to him, had been drowned out by the sounds of the aeroport. What wasn't drowned out was the yells of pain, nobody took any notice, nobody cared. Pickpockets were dealt with in harshest possible terms in aeroports, you did it at your own risk and took your lumps if you were caught.

One went for Reeves, perhaps even less of a sensible idea. Like Wilsin had, he caught the hand, leaned in close to the thief and murmured something close to his ears. The thief's eyes went strangely blank, he stepped backwards as if in a haze and wandered off, almost tripping over his own feet. Reeves gave Wilsin a rueful look. "He decided to rethink his life choices. Good for him." After that, they didn't have too much trouble. The key to surviving Vazara was not to look like prey. More than any other kingdom Wilsin had been in, the locals gave the impression they were sharks waiting for any bit of offal in the water. If you didn't look like offal, they wouldn't go for you.

Outside, Brendan came to a halt, gave a wave to two men stood across the lounge. One was Vazaran, heavyset with glasses and a prominent scar on his neck. The other was taller and thinner, his skin paler and his hair lighter. Both wore clothes that suggested they were ready for an expedition, they looked painfully out of place here, Wilsin had to admit. They'd never have passed the Unisco test about blending into their surroundings.

They met them halfway, Brendan exchanging handshakes and greetings all around. Wilsin looked at Reeves, shrugged. He shook the hands of both men, the Vazaran stank of sweat and goat meat. The other guy, from Canterage if his accent was anything to go by, grinned at them, his eyes half-closed and his words slurred. He sounded like he'd been drinking, his breath reinforced that notion. Wilsin had been in breweries that stank less of alcohol.

"David Wilsin, Ben Reeves, these are Doctors Alex Fazarn and Shane Bryce. They're both part of the expedition..."

"In charge of," Fazarn said snippily. He didn't sound impressed with Brendan's choice of words. "Discovering the secrets of the Green is perhaps the single most important task of our lifetime. This is a brave new world and we need to be at the forefront. We do this right; our names will go down in history. Yours. Mine. His." He gestured at Price. "It's a joint effort between the three of us to lead this thing. My academic reputation. Brendan's professional reputation. Shane has a reputation as well, logistically. He's the guy you want for this sort of thing. There's nobody better, I assure you all."

"Hells yeah," Bryce said. "Don't worry about Alex. He's wound a bit tight. We're glad to have you all. Every hand makes it easier, right?" He clapped his hands together and yawned, clamping one of his hands up to cover his mouth. "Excuse me, long day. Got here not too long back myself. A bit of a circus here, no?"

Wilsin wondered how long he'd been drinking if that was the case. He didn't want to think about what that might mean for the mission if one of the planners was already inebriated out of his mind.

"Anyway, we'll hit our inn for the night, we'll set off for the Green in the morning," Bryce said. Another yawn. Wilsin wondered if he was being overtly critical. Maybe it was just a bad day. Maybe he didn't like flying.

There'd been enough bad days recently. What was one more?

"I think we could all use some rest," Brendan said, hefting his pack over his shoulder and rubbing his hands together in eagerness. "Lead us on then. We have jungle to explore and they won't wait for us. The sooner we turn in, the sooner we can get this expedition underway."

Wilsin wasn't used to seeing this level of enthusiasm from his boss, he suppressed a smile and folded his arms. "I can agree with that," he said. "Lead on, doctors."

Chapter Ten. Process of Elimination.

"For as long as I can remember, this academy has been a place where the training has only been second to actual field experience by the tightest of margins. Training should be a prelude to an experience, not the experience itself. A grounding, if you like. I want it to be as realistic as possible. Within reason, push them to their limits and see what they've got. This isn't a summer camp, I want the training intensified and hard. It is only through fire that the glass is formed from sand."
Message from Tod Brumley to Kinpatso Takamishi and Nandahar Konda at the Iaku Academy, RE the training of fresh cadets.

Three months ago.

They'd dragged them out of bed early in the morning, four am and Pete hadn't been expecting it. It wasn't a figure of speech, the doors to the dormitory had been kicked in and they'd been forcibly removed from their beds, faces forced into the cold floor. He'd yelped as his face hit the stone, felt the knee in his back holding him down, his arms yanked behind his back as they secured his wrists together with cuffs. Around him, they were doing the same thing, he heard Theo swearing forcefully and trying to fight back. He was making a good go of it as well, he could see four of them trying to hold him down, fists and feet flying everywhere in clumsy fashion. He knew the moves, he hadn't entirely mastered them yet. None of them had. The four around him were practiced, they ducked and weaved away without getting hit and Theo had to be tiring. He couldn't keep that up forever. Pete was subsequently proved right, a fist came from his blindside and caught him across the jaw, he hit the ground in an undignified manner and didn't move. In moments, he was restrained in the same manner as the rest of them.

A trickle of blood dribbled down his face, he could taste its coppery tang in his mouth, mixing with his saliva. It made him want to spit. What the hells had happened here? He wasn't sure he knew what was going on. These people, who were they? This place was a Unisco academy, it was supposed to be a heavily protected secret. To get the forces together to storm it... He'd heard the stories about what the Coppingers had in their arsenal, what they'd do to try and overthrow the kingdoms. He'd heard too much about the riots in Burykia and Premesoir, how they'd incited people to public disorder in deadly fashion. To hit the Iaku academy though... That was something else.

Eventually any sounds of resistance died away, those who continued to make them were beaten, one blow to force the fight out of them. Pete tried to look around, didn't see anything that made him think his choice was the right one. The dormitory had become chaos, it looked like an explosion had hit it. He tried to crane his neck to look at the faces of those who'd attacked, felt the presence of someone stood next to him clearing their throat.

"I wouldn't, boy. You see our faces, it won't end well for you. You're on thin ice already. Don't give us excuses." The voice was distorted, almost mechanical in its lack of emotion.

He let his face sag into the stone, felt the sharp sigh of frustration slip out of him. He heard the figure above him chuckle. He was glad someone found it funny. He didn't. He wasn't laughing right now. Wasn't sure he'd be laughing again for a while.

"Okay, freeze it up."

That voice he recognised, the silence was cut in an instant and the voice of the academy administrator spoke up once again. "You might be wondering what has happened here," Kinpatso Takamishi said, striding through the maze of fallen cadets as if they were his property. "Here is your lesson for the morning. You never know when the enemy will attack you, it is when you feel most secure that you are always at your most vulnerable. It is a time of war and safety is a sense of luxury that none of us can afford to feel. You all need to learn that more than most. If you are lucky enough to graduate this fine institution, you put a target on your back. There are always people out there who will have wished for the death of Unisco agents. Thanks to Claudia Coppinger and her band of dissidents, that number is only going to increase over the coming months."

He paused. "We're not going to let you out, you know. Just think on that. You're going to get yourselves out, no matter how long it takes. Pain, discomfort, hunger, humiliation, these are all fine motivators we have found over the years. Once you go out into the field, this could happen to you. It has happened to more agents over the years than we can count. Being able to master your environment when you are confined is a skill that will be amongst your most valuable."

Pete tried shifting into a better position, felt a foot press against his back in warning and thought better of it. He didn't want the shit kicked out of him just yet. They gave the impression they'd do it. Unisco training wasn't for the weak, they didn't do things by halves. He'd worked that out months back, in his first week here. Hells, he'd worked it out that first day when they'd thrown him out the aeroship. There'd been a few who hadn't made it as far as the academy there. They'd been sent out to clean up the bodies. Horrible, it had been. He hadn't known what a human body looked like when it hit the ground from a couple thousand feet before, but he did now, and he could have done without earning that image. Saying it made a mess didn't even come close to describing it. The words were inadequate. He could still remember what they'd said to the cadets after it had happened, and they'd been brought there.

"In this line of work, you are going to see some truly messed up things. Enjoy." Those short words and they'd been left to work the day away with nothing more than a single pair of gloves and a strong black disposal bag each. He could remember the heat that day, the buzzing of the flies and the smell of vomit. He hadn't thrown up. He'd wanted to. He doubted he'd been alone in that urge, a thought proven when several others had relieved themselves of their stomach contents.

"You see," Takamishi said. "Not too long back, we went through a phase where we tried to do it as nicely-nice as we could for you guys. We didn't want you to suffer unnecessarily. After all, this is a training camp, not a torture centre."

"Then y'all started to die in the line of duty. And we decided to kick your training up a notch or two." That had to be Bruno Hans. He put that accent on when he was trying to be taken seriously. His accent was normally heavy with inflections from the west of Serran, quite emotionless in his delivery. The change to laidback Premesoir cowherder was a shock to the system. Especially since Pete wasn't sure he had a sense of humour. He quickly went back to his normal accent. "Yes, you all didn't pass the muster and as a result, our future cadets have to be regarded as the best yet, yes?"

"Anyway, have fun," Takamishi said. "There are ten of you in here. Ten ways of getting out of your cuffs. One for each of you. Five are obvious. Five are harder to discover. When you get free, do not stop to help your fellow cadets. You are all being scored out of one hundred by myself, Instructors Hans, Khazeer and Christophe as well as Professor Melane. We will judge you on your attitude, your creativity, your speed, your technique and your composure and commitment. The highest three scorers will be rewarded." He sounded like he was grinning. "They won't have to clean this room up after the last of you end up shitting yourselves."

Pete kept his face clear. It didn't do to show too much emotion. Instructor Christophe had told them that. He looked like he couldn't raise an emotion if his life depended on it. Learning all the Unisco directives was the driest part of the learning experience, he found it a little dull but had to admit that it was essential. You couldn't do the job if you didn't know the rules. Christophe's frequent tests made sure they were all up to speed. Repeated failure was not tolerated, he'd seen someone thrown out of the academy for not being able to give the correct answers in time. Regardless, the point had been made. If people didn't know what you were thinking, then you were at an advantage.

"Enjoy," Instructor Hans said. Before Pete knew it, the doors were opened and closed above him, the extra sounds of breathing gone from the room. Just the ten of them remained, ten of them all tied up and unable to really move. But they had to be able to move a little. It wasn't going to be easy, they wouldn't have made it that way. He'd expected them to start off slowly and gradually increase the trickiness of the tests but once they'd had their initial training, they'd been thrown in at the deep end more than once. They'd always said they found recruits learned more through failure than they did through success.

That was a very spirit caller attitude to the process and Pete had to appreciate that. The irony of it was that his skills in that respect hadn't really been tested since he'd come here. He'd been at the Quin-C though and so had Dan Roberts. Theo had gotten to the final and could well have won it if it hadn't been for circumstances beyond his control. He certainly couldn't say that he'd lost it, given the official result had been declared as a draw. Rumour had it they'd offered to split the prize purse between the two finalists, but Theo had declined it. They'd given Scott the full pot and Pete knew his best friend had had no qualms about accepting it. He'd have been more surprised if he'd turned it down.

That wasn't important right now. Getting out was.

Pete rocked himself side to side, trying to see how much of his body he could move. His legs weren't secured, he wondered if they'd done that deliberately. Trying to second-guess the instructors made his head hurt. He didn't know what they had or hadn't done, wasn't sure if he'd ever be able to work them out. Again, not important. He wondered if this was what the attitude part of the test was about. Seeing how they adapted to circumstances out of their control and reacted to them. That could have covered composure as well. If he were to dwell on what it meant to succeed, he'd probably end up failing.

He continued to rock, lifted his head to try and get a better view of the surrounding area. If five means of escape were obvious and five not so, then he'd wanted to find one of the easy ones. He couldn't move his arms, not easily anyway and he had to grimace as he stared around the room, his neck muscles on fire. All he could see was the shadows under his bed. No joy there, not unless his eyes adjusted to the dark and soon. It wasn't impossible that something could have been hidden under there but short of jerking himself under there in some sort of clumsy roll, he wasn't about to find out. He certainly couldn't reach under and have a good root around, no matter how easier that would have made things.

"Pete? Theo?" That was Dan Roberts and he sounded a little thick in his words, like he'd taken a punch to the mouth. "You guys okay?"

"Clearly," Theo said. He hadn't lost the sarcastic touch, even despite the kicking that he'd taken earlier. Pete had been hoping that being beaten up would have calmed him a little. He'd been hoping that for the best part of the last few months. If anything, it had made him more obnoxious. He clearly wasn't someone who took hints about his attitude. Divines alone knew what he'd be like when he was fully minted as an agent and had the skillset to back up his mouth. "We're all just peachy pie over here. Wonderful, even."

"What he means to say, I'm sure," Pete said. "Is that they've not punched the sarcasm out of him yet. Doctors remain hopeful, but the verdict is that it's unlikely at this point. He's terminal. No hope for him."

"Are you still beating your gums, Jacobs?" Theo asked. "Or are you looking for the way out of here?"

"Ways," Dan offered. "He said there were more than one. Ten, yeah?"

"Here's hoping that there's not an unpleasant one like breaking your own thumb to get out of it or cutting your hand off," Theo said, a little unhelpfully Pete thought. He doubted they'd leave some sort of cutting implement about for that purpose. Training for the real thing would only get you so far. Having your cadets maim themselves in an exercise like this would be futile. "Mind you…"

Theo tailed off, Pete heard the crack followed by a high-pitched yelp an instant later, a sound he thought he'd never have heard Theo make. Seconds later, he saw a wincing Theo stand, clutching his hand to his chest. He didn't look badly hurt, more pained than anything else, his face pale and his breathing heavy but he was free and moving.

"Seriously?" Dan asked. "Did you just break your own thumb? Hard core, man!"

"Which one of us just got out first?" Theo asked, heading for the door. He paused to blow the two of them a kiss. "See you in a few days when you work it out. Top score all the way."

Silence reigned as the door slammed behind him, Pete had to fight to roll his eyes. It wouldn't have done much good for anyone. Theo wasn't going to see it, he decided to try and roll onto his other side, get a better view of his environment around there. He rocked his body back and forth, winced as he trapped his arm underneath him, managed to drag his full weight off it and look around. He could see Roberts' foot almost in his face.

"What're you doing?" Dan asked. "You trying to wriggle free?"

The door opened again, a voice came in from outside. "One more thing. Anyone else who tries escaping by breaking their own thumb is immediately dropped to the bottom of the pile. That was one of the hidden ways, just so you know. It's crude but effective in the right set of circumstances. Some more recent models got adapted so that they couldn't be broken out of that way. We gave you an old model. Because we're kind like that."

If that was kind, he wasn't sure what their cruelty looked like.

"Trying to get a view of my surroundings," Pete said. "Remember what they said on the first day? Always check your environment." Dan added the last four words in unison with him and Pete grinned. "There's got to be something here that we can use. There always is."

"No matter how small, there'll always be an opportunity," Dan added, echoing the words they'd heard. That first full day had been one hells of a memory to look back on. Whatever else could be said about it, the lessons had stuck. They'd been driven home under the reminder that if they didn't follow them, then there was a good chance that they'd wind up dead once they were in the field. Then the instructor had thrown a stun grenade at them to push the point home. "You just need to know when to take it."

"Think it might be one of those things that comes in with experience," Pete said. He couldn't see anything leaning over his other side either, just more stone floor and people struggling to get free. He couldn't tell if anyone was succeeding. If he closed his eyes, he could hear muttered voices and sounds of disgruntlement. He'd learned his fellow cadet's names, unlike Theo and he could tell them apart, hearing what they were saying nearby.

He couldn't move his arms, wouldn't resort to breaking his own thumb like Theo had, not least because of the consequences that had been outlined to him. If he couldn't move his arms, what could he do? He tested his legs, stretching them out and spreading them to their full width. He could move them. They hadn't restrained his feet. That felt like it meant something. Could he get to his feet without using his arms? Wouldn't be impossible, would be very difficult. He gritted his teeth together, tried sliding into so his body was in a better position for it. Rolling onto his back, he at least managed to get up into a sitting position with his arms behind him. Now he was perched upright, he could see the room a little better.

The lights had all been switched off, barring one above Hill's bed that had never quite switched off properly, the faintest glow of light stubbornly clinging to the glass. There'd been a big fight to decide who didn't get it and Hill had drawn the short straw. Hill was a tall youth from Canterage with dark hair and a thick beard that must have taken some impressive maintenance. Pete found it an effort to get the time together to comb his hair since he'd gotten here.

In that flickering light, he glanced about the room, cast his eyes across the bound wrists of anyone he could see. By the looks of it, the cuffs were all the same model. That was good. The same set of cuffs would have the same sets of weaknesses. If they had the same weaknesses, they could be manipulated in the same way. They looked to be made of steel, a thin chain connecting them. It looked like silver string, it gave him something to think about as he wondered how strong they really were.

He'd always fancied himself to be strong, certainly a bit more well-defined than the average man. He liked his muscles, he'd encountered plenty of women who liked them as well. He'd not touched meat in recent years, but he'd ingested a lot of artificial protein powders over the same time to make up the substitutes he needed to build them up. He was pleased with the effect. Up in the north of Serran, he'd heard stories about men who injected a designer drug into their arms, filling them with fluid to make the muscles swell and look larger. He'd always thought it looked unnatural, the inflammation reminding him of disease and sickness.

Seeing that thin chain, he considered it for a moment. Tensed his muscles, counted backwards from five and then gave them a hard yank in hope that it'd give. He quickly realised it hadn't done even the slightest bit of good. That chain might be thin, but it was strong and durable. Exactly what you wanted if you ever bought a pair of restraints.

They weren't going to make it that easy for them, were they? If they broke under the slightest of pressure, then they weren't much good for anything outside of the bedroom.

Still, he'd tried it. He'd considered it as an option and he'd decided not to. It wasn't viable. When you went through everything, you had the chance to eliminate the stuff that wouldn't work and hopefully you'd be left with the options that might. Process of elimination. His mind went back to the cuffs. How much pressure before they did break apart? He didn't know. Maybe this was the sort of stuff a seasoned agent of Unisco might know, but he didn't. He'd not studied up on it. There'd never been any sort of hint that he'd need to. Not that it was possible to plan for everything. That'd just be a fool's errand. Try to plan for everything and you'd get stuck in a quagmire of details.

There was an excited squeak and Tamale stood up, a length of wire clutched between her fingers in triumph. Pete studied the look on her face, giddy glee at her own success. And she hadn't had to brutalise herself to do it.

"Excellent work, Cadet Tamale," the same voice called into the room. "Come out now and bring your makeshift lockpick with you. Always this should be your first thought when you find yourself cuffed and restrained. What is the easiest way to escape? Can I do this with tools to hand? She could. She did. Most cuff locks are easy to tinker with if you know how and you have the tools."

Pete watched Tamale leave, had to admit to himself that she looked adorable in her sleepwear and with her hair all mussed from the nights rest. Cute girl. Very cute. He liked the pink streak in her hair, though it had almost grown out in recent months.

They'd insisted that men and women share a dormitory in recent weeks as their numbers had thinned, although there were at least separations via a wall that gave the same impression as a mirror on both sides. Any sort of sexual liaisons between cadets, they'd warned them in their first days, would be severely punished. It was highly prohibited. He'd have risked it for Tamale, he got the impression that she was the sort of girl who craved the approval of older men. He'd seen it in the way she was around the instructors, always going out of her way to get the best possible praise she could from them. It was a little annoying, but he'd forgive her on the grounds of how her ass looked in her trousers when they were training.

To each their own. What Theo called shameless bloody cock-sucking her way to graduation, Pete called something else. Maybe she was just trying to get the best possible feedback she could on where she was. A little desperate in the way she went about it perhaps, but who was he to judge? If it got results for her, maybe it was the right thing to do. She had to have something going for her. They wouldn't just hire sycophants for this or because she looked pretty. There had to be hidden depths to her.

Dominic Hill got out next. Pete heard the clank, saw the chain fall away from one of his cuffs and the tall youth stretched his arms out, flexing the muscles with relief. He didn't know how Hill had done it, at least not until the voice filled the room upon his exit.

"Congratulations, Cadet Hill. You were aware of your surroundings and that metal degrades faster in some environments, particularly if it's old and worn. Using the spillage of water, you managed to wear them away enough to break free. Less perhaps of an obvious method but clever thinking regardless."

Some of these were getting tenuous, Pete thought as he took another glance around. He had to find his way out and quick. Already three out of ten were free and he didn't want to get a low score here. It'd reflect badly on him. There was a bit of an age divide between the people who'd been selected for this class, from kids just about legal to start spirit calling like Hill to him and Theo who roughly had to be about the same age, to Lamine Lavern who was a couple of years older than either of them. He'd heard it said that the best cadets were those at the younger age, he'd aimed to prove them wrong.

Finally, his gaze settled on the bed he'd just been dragged out of, he studied it for a few long moments, specifically the legs planted hard into the stone floor. They were thick and sturdy, and the bed was heavy. In an environment like this, it was important that the furniture couldn't be moved around easily. Not impossible but difficult. He wondered how tough the chain truly was if it took some weight to it.

It was an effort jerking himself over there on his knees, he had to take it slow, small efforts at a time or risk toppling over, especially without his hands to balance him. He tried to shut out every other sound, especially as someone else got free of their restraints, tried to block out hearing how they'd done it. It wasn't important. There'd probably be a recap session at the end of it, going over how each of them had done it. He'd just pay attention then. For now, he wanted to focus on one step at a time, not get distracted and make it into a position where he could do what he needed.

Kneeling at the foot of the bed, he considered his position. Lifting the bed would be awkward, lifting it and manoeuvring himself under one of the feet so it came down on the cuffs would be tricky on his own. If he'd been able to, he'd have stroked his chin in contemplation before realising how ridiculous the notion was. It didn't make a damn bit of difference to his progress.

Instead he turned so his back was to the bed and scrunched down, trying to get his shoulders underneath the frame. His breath caught in his chest as he got an up-close look at his own knee, almost folded in on himself as he tried to give himself that little bit more room. His abdomen started to complain at the efforts. He'd taken a punch there a few days earlier, this was only aggravating it.

You might not be one hundred percent when you do this, the words flashed through his mind. If you were fully fit and fighting able, chances are you might well have avoided capture in the first place. Since you didn't, you probably aren't.

He'd thought little soundbites like that weren't helpful at first. He'd later come to the opinion upon suffering through similar experiences, albeit at a much lower level, that they'd been borne out of years of experience and should therefore be listened to. That last one was a little twee for him. You could be at your best and still be outnumbered, still captured. If half of the lesson had a point, was it still valid? In this circumstance, given the ache in his stomach, he thought it might be.

In as best position as he was going to manage, he took a deep breath and tried to push up with his shoulders. He felt the bed give a few inches before clattering back down on him. He felt the pain scrape through him, the weight horrific across his back. His vision flashed, he was sure he saw stars, before he shook his head to try and clear it of thoughts. If the weight was like that, chances were that he might yet be able to scrape through this given the chance.

He permitted himself a quick glance around the room. He was still one of six. He hadn't seen or heard who'd gotten out fourth. Pete didn't want to think about what might happen if he was the last out of here. Especially if this didn't work. He tried to mentally push the pain away. Fixating on it wasn't going to do him any good. You suffered pain because your body was telling you that you were engaged in a practice that wasn't good for it. Being secured in here for as long as it took to break out wasn't going to be good for his health either.

Around him, the other five were already engaged in frenzied activity, they were desperate to escape their shackles and he couldn't blame them. Nobody liked being restrained. He wasn't sure how successful their efforts were, he just didn't want to take the chance that they'd beat him

Dan Roberts had already gotten into a standing position, towering above the rest of them and engaged in as wide a search as Pete was. Their eyes caught each other's, and they shrugged in unison. This felt futile. That settled it for him. He turned his attention back to the bed, moved a little closer to the leg, scrabbling sideways across the floor like some sort of misshapen crap and eventually he felt it with his outstretched fingers behind him. The post was thick, he couldn't even get his hands around it, no matter how much he tried. Pete grimaced, tried to lift it, but with the restraints on, he realised that getting the leverage to do so would be nigh on impossible. It was a case of he'd need to time it right and try not to think about what would happen if he got it wrong.

This time he tried not to think of the pain as he shoved the bed onto his shoulders, let out a curt wheeze of pain, tried to throw his restraints under the foot. He didn't quite manage it, felt one of the bed posts catch the edge of the chain with a clang, sent it skittering back into the small of his butt. Didn't hurt, the only blow was to his pride. He tested his strength against them again, curious if that bang on the chain had weakened them, yet he was sorely disappointed. Once more?

He had to try. He felt like he was onto something here and he wasn't willing to give up unless he'd been absolutely proved wrong beyond doubt. He'd come this far, he might as well go a little further. Deep breath. Come on, third time he needed to do this. He wet his lips with his tongue, tried to flex his shoulders best he could. Get the circulation flowing. The sensations running through his back weren't so much painful as uncomfortable. Stabbing aggravations burned through his shoulder blades as he scrabbled the chain back as close as he could towards the post. Come on. Come on!

He didn't realise he'd been muttering it to himself under his breath until someone yelled at him to shut up. Pete managed a wry smile, heaved once more and with the grateful imaginings that it was coming down on the shouters head, heard it come down on the chain with a clang. Okay so it hadn't broken but that sound was reassuring. Very reassuring. It sounded heavy. Blunt force smashing down onto potentially aged metal links. He drew several shallow breaths, went again, heard it come down once more. His shoulders were on fire, he could feel the pain burning down the length of his spine. Much more and he'd risk fucking himself up.

He didn't want to wind up in the infirmary either. That place depressed the crap out of him, he'd been in there for some mandatory shots a couple of months back and hated every second of it. For a Unisco facility that was supposed to have the best of everything, it had fallen a little short in that respect for him. He'd found himself surrounded by the gloom, wishing that there were more windows. It made things more cheerless than they really needed to be. A paint job and some natural light would have made a world of difference. He'd suggested as much to the doctor who'd smiled good-naturedly. Still remembered what she'd said in reply, hadn't been entirely sure if it had been a joke or not.

"Son, we're all aware it needs a paint. You know what we're waiting on? One of you cadets to screw up something fierce, then it's your punishment detail."

Doctor Stenner had been nice at least, friendly smile and more cheerful than most of the staff at the academy. He'd been more than a little taken by the trio of moles lined up under her left eye, a visual identifying marker you didn't see every day. He remembered these terms. VIM. He liked that one. Always remembered it with vigour. She'd had him rolling his sleeve up, had shaken her head as she'd administered the shot. Maybe she did it with everyone and his feeling special was unwarranted.

"You're going to need this," she said. "Where you're going next few days, you might pick something up without them. Just to be on the safe side. Son, I hope I don't see you again for a while."

She'd meant it in a nice way, he hoped. Not seeing a doctor again for a while was usually a good thing. It meant that your health was good, therefore they weren't needed. It was something he'd reflected on in the next few days when they'd gone training in the marshes to the east of the academy. He'd seen her in the halls but never really had the chance to stop and talk to her. She wasn't the only medical professional on site, but she was the most senior. Hence, she always looked like she had her hands full. Tough job, by the looks of it, but she always gave the impression that nothing fazed her.

Fresh pain shot through him as he lifted the bed once more. Dear Divines, was it getting heavier? This time, he only felt it give a fraction of the way it had earlier, before having to let it go again. Still nothing. He jiggled about a little, tried to see if he could get the cuffs loose without pulling them free from where they'd wedged the bed post up. He tried pulling upwards, using the weight of the bed as a pivot point to pin them down. His shoulders screamed with the strain, he heard a series of grunts break from him that didn't even sound human. If he rattled the cuffs, he could hear the chain shaking. They sounded like they were loosening, maybe he was imagining it.

He didn't think he could bear it if everything was in his imagination. To have gone through all this for nothing would break him. Already the dark thoughts were sweeping through his mind about failure, he'd put the effort in and it could come to nothing.

At least he'd been doing something. Some hadn't moved. Dan Roberts was back on the ground, the front of his body pointing up as he arched himself, his hands fiddling about behind his back with something too small to see entirely. Maybe he'd found another lock pick like Tamale. The idea that there were these things laid about on the floor just in case, was something he found fanciful. What sort of lesson was this teaching?

Of course, he had to remind himself, they were still technically training. So maybe restraining them and the offering of an option was the best of a bad bunch of selections. He didn't know the thinking behind their actions, but he had to trust they knew what they were doing.

Once more. If he didn't do it this time, he'd have to consider another tactic. Dropping the bed post on the handcuff chain was proving to be a lot more ineffective than he'd thought it might. He didn't want to think about what his shoulders looked like. There was a great chance that he'd be sleeping on his stomach when eventually he got back to bed. His back would probably wind up a canvas of bruising. That wasn't a pleasant thought, an even worse mental image flashing into his head, of skin mottled purple and black. Pete shook himself, tried to displace them. They weren't helping.

For the final time, he heaved, drove his complaining shoulders up into the bottom of the bed with unrelenting force. He didn't dare let out any sort of sound. He reached the biting point where he'd let it go before, felt the growl break from him as he held it there for a long moment. He twitched, felt the weight give slightly. He couldn't hold it up forever.

He didn't need to. He let it go, felt the smash as it hit the chain. Spread out his fingers and felt wooden splinters scatter over the backs of them. He wasn't lifting it again, all he needed was a little bit of extra pressure and he'd have it. Getting on the bed and adding his own weight to it wasn't viable, due to his position. Getting the cuffs' chain under the bed post had been hard enough without being able to move his arms behind him. Nor was asking everyone else to jump. Pete pushed backwards and felt the chain slip under the post, it hit the half inch distance from the ground with a clatter and suddenly he had himself something to test his strength against.

He pulled. Felt the tug as metal met wood, screwed his face up in concentration and tried to ignore the howling of the muscles in his arms as they started to tremble from the effort. Sweat poured down his face despite the coolness of the room

Something gave, he heard a crack, a faint sound amidst the silence but a tiny crunch regardless. His spirits leaped, buoyed by that encouragement and he thrust himself forward, some part of him hoping it was the cuffs, not the bedpost that had given way. His arms almost bent back double, he felt his shoulders ease back into their regular position and he nearly screamed with relief as he lay there on his chest, just glad to be able to get some feeling back in his limbs.

"Step out the room, Cadet Jacobs. An interesting technique there, to be sure. Brute force is perhaps not always the way, there always needs to be some thought to your actions. If you're not strong enough or smart enough to do something, then you need another way to do it."

Pete got to his feet, walked past Dan Roberts and shrugged at him. Mouthed the word 'sorry,' didn't know if he'd seen it or not and stepped to the door. He slipped a hand to the handle, not entirely sure what he was going to get on the other side. He wasn't surprised to see them all waiting for him, even Doctor Stenner who was working on fixing up Theo's thumb. He wasn't surprised to see the exasperated look on her face. Theo had a face like thunder, he didn't know why, and he didn't want to know. He had a feeling it'd be something best left to the imagination.

"Congratulations, Cadet Jacobs," Takamishi said, offering him a hand. Pete shook it reluctantly, trying to ignore the aches in his back. He found it a little hard to look someone in the eye who'd just done what they had mere minutes ago. "Interesting improvisational skills in there."

"Well I wanted to get out," he said. "That floor is not comfortable." The words felt a little hollow, but it was all he wanted to say on the matter.

"Few things in this life are," Takamishi said. "Go hit the track. Five miles around that, then report to the mess hall."

Oh, come on!

He was proud of the way he'd kept the straight face, managing to push the rising sense of disgust into his gut. Some bloody reward that turned out to be. Takamishi must have seen something, for he let out a harsh bark of laughter.

"You might think it harsh. Those that come out after you are getting ten miles, not five" he said with a smug grin.

Chapter Eleven. Rocastle's Secret.

"A lead, is a lead, is a lead. Never hesitate to follow something, no matter how tenuous, for if you have nothing else, then even the slimmest leads can be a lifeline to grasp on to in an investigation. They can be the difference. Sometimes, it is better to do something than nothing, for the brain works best in activity than being sedentary."
Excerpt from Unisco lecture at the academy on investigative techniques.

Wade's summoner rang, broke through the night like a siren and he rose to a sitting position in bed, blaster in his hands. He heard the second ring, relaxed his weapon. Ever since that attack in Ryoti and the death of Davis Teela, he'd been expecting the worst. He'd been expecting the door to come crashing through and that bloody woman to make an appearance. So far, they'd not been found. They'd kept out of sight, they'd survived, much to his relief. He didn't fancy another round with her. Not after the previous one had resulted in them having their arses handed to them in spectacular fashion.

With Teela dead, he'd expected them to head back to Unisco headquarters, engage their attentions to much more useful avenues of investigation. Not so. Pree had shrugged her shoulders at that suggestion. He didn't like to defer to her, yet there'd been something compelling about her argument, even if he couldn't remember what it was. She'd convinced him, and in Burykia they'd remained for the time being.

He looked at his caller, dropped the X9S onto the bed next to him. Caller ID showed HQ, an interesting coincidence. Wade glanced across the room, saw Pree's bed was empty. He scowled at that. More and more since they'd decided to stay here, it felt like she'd been vanishing for hours at a time, only to return as if she'd never been gone. He had to wonder at her intentions.

If there were to be answers, they weren't going to be found here. He thumbed the answer button on his summoner, saw the video image of Liam Caulker on the miniature screen. The main man himself. Since Unisco had been reformed, Caulker had been put in charge of the intelligence division. Wade didn't know him well, an unassuming-looking man approaching middle age with a prominent bald patch and watery eyes. Just that they'd judged him the best man to put in charge.

Why he was getting a call off him this time of morning, he didn't know. This couldn't be good. He shook his head, tried to brush the sleep out of his eyes. They still ached from the burns at times like these, he did his best to ignore the aggravation.

"Good morning, Agent Wallerington," Caulker said. He had that lilting accent from the west of Canterage that Wade found about as endearing as having teeth pulled out. "Apologies for waking you but this couldn't wait."

"Not a problem, sir," Wade said. He appreciated the comment, not that it made much difference. Unisco would disturb you in the build-up to a championship bout if they wanted to, never mind if you were sleeping. You worked for the agency, your time was theirs to do what they wanted with. "What can I do for you?"

"We've had a breakthrough," Caulker said. "Three hours ago, not a dozen miles from where you and Agent Khan are based, we had a hit on a person of interest regarding the Coppinger fiasco."

Wade was awake now, he hid a yawn behind his hand, and sat up a little straighter in his bed. "We have? Who?"

"As you know, we've made it out mission to talk to everyone related to any known Coppinger sympathisers, just in case they know where they might be hiding out. We've been looking for the family of a prominent member of the organisation for a time now. Last night, she used a charge card and we got her."

"Who?" Wade asked. Maybe Pree had been right about staying here. They had to be somewhere, Burykia hadn't seen much Coppinger presence since it had started, it could mean two things. Either Burykia didn't interest them yet, or they were doing a better job of hiding their presence here. Both thoughts he found equally troubling, he didn't know which he'd prefer to be the case. The former, maybe? Just about.

"We've managed to locate the sister of Harvey Rocastle. I want you and Agent Khan to talk to her, find out if she knows anything of value about where her brother might go. Anything we can use against him."

Wade nodded. "It'll be done, sir. We'll head out as soon as we can."

"Good. I'll have someone send you the address, any relevant information. Don't disappoint me, Agent Wallerington. This could be nothing, it could be something. We won't know until you ask."

As promptly as it had started, the call ended, the video image dying away from his sight. Wade shook his head. He could see why, he just didn't see the value in it. It was Unisco protocol, at the same time, it felt like wasted effort. This wasn't a caller who had gone to ground, and the family interrogated in case they knew something. This was so much bigger.

He threw the covers back, went looking for his trousers. It needed to be done, he might as well make peace with that.

Just a case of where the hells was Pree?

Pree had met him in the speeder bays of their motel, a mug of Willies coffee in one hand and a sandwich in the other, a bemused grin on her face. She looked altogether too chirpy for his liking, she'd had even less sleep than him and came across twice as happy. It irked him some people could do that, always had.

"Good morning," she said, almost singing. She took two big bites out of her sandwich. "Sleep well?"

He grunted at her. Couldn't say too much more.

"That good, huh?" she asked. "You want to fly? Don't want you falling asleep at the stick and killing us both. Plenty of people out to get us without you killing us by accident."

Wade ignored her. "Just got a call from Caulker?"

"Oh yes?"

"We've got a mission."

"Outstanding," Pree said, through a mouthful of coffee. "Who are we tracking down now?"

"They found Harvey Rocastle's sister last night," he said. "Want us to go talk to her, see if she can give us anything about where he might be."

"Cool," Pree said. "Rocastle, huh? You met him, didn't you? What was he like?"

"Big fucking freak," Wade said. "Not the sort of person you'd want to meet twice. He tried attacking me, this after he'd gone for two spirit callers and a dancer."

"I imagine that went well for him," she said, finishing her coffee. She glanced around, hefted the cup back and tossed it into the closest trashcan, all without looking. He tried not to stare, didn't want her to see how impressed he'd been by the blind shot.

"Didn't do much good in the end, did it?" Wade said. "He still got free to kill, didn't he?"

Pree shook her head. "What he did or didn't do, it's not your fault. You took him in, it's not your fault Unisco couldn't keep hold of him."

Wade nodded. "I know, I know. I did everything, short of putting him down." He shrugged. "Maybe it…"

"You can't think like that," she said quickly. "You've got a job, you're beholden to the law. We can't execute someone for what they might do, as Unisco agents. That'd just create the sort of world Claudia Coppinger says we're trying to build."

"I know, I know. But shit happens when you're trying to arrest them," he said. He was thinking idly now, he didn't mean a word of it. "You know what I'm saying?"

"I'm think you're saying that that's power," Pree said. "You know what the biggest crime is? Having power and not possessing the balls to use it. They say it's all about self-control. It's a justification. A sot to make themselves feel better. They don't use it because they don't want to see the way people look at them if they do. It's about courage and the lack of it."

"You sound like you have experience of power," Wade said. He slid into the speeder, turned the activation key. She smiled at him as she got in next to him. Despite her jokes about his fatigue, he knew she wasn't worried about him crashing the vehicle. He'd never crashed anything, except the occasional party. And only then in an official capacity.

"Everyone has power in their own way," she said. "You think power is carrying a blaster and a badge? Having access to your kingdom's weapon systems? Hells, you even think it's about carrying a laser sword and being able to touch the Kjarn?"

Wade blinked. Underneath him, the speeder pushed off from the ground, engines roaring. He twisted the steering, pointed towards the exit of the motel bays.

"What is it, then?" he asked. "Since you're proclaiming to be the expert?"

"I'm claiming nothing, Wade. Just that I don't believe in wastage. If you have something that you can use to make a difference, then is hiding it away really the best thing to do?"

Something about her words stung. He wondered how much she knew. Hells, he didn't know how much he knew, never mind her.

Pree had come out of the store with six bottles of water, two giant bags of potato chips and a giant bar of chocolate which she tossed across to him. "My treat," she said. "Since you're looking rough."

He didn't know whether to be pleased or indignant. He settled for thanking her, she shot him a grin.

"Hey, what are partners for." She held up her summoner, a picture on the screen. The woman didn't look unlike Rocastle. Similar build. Similar hair. Eyes were kinder though, nor did she happen to look like a complete bastard. "Even asked the clerk if he'd seen her before. He said she came from that direction." She pointed up ahead. "Every time."

"So, she comes here a lot?" He ripped open the packaging, bit out a huge chunk of chocolate with his teeth and started to chew. She'd been right, he did need the sugar. She broke a bottle of water out the pack, tossed it to him and then kept one for herself, dropping the rest of them under her seat.

"Every couple of days to a week, does a supply run, pays in credits and then vanishes. Never seen her otherwise. Makes out she's some sort of hermit which is interesting."

"Hermit, huh?" Wade looked out across the distance, followed Pree's gesture. He could see the tops of the trees swaying gently in the distance, great thin things that looked like they'd break under pressure. Burykian barepines if he had the right of it. "Let's go rouse her then. Nobody hides away like that."

"Well you've got the right of it there," Pree said. She cracked a bottle of water, brought it to her lips and took a long draw, leaving moisture coating her top lip. "She's definitely hiding from something."

"Or someone." Wade shrugged. "More and more I'm starting to think this is going to be a waste of time." He bit into the chocolate again, tore it out the paper. This wasn't a rare occurrence. His body felt like it had been all over the places recently, demanding more and more from him than he'd been giving. He'd sleep for as many hours as he could, yet it never felt enough. The hunger was a constant companion, he'd try to ignore it but found it hard to concentrate over his complaining stomach. A temporary respite like this was just that, temporary.

"Guess we'll find out sooner rather than later, won't we," she said. "We've got our orders. We follow them."

He couldn't argue with that. No matter how pointless this task might seem, he knew that even routine missions could yield surprising results. Life always had a way of shocking you, even when you thought you knew what was coming.

There'd been a time in recent months when he'd worried he'd go blind. There'd been an incident, he'd wound up in a fight with Claudia Coppinger and her taccaridon, his eyes had been injured. He could remember waking in the hospital, not being able to see properly. The pain had been horrific, he hadn't taken a direct hit, but the light had been blinding. If he closed his eyes and thought back to what little he could remember of that day, he could recall the odour of singed skin, of seared flesh and muscle. He could remember what it sounded like to hear your own eyes sizzle. The doctors had pronounced his retinas badly seared, it had sounded like a death sentence in the quiet of that hospital ward.

Facing the prospect of being crippled, he'd had a choice to make. He could accept it, accept the pain and suffering, secure in the knowledge that modern medicine could do so much, but it couldn't work miracles. Practically blind in one eye. Vision spotty in the other and getting worse. It would have been the end of most aspects in his life he held dear and he'd arrived at his other option. Investigate. Do what any good Unisco agent did. Find another way. Experimental treatments.

He might have scoffed at them, had he not bumped into Ruud Baxter.

For a long time now, he and Baxter had known each other. Back when they were rookie agents, they'd done their practice silent hunt together. That was a great memory. Some found that traumatic. Wade had found it liberating. All trainees went through it, even with the mixed message hanging above it that should they ever be the victim of a silent hunt, they'd be in bad trouble. Silent hunts were reserved for Unisco agents gone rogue. The training was only to help with evasion should they ever find themselves in unfamiliar territory, outnumbered and outgunned. The silent hunt test had originally been called the Evasion Examination. Some names just stuck.

His and Baxter's friendship had remained long through those early years, they were of a similar age and they'd done some time together as partners. They'd both been in Threll when the dragon of that village had gone on the rampage. (He'd been amazed to see said dragon again, some twenty years later, under the command of one of the finalists in the Quin-C. Strange how some things worked out in the scheme of things.) He'd said as much to Baxter during the final and his old friend had chuckled mysteriously. "The Kjarn does what the Kjarn will, Wade. You cannot reason or argue with it. You are neither for it nor against it, for it is a part of all of us and to go against its designs is to go against ourselves."

He might once have thought it silly. These days, he didn't know. Not after what Baxter had done to him. He'd shown him things, taken him by the hand and walked him through it all, stayed with him while it was ongoing. They hadn't seen each other for years, he'd done all that for him.

Now, his vision was better than ever, and he knew what he did, not just about his cousin but his entire family line. The Wallerington family had strong heritage with the Kjarn, Baxter had told him. Some families do. We've considered it countless times, well the old order did. Lately, it's not been much of an issue. Most of them were here when the Fall happened. A lot of old blood was wiped out there. Hence, we look at the new. That's what I've been doing. Fresh ideas. Fresh people. Scratch off some of what didn't work, focus on what did. We are the New Vedo Order.

He'd wanted him to join. Wade had refused. He didn't need the stress. He'd seen what Baxter's Vedo could do in the final of the Quin-C and it scared the living hells out of him. That sort of power shouldn't be wielded by man. That day, he'd suspected Baxter had known what was going to happen, how many people would die, but he hadn't warned them. He'd wanted his people to be in position to look like heroes and they'd achieved that goal. The very thought churned his stomach, made him want to purge. He couldn't live like that. He wouldn't live like that.

Power corrupts. The oldest tenet in the Book of Gilgarus. He'd heard it so many times that the words threatened to lose their edge, a soundbite that didn't convey the true magnitude of the words.

Baxter and his lot were supposed to be the good ones as well. Apparently, they had enemies who lacked most of the compunctions that the Vedo did. Wade couldn't prove Baxter had done what he'd done but he wouldn't like to meet the enemies of the Vedo if it were true.

His thoughts were interrupted by Pree clearing her throat. They were reaching the edge of the forest. He took one look at it, rolled his eyes. Typical Burykia. Even the forests were smaller, more compact than those in other kingdoms. Smaller was relative, of course. The barepines still dwarfed either him or Pree. He looked across at her and shrugged.

"Are we in the right place?" he asked. Up in the distance, he could see a plume of smoke from his seat in the speeder, a hint of life. Someone was out there, and they'd made a fire.

"Only one way to find out," she said, unbuckling her belt. She stretched out her arms, slid from her seat. He removed the key, moved to join her, locking up behind him. Neither of them left their weapons in the speeder. Not if they were moving into unfamiliar territory. The risks were too great to ignore. "I had a look through the intelligence. We're in the right area. That guy pointed us out here. Can't really be too many more places."

"What are we waiting for then?" Wade said. His stomach was already starting to growl again, he rubbed at it with his free hand, tried to ignore it. That chocolate hadn't been that long since, he probably should see a Unisco doctor the next chance he got. Couldn't hurt.

"After you," Pree said. He rolled his eyes, stepped away from the vehicle and out into the ocean of trees.

They'd found the cabin, followed the plume of smoke lazily peeking above the treetops. It wasn't hard to find, just out of the way enough for someone not to want to bother unless they had to. Wade had seen worse places to live. He could see the attraction. He and Clara had set up their reserve in Canterage, they lived in places like this when they were there. All the staff did. Their other jobs took their time away from the dragon reserve more and more these days. He didn't like to have regrets. What he did was important. Wishing things were different felt like it cheapened their work.

First sign they got of life was the woman on the porch, kinetic disperser across her knees, her expression not even close to being welcoming. Life looked like it had hit her hard, she raised the weapon as they approached.

Neither of them went for their weapons. It would have been suicide. The woman definitely had the Rocastle look about her, they saw that immediately in a way the picture hadn't been able to emphasise. Same heavy build. Same sort of wavy hair, even if it was greying black rather than the rich purple they'd come to associate with Harvey. She didn't raise and point it at them, neither did her hands move away from it.

"Private property," she grunted. The voice was different. Deeper than when her brother spoke, ironically, Wade thought. "Can turn around or you can…"

"Are you really going to threaten to shoot us?" Pree asked. She sounded delighted. "For walking? That's adorable, I didn't know people still did that." She shot a sideways glance at Wade. "Did you know that?"

"I didn't," Wade said. "But I suspected." He looked away from her, gave the woman a weak smile. "Ma'am, we're from Unisco. Are you Lola Myers?"

"Yep," she said. "And I'm not talking to you."

"You're not in any sort of trouble," Pree piped up. "We just want to talk to you about your brother."

"I'm definitely not talking to you. I don't have a brother."

"Big guy, similar height and build and acts like he'd rather be your sister…" Pree offered. "That guy. Ring any bells?"

"Why are you out here?" Wade asked. He glanced around the forest, made a big show of it as he did. "There's not much here. Not unless you're hiding, then it's good. Add in the paying solely in credits at the nearest store… You're trying to stay hidden, aren't you?"

"Ain't a crime now, is it?"

"No," he said. "It's not. You've done a good job of it. We didn't find you until last night. And we've been looking for you." He nodded as he said it, hefted his fingers into his belt. "If we struggled to find you, I doubt your brother will have much luck."

"Harvey's tenacious. When he wants something, he sticks at it," she said. "He might not have many good qualities, but I suppose that's one of them."

"Can we ask you a few questions about him?" Pree asked. She sounded almost gentle, Wade was surprised. He'd never associated the Spectre with being gentle. More the sort who'd hook extremities up to electrical outlets to get answers. "Just a few and we'll be gone. We don't want to take up your time, but your brother's a bad man, I think you know that, and we want to make sure that he's dealt with appropriately."

She considered it, thought about it for a few long moments, her lips wobbling as she thought. Wade stroked his chin. Eventually she looked up at them, slid the disperser down onto the ground, resting it against the wall. "You better come in."

Whatever he might have expected to see when they entered the cabin, Wade thought, it hadn't been this. Outside, it looked dumpy. Unimpressive. Not unlike its owner. Entering, he could see that the inside held hidden depths that hadn't even been hinted at. It had been outfitted, waterproofed. Derenko had done it to their base on Carcaradis Island, not a big job but he was surprised that she'd bothered. She'd clearly expected to be hunkered down here for the long term. The walls had been painted white, something strangely sterile about them. He'd been in hospitals that had more character.

"Nice place," Pree said. He'd always found her sincerity a little lacking. This instance was no difference. She kept her face neutral though, even to him. If she had any strong emotions about the place, she wasn't displaying them.

He couldn't ignore it but from the woman, he got only fear. Sheer naked terror, not for herself but for someone else. Wade glanced past her, saw the bed at the far wall and understood.

She saw him looking, bowed her head. "That's why I don't want to talk to you. I just want to hide here until the end. Then I guess I'll leave. Go somewhere else and live out my days."

They both moved to the woman on the bed, her eyes closed and her breathing light. He studied her, could barely see the rise and fall of her chest. Her bones stuck out against her flesh, protruded almost vulgarly into the air. Veins crawled across the translucence, gave her skin the colour of old bruising.

"Damn," Pree said. Wade glanced at her, saw the way her face fell. He guessed why. Maybe it was just him but the whole place stank of death. The companion was near. She wasn't long for this world.

"She's not got long left now," Lola said. She stepped up to join them, a hot water bottle in hand, swaddled in a towel embroidered with tiny red cherries. "Months at most. She's just waiting for it to come."

"I'm sorry," Wade said. It felt painfully inadequate. Maybe they could have helped her if Baxter was here, if any of his Vedo were here. They had healing abilities. Baxter had healed him. Shown him how to do it himself if ever it was needed. He'd proffered more but he'd refused it.

Right now, he hated himself for doing that. Seeing someone in pain like this rammed home the implications of that decision. Could have done so much. In the end, he was doing nothing.

"It's fine," Lola said. "Not your fault. She had a good life. Well, my bastard brother aside." She spat the words aside with bitterness, the bile in them startling him as he looked at her.

"I take it he's not been here then," he said. "That's who we're looking for."

"If he showed up, I'd shoot him," she said. She meant it as well. He could tell. There wasn't a hint of hesitation or doubt in her voice. Just conviction. "I wouldn't stop until my cells ran dry."

"Ma'am, you do know that you can't say that to law enforcement professionals," Pree said, not quite admonishingly but with a hint of amusement in her voice. "On the other hand, you'd be doing the kingdoms a favour and neither of us were listening to what you just said. Carry on."

"Either of you got brothers?" She looked more at Pree as she said it, who nodded. "It's always fun, if you're their only sister. You're in a rivalry from the moment you're old enough to realise it. Maybe even before then."

Wade looked at Pree. "That true?"

She nodded again, her eyes distant. "More than you'll ever know."

"You know how parents aren't supposed to have favourites? Well ours did. No dad after he ran off, mum… Well she liked me more. I know you probably don't see it now, but I used to be happier. Light up a room with your smile, they said. I did that." She didn't sound sad as she said it, more wistful. Like she didn't miss the past itself but missed what it had meant for her. "This came out of the blue. It took a lot from me. I've given her everything to try and help her. None of it did any good."

"And what about your brother?" Pree asked. Still gentle. Whatever else she might lack, she knew how to handle an interrogation. Knew how to get through to people. It was a skill you couldn't teach. You either had it or you didn't.

"She never liked him. Well, she might have at first. As he got older, Harvey got harder to love. We still tried. We tried like hells. But it's not always possible. Childish pranks turned mean. Mean tricks became spiteful. He'd do stuff out of spite that was just plain nasty in the end." She sighed, her voice laced with sorrow. "We never knew why. Someone told us that some people are just born nasty. I never wanted to believe that. Mum found it harder to forgive him with every passing antic. Sometimes I wonder if that made it worse."

She paused, slipped the heated water bottle between the covers, tucked them back up beneath her mother's chin. It wasn't cold in the cabin, but Wade wondered how suitable it was to have someone in her condition here. Mind you, if she was dying and the hospital had accepted there was nothing they could do, it was hardly going to make her condition falter further.

"Eventually he did something he couldn't take back. Mum kicked him out of the house. He tells people he ran but he was cast out. She couldn't put up with him anymore. Typical Harvey. A born liar. Sometimes he'd pit me and mum against each other, just because he could. She tried but she had a temper. And me, well, I was younger then."

"Lola, you can't blame yourself for this," Pree said. She reached up, patted her on the shoulder. "Harvey Rocastle made his own choices. Nobody put a blaster to his head and made him do them. Some people ARE just born bad, that's been my experience. Your mother shouldn't blame herself either."

"She doesn't." Lola shook her head. "She blames him. Harvey was a sick puppy, she's said so herself on many occasions. We always expected to hear about him winding up dead, she wanted to write that on his headstone. You know what you need to do with a terminally sick puppy?" She didn't wait for them to respond. "You drown them before they start to harm anyone around them because they don't know any better. You know how bad someone must be for their own mother to even think about that? Unconditional love went out the window in our family a long time ago."

"Is that why you're hiding?" Wade asked. "So that he can't find you?"

"Something like that," she said. "I got in touch with him a year or so back, told him what had happened. I wanted him to know what was happening with his mother, even if he wouldn't care or not. He deserved that."

"I imagine he didn't take it the way you thought he would?" Pree said, raising an eyebrow in amusement. "It would be a very troubling world if people did act the way you wanted them to."

The disgust in Lola's voice was palpable. "He wanted to help."

"That bastard!" Wade said. He tried to hide the sarcasm, couldn't quite manage it. She shot him a venomous glance, he was suddenly very appreciative of the fact that she'd left her weapon outside.

"My brother left," she said. "He didn't bother when she was well, all the shit he got up to ruined mum. The stress did for her. We got on without him. We moved on. Even when I married, we stayed close. Mother and daughter. Together. We didn't need him then, we don't need him now." She laughed, bitterness in her voice. "Some people just don't take no for an answer. You say it so many times and it runs off their back. Then you start to ignore them. Hope they'll go away."

"They never do though, do they?" Pree said.

Lola shook her head. The bitter mask slipped, replaced with glumness. "He started sending credits," she said. "More than we'd ever be able to spend. He was throwing them at the problem. Wouldn't do any good. I never spent them. Cheques would come, letters begging to talk would be with them."

"Do you still have them?" Wade asked. He tried to sound offhand, wasn't sure how much he was succeeding. Lola nodded. "Any chance we can examine them? For clues." He looked at Pree. This could be interesting, an opening they'd looked for. Since Reims had been stripped from her, Claudia Coppinger had still been able to move her credits around and they had very little evidence as to how. If she was paying Rocastle and Rocastle was sending it along to his sister who hadn't cashed it all in, things could have light shed on them very quickly.

There were people at Unisco who made it a habit to follow the credits. They'd gotten very good at it as well, for credits spoke a lot louder than most other evidence in Wade's experience.

"I'm not spending them," she said. "It's blood money. I know some of the stuff he's done in the last year. None of it was exactly shy about being kept out of the media, was it? The psycho dancer aiding Claudia Coppinger. One of her hands." She was shaking now, her voice rising in the confines of the cabin. "You know why else I don't want him here? I know what he's done. I know what he's capable of."

She gestured towards her stricken mother, Wade got the impression the tears were being held back but barely. "If he sees her like that, he might do something he can't take back. He'd say he's doing it out of mercy. We'd both know he'd do it just to stick it to her." She wiped her eyes, straightened herself up. "My mother is going to die when she's ready, not when Harvey decides to try and stick a pillow over her face as some demented act of what his addled mind sees as mercy. I'm not ready to let her go yet."

"To move on is the nature of being human," Pree said. "Without death, life is pointless. Everything needs a culmination. You can only validate a life when it comes to an end."

"Divines, Pree," Wade said. He shook his head, the sound of disgust slipping from him. "Cheerful much?"

"You want hope, go see a zent," she said, turning back to Lola. "Mrs Meyers. We can't promise you much. But if your brother ever finds you, I hope that day doesn't come, but it won't be because of us. We're obligated to tell our bosses that we spoke to you. We don't need to tell them where you are. That's going to remain our secret." She shot a glance at the comatose woman, shook her own head. "I'm very sorry for your loss. I know she's not dead yet, but…"

"You'll have to forgive Agent Khan," Wade said. "She was out sick the day they taught people skills. She's good at other stuff though."

"You have no idea," Pree smiled. Even though her mouth had curved into a grin, her eyes narrowed at him. An implied threat? He couldn't tell. He didn't want to know.

Lola Meyers vanished towards a cupboard at the back of the room, Wade took the opportunity to study her mother once again. He shook his rust-coloured head. Such a waste. He didn't want to inquire about the disease. Something wasting. Something terminal. Something that took life and ruined it beyond recognition, made it barely worth living.

That was what was wrong with what Claudia Coppinger preached. She spoke of creating a perfect world, a better one than what they had. She'd never wipe it out. Nature would always win. There'd be a culling sooner or later. Something she couldn't see coming and it'd be the thing that damned her cause. He didn't believe in someone giving them a better world. He'd always thought the way to make it a better place was for everyone to do their small part rather than it being gifted to them.

He cast his thoughts aside, watched as their host returned with a cardboard box, they could hear it rattling with every step she took. "Everything," she said. "Everything he ever sent after he found out she was sick. I remember the one time he made a call, she spoke to him once. Never again. Demanded that I not let him through. She took a turn for the worse not long after that." She sighed. "I hate being their referee. But what can I do? It's family. Nobody said it would be easy."

"You need anything to help make this easier?" Wade asked. "Anyone to come out here?"

She shook her head. "I got this. I used to be a nurse. I know what I'm doing. Get the medicine every week, it's delivered to the closest store, I walk out and get it. They weren't happy about me doing it this way, but they were relieved I guess. Not many beds in hospitals around here. Especially not for a foreigner who has no hope. Occasional progress report sent in and they're happy."

"There's always hope," Pree said. Her words surprised him, he shot her a sideways glance. She'd never given the impression much that she was one to believe. "If you don't have hope, you might as well give up."

He knew what she meant. Maybe Lola Meyers did as well, she hugged them both. "I can't say it's been a pleasure. I'd rather you hadn't found us. But if you get the shot on my brother, take it. He's dead to me. Soon I'll have nothing. But maybe that's better."

Sad, he thought. Nothing should never be better than something. Still, he wasn't sad to leave the cabin behind. He'd be getting the smell of death out of his cape for days, he imagined. Hopefully, there'd be something in Rocastle's correspondence they could use. If there was, it wouldn't have been in vain.

Chapter Twelve. Creating the Unstoppable.

"Project Apex continues to exceed all expectations. Rocastle made an excellent choice in his selection of test subject."
Message from Doctor Hota to Claudia Coppinger on the progress of their newest pet project.

Memories.
Flashes of before. The sights. The sounds. Someone else's life. Now, all felt so far away. Like a dream. Impossible for she does not dream. She does not sleep. She simply exists. They have their bidding and she carries it out. She can't do anything else. A puppet on invisible strings. A slave.

She hated that word. Hated what it implied. To be a slave is to be less, to have the very thing that makes you taken away from you. It was about more than just a loss of dignity, it was having the choice stripped away from her. Every little implication of it brought bile to her throat, made her want to choke it all out. Just purge it all out of her until she had nothing inside, her body just the hollowed-out husk she felt like. Empty.

He'd taken her freedom. They'd taken her life. She could never go back. Didn't even recognise herself in the mirror any longer. When she stared, a stranger looked back. Her eyes had once been so full of life, everyone who had met her said so. Now they were the eyes of a dead woman. Someone who didn't want to go on but didn't have a choice, driven on by desires no longer her own but rather the whims of those whom stripped everything from her.

If she could, she'd have killed herself. She was certain of that. They wouldn't let her. He'd told her that as he'd stood above her bed and laughed himself stupid. "Oh no, no, no, dearie. You don't get to die. You're going to live for a good long time left." He'd leaned closer, that face that she'd liked and trusted, the lips splitting into a cruel smirk. Right then, she'd seen all the rumours were true about him, everything everyone had hinted about, but she hadn't wanted to believe. She'd chosen to try and see the good in him, knew some spark lingered in his heart but now she realised she was wrong. "Thank you!"

Back then, she'd not known what he meant. Hadn't known why he was expressing gratitude to her. Every urge in her body had wanted her to reach up, snap him in two, see him bleed like a little bitch, hear him scream. She hadn't been secured to the table, her arms laid limp at her sides. She'd willed herself, get up and hit him. He'd always been big, but she knew he wasn't as tough as he made out. Any hint of standing up to him and he'd fold, run away and lick his tail. She'd seen the true side of him. She knew what he really was. A coward and a bully, a bad dog with a bark that outstripped its bite. Or so she'd thought. The truth had turned out to be worse than she'd thought possible. Hindsight was a marvellous thing.

She just wished that she'd worked it out sooner.

Even though most of her past life was a struggle, the only name she could recall being the one that they'd given her when she'd awoken, she remembered that night all too well. Harvey had been there, he'd met her at one of the fanciest restaurants in Haxfold, his suit pressed, and his shirt crisply ironed. He'd toned down his normal clothes, was wearing a classy midnight blue suit rather than the acid green number normally employed. He looked respectable, for him, as well as altogether too pleased with himself, almost bouncing with glee. She'd dressed in her finest, chosen to clad herself in blood red, tied at the front around her neck for maximum uplift in the cleavage, leaving her shoulders and upper back bare. Some might say it looked daring, others might have called her slutty. She didn't care. She'd worked hard to craft this body, she'd damn well wear what she chose. They always said spirit dancers were eccentric after all. Some stereotypes existed for a reason, like Vazarans were all thieves and murders, that the Serranians were all great between the bedsheets. Just because there might be one or two who buck the trend, the majority had come from circumstances which meant it was the case. She'd got the Vazaran thing. It was a poor kingdom, sometimes people killed for what they needed, just as they sometimes stole to eat. She'd never understood the Serranian one though, how the reputation for being skilful lovers had emerged. Something in the water perhaps? A musing for another day.

"Well you look happy," she'd said, smiling at him. When Harvey was happy, his glee was infectious. When the black moods took him, he was someone to be avoided. He'd never been anything but kind to her though, she'd taken him under her wing when he'd first reached the spirit dancing circuit. He'd become her protégé and she'd done her best to teach him a portion of what she knew. Never everything though. They would one day be competitors, the last thing she wanted was him to know all her tricks. Shaping someone was a worthy path, not at the expense of your own success though. There was decency and then there was self-preservation. Her own brand might need propping up with key victories one day.

"I am happy, hope you're happy too," he smiled. "All things considered, anyway."

"How's your mother?" He'd confided in her with it, she'd always done her best to make sure that she'd offered her sorrows. She'd never met the woman, but she had to be some character to have a son like Harvey. Not necessarily in a good way either, she guessed. Either it was the mother or the father who'd been a real piece of work. She'd never heard him mention his father, had never asked. If he'd felt the need to avoid confiding in her, she wouldn't push him.

He shrugged, made a rasping sound with his tongue. "Still alive. I've been looking into things, seeing what I can do. That bitch Lola won't let me see her. She's happy to take the credits I send though. Grasping little harlot." He cackled inanely. "Still never forgiven me for saying I was glad her marriage broke down."

"Just think that you're doing what you can," she'd said. "You're helping in your own way. If they truly hated you, they wouldn't accept that help, would they? Maybe there's some chance of reconciliation."

"It's a strange world," Harvey said. "The sort of place where you can have everything or nothing. It doesn't do halves, I've found, Sweetums. Either you're happy or you're not. There's no middle ground. You can't be a little bit content."

"I think plenty of people manage."

"I want to do more than manage, dear heart. I want everything. I want her to live. I want her to be proud of me. I want to be the one that saves her, and I want to rub it in her face that I did, make the bitch admit she was wrong about me."

She could remember the disgust that flowed through her. She liked Harvey, there were always parts of him she found distasteful. Everyone had a dark side, she could testify to that. Everyone was capable of hideous acts that would make the right-minded flinch with horror. She'd always wondered if she was capable under the wrong circumstances. The answer had come to her and she hadn't liked it one jot. Everyone was capable of doing the dark thing, they were back to circumstances. Sometimes you found yourself in a situation you couldn't climb out of, no matter how hard you dug in.

She looked at her own hands. They'd once been so delicate. Slender. Now, they were covered in blood. She had death clinging to every line, every print. If she closed her eyes, she could hear them scream. She wanted to remember their screams, hear their echo through her mind as she felt the disgust resonate around her being.

She knew what she'd become. Killer. Murderer. Disgusting bitch. Unclean. Evil. Tags she could throw at herself, others would too if only they knew what demons lurked inside her.

"I'll do anything," he said. "You know that? I'll do anything to make sure that my dream becomes a reality." She didn't like the way he looked at her as he said it. She'd seen that look before, countless times.

It was a look that never had good consequences for the recipient and with hindsight, she'd have run.

Still she'd believed in him. Comparing what she knew now about Harvey Rocastle with what she'd known then, she felt her situation an apt punishment for just being so fucking blindly stupid as to his intentions.

She'd always known she'd wanted to be a spirit dancer. She'd heard stories of those who'd stumbled into the sport because they couldn't make it as callers, though she'd never personally met any of them. People always assumed you could be one or the other, they were usually right, though there were some who'd managed to combine the two. There wasn't anything wrong with it, just plenty didn't make the effort. Those who did were usually formidable.

Privately, she'd always wondered if it was too high-form for those who sneered at it, they didn't understand the subtleties of what happened on the dance floor. They clamoured and cheered for blood and violence, they wanted to see creatures get mangled beyond recognition, smashed into the ground and otherwise murdered in a way that would make the right-minded flinch in disgust if it happened outside an arena. The talented spirit dancer never needed to draw blood, often never needed to look as if they were exerting themselves. That was the mark of prestige, she'd always found. The more effortless the dancer looked in conjunction with their spirit, the better they were. Some performances, she'd never broken sweat.

It had been her dream for as long as she could remember, those early days felt so long ago but their impact had never been lost on her. Perhaps the gulf in class was more pronounced in spirit dancing rather than calling, there was always a chance for a favourite to lose to a relative unknown in battle conditions, a lucky shot or the perils of overconfidence. Not so in spirit dancing, for the favourite if such a term applied, had worked their routines out over the years, developed their bases and tailored each individual performance to match the circumstances, never the same routine twice at the same event. Judges didn't like that, it was as much about knowing how to play the officials as the opponent. She didn't hate spirit calling as a sport, she didn't like that aspect of it though, how human referees had been replaced with automated video ones who called every decision to the correct letter of the law, no room for interpretation or leniency. Sometimes, automation was the wrong way to go, not that she'd ever be surprised by anything Ritellia had done while in office. He'd championed himself for making what he'd called a tough decision. It wouldn't have surprised her to hear he'd taken a huge bung from the company who made them to introduce the technology.

She was starting to sound as cynical as Kinsella, if she wasn't careful. She knew her from way back, Kate 'No Fucks Given' Kinsella, the nemesis of Ronald Ritellia and all those who'd take the people for a ride with their own whimsy given half a chance. She could remember all too many chats she'd had with the woman when she'd reported on the dancing, remember them happening if not the actual details of the conversations. That hurt. It hurt a lot, like a part of her life had been lost irrevocably to her.

One day she'd get them all back. The memories weren't lost, if she pushed she could feel them swirling around in her brain like shiny rainbow-coloured oil atop the ocean but trying to pull them free only left them slipping through her fingers, the pattern returning to normal in a matter of moments.

One day.

Sometimes when she was alone, she muttered that mantra to herself, over and over to try and keep the hope. She could fake the confidence in her voice, wished she could fake the feeling she truly believed it would happen. For better or worse, she belonged to them. She might as well have Coppinger's name branded into her rump. Property. That was all she'd ever be, barring a huge surge of fortune.

Harvey had called them a cab, he'd led her to the sidewalk out through the front door, a simpering grin on his face. If there'd been darkness before, now there was light. He was like this, she knew all his little fads and quirks by now. You had to take him as he was. Couldn't have one without the other. To remove one would diminish him as a whole. She suspected it was what made him a ruthless spirit dancer. It was a brutal circuit, spirit callers always thought that it was just one giant love-in between foppish individuals who didn't have a bloody streak in them.

They couldn't be more wrong. People like that didn't last five minutes in the dancing arena. The art swallowed them up, broke them down and spat them out. Everyone had to break before they could be rebuilt. Some handled it differently than others. Some faded. Some flourished. When she'd first met him, Harvey had been like that. A timid boy, a lack of confidence, hiding behind an eating disorder. She'd witnessed his breaking with great interest. Perhaps what was most remarkable was the man he'd become out of it. He'd definitely been one to flourish.

Always there were stories about the streak he'd come to possess, for to call it mean wasn't doing it justice. Though, some she doubted were true. They told each other everything. She'd know if they were true. There'd always be those with cruel tongues. They told the same stories about her. They couldn't beat them on the stage, so they tried to do them down wherever they could, tried to prick confidences with needling lies. The women were whores, based on the way they liked to dress on entering the arena, the men were seen as less because they'd decided to compete in something many didn't place as high a value on.

The cab had come, he'd let her enter first and he'd given his usual flamboyant greeting to the driver. She tried to ignore it, keep a straight face through his words. She knew what he was like. Chickenshit. He might talk a good game, but he was timid.

Harmless.

Harmless Harvey.

She'd called him that more than once. She'd believed it. He was like a noisy little terrier, all bark and couldn't bite to save his life. She'd been secure in that knowledge. All until he'd put his hand on her knee. That should have sent the alarm bells ringing, she knew he didn't think of her that way. There were plenty out there who desired a night with her, yet she knew all too well she wasn't Harvey's type, somewhat lacking in the cock department. She smirked at that thought.

"Sweet pea," he said. "You should know that there's something I need to tell you, and I've been so bad." He grinned at her, his teeth glinted in the light from the streets. He looked positively ghoulish. "But I've been putting it off. It's great news!"

She wanted to move for the door, she could remember that feeling. Fight or flight and every instinct was telling her to run. Jump out of the cab, even while it was moving if need be. She might look delicate and waif-y, but nothing was further from the truth. She knew what she'd need to do if it ever came to it.

"Did you know I'm quite good friends with a doctor?" he said, his voice low and soft. The driver wasn't paying them any attention. Just kept his eyes front, far away from either of them. He wasn't interested. She cursed Harvey. That flamboyance served its purpose. Men of a certain orientation found it uncomfortable. She knew that. She'd have been amazed if Harvey didn't. He did a lot for effect, it was as easy for him as breathing for some. You had to forgive men like him their little affectations.

"What does he say about your mother?" she asked. Her lips felt heavy, her words coming out almost slurred. She narrowed her eyes, tried to rub her mouth. Her hands felt like they'd been coated in lead, she could move them, but it was an effort. A real struggle to lift them the distance between the seat and her face.

"Oh, I didn't talk to him. He's not that sort of doctor. He's the sort that you go to if you want something…" He tailed off, his eyes glittering with malice in the moonlight as he spoke. "He gives me stuff, you know, stuff I probably shouldn't have, but hey he has more credits than integrity. Gave me a great deal on Urcazine. Got a few bottles of the stuff."

"Ur-Urcazine?" she asked. She wanted to let her head loll back, knew that if she did, she wouldn't move again. "Isn't tha'…?"

"It's a muscle relaxant," Harvey smiled. He patted her hand, a gesture strangely affectionate. "A strong one. I slipped it in your drink just before we left the restaurant, you know?"

She remembered. Harvey had paid, they'd finished up their drinks; him a rose water soda, her a pink wine which had come with decoratively edible petals on the top of the surface, she'd smiled at him as she'd sipped it, remembered the funny taste as she'd swallowed it, she'd put it down to the petals being past their best. It had been that sort of restaurant. "You know how it works? Doesn't kick in until your muscles relax. Like say, when you sit down. Then it's got you." He trailed his fingers off up her arm, smiled at her. His grin grew and grew until it threatened to split his face into two pieces before he made a popping sound with his lips. "Just like that!"

They'd met the speeder outside a building, she'd not seen much of where it was or what it was like, the drug kicking in, a chore to keep her eyes open. Her mouth had fallen open, she didn't have the strength to close it and her tongue was lolling out across her chin. A stray fleck of drool tickled her chin for several long seconds before falling away. She didn't see where it dropped. Forming thoughts was hard too, her mind lost amidst a whirlpool of torpor and haze. She felt the speeder grind to a halt, saw a face on the other side of the door. She could still hear fine though, could hear the slam of Harvey's door as he stepped out. He sounded way too cheerful, even by his standards.

"Present for the Mistress," he said. "Just what she asked for." Out the corner of her eye, she could see him rubbing his hands together. "One woman. Exact height. Exact weight. No prior medical history."

The face peered through at her, the features hazy and blurred, she couldn't make them out even if she wanted to. All she wanted to do was sleep, just let her eyes make their final slide shut. Her body had become her prison. She thought she saw the recognition dawn in his eyes, she got that a lot. Why should this be any different?

"Are you out of your mind, Rocastle?" That voice was rough, angry. Like the speaker had gargled sandpaper.

Harvey cackled. "Not even close. I'm seeing things clearly for the first time. I know what I need. I know what you can do for me."

"We said nobody who's going to be missed!"

"And sweeping up street scum in hope is why you haven't found anyone who matches the profile!" He sounded outraged, petulant even. She knew that tone all too well. It was the voice he used when he was determined to get his way and to hells with the consequences. "With a venture like this, you need some prime material. Not the shitty little people nobody else gives a crap about. You want to make a deluxe meal, you use premier ingredients and I bet the Mistress would agree with me."

"You've not heard the last of this, Rocastle. The Mistress is going to be furious with you despite what you seem to think. You broke her rules, she's a real bossy bitch over stuff like that."

"Perhaps. Perhaps I might get rewarded beyond my wildest dreams for doing what you fuckers couldn't! You ever think about that? What's more valued? People who say they can't? Or people who just do it? I'll let you think about that." She heard him cackle with laughter. "And maybe I won't repeat to her what you think of her. I'm sure she's the sort who'll laugh along with you over it." The laughter stopped, the mirth in Harvey's voice fading to be replaced with grim certainty. "Or maybe she'll have you beaten to death. I've never seen it happen before, I get a little excited over the thought if I'm honest. Little dribble's creeping out in me kecks, you know."

"You're disgusting, Rocastle."

They'd stripped her, shaved her beautiful hair away until she was balder than an egg, strapped her down to the table, secured her wrists, neck and ankles. She felt cold and exposed, the table hard against her back. She didn't know where she was, just that she wasn't alone, two uniformed guards stood across the room from her. If she tilted her head, she could just about see them. They both had weapons, but not ready to use on her. They looked relaxed. Calm. They couldn't see her being a threat and they were right. She gave a token struggle against her restraints, didn't feel them give even an inch. They couldn't even be bothered to give her their attention. For the first time in her life, she felt like she didn't matter.

That bothered her more than being captured if she was honest, she knew it was strange but the disconnect between them and her troubles was the most unsettling thing about it all. This wasn't normal. There'd been a kidnapping attempt on her some years earlier, that had been entirely different to this. They'd tried, they'd not even gotten close to her. She'd thanked the Divines for incompetence, as well as the interference from Unisco. She realised she'd give anything for one of their agents to charge through the door right now, a blaster in hand and murder

Then there'd been the doctor, he stepped across to her, a grin on his face. She wanted to spit, show some defiance. Nothing. The fight had gone out of her, she knew it even if she didn't want to admit it. Her entire body felt relaxed, she wondered if she could feel the chemicals already flooding through her if she closed her eyes and just let her mind open up to all the possibilities ahead.

"Now then, my dear," the doctor said, running a gloved hand over her body. "Thall we thtart?"

She wanted to beg and plead him to let her go, she knew it'd likely do little good, but she had to try. What would happen if she didn't? Her mouth wouldn't work, she'd already been warned she'd be gagged if she started screaming. Somehow, she doubted it was something they were bluffing over. Those who'd kidnap wouldn't hesitate to make her life worse. No, more than that, she realised then, her life as she'd known it was over. She'd never go back. Either she'd die here, or she'd be whatever they made her.

The pain. So much of it and unending. Being flayed was horrible. What they'd done to her while her skin was off, that was worse. They'd tried to keep her under as long as possible while doing it, they'd professed that they weren't monsters after all. She didn't believe them. She couldn't. Anyone normal wouldn't be able to do this to another human being. It could have been minutes. It could have been weeks.

People had to be looking for her. They had to be. Sooner or later, they'd find her. They'd find her, and they'd save her. Unisco would be on it,

Days ran together, she slept for weeks and was awake for months it felt, forced to stay conscious until she couldn't tell which of her captors were real and which were figments of the twisted images running through her mind. Fire burned through her veins, iron through her muscles. Alien blood made her stomach twitch, her skin scald until she was ready to cry so hard her ducts would shatter. Then the chills would set in, she'd go from fire to ice and she wouldn't be able to feel her extremities through the cold. Maybe she was dead, and this was punishment. Sometimes they'd pull a helmet over her head and bombard her with sights and images, try to make her feel things she'd never felt before and likely never would again. Some of it took, she knew that, others felt like they'd had no effect. That worried her, she wondered how much of it was her own opinion, how much of it was what they'd made her.

She hadn't led a bad life. Never intended to. Nobody was perfect though. Some things felt trivial at the time but later, they mattered more than anyone could realise.

She'd always wondered about the woman long before she'd known her name, the doctor with the lisp had deferred to her, even Harvey had shown up and shown the same submissive streak, she'd never seen him act like that around a woman in all the time she thought she'd known him. She had to be in her forties, showing signs of her age, hints of grey creeping into the chocolate of her hair, and when she turned towards her, she saw a stone embedded in her wrist, the light winking off it, twinkling happily at her.

"She's awake?" she asked of the doctor who nodded at her. "Good. Good." She turned to look at Harvey. "Untie her."

"Mistress?" he asked. "Are you sure that's…?"

"Do not ask me if you feel my opinion is wise," she said quietly. "I'm still not happy with you. You know what my displeasure already cost you." Out the corner of her eye, she could see Harvey walked with a limb, that bit of knowledge she found interesting, his step uneven compared to what it once had been, his footstep heavier than before. Were her senses improving? It certainly felt that way, she'd awoken to the scents of chemicals, a tang of body odour she could have done without experiencing. "Do not assume I'll be any more lenient with you a second time."

She couldn't help but laugh, she saw the look of hurt on Harvey's face as he fiddled with the restraints, hurt replaced with anger and he slapped her, one of his fat hands cracking off her face with a sound akin to a whip and she winced, glared at him. Too late she realised any pain had been beyond her notice, the slap hadn't hurt as much as he'd meant it to. Sure, her face stung but already it was fading.

"All you got?" she asked, the words clumsy and uneven, her tongue felt alien in her mouth. "Bitch!"

Harvey had reacted the way she'd expected him to, had spun on his heel and driven his fist hard into her mouth, she'd felt teeth shatter, blood dribble down her cheek. Still no pain, not as she'd expected. She touched the gap in her teeth with her tongue, some part of her still dismayed at the way he'd just ruined her smile, tried to fight the urge to react as she felt something hard forcing its way through the gum already. It didn't feel as if her cut were bleeding any longer either.

"Huh, guess it took," Harvey said, looking back at the woman. "How about that." She saw what he was going to do, the most miniscule twitches in his body and he went to hit her again. This time though, she'd already decided she wouldn't let him, ripped her arm free of the restraints he'd already loosened, caught his wrist and started to squeeze, somewhat aware of the way her mouth was contorting into a manic grin. He tried to pull away, his eyes wide with fear, little moans of pain slipping from him, it only made her hold him tighter. She'd rip his arm off if she could, would enjoy beating him to death with it.

"Let him go, Apex," the woman said, and it was as like hearing the voice of Gilgarus, the notion of disobeying didn't even pass through her head, she didn't know if she could even think about it, just let go of Harvey as quickly as she'd grabbed him. Apex, huh? The name didn't sound familiar, not back then. Now though, it felt like the only one she'd ever answer to, each time she found herself involuntarily responding to it was like a knife to the heart. The knife wouldn't even kill her now, thanks to what the Mistress had done, made her a mockery of humanity, a good little flesh and blood endroid to do whatever she said.

One day, she'd get it. One day, they all would.

She'd been following them for days. The two of them she'd encountered outside the stadium. They were Unisco, she wanted to know what they knew. Taking them would have been easy. Stalking them was harder. They were both highly trained. In different ways though, observing them had told her that. The man was like a dog. Aware but trained to be aware. Confident if misguided. He didn't quite know the threats he faced but he'd rush in regardless and he'd probably end up bitten for it.

The woman though, she was different. If he was a dog, she was a lioness, an imperious presence who knew what she faced but didn't care. She'd see the challenges, she wouldn't be beaten by them. She'd be the trickier to deal with. How people acted when they thought they weren't being observed said a lot about them.

Finding this place hadn't been tricky, she'd beaten the information out of a shopkeeper. He'd tried to put up a fight but only briefly. He might live if he got the treatment, had lapsed into unconsciousness after giving her the information. She'd gotten the rifle, had been watching the cabin for minutes now, setting herself. They'd put her through the same systems they put the clones and the angels through. All the combat training. None of the experience. None of it was real. It was all in her head. She believed she could do it, she'd been conditioned to do it, therefore she could.

Her rifle was an old Femble, one of the projectile ones rather than an energy-based weapon. They were a lot harder to get hold of.

Especially in these circumstances. The Burykian government weren't wanting to let the population arm themselves in case Coppinger turned her attention to them. These things were easy to buy, most people who had them wanted rid of them. They still killed very effectively.

She studied the two of them through the crosshairs on the scope, their impressions gave that it had been a productive trip. The man had a box under his arm. He looked thoughtful, her excited. The woman was going to be the one to die first. Everything about her gave off bad vibes. She couldn't explain it, but she wasn't going to take any chances.

Line it up with her head, wait for her to stop, wait for the wind to die away and then pop her. She wouldn't see it coming. Adjust, put the man down while he was trying to work out what had happened. Maybe his reactions would save him for a few moments more, but he was marked. It wasn't reasonable to expect him to stand there and be hit. He'd duck down, find cover.

In the next few seconds, two things happened. She lined up the sight on the woman's head, saw the target turn to look in her direction. Her face lit up in a smile, she shook her head playfully. Before the shock could register, her summoner rang, and she dropped her hand down to silence it before it gave away her position. She wasn't so far away enough that it would go unnoticed. Maybe, just maybe they'd mistake it for the call of a bird if it was a solitary trill.

"Yes?" Her voice no longer sounded familiar to her. They cut her open, stitched the medical webbing to her muscles, given her transfusions, some of those had been on her throat and it hadn't been the same since. Doctor Hota had explained all of this to her in very simple terms, he'd drunk in her despair. Finding herself a stranger could only be expected.

"You have not returned to base," the emotionless voice said. Not Rocastle. He didn't do composure like that. He was like a fire. He had to take everything to extremes. "You have not been assigned a mission. Cease whatever you are doing, return to base immediately."

Her breath caught in her throat. She was on the verge of telling him what she was about to do. Two dead Unisco agents had to be worth a delay.

The memories flooded through her. They hadn't given her an order to exterminate. She had no bounds to do so. She didn't owe them anything. Not after what they'd done to her. Why should she volunteer to help push their agenda?

Maybe, one day, Unisco might be able to help her break free of them. The lump at her chest felt heavy. More than anything, she wanted to tear it away and fling it into the forest. She feared what would happen if she did.

Maybe. One day. For now, she'd play their game.

"At once," she said. She got to her feet, put the rifle away over her back. "I'll report to you when I get back. My apologies. It won't happen again."

"Best see that it doesn't. We don't want to have to teach you a lesson now, do we?" Only an implied threat but it chilled her blood. She might be strong, she might be almost invulnerable, but they knew how to hurt her.

They'd created her after all. Nobody made a weapon they couldn't control. Even loose cannons were eventually tied down, they might harm all around them but sooner rather than later, they'd be secured down again. She had no illusions the same would come to pass for her. They'd gotten her after all, they'd made her strong and unbreakable, at least in her body. In her mind though, she'd been shattered, she could feel the fragments of her psyche rattling every time they made her do another horrific thing against her will.

Chapter Thirteen. Into the Green.

"What qualities do we need in our team? Experts, man, experts in whatever we may face! We are to be the first scientific team to enter the place. Only the best should be involved. Or at least, the best we have available. Me. You. My assistant, Ms Aubemaya. Get Suchiga… Yes, I know he'll not want to go but it's our job to persuade him. His expertise will be vital. Brown, well, yes, he's a weed but again, he's our weed. Whomever Brendan brings as well, damn the man. He flutters back into our life and demands every consideration! Find a doctor as well, just to keep the bastards upstairs happy."

Alex Fazarn to Shane Bryce ahead of the expedition into the Green engulfing Vazara.

Wilsin remembered.

There'd been that moment before they'd entered the jungle when they'd studied it from a distance and he'd been impressed by the sheer majesty of it all. He'd never seen true jungle before. A lot of it had vanished from Vazara years since, cut down and built upon. The people back then hadn't considered the impact of that. Small wonder that they were considered savages, a stereotype that had never faded with time.

Brendan had pulled him aside, moved over to the back of one of the hover wagons they'd brought out. He didn't look his normal self; the weather had been growing warmer and warmer the longer they'd been here and Wilsin couldn't wait to get back to somewhere cooler. It hadn't been this bad on Carcaradis Island, he'd stake a claim on that, or perhaps he hadn't noticed it as much. King's skin had been bronzed the colour of aged walnuts, his eyes hidden behind sunshades but still there was no mistaking the intensity through them.

"David," he'd said. "We aren't in a good situation here."

An understatement, Wilsin had thought at the time. Regret had never set about him on a mission. Everything he did, he'd always done for the greater good. He'd tried to follow that path. You couldn't work for Unisco without questioning your moral compass sometimes. All it took was the conviction to know that every decision was not an easy one. None could be taken lightly. Coming to Vazara under these circumstances weighed on him. They'd be shot as spies if they were caught. Him. Brendan. Everyone with them. They'd be guilty by association. That was a burden to bear. They couldn't afford to be caught out in a lie of their own making.

"Okay, sir," he said. "Uh, Brendan, sir." Years of Unisco had ingrained a healthy respect for the chain of command into him.

Adapting was tricky, not in public but in private. Brendan had insisted. A slip in private could just as easily happen where people could hear them and then the game would be up. "I hear you."

They'd seen Vazara on their way to the edge of the Green. Not the parts that the tourist videos showed. The real Vazara They didn't focus on places like this, with good reason. They didn't come for the squalid conditions and the poverty, to see the desperation in the eyes of people they considered lesser than them. It had never been good, it looked worse than ever now. Humanitarians would have wept had they seen some of the sights Wilsin had on their journeys through the kingdom. People came to Vazara for the sun, the small parts of luxury they could afford and the deference from the natives. Those were on the cities towards the outskirts of the kingdom. A slip, he realised. That had been the cities on the outskirts of the kingdom. Anyone who came here for a break now would be risking their lives. Mazoud had seen to that. Overnight he'd declared that foreign tourists were no longer welcome in his kingdom and that any Vazarans who'd left were invited to return to make their kingdom great.

He'd branded them race traitors, those who hadn't come back. Warned them if they hadn't come back when asked, they best not return later. They weren't wanted. Their betrayal outranked anything they might bring to the kingdom. The same had gone for those who'd worked for companies based in other kingdoms, the hotels and the transport divisions. They'd been rounded up, locked away, publicly mutilated. Mazoud had ordered they give their left hands for the kingdom, given they'd spent so long making sure the credits went somewhere other than Vazara.

"Fucking lunatic," Wilsin had muttered to himself when he'd heard that.

Wilsin was just glad that the order had been given for Unisco agents to get out of the kingdom as fast as possible. The order had been made the moment the Coppinger fleet had approached Tripoli. The Senate had told the right thing to do, they'd abandoned Nwakili and Vazara to their enemy. Just because the order had come, didn't mean that he had to personally feel good about it. He'd met Nwakili, had liked him despite the undisputable fact he'd been a slippery son of a bitch who could talk his way out of a snake pit.

A snake pit, if not a full-on invasion of his city. No matter how talented or skilled you might be, there always would be events beyond your control. Overwhelming force was a good way to win a battle, if not a war. Outnumbering and outgunning your opponent was a hard tactic for them to counter.

Brendan sighed, reached into the wagon and fumbled with the tarpaulin, callused hands playing with the edges of the sheet. "I don't expect it'll go to hells for us. But I need to be sure. I asked a contact here to procure us a little something as insurance, just in case things go south."

Wilsin wasn't surprised. It would have been irresponsible not to have done so. He didn't have many contacts in Vazara and most of them had run for cover, or he would have done the same. Brendan yanked the sheet back, Wilsin nodded in appreciation at the boxes beneath, the sleek black blaster rifles. They still carried their weapons, neither had found cause to draw them so far.

"Managed to have them stolen straight from the Suns," Brendan said, pride in his voice. "Brand new BRO-80's. No arguing with these. We run into a situation we can't talk our way out of, we break them out and to hells with the consequences. Consider yourself under silent hunt conditions if that's the case. Split up. Run like the hells are trying to swallow you up. Don't worry about me. Don't worry about Reeves or these doctors."

"Sir, I'm not sure I can do that," Wilsin said. He heard the order. He acknowledged it. He wanted to voice his discomfort with it. "I have a duty…"

"To a group of kingdoms that have been broken, David. Remember the oath you took when you graduated the academy? To serve the five kingdoms? They're no longer acknowledged as the five kingdoms. I'd say you've done your duty and that oath has been nullified."

"Brendan, that isn't what I signed up for. I signed up to do my duty and protect the people that needed protecting." The urgency in his voice must have registered as Brendan let out a snarl of bitter laughter.

"David, I appreciate your show of loyalty. I'm glad you're here to watch my back, but I don't want you dying for me here in this shithole kingdom. This mission isn't worth it. I'm here as a scientist. Nothing more. I want to know what's in that jungle and where it came from. Maybe something'll come of it. Maybe Coppinger is building weapons there. She didn't do it just for the people, I'm sure of that. If I'm wrong, I won't lose sleep. I don't have much time left with Unisco. Hells, maybe the organisation doesn't have much time itself. We've reorganised at a time of crisis, we've made ourselves weak when we should be strong."

He reached out, patted him on the shoulder. Wilsin fought the urge to flinch, the gesture was strangely familiar, something almost paternal in his face. Maybe the heat was getting to Brendan. "David, I'm giving you an order with this. If you must, you run. You don't try and save me. Reeves can look after himself. The doctors won't be harmed if we're not here to taint them by association. They're here on an official visit. They can't be harmed without serious repercussions from the Senate. They might not have an official relationship with Vazara any longer but that works for them. They will go to war over it if they need to."

Wilsin blinked. He wondered if there was some deeper meaning here. It was too hot to start delving into double-speak. He'd heard Nick Roper talk about how much he despised it and if he was honest, he felt the same way about it. Out in the cold and the wind, he could tolerate it all, play along with it. Here where it was hotter than the damn hells, he didn't have the patience.

Brendan smiled at him. "Mazoud knows that. He was sent a message by Cosmin Catarzi upon this visit being approved."

Wilsin said nothing. He didn't think much to Catarzi and whatever he might have to threaten Mazoud with. Catarzi hadn't exactly shone during his time in office. The kingdoms had broken apart under his watch for one thing. That was the sort of thing that history tended to remember. He'd become a typical modern politician, in Wilsin's opinion. Anything beyond posing for photographs and memorable soundbites, he made look difficult. He wished that they'd had a say in voting for Catarzi for Chancellor of the Senate. That hadn't been the case. They'd vote for their own senator to represent them, the senators as a collective voted for their leader. The problem with Catarzi was the charisma he'd spent his entire life working to develop had finally flowered, he'd managed to get the majority on his side and he'd been all smiles as he'd accepted the role.

"Catarzi wants this resolved peacefully," Brendan said. "He doesn't want to turn this into war unless he absolutely has to. He wanted Mazoud to know what would happen if he interfered with this investigation."

"So, if we get attacked…" Wilsin started to say. The gears in his head might be rusty but they still turned under encouragement. He rubbed at his temple. Normally, he wasn't this slow. Months of recuperation had left him out of mental shape. That was the problem with healing. You could do it fast or you could do it properly. Too many agents went for the former option and found themselves sensationally fucked up later in life. He hadn't wanted that, not this time. With the way things had been going, the way Coppinger had declared war on the kingdoms and Unisco, he'd made the quiet choice that being out of the line of fire might not be the worst thing.

It was probably cowardly. Doubtless if he ever aired those private reasons, they'd condemn him. Screw them. It was his body, it was his choice. He might live long enough to reap the benefits. He might not. Only time would tell.

This mission was ideal to get back into the swing of things, really. If they kept their heads down and didn't attract attention, it would be a cinch.

"If we get attacked, you want me to run. You'll do the same?"

Brendan nodded. "Catarzi doesn't want a war. Intelligence from Five Point Island though says that if these scientists are attacked while on a research mission, he might just take it as an excuse to crush Vazara and Mazoud. It'll be bloody." He glanced to the sky as he said it. Wilsin didn't have to follow him. They'd seen enough Coppinger ships in the air since they'd gotten here. An entire kingdom occupied by the enemy wouldn't fall easily. It had taken Coppinger three months to bring down Vazara but that didn't tell the full story. Leonard Nwakili's support from the Senate had never come. They'd been betrayed from within, collaborators to the Coppinger cause doing their best to destabilise any effective defence against the conquerors. The Vazaran Suns had shown their true colours early and finally they set about their attack, bases had been assaulted and aircraft shot down before it could be mobilised properly.

Three months. It could be five times that if the circumstances weren't as favourable. A year or two assaulting Vazara to try and drive out Mazoud and his Coppinger allies wouldn't do anyone any favours. The casualties would be huge. More than that, it would be manpower and equipment that the Allies would lose elsewhere. They'd leave gaps in the formations they'd prepared to counter the Coppingers should they move elsewhere.

"War wouldn't be good," Wilsin said softly. "Let's hope it doesn't come to that."

"David, we always have to hope for the best but prepare for the worst. To do anything else is an exercise in foolishness. In our position, we cannot do that. It is not only careless, but dangerous. There is enough danger in the kingdoms without adding to it, therefore we must always be prudent."

"I know, Brendan, I know." He jerked his head towards the rifles. "That's why we brought them, right?"

"Correct."

"I'm still not happy about leaving you, if it comes to it, Sir." He recognised the use of the final word, he decided he didn't give a damn. He had a lot of respect for Brendan King, he wasn't about to let it go without him knowing that. King had done plenty to earn that respect. He'd had the chance to work with him, not just here but on Carcaradis

Island and he'd considered it an experience. He'd looked up to him growing up as a boy, then as a teen, then as a man and a spirit caller.

"You aren't paid to be happy, David. You're paid to follow orders. Report. If this goes badly wrong, then make sure that every story is told in full details. Make sure that everyone who needs to hear it, hears it."

Bryce had a bottle in his hand, Wilsin could hear the low hum emanating in his throat, he sounded far too cheerful for a place like this. Fazarn shot him a bemused look then returned to his data pad. The two made for mismatched companions, almost as unlikely as him and Brendan. They'd set up camp for the night in as good a spot as they were to find, far enough outside the closest town to avoid attracting unwanted attention.

Tomorrow, they would reach the edge of the jungle. At the rate it was rumoured to be advancing, perhaps it would reach them first. That felt, to Wilsin anyway, just a little depressing.

Mind you, he thought, it'd solve the problem. Let Mazoud rule over a jungle. What happens when it swallows him and his whole messy kingdom up? He'll rule over trees and planets. Wilsin laughed, couldn't keep the bitterness out of his voice.

Bryce looked across at him, extended his hand with the neck of the bottle pointing at him like the barrel of a blaster. "Drink, Davey?" His voice was slurred, thick with drink and emotion. Maybe he wasn't as cheerful as he'd thought. Now he turned his face to the dimming half-light of the fire, Shane Bryce looked tired. His shoulders sagged, like the weight of his own thoughts were forcing him to the ground.

He shook his head. "I'll pass."

"Shame, it's good stuff, yeah?"

"You'll have to excuse my inebriated friend," Fazarn said. His eyes rose from his data pad, he set it down in front of him. The screen glowed for a moment, dropped to a dimness that his eyes missed immediately. "He does this on a night."

"Damn rights," Bryce said. He dropped back in his seat, folded one long leg over the other and let out a contented sigh. "If I could be a poor man…" He started to hum again, mingling occasional words into his moans. He probably didn't have a future as a singer, Wilsin thought.

"Why though?" Wilsin asked. Regret that he'd let it slip out filled him the moment that the question left his lips. It wasn't any of his business. Curiosity didn't do him any favours in this instance.

Fazarn only smiled at him, showed fake teeth beneath his toothbrush moustache. Most Vazarans who'd worked their way up from nothing to something had fake teeth. If you were poor, the dentistry in the kingdom was nothing short of shocking. About the best you could hope for with toothache was that they'd take the right one out and give you painkillers you wouldn't have an allergic reaction to. "You'd have to ask him yourself. Preferably when he's sober, though. He throws a mean punch."

Not at me, he wouldn't. "Oh yeah. Shadow fighter and all that," Wilsin said. He tried to sound impressed. He couldn't manage it too much. Shadow fighting was an art more than a serious form of combat. Something for people to judge the artistic merits of. He appreciated the skill involved, but most of them folded with one good punch. When you were a master in a sport where they weren't allowed to touch each other, it tended not to do wonders for your jaw.

"He's got a temper," Fazarn said.

"He's got a lot of pain in him," Reeves said, sitting up from behind the bags. Wilsin hadn't seen him, realised now that he'd laid out across the ground on his side. "He does a job of hiding it. Not as well as he thinks."

"We've all got pain," Brendan said, moving himself closer to the fire. He gingerly took the bottle out of Bryce's hand and put it on the ground next to him. His nose wrinkled as he caught the smell. "Filthy stuff," he said. "I'm surprised he's not pickled himself drinking that."

"Shane's got a high tolerance," Fazarn said. "I've known him years. We were students together, he always liked his drink. Even when he was fighting, he still drank more than he should."

"Probably the reason he got injured," Reeves offered. All eyes went to him. "Sorry. I remember that. You know how they don't touch each other in shadow fighting?"

Wilsin did. It was a display that involved anticipating what your opponent was going to do, reading their body language and countering it with a mirror of the move. They'd done it back at the Unisco academy in combat classes, used the theory to teach them to read an opponent. Shadow fighting on its own was like teaching spirit calling without showing your spirits how to go for the kill.

"Bryce got touched. He got touched badly."

Wilsin smirked at that. Reeves could have made that sound so much better. He made it sound like someone had interfered with him in the ring. Maybe they had. If they had stuff like that involved, it'd have been worth a cheap laugh or two. The first time it happened anyway. It was a joke that would get old very quickly.

"Misjudged an opponent, took a strike to the knee. Snapped his ligaments and his Achilles when he went down. Messed up bad."

"It's true," Fazarn said. "I was ringside, he was a real mess. Never heard anyone scream so loud." He drew a deep breath, swallowed from his water canteen. His eyes shone with nostalgia in the firelight. "Those were the days. Shane was in the hospital for weeks. They thought he might not walk again."

"Damn," Wilsin said. He couldn't think of anything else. Wasn't sure that he wanted to dwell on the subject. Getting crippled was an all too sensitive subject where he was concerned. Not something he wanted to think about. He'd been luck to avoid serious damage during the last fight he'd had. Permanent damage. They'd fixed him up well, he accepted that. Every little twinge of movement no longer set his nerves on fire. "And now he's a botanist."

"Oh, he's always been a botanist," Fazarn said. "Now he just does it full-time. Says it keeps his mind focused."

Wilsin looked at the slumbering Bryce. A snore broke out from him. Poor bastard. He nodded. "I get that. I really do."

"Everyone has their sore points," Brendan said. "I have a feeling we're all going to find ours before the end of this expedition."

"I hope not, Brendan," Fazarn said. "I want as little extra-curricular excitement as is possible. I hope we find a logical explanation, we can record it as harmless and we can get back to civilisation without being harassed by the local militias."

"We all hope that," Reeves said. "Doctor Fazarn, don't worry. We'll be fine."

A Vedo Reeves may be, Wilsin thought. He had a lot to learn about not tempting fate. He'd have a word with Baxter about that when he next saw him. Hey Ruud. When you're teaching your students, tell them not to jinx the mission.

He laughed at that, saw the looks they gave him and fought the urge to explain. They wouldn't find it funny. Hells, he didn't find it that funny and he'd thought it up. The morning would be here before they knew it and the first day of their expedition proper.

Exciting times, he wanted to think. Some part of him couldn't allow him to do that. Experience. Intuition. Maybe an inbound sense of pessimism that had accompanied this whole damn war. Whatever he wanted to call it, the sensation lurked out in the back of his mind. Watching. Waiting.

This was supposed to be a simple mission. He knew it was going to be anything but.

The rest of the team had long gone ahead to arrange their route into the jungle with Fazarn leading them into the distance. Wilsin preferred that. Large groups of people attracted attention. They'd made their way into the closest town to the jungle just before mid-morning. Him. Brendan. Reeves and Bryce. If he was suffering the ill effects of the previous night, Bryce made no show of it. Just meandered, hands in pockets and a grin on the face beneath the sun shades. He didn't take to the sun well, Wilsin thought, his skin had already taken on a reddish tingle. If he didn't take precautions, he'd look like a lobster.

He'd already lathered his skin in protection, he didn't feel much different. The heat bore down on them all, stifling them until the air choked from their lungs and they wanted to drink all week. They'd need plenty of water for the jungle. Water and sterilisation tablets for any that they found. They could be out there for a very long time, he realised. With the wave of Green getting bigger every day, who knew what would happen. They could enter, come back and find that their starting point had been overrun.

Brendan dropped into a walk next to him, his weathered face thick with sweat, his clothes already bearing white stains across them from the salt. He gave Wilsin a weary grin. "You know, it's not too late to back out, David. I won't think less of you for it."

Wilsin chuckled. Would have laughed more, the heat made mirth oppressive. Anything more, he might have passed out. Would it be as bad as this in the jungle, or worse? He didn't think this could get worse. Up above their heads, the sun bore down hard, didn't care that they were suffering.

It could always get worse.

"I'll pass, Brendan," he said. His tongue felt thick and heavy in his mouth, a useless muscle he couldn't control if he wanted to. "I made a promise to come out here and help you with this whole damn thing. I don't break my promises." Sweat dribbled into the corners of his mouth as he smiled at his boss. "Besides, who's going to come save you when it does go wrong?"

"David!"

"I know, I know. Run. Save myself. Figure of speech."

"I figured Reeves'd be the one who would fight me on this, you know. Not you."

He didn't know whether to be hurt or not. Wondered what Brendan meant by the words. They didn't sound complimentary, although maybe he'd meant them to be anything but insulting. Their weight had struck him though. What did Reeves have, that he didn't, other than Vedo skills and the ability to manipulate the Kjarn? Wilsin knew he had a lot of years of experience behind him. He was as fit as he'd ever been, maybe a little rusty but this was the mission to smoothen that out.

Brendan must have seen the look on his face, he raised both hands as a sign of deference immediately. "My apologies. I didn't mean it like that. I wasn't questioning your character."

He didn't sound convincing. Like he was trying to tell himself that rather than he was Wilsin.

Up ahead, Reeves and the rapidly-reddening Bryce were chatting animatedly as if they'd known each other all their lives. Reeves, damn him, Wilsin thought, didn't look like the heat was bothering him in the slightest.

Sometimes, he thought, they'd all been a lot better off when the Vedo had been a footnote in a myth that none of them had ever heard. He knew things had been a lot less complicated before Baxter came back out of the woodwork. Nobody could dispute that.

Probably not even Baxter himself, given what he had to deal with these days.

Brendan coughed. "Just so you know. Not even Fazarn knows this. Should something go wrong in that jungle, there's an emergency beacon in my pack. If things move beyond recovery, push it. An emergency Unisco recovery vehicle will move out for you."

Wilsin whistled. Up ahead, Bryce and Reeves paused, the older man glanced back at him, shook his head in a painfully condescending manner. Wilsin considered going over and punching him for the look. Decided against it. Too damn sapping. He didn't want to expend the effort. Not with the bombshell Brendan had just dropped on him.

"That's incredible," he said. "They do know that they run the risk of being shot down if they come here, don't they?"

"That's why it's only to be used in a major emergency. Only if things are so bad that pushing it can't possibly make them worse." He saw the look on Wilsin's face and laughed. "I don't expect them to get that bad. I can't imagine what would precipitate needing to push it. But remember. Preparation. Good not to need it, better to have it."

Their numbers were few, even when they'd joined up. They'd set their rendezvous point at an old storage yard just on the outskirts of town, their wagons would be stored there while they made their trek into the jungle. "Can't take them into the jungle," Bryce had explained as they'd approached. "It's uncharted wilderness. No paths. We rise above the treeline, we run twice as much fuel. Those wagons aren't good with heights, not with the weighs we're talking."

"I didn't know you were an expert on jungle navigation," Wilsin said to the botanist. It felt petty letting the words slip his mouth. He couldn't bring himself to care.

"You learn new things wherever you must, David," Bryce said. Now he knew what to look for, he could see the limp. It wasn't noticeable at first, but now he could see the slightest misstep every time he walked. He never quite looked like he'd topple over, but the threat was there. "That's the way the species survives. Dogs and tricks. Learn them."

Yeah, I want to learn how to take a beating in the shadow fighting ring, I'll come talk to you, Wilsin thought. A smirk played across his lips. He'd loved to throw that at him, see what he had to say in retort. Decided against it. It wasn't worth the argument that would follow. Plus, he might not be here as an agent of Unisco but still there was a professional demeanour to follow.

"I suppose," he said instead. "I don't know, I've never gone trekking through the jungles. Couldn't tell you the first thing about it."

"Not as easy as it sounds, David," Brendan said.

"Really, because I thought the whole process sounded like it would be horrific," Wilsin smiled. Brendan had to turn his face away, he thought he saw the older man's shoulders shake.

"Anyway," Bryce said. "We leave the wagons here, all bar one. This jungle might be swallowing up everything it touches but there's one thing that it hasn't touched so far. At least, not in a bad way. We've got a boat. We're loading everything into that and we're heading upriver."

Wilsin remembered that story. That was how this whole thing had been reported, back at the start, if his memory served him. The first thing people had noticed in Vazara was that the rivers were filling up. A good chunk of the kingdom had been scar-mined over recent years, chunks of the desert sands heated up and solidified into glass, melted down into liquid to be transported to a site where the valuable minerals within could be reconstituted. Easier than traditional mining, very much cheaper as well.

Claudia Coppinger had laid claim to be the main culprit, most of the materials to build the resort and the stadiums on Carcaradis Island had come from here. Then the Green had appeared, and the cracks left on the landscape had started to fill with water. She'd claimed to have done it deliberately as her gift to the people of Vazara, a country that had so much and yet received so little of it. "At least," she had said in a broadcasted interview, "they can at least have some fresh water. Courtesy of me."

No wonder she was so popular here. They'd seen pictures of her plastered up across several of the towns they'd been through. She was more popular than their Premier. He wondered if they only tolerated Mazoud because he had been put in place by Coppinger. More than once, he'd seen a shrine to her. Offerings. These people didn't have much but what they did, they were willing to give up in supplication to her. They believed in her.

Brendan had shaken his head at the sight of the last one. "Disgusting."

The yard was about what he'd expected from a town like this, the sort of place where old speeders went to have parts recycled into slightly newer vehicles. He thought he'd seen junk before, none of it had anything on some of the stuff piled up here. On second glance, not all of it was old. Some of it could have passed for new. Calling it junk was an unfair assessment. He could have sworn a few of the items looked newer than the ones on the wagons they'd rode down in. None of the stuff however looked as old as the Vazaran with one hand stood leaning on a stick, chatting to Fazarn and his assistant. Fazarn spoke, the girl to his right translated. Out here in the outback of Vazara, every other village had their own variation of the same dialect. It was, putting it mildly, a real pain in the arse.

They'd not had much to do with the rest of the team so far, beyond introductions. Fazarn's assistant, Tiana Aubemaya continued to translate away into arguments with the old man, his face not giving anything away. Living in this part of the world probably did wonders for recognising when someone wanted something and being willing to negotiate hard. Wilsin smiled, broke open a bottle of water. The heat had died away, still stifled but at least they were out of the full force of it for now. The entrance to the yard had shade, enough for one or two but seven was pushing it. Two more of the team, Suniro Suchiga and Ballard Brown were already there, crammed up against the back, the latter mopping his head from perspiration. Brown grinned as he saw them.

"Look who showed up," he said, pale teeth flashing against mud-coloured skin. At some point, someone had told him that dying hair green and blonde was a good thing to do and he'd believed them. "Told you, Sunny. They'd be here sooner or later."

Suchiga looked at him, chose not to respond. The sun shone off the polished skin of his hairless head, the lack of hair in conjunction with the slant of his eyes granting him an aura of wisdom. People from Burykia didn't come to Vazara often. Historically, they didn't trust each other. The former thought the latter were subhuman, the former thought the latter were thieves and cheats. Suchiga had the air of someone who'd rather be somewhere else but that the opportunities were many here and he was willing to swallow the indignity of suffering the sands.

"Doctor Suchiga. Doctor Brown," Brendan said, inclining his head as they returned the greetings. Wilsin returned them, wandered past the one-eyed doctor who glanced up at him from where he was sat on the sand and smiled. If they found themselves in need of medical attention, Nordin Nmecha was going to patch them up. He reached down, shook his hand. The doctor was going through his pack, checking their medical supplies. He might only have one eye, Wilsin had noticed that immediately, seen the bright white patch covering it, but he looked competent enough. He'd rather his doctor had two hands, unlike the yard owner.

That was where he'd found himself heading. Towards Fazarn, Aubemaya and the one-handed man, curiosity filling him up. He couldn't speak the tongue, he fancied he might be able to get a glimpse into what was going on. They weren't exactly going to great lengths to conceal their body language. Nobody did unless they realised what it said about them. Teaching it at Unisco was a subject that nobody enjoyed learning, yet when they got out into the field, they realised how valuable it was. It was the sort of skill that saved your life.

Those days felt longer and longer ago with each passing week, yet the lessons had never faded. He looked across at Fazarn, righteously annoyed that the negotiation was taking so long, arms folded, trying to stand taller as to intimidate. He could see the stubborn confidence in the owner of the yard, leaning forward, face set in pride. He wasn't going to give an inch. Every sinew of his face bore the contours of determination, here was a man not used to quitting.

Aubemaya looked fed up as she translated, rapid-fire dialect into something they could understand. Her voice was like honey poured over biscuits. "He says he knows that we make arrangement already, he say circumstances have changed."

"Not that bloody much, they haven't," Fazarn said. None of them were looking at him on approach, still embroiled in their own little argument. "We had an agreement, he's been compensated."

Aubemaya rolled her eyes, stretched out her fingers in front of her and chattered in the dialect, it sounded harsh and alien to Wilsin's ears. Saying it sounded like conversational chimp might be doing it credit.

"He says again, circumstances have changed. We go upriver, he never sees his boat again. He's not happy about it."

"My good man," Fazarn said. He looked to have found another few inches of height from somewhere. He towered over the one-handed man who didn't look impressed in the slightest by it. Fazarn was large, that couldn't be disputed but it was the shape of a man for whom the easy life had started to take a toll. Height and size only intimidated when they looked deadly, not when it gave the impression throwing the first punch would lead to passing out from exertion. "We are not shysters out to con you. We are academics. We seek the answers."

No response as Aubemaya translated. Her face had only taken on more resignation, her eyes lowering to the ground.

"Why does he think he won't see his boat again?" Wilsin asked, breaking his silence. The old man jumped, turned with his stick held up high like a sword in the one hand. For the first time, that face lit up in delight and he shuffled forward, the stick dropping. Wilsin saw the hand come up, offer itself to him. He grinned, shook it. It was like gripping old teak, solid but without the threat of crushing. At the same time, you knew that it would outlast you if it came to a show of force.

The words broke from his mouth, two that he recognised amidst them. David and Wilsin. He grinned, wished that he was stood somewhere else right now. Anywhere else would do. He glanced towards Aubemaya. "What did he just say?"

"Big fan," Aubemaya said. "He said they have an old viewing screen in the hut, he saw you on it during the Quin-C." At least it had brought some enthusiasm out of her, the smile lit up her face. "There's always one somewhere, huh, Mister Wilsin?"

"David, please," he said, giving her a wink. "Tell him it's nice to meet him. And ask him my question. Why does he think he won't see his boat again?"

She didn't hesitate, launched straight into the questions while Fazarn muttered under his breath. They sounded angry, threatening even. Another reason to potentially regret this whole expedition. Bryce was turning out to be difficult to work with, Fazarn wasn't much better. He found himself wondering why he'd bothered. He wasn't an academic like Brendan, Reeves had been volunteered for it. He'd had a choice and he'd made the one to come.

"He asks if you'd like wine, though I'd decline before Doctor Bryce hears about it," Aubemaya said. "Otherwise we'll never leave."

Wilsin grinned. "Thanks, but no thanks." He pointed up in the sky, towards the sun. "Doesn't agree with me in this."

"As for your other question, he says he see travellers come through here towards the jungle all the time now. One, maybe two a week."

"Popular destination, huh?" Wilsin asked. He glanced to Fazarn. "You know anything about this?"

"Thrill seekers and scientific charlatans no doubt, seeking that their name remains immortal whereas we who do it for the contribution will be left seething in the background," Fazarn said. If he'd sounded any more theatrical, Wilsin would have felt bad about not buying a ticket.

"People come," Aubemaya said. "They go into the jungle. Six months it's been advancing. He worried that it'll swallow everything he has soon." The old man continued to jabber, the translator nodded and nodded, looked him up and down as he said it. "He says he's going to throw himself into it if that happen."

"Nice," Fazarn said. The disgust was palpable in his voice. For someone who looked like he'd been born not a few miles from a place like this, Fazarn's attitude bemused Wilsin. Maybe he'd gotten too used to city living and a cushy life. Going from the top of your field, as Brendan had told him, to a backhole like this must have hurt.

It was nice to know he wasn't the only one having second thoughts about the validity of being here then.

"Six months, he's seen people going in there. A few at first, one or two in the first months. Then many more. Much more after that. We're the..." She cocked an eyebrow, said something that might have been a request for clarification. A due response came, she nodded in agreement and smiled her thanks. "Thirteenth party to have asked him for help."

"Unlucky for some then," Wilsin said. He glanced around the junkyard again, realising some of the stuff here suddenly made sense. Crafty old bastard. He'd been recycling the parts of the equipment the previous parties had left here. Running a con. The implication of it all made his eyes want to water. How many had been through here and not come back. Thirteen parties. Given there were nine of them in theirs alone, that could be a horrific number of people. What the hells were they getting themselves into?

"How many have come back?" Fazarn asked. "Has he heard from any of them again?" The look in his eyes said he was serious. Wilsin shook his head. Oblivion was nice for some people. Being able to listen between the words wasn't always the best thing.

"Just one speeder," Aubemaya said. "With an interesting cargo." She jabbered some more, he found himself watching the fascinating shapes her mouth made as she spat the dialect. "In the shed, he says. We want to see?"

"I'll look at it," Wilsin said, not giving Fazarn the chance to cut in. "Forewarned is forearmed, after all."

The shed was probably anything but. Where Wilsin came from, they were small huts at the bottom of gardens. Not everyone had one but those that did considered themselves to be a cut above the rest. There'd never been one in his family growing up, if his father wanted to get away from his mother, he went to the local tavern and didn't come back until the young David Wilsin was asleep.

This was several sizes bigger than any shed he'd ever experienced before, larger and darker. He could smell engine oil in the background, the floor sticky beneath his boots and he didn't want to think about what it might be. Something nasty, no doubt. The relief from the heat outside was instant, his skin cried out with the relief. He licked his lips, tasted the salt on them.

The speeder in the centre of the room had seen better days, he was amazed it had made it out of the jungle. Deep gouges ratcheted the frame, cut the metal almost back to what lay underneath. He could see the engine through the ones touched by the light, it looked about as healthy as the rest of it. The windshield was more cracked than whole, as if something heavy had struck it and come off better in the ensuing confrontation. He'd be amazed if it flew again.

Everything about the speeder was incidental, except the figure sat in the pilot's seat. Wilsin hadn't seen one for a while, they were becoming rarer and rarer in common society. Humanoid, but not human. A slave that wasn't aware it was a slave. The skin that covered it looked flesh-coloured, but if he touched it, he'd find it was harder than steel. The eyes, though they looked real, stared unblinking into the light. Some of their owners programmed them to blink. When they looked like this, it was disconcerting. Some used them as labour. Some as butlers. Others as bodyguards.

"Endroid, huh?" Fazarn said. "One of the parties must have been wealthy."

Wasn't that the truth? Endroids were expensive, marketed only to the rich and the important. They cost more to run for a month than most people made in a year. They were effective, efficient, trustworthy, all the things that they'd been marketed to be that human employees weren't.

The old man jabbered, gestured to the endroid. Aubemaya rolled her eyes. "It's always about credits with some people. He says he's going to rebuild him…" Wilsin smirked at that. If the old man was capable of that, there was more to him than met the eye. Nobody in their right mind would buy a second-hand endroid that had been tinkered about with. There were easier ways of committing suicide. Assuming they didn't blow up, there'd been a rumour about that some months back to avoid illegal modifications, their programming was unnaturally sensitive. Each was made for a specific purpose, they did not respond well to having that purpose subverted.

"Just make sure we're far away from here when he does," Fazarn said. Sounded like he'd heard those same rumours to Wilsin. "Does that blasted thing still work?"

Wilsin turned away, studied the thing while Aubemaya relayed the question. He saw that single hand reaching out, touch it on the neck, fingers dancing across invisible switches. The eyes, previously unblinking and dead, changed. A light shone through them, the difference between them and human eyes suddenly indistinguishable. The mouth moved, though not in time to the sounds coming from it.

"I appear to be unfunctioning. I cannot move."

The voice was neat, clipped, upper-class southern Canterage at its finest. The voice of one who knew their place was to serve. Wilsin glanced into the cockpit of the speeder, saw the problem immediately. The endroid didn't appear to be aware that its body ended in a trail of wires and synthetic fluid, the seats thick with the scarlet fluid. Blood that wasn't blood.

"You had an accident," Wilsin said. "What happened to you?"

The head rotated to face him, nothing even remotely human about the gesture. A human neck craned, the muscles tensed, and the bones twisted to allow the gesture. Here, it was simply a rotation, the neck turning idly on the shoulders.

"Vocal or facial recognition unavailable. Not an authorised user. Request for information denied."

He smiled. If that was the way this thing wanted to play, he could play that game. He folded his arms in front of him, tapped the mangled roof of the speeder. Even that hadn't escaped damage, a quad of rips torn through the metal. Light from the dim bulb above poked down onto the seats, leaving the cavities bathed in shadows.

"Bet I can make you talk," he said.

Endroids had been approved by the Senate following a concession by their creators. They would be permitted to make them provided they were subject to recognise the authority of the kingdoms just the same as their owners or their designers. They would not be above the law. The law had been updated to include their presence, the punishment for a rogue endroid being deactivation. Every Unisco agent past a certain rank knew the access code needed to prod them into compliance.

"Endroid," he said. "This is a tango-alpha-four-one-one-U request for information as to how you arrived in this circumstance." That code would prove he was who he was, that he was to be granted aid immediately and the consequences would be dire should it not comply with instant effect. "Answer my question."

The eyes blinked, normally too fast to see but there was almost something deliberate about the gesture here. If these things could think for themselves, he'd have been worried. Not that it could have done anything to him. It didn't reply, just sat inscrutable like a cat.

"Answer my question. Where is the rest of your body?"

If it could have looked sulky, no doubt it would. The words were reluctant, but it didn't have a choice. "I do not know. Perhaps where I left it. I remember... Oh dear. My goodness. How horrible."

"What is?" Fazarn looked at the endroid, the face turned to look at him. "What's horrible."

"Vocal authority unrecognised. Cannot process information at this time." The level of snootiness in the voice was remarkable, Wilsin thought. A part of him wondered if it was doing this deliberately. They shouldn't sound like they were enjoying bundling themselves up in the protocols of their programming.

"Who is your owner?" Wilsin asked. He gave Fazarn a look, one that made him retreat to his original position, muttering under his breath. The doctor being unhappy wasn't even a problem that registered with him right now. Brendan would back him, he hoped. Finding out what the endroid knew was more important than stroking Fazarn's ego.

"I am the property of Lord Ronald Carston of Wyndsar, Canterage," the endroid said. The pride that layered the words made him feel sick to his stomach. The thing knew it was a slave and was happy about it. Its eyes flickered, sputtering sounds broke from its orifices. "My master sought to travel here..."

"I know of Carston," Fazarn said, unable to keep his mouth shut in excitement. "A gentleman and a scoundrel. The sort of man that..."

"Alex, that thing will break you in half if you insult its master," Wilsin said from the corner of his mouth. "Just a friendly reminder." He didn't know if Fazarn had seen that it couldn't walk but it had the desired effect. He didn't want to listen to him go on. He'd heard bits about the lord, not all of it good but most of it irrelevant. That he'd gone off on a trip like this wasn't something he found surprising. Few things could trump a rich man's ego.

Wilsin turned back to the endroid, glanced into the cockpit of the speeder. The synthetic fluid was gushing out of it now, flooding the seat below it. It smelled of unripe cherries, he was sure he could taste it on the buds of his tongue. Firing it up, getting it going like this couldn't have been good for it. Its limbs were twitching, he jumped back as an arm flailed into the side of the speeder, only ruined metal protecting preventing it from hitting him in the groin.

"You're dying," he said. Two words but he felt the weight of them. Death was a ridiculous notion to apply to something that wasn't alive, yet they felt apt. "You don't have long."

"My systems have been compromised. Suspended state has been disabled. Cannot be reactivated. Yes. I do not have long." It looked at him, their eyes met. "I will not betray my master."

"I'm going in there," Wilsin said, pointing in the vaguest direction of the jungle. Out the corner of his eye, he could see it looming, a green cloud on the horizon. "We're taking a boat upriver. If he's alive, I'll get him out of there."

Experiencing the laughter of a synthetic being was a first-time experience for him, not one he wished to repeat. It was laughter at its most joyless. The mirth of something missing that vital spark of humanity. "You are going there?"

More laughter. It couldn't hold itself up any longer, the body fell backwards. "I am," Wilsin said. "I'm leading a party in there very shortly."

"Well actually…" Fazarn started to say, went silent as Wilsin's hand went under his jacket, came back with the giant T6 blaster pistol. The angry black eye pointed in his direction. Wilsin tried to ignore the weight of the weapon, just kept it steadily pointed at him. He was probably going to be reprimanded for this. Aubemaya shrieked and threw her hands into the air. A little unnecessary given she wasn't the one he was pointing it at. The old man just looked amused, like it wasn't anything he hadn't seen before. Maybe he hadn't. This was a rough kingdom.

"You won't come back," the endroid said, breaking the silence. Four little words but he could feel the effort behind them. "You'll die with my master and his men. They'll come for you. Can't fight them. Too many of them. They're everywhere."

It forced the last word out, emphasising the first part with effort. He didn't know if it was in pain or not. Didn't look like it was comfortable.

"What?" Wilsin asked. The timer was running out. They could have minutes or mere seconds, he needed to make the questions count. "What's out there in the Green?"

It answered, voice almost silent, the vocal receptors fading but he heard it. A single word just about audible.

"Monsters."

Any chance to ask further questions was lost to him, the thing started to spark and spasm, head twisting around on its axis, arms smashing out blindly into whatever was in reach. Wilsin jumped back, saw one of them punch through the side of the speeder. He brought his weapon up out of reflex, aimed and pulled the trigger, felt the vibration all the way into his shoulder. His aim had been true, right in the centre of its twitching face. It had been in its death throes and now it could rest. The old man went crazy, would have leaped at him had the barrel of his blaster not still been smoking. Still he yelled in fury and Aubemaya stuck her head up to translate.

Wilsin raised a hand, cut her off. "I don't care," he said. "I don't care how pissed he is. Tell him that our initial agreement stands, and he doesn't need to thank me in advance for saving his life." He holstered his weapon. "I'll be outside."

He moved to leave, not before taking in the speeder and the headless body in the cockpit. The old man still looked furious, Aubemaya was relating back what he'd said, or at least she should be. He didn't need to justify what he'd just done. He was right, he probably had saved the old man's life. First time he tinkered with the endroid, he'd have blown himself up.

More than that, he'd seen the look on its face. It had been suffering, these things weren't human, but it didn't mean that they weren't exceptionally capable of making you forget that sometimes. Just for a moment, he'd seen that pain and he'd acted, moved to put it out of its suffering. Improper conduct.

The sun beat down on his face as he stepped out, ready to face whatever wrath Brendan was about to bring down on him for the way he'd acted. A wry smile flitted across his face. The prices they paid for the things they did sometimes.

Chapter Fourteen. The Harshest Lesson.

"I never liked lone survivor scenarios. Too eager for the cadet to develop a Divine complex, fighting for the sake of it. It's habits we'd like to break out of them, not encourage. If they treat every exercise like they have nothing to lose, sooner or later we're going to have to teach them how to fight for something. They've all got their reasons for being here. They should never forget that. It should be their motivation to succeed. Any idiot can die. It takes someone special to live against all odds."

Memo from Tod Brumley to Inquisitor Nandahar Konda at the Iaku Unisco Academy.

Two months ago.

"Killing a man in hot blood is easy. If someone is trying to kill you, then natural survival instincts to kick in. Those instincts are the basest of human need. It is these moments when you realise it comes down to you and them. A crystal-clear choice. And I never met someone who actively wanted to die in those circumstances." The instructor looked around the room, cleared his throat. "None of you have ever experienced it yet. Should you graduate, you'll miss your time of innocence. Your first kill changes you just as much as your hundredth. As your thousandth."

Pete blinked. One thousand kills. Were there really people in Unisco who'd killed a thousand times? He didn't even want to consider that. Surely it was exaggeration.

Next to him, Theo looked disinterested. That was how you knew he was paying attention. The silence. He'd come to work that out in the last months, since they insisted on grouping him and Dan Roberts with Pete in exercises. Never all the time but more often than they didn't. He wouldn't have described any of them as friends. Theo never gave the impression he'd learned more than the rudimentary about human behaviour. Looked like a human, behaved like an endroid sometimes and not a particularly friendly one.

Dan Roberts, on the other hand, was friendly enough without being over the top about it. Neither of them would replace Scott any time soon. He missed his friend. It felt like too damn long since he'd seen him, since they'd had a chat and shot the shit. After Carcaradis Island, they'd gone their separate ways. Scott had his own life, he had Mia and that bloody ghost, and Pete felt like he had a hole in his gut where his life used to be. Since that day, he'd asked himself over and over if he'd made the right decision joining Unisco.

Every time he'd asked himself that, the answer had always been a resounding yes. He couldn't have done anything else. Alone, he didn't have the skills to take on Coppinger's group, bloody their nose like he wanted. He owed them that, for his sister. He couldn't forgive them for Sharon. He was young, he was a talented spirit caller if he did say so himself, he'd thought himself fit and in good condition. Why wouldn't Unisco want to take him?

Revenge was a powerful motivator. He'd said as much in his interview with the recruiter, they'd sat there and listened to him talk before saying their part. They'd made him want to belong, realise when his chance came to get revenge, it would be his to take. That feeling alone had been enough to make him sign up, even with the caveat that the revenge he wanted might not be the one that he'd get.

"Because," the recruiter had said with a smile, showing a single broken tooth amidst a mouthful of pearly whites. "Stopping her is revenge enough. Doing your part in making sure her plans don't come to fruition hurts her far more than wiping out a hundred faceless underlings. Remember, there's always a bigger picture."

Those words had comforted him through the first nights in the academy. First doubts were natural. His part in the bigger picture was to get through here, graduate and do his part in the war effort.

"Cold blooded murder is never condoned by Unisco," the instructor said. Waul Paddington, his name was, he'd written it on a screen at the front of the room at the start of the session. His accent wasn't hard to understand, a bit abrupt and harsh but he made his point. As he rose to his feet, his bulk trembled. He might have been fit once, his lifestyle was catching up with him and his belly crowded over the top of his uniform trousers. "Never. There are circumstances in which it needs to be done sometimes, but already you have failed should that arise. Every other option has been exhausted. Should your cause be just, then you need not worry. We back our agents wherever we can. In the field, your judgement is the final call."

He paused, ran thick fingers through straggled hair. He looked like he hadn't seen a groomer in months. Maybe he hadn't. This place wasn't exactly a centralised hub of commercial activity. The academy had been placed here for isolation. When you were here, you were here for the long term. Communication with the outside was limited. It was the only reason he hadn't spoken to Scott for the four months he'd been here.

"Of course, you will be investigated. Every kill you make needs to be investigated, hence the reason we have inquisitors. All of you will talk to an inquisitor at some point. Some of you may go on to work for them. It's an honourable role, no matter what some agents might tell you. Of course, some are decent guys, others are assholes. Kind of the kingdom. The only agents who dislike them are the ones who get the call from them every other week." Paddington smiled. "And for every innocent agent who acted true in the line of duty, there's one who tried to get ahead through less than scrupulous means. Nobody likes a dirty Unisco agent. We have a duty, a higher calling to make sure that the laws of the kingdom in relation to spirits are upheld. We have to be better than everyone else, not just physically but spiritually as well."

He folded his arms in front of his chest and exhaled. "We set the standards we expect the rest of the kingdoms to follow, it does not matter whether there are four of them, five of them or just one. Our mandate is what it is."

The lessons had come thick and fast, punishing his mind with their constant onslaught of information, tests for things he was expected to remember. Even the combat didn't let up, though he thought he was getting better at it. When they showed Unisco agents in shows on the viewing screens, they never revealed how much documentation was tied up in it. Some part of him had thought that it would be like that. He'd been mistaken.

His latest appointment was with the academy inquisitor, a sallow-featured Burykian whose eyes locked on him the moment he entered the room. Deep pools of brown followed him, the slash of mouth curving into a smile.

"Sit down, Cadet Jacobs," Konda said. He'd seen the name on the door as he'd entered. Inquisitor Nandahar Konda. The office wasn't much but that kept it in line with most of the others he'd been in here. Calling it sparse was being generous, a few filing cabinets loomed at either side of the desk, an elaborate teapot sat atop one of them. Steam puffed merrily from the spout, he tried not to study the designs on it and instead looked at his host. "Drink? Tea? Water? Coffee? I'd offer you beer but that would be highly inappropriate, no?" His grin split larger, almost pulled his lips back over his gums.

"Tea, please," Pete said. That steam escaping the pot smelled good, a little herbal and he'd found himself trying not to make a show of sniffing it too enthusiastically. Never good to show eagerness. "It smells good."

"Is my own infusion of herbs, fruits and leaves," Konda said, rising to his feet. Small hands clutched the pot, he brought it down onto the desk between them with a delicate clunk. "Isn't just good, is pretty damn fantastic."

"I don't normally drink it," Pete said. He meant it as well. Tea wasn't the drink for him, it was coffee's inferior younger brother in his opinion. Up close, he could see the colours of the Burykian flag on the kettle, designs of suns and moons, stars and sigils whose meaning he couldn't even start to guess at. Konda placed a cup in front of him, a cup in front of himself and slid back into his seat.

"Well, help yourself," the inquisitor said. "Relax, you're not in any kind of trouble. This is just an informal chat, you know? I do it with every trainee at some point, sometimes twice or thrice."

"You need that many informal chats with some cadets?" Pete asked. He didn't want to touch the teapot, saw how delicate the handle looked. He could well imagine himself breaking it off, the accident leading it to smash against the desk, hot tea everywhere. Bad enough he scalded himself, even worse should he burn Konda.

"Those I deem problematic," Konda said. "Not everyone is cut out for this work, you know? Some burn long before they reach the pinnacle of excellence we demand."

"Yeah, I can imagine." It didn't take a lot of thought really. He didn't think he was struggling with the training. So far, it hadn't been an insurmountable challenge, he'd had to work for things but nothing that he wasn't capable of. Some weren't so capable, he tried to blot them out of his consideration. Dwelling on others wouldn't help his case any. Wherever he could, he tried to offer advice should he see someone struggling, yet that could only go so far. He couldn't make someone stronger or faster or fitter, so it was halfway to a losing battle before he'd even started.

"Can you?" Konda didn't sound impressed. "Imagination isn't perhaps the skill we value above all others here, Mister Jacobs. We value many things. Commitment. Talent. Consistency. Effort. All these things stand above the imagination. We prefer to focus on what is, rather than what it could be."

"Naturally," Pete said. "You don't need your agents thinking too much, huh?"

"We don't desire our agents to be automatons," Konda said. "Too much of the job is down to human judgement. Many of our successes and many of our failures boil down to that same thing." He sighed, fixed a pointed gaze onto him. "Have some tea, Mister Jacobs."

He reached for it, trying not for any sudden movements in case it slipped from his hands, moved the spout to the empty mug in front of him and started to pour away, hearing it slop down into the porcelain. The tea was the same colour as Konda's eyes, rich dark brown, although twice as warm. "Making the choice that was right at the time. Never as easy as it sounds afterwards. Tell me, Mister Jacobs, do you know what an inquisitor does?"

"Instructor Paddington mentioned it," Pete said. He put the teapot down, careful to make sure it didn't spill in front of him. "He said that you made sure we all followed the rules. Unisco agents."

"You're not an agent yet," Konda said, his tone gentle but firm. "Walk before you run, cadet. Instructor Paddington is right, essentially. If Unisco is the sword that defends the kingdoms, the inquisitors are the guard which prevents you wounding yourself in battle. If Unisco works for the kingdoms, the inquisitors work for Unisco. We are the ones who watch, we ask the questions and we never give up. We are the deterrent and the punishment." He grunted, cleared his throat. "That's the pitch anyway. We also need to make many speeches in that mould. You know what it's like."

Pete opened his mouth, about to say that he didn't, found himself cut off as Konda sat bolt upright in his seat, a big grin on his face. "Okay, so every cadet comes to me at some point for testing. What I'm going to do is give you a few questions, see that you're taking in what you learn. We throw a lot of information at you, normally it's less dense than this but needs must. We need agents, we have one less kingdom to recruit from." He shrugged. "By my notes from your instructors," he tapped a pad on the desk in front of him, "you've had about thirteen months of training condensed into four and a bit. These questions aren't hard, they have all been covered by your instructors so far. There's no further action for success or failure, rather this all goes into your file. Should you succeed, we'll look at advancement. Should you fail, and if you don't know, I implore you not to take your best guess, we'll give you further training. No harm, no foul."

"No guessing then?"

"Guess in the field, get it wrong, it could be disastrous."

He must have seen the look of disgust on Pete's face, a smile broke out. "I know, I know. Everyone feels eager to get ahead when they get to this point. We don't hold you back out of malice. We do it because it's the best thing, because you're not ready." He smiled wider, Pete could see the kindness in it, hear it in his voice. "Inquisitors have a bad reputation because of one of our former top guys. He was a great inquisitor, a shitty human being. That sort of thing sticks, and you can't ever get rid of it. Just consider this. We're doing it to protect you. Not punish you."

Konda leaned back in his seat. "Punishment implies that something has been done wrong. You can never be wrong when you learn. Only if you fail to address your errors."

"So, you're like a final exam?" Pete asked. "You're here to judge me?"

"Something like that. What I prefer to think of myself as is a challenge. Life is full of challenges and like a glorious firebird, you must rise above them all. The Unisco education doesn't cease when you graduate, every day will teach you newer things, until you retire." He shrugged. "Or you die. Whichever comes first."

To that, Pete had nothing to say. He'd never thought about dying. They'd repeatedly hammered home the notion that being killed in the line of duty was a very real possibility, but it hadn't been something he'd chosen to dwell on. He was willing to give it up if he needed to. It wouldn't be first choice but coming to terms with that hadn't been as hard as he thought it might.

"Cadet Jacobs, explain appropriate force to me, in relation to the Unisco directives," Konda said suddenly.

"Appropriate force as laid down by the Unisco directives invokes that the measure of retaliation against a suspect must be equal to the action being levelled against the agent at the time of the intended apprehension," Pete said. That one was easy. They'd done a whole morning on the theory.

"Causes us a lot of problems that one," Konda said. "Us, the inquisitors, not us, Unisco. Good answer. Word perfect in fact,"

Pete said nothing, just took a swallow of his tea. It was bitter but not unpleasant, he'd had a lot worse. The aftertaste lingered, perhaps more pleasant than the first initial impressions.

"Good tea, no?" Konda smiled. "Tell you, it's good for you. Cleanses the mind, the body, the soul. Never too much though. Make you see things that aren't there. One cup a day does wonders for you. More than that, you're asking for trouble."

"Uh-huh?" Part of him wondered why. He didn't know, maybe he didn't want to know. It had left his taste buds throbbing, his tongue twitching like it had a will of its own. Unusual feeling, he wanted to stretch his tongue out, wiggle it like a snake. If Konda hadn't been staring at him, he might have done. He grinned at the Burykian, knew somewhere in the back of his mind that he probably looked an idiot for it. Konda's face was dancing now, spinning side to side, he had to follow him with his eyes to keep up.

"Sometimes there's an adverse effect. Never an accidental one though. Tell me, Mister Jacobs, did they tell you what a forty-two-alpha-six is?"

His words sounded distant and hazy, like he was hearing them through water. They didn't even match up with the movement of Konda's lips. They moved, and no sound emerged from them, failed to move and Pete could hear the voice.

"That's an…" Words failed him, he shook his head. He felt numb, his eyes like leaden weights, his head heavier. "That's an executive order, right? Top priority to be obeyed? Every Unisco station head gets one to use…" How long was it they got to use one? The lights on the ceiling winked at him, tried to grab his attention. They wanted him to stare at them. Cheeky little lights. He broke into a grin, tried to rise to his feet, felt his stomach give a twist of protest.

"… Every year, right? They get a year and one chance to do whatever the hells they want." Part of him wanted to giggle. The options were endless. He'd send his guys out for supplies if he had the power to do that. They'd think he was crazy, and it'd be funny when he sent them out to get the biggest bag of nuts they could find.

"Bags of nuts, fascinating," Konda said. His voice was quieter, harder to hear. Pete stared at him, he guessed the surprise must have been stamped all over his face. Had he just said that out loud? Didn't feel like he had. Unless Konda could read minds, that meant only one thing.

"Okay, wow, wow, wow. Are you a Vedo?" he asked, unable to keep the glee out of his voice. "I always wanted to meet another one of you guys. At least, one I know that was a Vedo, because see my sister…"

"I'm not a Vedo, Cadet Jacobs," Konda said. "That is a story for another day, one we do not have time for now. Have some more tea. It'll make everything feel so much better."

Something screamed at the back of his mind how the idea was stupid, that it was one he shouldn't follow through on. Something wasn't right with him; any idiot could see that. He wasn't well.

"Finish your cup, Cadet Jacobs." The voice was like honey in his ears, soft musical words being pushed into him and he wanted nothing more than to receive their wisdom and be blessed. He lifted the cup, realised how light it felt in his fingers now he wasn't worried about trivialities. He brought it to his lips, started to swallow the contents inside, felt dribbles slide down his chin.

Now he had the chance to exercise that tongue, sliding it out, desperate to get every single last drop. Through the corner of his eyes, he was sure he could see Konda smiling at him, proud like a penguin through the haze. His arms felt weary, he wanted to lift them, they were fighting him all the way. Sitting up had become an effort, his legs didn't want to hold him, he felt his body relax and he wasn't in the chair anymore, sliding down to the ground.

The carpet rushed up to greet him, ready to cradle him in its embrace. He'd never felt anything more welcoming. Face met rough fibre, he found he didn't have the urge to fight it any longer.

Darkness fell, landed on him with all the force of a hunting eagle, swallowed him up. He wouldn't have had it any other way.

He wasn't sure what had awoken him, just that something had broken him from his slumber. Pete slid his eyes open, glanced around the room. Nothing. Silence. In the past, he might have just gone back to sleep. Since he'd been here, things had changed. The scales had been sliced from his eyes, he knew now more than ever before that things were not always what they appeared to be. That sort of lazy assumption might kill you.

Silence wasn't normal in the dormitories. Those early night, he'd laid here questioning his choices, he'd realised that. With sleep came the absence of silence, the breathing, the snoring, the tossing and the turning. He couldn't hear any of it.

He threw back his sheets, realised he'd fallen asleep in his training clothes. Embarrassing but not uncommon. It meant he'd worked his butt off and that was something to be proud of. He couldn't even remember getting to sleep, climbing into his bunk and throwing back the sheets, yet he must have. His presence was evidence.

His head ached, more than that, clamoured for his attention. He slid out of his bunk, bare feet meeting the floor and he winced as the cold shot up through him. Pete tried to shove it out of his mind. Where were his boots? He couldn't remember getting here, never mind finding out where he'd thrown them.

What could he remember? Konda? If he thought, he could recall the smiling Burykian and the bitter taste in his mouth, but nothing concrete. Felt like it had happened to someone else, not him. Like he'd seen it on screen. Pete rose to his feet, shook his head like a dog. Cobwebs cluttered his brain, he needed to clear them away.

There was no curfew in the academy, they'd had that made clear to them. If they wanted to go wandering late at night, they were welcome to. After all, it had been pointed out to them the job in the future might entail that. However, should they be unable to complete their tasks the next day due to fatigue, the consequences would be harsh. He didn't even know what time it was, if the night had come or if the evening was still young. They'd taken his caller and his spirits when he'd entered, promised that he'd get them back when he left. That was reassuring, even if their absence wasn't. Those spirits had been with him a long time, being parted from them hurt.

Everyone had to make sacrifices. And if they were pleasant experiences, they wouldn't be called sacrifice, would they?

He pushed the door open, stepped out. Nothing. Nobody. The corridor was empty, one light flickered weakly, like it wanted to shine but the effort to do so was too much. Strange. The maintenance here normally was on top of things like that. If something broke, it was fixed within a few hours. A strange smell hung in the air, a scent he couldn't place. Coppery with a hint of a tang. He didn't know where it came from. Something felt off. One of the first things they'd told him was to listen to his instincts. If something looked like a bad situation, it probably was. Situation judgement was an important skill, more than any amount of unarmed combat or blaster training.

He decided to head for the canteen, see if there was anything there he could use. Trying to swallow was like sucking sandpaper, his mouth felt dry and his head continued to pound at him, demanding every inch of his attention. As much as he wanted to ignore it, he wondered how long he could fight a losing battle.

Some water would go down well. Maybe some food. Doubtful they'd be serving, but there were a few vending machines in there. Better than nothing. If he'd been asleep, he'd missed dinner last night. The food wasn't terrible here, it kept you going. All the various nutrients you'd ever need, masked with some attempt at flavour that nobody could recognise. Feeding time was about the only time he ever saw Theo smile. Once he'd asked him about it, received only a cryptic answer in exchange.

"Better than I got when I was growing up."

He didn't like to think about that. Ever since the revelation about his heritage, Theo had been touchier than normal. Anyone who mentioned Cyris or Cyria to him better watch out. He was too subtle, just a little too clever to get caught retaliating in the classroom, he waited until they were practicing unarmed combat. A few blows would be harder than normal, just a little naughty in their placement. He shouldn't have been surprised Theo had turned into a dirty little bastard of a fighter.

Pete turned the corner, saw the man before he saw him. He froze, realised any little movement could betray him. The man had his back to him, a blaster rifle pointed at the ground. His armour didn't look Unisco issue. He'd seen it in the armoury, wrong colour, wrong style. Past him, scarlet stained the wall, a thick gout of it and he realised he knew what the smell was. He'd missed the body at first, saw it perched at the base of the stain, eyes wide open and unseeing. He couldn't see who it was, saw the barest hint of a twitch in the armed man's neck and he went for him.

Too late he saw Pete coming for him, the rifle was coming up even as Pete hit him with his shoulder, the other man might be bigger, but the element of surprise had won out. The rifle hit the ground, knocked aside and Pete watched him stagger back.

"Don't give them a chance to recover!"

They had a guest instructor for the day, Tod Brumley himself had come to the Iaku academy, currently stood watching them go through their paces. Pete never would have guessed Brumley held a position like this. Someone had told him he'd recently been promoted to overseeing all the academies and recruitment, currently he was checking them all out to see they passed muster, he wasn't sure if it was true or not. Yet there he was.

They'd drawn the short straw that he'd be stepping in on their unarmed combat session, it didn't help that Brumley looked like a fighter. Even in his suit, he towered over Pete. He could have sat on Theo's shoulders and he might still have only just reached eye level with Brumley.

It wasn't a fight. Not in any sort of recognisable sense. At the same time, they'd been warned to train at their maximum, to treat it as if the danger were real. Train like their lives depended on it to survive. Because one day, they might.

He'd caught Roberts flat in the chest, hit him with the heel of his hand and knocked him back. He hadn't seen it coming, had watched him rub the sore area with an annoyed look.

"You, boy! Jacobs!"

He straightened up a little, fought the urge to salute. It wasn't that sort of academy. You showed your respect in other ways. "Yes, sir?"

Still that though. You gave them the appropriate form of address without hesitation. That was just great preparation for the future ahead. That had also been a lesson. Kiss ass. Get ahead. Disturbingly vivid in the way it had been described then, but it had stuck. That was the art of teaching, he'd guessed. Get your point across and make sure they remember it.

"Did you hear what I said? Don't give them a chance to recover. You get an opening, keep hitting them until they can't get back up. In the field, you'd be dead by now." He made a blaster shape with his fingers, pointed it at him. "Bang. You understand me?"

He nodded, chewing over the words as he studied him, then looked back towards Dan Roberts. He still had his hand on his sternum, his irritation hadn't faded. He wondered if it was directed at Pete for landing the blow or himself for not blocking it. "Sir, yes, sir!"

He staggered, and Pete didn't stop. That would be a very bad idea right now, the rifle might be on the ground, but he had other weapons on his belt, a blaster pistol and what looked like some sort of knife. Knife training had been the simplest lesson of them all. If you fight someone with a knife, don't let them get into a position where they can use it on you or you'll regret it.

He'd go with the basics, hit him again, shoulder to the stomach. Unrefined but effective. Some of the instructors made actual fighting look like shadow fighting, a display of art and poise. They made it look simultaneously deadly and beautiful. He raised his fists, jabbed out twice towards the man's face, tagged him and watched him go down.

Don't give them a chance to recover.

The element of surprise could win him this fight and he didn't want to squander the opportunity. Even as the man tried to scramble back to his feet, he was on top of him, raining blows into his unprotected face. Best area to hit him. He didn't fancy the chances of bare fist against body armour. That'd be a sure way to maim himself.

Blood stained his knuckles, he'd felt cartilage smash minutes ago, chokes lapsed into silence and he was sure that the last few had been unnecessary. He was breathing, but not well, the laboured gasps of a man not dead yet but on his way

Always be sure. Too much is more than too little.

Had he just made his first kill? He stood up, not entirely sure, just knew it was scary how quick it had happened. Pete blinked, felt the bile course through him, threatening to overspill. It wanted to come out, he fought it just as hard as he'd fought for his life seconds ago, determined that he wouldn't upchuck the contents of his last meal. He didn't feel guilty. The scene had told no lies, it didn't take a genius to work out what had gone down here, the man had deserved to die. He glanced at the body. Hadn't known who it was before, hadn't even realised the gender. Now he had the chance. Professor Melane, blood the same colour as her hair staining the ugly mess her throat had become.

Poor bitch. He looked at her one last time, turned his attention towards the man he'd killed. He wasn't twitching anymore. He was a goner, if he'd ever seen one. He'd seen Sharon's body, she'd looked a lot more peaceful than this guy had. The funeral guy had done great work with her. This bastard wouldn't be afforded that honour. If he'd killed Melane, how many others had they taken with her? How many more of them were here?

Questions. He wasn't going to get the answers stood here in a corridor feeling sorry for himself. They always spoke about how duty didn't call, duty demanded. Right now, it demanded that he do what needed to be done. He might be the last one left, they might have missed him through his own fortune and he couldn't pass that chance up.

He was the last one alive. He had to make that count for something. If he didn't, then the training was for nothing.

He bent, picked up the blaster rifle he'd knocked away from his foe. It was an unfamiliar weapon, an awkward shape and boxy. Nothing he'd had the chance to practice with. They had trained with rifles, if briefly. Far more focus had been devoted to the pistols, now that was a weapon he felt confident with. He continued to search, drew out the pistol and the knife from the dead man, several other charge packs for the blasters. They'd come ready for war.

Little did they know, Pete thought, that he was going to take the war to them. He checked the rifle, ran the basics. Safety off, charge pack loaded, ready to be fired. Blaster pistol in his waistband, knife in his pocket, he took that first step, before wondering if the dead man's boots would fit him.

Come to Unisco, they'd said. Learn how to fight the good fight, defend the world from those who'd wish it harm. Now he was reduced to robbing corpses in the middle of a war that people better trained than him had failed to stop.

His first initial thoughts had been to run around, weapons blazing like some sort of maniac, kill anyone who he came across. He'd found it disturbingly easy to kill already, had to force himself away from memories of the sounds and the smells that had assaulted him as he'd beaten the man. He'd not just killed him, he'd snuffed him out. He'd taken the lessons to heart and he'd made sure that he wasn't going to get back up.

Could he do it again. That hadn't been an option the first time. It was him or me, Pete reminded himself. If he hadn't acted, he'd be dead. The shots would have hammered him to the ground, the last thing he'd have seen would have been the enemy stood over him as he went for the killing shot. The rifle trembled in his hand, he clutched it harder, determined to cut the shaking out. It wasn't bothering him, he told himself.

That had been a fight. If he turned the corner, saw one of them stood unaware, could he pull the trigger and watch him fall? He might never see that Pete had been the one to kill him, he'd die in the dark alone like a dog.

You never know what you're capable until it comes to it.

That sounded like a lesson they might have imparted here. Far from it, he could remember that Sharon had said that to him once. The words had stuck. She might never have said them to another human being in her life, but she'd said them to him. Him. Her only brother.

Thinking of her was a mistake. He couldn't afford to feel sorry for himself. That way lay failure. Only one thing that drove him on more than desire for success, the fear of failure. He wouldn't allow himself to die here. He'd avenge those who had died here, honour their memories by giving their deaths purpose.

He'd cooled down a little after that, realised that storming out looking for a fight would bring nothing but that which he desired. It only took one stray shot, one alarm and anyone who wanted to kill him would be down to join in the fracas. It'd be a Peter Jacobs free-for-all. He didn't have unlimited ammunition, he couldn't fight them all. There could be a hundred men.

What he needed was some sort of advantage, a way to work out where they were and what they were doing here, a way to see if there were any survivors or what sort of force was being marshalled against him.

The security centre it was then. Part of him wondered if subconsciously he'd already been heading there. It made sense. It was well fortified, enough weapons to hold out there until reinforcements came, recording equipment that covered the whole academy. It was his best bet on a night when the simplest of gambles could either pay off or see him go home dead.

Melodrama much, Pete?

He grinned to himself at his own quip, let the smile fade away into a grimace. He couldn't allow himself to joke around now. He had to take this seriously. Anything less wasn't good enough.

He'd never been inside the security centre before, cadets weren't permitted in there under regular circumstances. He bit back bitter laughter at that, circumstances couldn't get much less regular than these. He'd seen inside, glanced through a crack in the door when he'd seen Hans walking through. He knew where it was though, he'd been here at the academy long enough to have the advantage of the ground. Whatever they might have in numbers, they couldn't match that.

In battle, one uses every advantage one can get. How can you make the most of what you have and undermine what your enemy has that you don't?

All these little quotes had their uses. He'd thought them a little twee at the time, simple and not much use. In the classroom, they might have felt that way. Here in the field, they felt like they might be the difference between success and failure.

Several times now, he had passed dull black eyes that made up the lenses of the equipment watching the entire academy. He wondered if he was being watched even as he made his way to their hub. That'd just blow the element of surprise, wouldn't it?

He'd come too far. He needed to keep going. It felt like he was repeating those words to himself, just five little words but they'd become his life mantra. Just keep moving forward. Worry about what comes next after.

If they knew where he was, they'd have come for him. Surely! He couldn't see that there was any benefit in them letting him roam free like this. If those videocams were recording his location, they'd surely be closing in on him. Attacking the Unisco academy might be suicidal, but the way they'd planned it out so far didn't reek of stupidity.

He'd made it to within sight of the door when the first shots hit the ground at his feet, kicking up chips of stone. Pete bellowed, a guttural battle cry, and he brought the blaster up, sprayed hot laser out in front of him. Running backwards, firing an unfamiliar weapon while being shot at wasn't something they'd ever prepped him for.

Suck it up!

He hit cover, heart pounding and the weapon still shaking in his hands. Fuck, fuck, fuck, fuck! He chanted it under his breath, couldn't keep them from spilling out. There was a shooter out there, someone had known he'd come here. Realisation dawned on him like a kick to the chest. They hadn't come to find him because they'd known he'd come to them. Why chase when you can lure into a trap? He felt like a prize idiot, he clearly hadn't learned anything of use during the last months, other than how to do the dumbest thing he could without hesitation.

Idiot!

He closed his eyes, let the shame bundle over him. His head hit the wall, he let it bounce once, twice. A sigh slipped his lips, laser fire still hammered the structure behind him. They couldn't hit him. They didn't care that he'd fucked up, they just wanted to kill him. Tie up that loose end, put him down and then they could…

Do what exactly? They'd devoted this time to setting him a trap but why tackle the Unisco academy anyway? Killing cadets was a good reason, deplete your enemy's resources but it felt like a foolhardy excuse to waste troops. They couldn't have taken this place easily. Approaching from the ground, it was well defended across treacherous pastures. He knew that, they made all the cadets run across it. An invading army would have trouble, it might make it but not without heavy casualties. The defences were there, not just the visible stuff but the armaments you couldn't see as well. Aerially, it was fortified.

Unisco didn't screw around when it came to defend what was theirs. They'd made it that way and they intended to keep it that way.

Pete fired back, blindly shooting back around the corner. Didn't know if he'd hit anyone, but the enemy shots subsided, the silence blissful. He exhaled, slid closer to the edge.

Never stick your head up, they will shoot it off. This isn't like the serials. You try to be a one-man hero, you will get killed. Caution trumps carnage every time.

This would be easier, he thought, if the rifle were smaller. The awkwardness in his hands hadn't subsided, trying to keep it ahead of him, trying to keep it level and still, pointed at anything that might jump out at him, all while pressed against a wall, he wasn't having fun with it.

Nothing about this was supposed to be fun, he reminded himself. The barrel was around the corner, he couldn't see a damn thing. Couldn't hear anything. He wondered whether to peek, check the coast was clear. His ears hadn't told him anything untoward, hadn't heard a body hit the ground, the clatter of a rifle falling from hands, nor had he heard any more shots come his way. They could be patient.

He made his decision to move, span out of cover and went for the opposite wall, his heart screaming with silent prayer. He brought his weapon up, saw two of them and fired a cutting burst in their directions. If he hit them, he didn't know, hit the other side of the T-shaped corridor. One of them let out a groan, he thought he heard them fall, punched the air in triumph. Result. Maybe he was dead. He didn't care.

That realisation shocked him, didn't have time to dwell as laser tore through the wall ahead, leaving grooves in the concrete.

Don't think! Do!

He didn't even know where half of these sayings had come from, if he'd heard them and absorbed them, if he was giving himself a mental gee-up or if some part of him was doing all of it. He wanted out of here, unharmed and alive. He'd do anything. He couldn't stop fighting.

In fights, people died. They'd attacked. He'd defended himself. That was the sobering truth of it all. It was war. It wasn't murder. Killing someone in the streets couldn't be compared to this. It'd take a professional idiot to think that they were even close to the same thing.

He shot back, best he could, there'd been two stood there and out in the open, he risked retaliation. He dropped down to his haunches, made himself a smaller target, glanced off towards his left. Couldn't see him at this angle. Closer. Nothing. Edged his face even closer. He saw the boot of the man he'd killed.

He'd killed twice! Twice! There wasn't even a twitch in him. That was good. He couldn't get back up. No sign of the other one, he heard a door slam shut and the unmistakable click of a lock moving into place.

Not good. There wasn't another way in there. He'd made it his goal and if he was locked out, then he'd failed before he even started.

"Fuck!" he shouted. It looked petulant, he didn't care. He raised his hand, extended his middle finger to the videocam. Maybe it'd lure them out. Perhaps. If only. It'd be nice, but he doubted they'd be that easily manipulated. Nobody was that stupid.

He needed another plan. This one had turned out to be a bust.

Part of him had dwelled on marching up to the door and kicking it, spraying his weapon into its frame and body until something had given. It would have been futile, he realised. Doubtless so important a door had been reinforced to protect against an attack like that. More than that, he might as well announce his presence completely, let them know that he was on the other side. The room was large, the door was not. Should he shoot through it, assuming he even could, it'd betray his position. They might even be awaiting his approach, wait for him to put his hand out, yank it open and blast him in the guts.

He hadn't studied the room, didn't know if there was another way in or not. Wouldn't be much of a secure room if you could just head upstairs and blow your way in through the ceiling. Besides, he had no explosives. Or any knowledge about explosives beyond 'pull this and throw'.

They hadn't covered that yet. He'd heard something about learning to defuse them, that didn't sound like fun. Theo, in his usual abrasive fashion, had stated that it'd be a challenge. How were they going to replicate the pressure and the circumstance of something that could blow up in their face?

Pete wasn't sure he should have challenged them like that. They had too many tricks up their sleeves, the instructors, they gave the impression that they'd prepared for any circumstances that might be thrown against them.

They hadn't for this though. This had caught them on the hop. They were dead, Pete guessed. Dead or captured. They'd been the last line of defence and they'd failed. A sobering thought. What chance did he have?

Better than them. Nobody would dispute that. Alone but alive trumped thousands of silent dead.

He'd decided to make for the armoury, extra weapons and armour felt like they'd give him a better chance of survival than stood staring at a door that wasn't going to open for him. He knew the route from here, had been in the armoury many times. Part of their duties involved cleaning and maintaining the weapons they removed, making sure they were put back in their proper place. He liked the silence in the armoury, he'd had some good times in there. Him and Dan Roberts, him and Tamale, even a laugh with Dominic Hill. In there with Theo, the silence was prevalent, he wouldn't have minded talking, but any effort was met with grunts that started out polite but grew less so over the passage of the hour.

It'd give him a tactical advantage at least; the first plan had been solid but a non-starter. Therefore, the second plan would have to suffice. Bemoaning what might have been might be nice, but it had little use in the scheme of things. Better to get on with it.

If he survived this, that sense of pragmatism felt like it'd serve him well. If he survived it.

Mind on the mission, Jacobs, he admonished himself. You let your mind wander and you'll fall into your own grave.

He ran into trouble outside the armoury, wondered if they were being guided to where he looked like he was going. They had access to the videocams, it might not have been impossible. This time, there had to be five of them, blaster fire screamed towards him, he hurled himself out the way. He hit the ground, rolled into a crouch and pointed his weapon. He felt his finger tighten against the trigger, stock crash into his shoulder as the weapon kicked to life. They scattered, their attention solely on survival as he turned to run.

More behind him. Too many to kill, they all had the same sort of rifle he did. If he stood his ground, those behind him would blast him in the back. He glanced to the left, to the right, to the doors. They crashed open, more rifles pointed at him.

Shit!

His own weapon felt painfully inadequate. As one, they advanced on him, footsteps beating the floor in unison. It sounded like the knell of drums, the oncoming death. His eyes darted back and forth, there had to be a way out. He hadn't lowered the weapon, wondered if they'd give him a quick death if he didn't.

Drawing things out had never been his style. Either do or die. That saying felt painfully uncomfortable in these circumstances, he shot them a grin. Maybe he could lure them into fighting him in hand-to-hand combat, one at a time. Better that than death by firing squad. At least that way, he'd stand a chance. A small one, but larger than the eternal struggle faced by man versus blaster. That score was tipped in favour of the man with the blaster come these circumstances.

The voice that rang out startled him into dropping his weapon, fingers slid open and he watched it clatter to the ground. He was lucky it hadn't discharged.

"Freeze simulation!"

He heard the words, brought himself to a halt as weapons didn't fire. Nobody moved, except him, a solitary figure. Now he wasn't fighting for his life, he took the chance to look at the faces of his enemies.

Not enemies. They bore the faces of people he knew, cadets and instructors in the academy, expressions contorted into anger and rage as they stared down the sights of their blasters at him. Dan Roberts was closest, his face frozen in time. Pete reached out, placed a hand against his face. Solid but not solid. His hand slid through the skin, moved about an inch and then stopped, whatever was underneath spongey with a hint of wire.

He knew the voice, turned to see the great bulk of the instructor behind him. He didn't know where he'd come from, only that he hadn't been there a moment ago. Behind him, Konda stood, an expression of serenity on his face, arms folded behind his back.

"Not bad, Mister Jacobs," Paddington said. "Not bad indeed."

"What is this?" The question felt insipid, he couldn't quite get his head around what had just happened. He shook his head, trying to clear his thoughts. None of it had been real, he got that much.

"A simulation," Paddington said. "Some of my best work, in fact. I told you about cold and hot blood. This is part of the test. A recent one. We used to, in past years, organise it pitting other cadets against the lone survivor scenario. It taught teamwork on one hand, survival skills on the other. It lost effectiveness over time. When you know about it, you are prepared. This is much better. Cuts down on injuries as well."

"It was a test? You were testing me."

"He wasn't," Konda said. "We both were. Part of a psychological profile I like to build on cadets who come through this academy. How you cope, how you adapt, how long it takes for you to throw away everything you value."

"Huh," He didn't know what to say to that. "So, it wasn't real? Any of it?" He felt a bit of an idiot, that was saying the least about it. "Nobody got hurt?"

"Nobody."

"Who did I kill outside the dorms?"

"He's not dead. Just a simulant frame that doubles as a living target. Uses a half endroid program to follow basic instructions..." Paddington said before shutting up. "He was modelled on Cadet Jameson, I believe."

"No wonder it was satisfying." Pete managed to find a grin from somewhere. He saw Konda tap something down on his pad, his brow furrowed in dismay. How complimentary would that be, he wondered. "How did I not realise it wasn't real? Everything felt so..."

"That'd be subterfuge on my part," Konda said, more than a little sheepish, judging by his expression. "Did you enjoy the tea, Cadet Jacobs?"

"Remind me never to accept a drink from you again," Pete said, not entirely joking. Konda only laughed. "So how did I do?"

"We'll get back to you on that," Paddington said. "Everything looks good. You did everything that could reasonably be expected from you. You fought when you had to, you didn't crack under pressure..."

"You made plans," Konda added. "You went for the security centre, a defendable position where you'd be able to gather intelligence. When that didn't work, you made a backup plan and went for the armoury."

"I didn't win though," Pete said. "I mean, if this had been real..." He threw out a hand, gestured towards the endroids or whatever they were. "I'd have been dead."

"Cadet Jacobs," Paddington said. "Do you want me to tell you what the point of the exercise was, or do you want to hazard a guess at why it ended like it did?"

He didn't know, or at least he didn't think he did. He wanted to shrug, instead shook his head in defeat. "I assume there is some purpose to your madness."

Konda and Paddington looked at each other, then at him. "If we both came to attack you now, Cadet Jacobs, what do you think would happen?" Konda asked. "Keep in mind your training isn't complete and we both have many years of combat experience on you."

"I'd fight," Pete said, making sure the defiance laced his voice.

"Yes, you would," Paddington said. "The odds are that you would lose. We could come and beat the shit out of you every day for the rest of your time here and chances are that you wouldn't be able to stop us."

The more he thought about it, the more he realised that it was probably true.

"I mean, you'd try to defend yourself and you'd probably still come out badly. Remember, we teach you everything you know but not necessarily everything we know," Paddington said with a smile.

"Always there are those things that you can't deal with. But you know what?"

Pete didn't. He felt more and more stupid by the second, an uncomfortable feeling. Maybe that tea was still messing with his mind, now the adrenaline had stopped pumping, his head felt woolly. Like a bad hangover, his brain rough around the edges.

"We give you the best chance we can. We can't prepare for everything. There's always going to be things outside of your control. No matter what you do, the little things will seek to screw you over. You know what the harshest truth about this job is, Cadet Jacobs?" Paddington smiled at him, not a pleasant smile. He'd seen sharks that looked friendlier. "You can't always win, no matter how hard you train. And the price for defeat is always high. All we can do is even up your odds the best we can."

That smile faded from his face, might as well have been scrubbed off. "Dismissed, Cadet. Return to your dorm. We'll be in touch with your full assessment."

Chapter Fifteen. Running Blind.

"We have certain items that we all require to be kept free from hands that might misuse them. If anyone is going to misuse them, it will be us. Therefore, they need to be hidden securely. One of you will be placed in charge of keeping them secure, will report only to me as to their location. The rest of you will never know. I name Lord Tarene as the Keeper of Curiosities. Anything we cannot use, is to go to him for safekeeping. He is our gatherer, our collector, our weaponeer. His is the finger on the trigger of the blaster we hold to our enemies' heads."

Vezikalrus, Dark King of the Cavanda making a proclamation to the princes and the lords of the collective.

"Well, we certainly suspected," Perrit said, looking up at them. They'd projected a holographic image of her into their speeder, both eager to hear what she had to say. The credit sniffer grinned at them, stifled a yawn. The image wasn't the greatest quality, picking out the finest details was harder than it sounded, but she looked tired.

Two days since they'd forwarded the information from Lola Myers to her and she'd come up a winner. He couldn't say he was surprised. Credits made the kingdoms run smoothly, Unisco's financial division was the one that made sure those credits didn't arrange bumps in the road. Too many were swayed by the possibilities of easy credits, they saw them, and it distorted their priorities, made people re-think what they were meant to do. Perrit had been investigating the Coppingers, mainly through Reims and other companies linked to them, for months now.

"Suspected?" Pree asked. "What did you get, Bev?"

"A lot of the credits Harvey Rocastle was paid came from a subdivision of Reims that since was closed down when Reims was seized by the Senate under the Reclamation Act. The credits stopped coming to him via that source, redirected to his sister via his instructions. There's all that information in here, a requisition of transfer, an approval of transfer and one of receiving."

"So, despite her saying she didn't want it, she was happy to take it," Wade said. He didn't know what to make of Lola Myers, he'd believed her when she said she didn't like her brother. Rocastle seemed like the sort of man that it'd be hard to enjoy a family dinner with.

Pree shrugged. "Can't say. Sometimes people say one thing and do another. Whatever helps them sleep at night, right?"

He couldn't disagree with that. Principle might sound like a fine thing at first. Turning down credits because you didn't like where they came from was a noble thing to do. Enough time passed, enough desperation came, a perspective might change. That was just people being people. Couldn't blame them, couldn't condone them.

"She didn't spend them though," Perrit offered. "Just kept them all stockpiled in a drawer. Wealthiest cabin in the Burykian forests by the looks of it. She could have bought the damn forest for everything here. Over a million credits."

Wade and Pree looked at each other. They hadn't expected that much. More than that, Wade found himself starting to wonder about Lola Myers' mental state. That many credits could have kept her mother alive and comfortable a lot longer than her current circumstances dictated. A conscience was nice, but family was family.

"That's a lot of credits," Pree said. "All from Rocastle?"

The small image of Perrit nodded. "Yep. Seven-fifty from Reims, two-fifty in the last six months from a different feeder company." Her face broke into a grin, she did a quick little two-step where she was. It made Wade smile. "One that we didn't know about. Constauri Holdings. They paid the credits directly to Ms Myers, there's one of their buildings just a few miles away from where you are. Closest building to her."

"That makes no sense," Pree said. "If this is the closest building to her, he knows where she's picking up her credits, why hasn't he come to find her? Since she was so worried about it in the first place, that's why she hid out in the Yulionian forest."

"Maybe he doesn't care," Wade offered. "Maybe he's not really looking for her and she's just running paranoid."

"Maybe. It's a big area this. Not densely populated," Pree said. "But definitely a lot of effort to search every individual place. Maybe he hasn't devoted his time to it yet. Maybe Coppinger won't let him. I don't think we should be too worried about Ms Myers. She seemed more than capable of handling herself, my read of her."

Wade shrugged. "I don't think she'd accept our help even if we offered it. Think we should?"

Pree shook her head. "I think when her mother dies, she'll be gone. Nobody's ever going to hear from her again. She'll hit the wind, probably burn the cabin and change her name. It's what I'd do."

"She's not you though," Wade said. Down below them, Perrit cleared her throat, let out a little cough that caught both their attention.

"Regardless, Constauri Holdings has quite a reputation. It's owned by Coppinger, very distantly removed, we had to dig for hours before we found that out. She's not the sole owner as well, the other's a man named Allison. We haven't found much out about him, just that he doesn't seem to have a life beyond a legal existence. No evidence that he and Coppinger ever met. We've got an address, near his place of work but nothing much more to go on. Listed as his place of residence but he barely seems to be there according to one of the neighbours."

"You got in touch with one of his neighbours?" Pree asked. It wasn't uncommon, she just couldn't picture Perrit doing it. The other woman shrugged, let out a snort.

"Of course not. That's what we have assistants for."

That. That was what Pree had come to expect from her. The financial division thought that they were a cut above, in her experience. Because they could spot a credit on the ground from the top floor of a high-rise building, they thought they were the hottest shit going. Divines forbid Perrit should make her own damn contact with useful leads.

"Not seen him for months. Either he travels a lot or he's dead. It'd be one hells of a cover for Coppinger to hide behind a dead partner. Someone associated with Constauri is funnelling credits out to fund the Coppinger war effort. When Reims was captured, all the assets were stripped. It was a big useless carcass of a company by the time we got our hands on it." The hologram of her shrugged. "Many piranhas can have the same effect as a shark. Small companies if they're run right and you have a collection of them can be just as effective. More so."

"Spare us financial conspiracy one-oh-one," Wade said. "We know this theory, we read your book?"

"You did?" Perrit looked surprised, a hint of colour flushing into her cheeks. "I mean, thank you. How was it?"

Wade said nothing, glanced towards Pree who smirked at him. You got yourself in this, you can get out of it. It had gone around Unisco in recent weeks that Perrit had released a book, plenty of agents who knew her had read it to see if they were mentioned in it. She'd told Pree it was a thriller set in the world of high finance, the story of a loan shark seeking to acquire flagging companies through shady deals and legitimise himself. Pree hadn't glanced at it. Wasn't her thing.

"I, uh, I enjoyed it," Wade said. "I enjoyed the character assassination of Mallinson in it. I assume that was who the…"

"Yes!" she said, almost yelling. Pree rolled her eyes. The joy there was something she didn't want to deal with right now. Or ever, for that matter. She didn't care about Beverly Perrit wanting to be an international bestseller, she cared about her doing her damn job.

"A little tasteless," she offered. "I mean, Mallinson… Couldn't you have found someone marginally less dead to insult?"

"Hey, he wasn't dead when I started writing!" She'd touched a nerve there, she saw, hid the smile. Somehow, she got the feeling that she wasn't the first one who'd said this to Perrit. Rumour had it, Brendan King hadn't been impressed.

"Bev, send us everything that you have on Constauri," Wade said. "Send us the file on this Allison fellow as well, there might be something we can use. Forewarned is forearmed." He rubbed his chin. "Good luck with the second book."

He tipped her the wink, a little shamelessly, Pree thought. As the hologram faded, Wade let out a huge sigh and sagged, letting his head rest against the leather.

"Did you really read her book?" Pree asked, her curiosity finally getting the better of her. She'd known he was lying all the way through the conversation, he'd done it skilfully though. It was doubtful Perrit had picked up on it.

"Nope," Wade said. He gave her an uneasy grin, the sort of smile that had gotten Perrit's attention, Pree noted. Doubtful he was trying to ingratiate himself to her, she didn't go for that. Wade wasn't her type. Perrit might fall for it, but they lived in different words. In her world, Perrit would be dead in minutes.

"Knew it."

"Just parroted what I heard someone else say about it," he said. He didn't sound proud of it, just a statement of fact. "I'm glad she interrupted me over it when she did, I was running out of compliments."

You can't bullshit a bullshitter, Wade, she thought with a smile. And in that regard, nobody at Unisco did it better than her. Her training in that regard had started long before she'd walked through the academy doors at Iaku.

They'd studied the files of one Robert Allison, found nothing of use in there. The image wasn't flattering, a gaunt-looking man with thick dark hair and the sort of smile that made children run screaming for their mothers. Something about him looked familiar, she couldn't place it despite the unease gnawing at the back of her mind.

Pree didn't like that feeling, the uncertainty gnawing at her. The Unisco academy taught them that there would always be things out of your control that you couldn't affect. Her other life had told her that was complete horseshit. If things slip away from you, tighten your grip and bring them closer to you.

Two conflicting views with her between them. Two sets of rules, she'd tried to live her life between the two of them, neither one nor the other. It would have driven anyone else insane. Keeping everything bottled up inside her, hidden from sight. That was the true challenge.

Maybe she'd seen Allison somewhere before. Across a room, on a viewing screen. What was it?

"Something up?" Wade asked, cutting into her thoughts. She shook her head. Couldn't shake that feeling about Allison.

"No," she said. "Just thinking." She didn't elaborate into what. It wasn't any of his business, he likely wouldn't understand anyway.

Constauri then. She'd considered the possible angles, decided it was the more likely option. Wade would too, eventually. Couldn't chase a man who was little more than a ghost. Allison was in the wind, ergo his company was the best place to start. Besides, co-owning a company with Claudia Coppinger was no indication of complicity. It was possible to be duped by her. She'd fooled a lot of people for a long time.

She studied her partner, could see the gears twisting in his head as he considered all the angles, working them out gradually. He'd get there.

The company sounded interesting, a no-mark place in a no-mark city. There wasn't even much around it to arouse suspicion. She read some more, smiled. That made perfect sense, if you wanted to funnel thousands of credits around without suspicion falling on you.

"I've never heard of it," she said. "You'd have thought Perrit would have mentioned it."

Wade shrugged. "I don't even want to consider what sort of security a place like that is going to have. I don't think that you're high on the priority list to know about them. I don't think you could afford their fees for a start."

She would have snapped back, retorted in anger, had she realised it wasn't worth it. He was right. As satisfying it might be for him to hear her say that, she wasn't going to give him the pleasure. They moved in different circles. Perrit might have been able to tell them more about Constauri Holdings but she wasn't here. Getting in touch with her had been hard enough in the first place, doing it a second time was unlikely. Everyone had their own places to be, their time was always more valuable than other peoples. They'd have to work this one out for themselves.

They could do that, Pree reasoned. They were both smart enough, she figured, both well-trained. It wasn't beyond them. Although maybe if Wade hadn't been too busy flirting with Perrit, they might have gotten the story from her.

"Robert Allison's pride and joy," Wade read aloud. "Constauri was established twenty-five years post-Unification with the aid of numerous silent investors who wished for an establishment to do business with that they could rely on. Originally pitched as a superior bank, Constauri soon evolved into investment, property development and even security, with several private vaults on site within which many of their clients have stored property since their inception. Their clientele contains the names of some of the most wealthy and influential people in the five kingdoms…" He paused, cleared his throat. "Document is a little out of date."

She'd noticed that, chose not to comment, instead gestured impatiently for him to continue.

"… Which is suspected where Claudia Coppinger comes into play. She inherited the family business early, it's not unreasonable to suspect that going into a partnership with Allison might have been one of the first things she did. It is supposition though. What has long been suspected and unable to be proven one way or the other…" He shrugged, rolled his eyes. "There's a reason Perrit hasn't made it on the bestseller list with writing like that."

"I'll come over there and read it myself," Pree said, finding it her own turn to roll her eyes. She didn't need to listen to Wade do little asides he thought were funny. She wanted to hear the facts and the theories, not him trying to do his best impression of Brennan bloody Frewster.

"What has long been suspected is that Constauri has been involved in offences of a criminal nature, credit laundering, transference of credits for illegitimate activities… Huh, says that they were the ones tasked with handling Lucas Hobb's finances, at least until he was taken off the board." He must have seen the look on her face, shrugged at her scowl. "I'll tell you the story sometime. It's a good one. Nick got drunk and told me one time."

"Heard the name, don't know why it's relevant. Hobb died a long time ago." She curled her lip in disgust. Traitorous Unisco agents disgusted her. Lucas Hobb, the Wandering Man. Gone, but not entirely forgotten.

"In short, they're a middleman. They do all this, though nobody's ever been able to prove it. Coppinger picked a good partner. Normally you'd need all sorts of warrants and requisitions to enter the building as a Unisco agent," Wade said. "That amount of wealth buys you a lot of insulation from the law."

Sure did, she thought. There was a reason that the rich managed to get away with murder and the poor had the book thrown at them for minor misdemeanours. That was the society the five kingdoms had built, it was the sort of society that Claudia Coppinger banged on about wanting to tear down.

When the richest woman in the kingdoms spoke about making things more equal without giving insights into her process at doing so, hells when she ploughed her own credits into building an army rather than investing in social care, it was hard to take her seriously.

They both looked at each other, smiled. "It's a good thing then that since this Coppinger crisis started," Wade said, smugness personified in his voice. "Normal circumstances have gone out the window. We have evidence that Constauri has a connection to Claudia Coppinger, more than just circumstantial. Those payments from Claudia Coppinger to Harvey Rocastle to Lola Myers via Constauri…"

"You know what I think?" Pree said. "I think we should have a look around Constauri. Preferably after everyone's gone home. See if we can get a look at Coppinger's vault. She must have one there. It makes sense. Find something that can break all reasonable doubt and throw the book at both Constauri and Coppinger."

Normally, anything they found on the scene without a warrant to investigate would be ignored in court as illegally obtained evidence from a place they had no business being anywhere near. The rules had been relaxed. The Senate wanted the swiftest possible resolution. Anything Coppinger-related was fair game.

Do whatever you need to do to resolve this, had been the message. The rules had been relaxed.

Of course, getting it might well prove to be a different matter, she thought with a smile.

Statistically, there was a reason why most attempts to break in, rob and get away with the contents of a bank vault ended in miserable failure. What made Wade so sure that this was going to be a success was that most attempts to break in there were doomed to fail because they had no right to be there. There'd be people trying to stop them from entering, from taking, from leaving. Every step was a hurdle to be overcome. You might surpass one, but to do them all was a challenge.

This would be different. They'd spoken to their superiors, they'd gotten approval, they'd even had some tech mailed to them to help them get in there. Anything and everything they'd need. The word from above was that they thought their lead was solid and they needed a win. There'd been some talk about some sort of violent fuck-up in Canterage, Wade had wanted to know more about it but been given the usual line of 'need to know' BS. He'd found himself wondering how much of it his friend was in the middle of. Violent situations did seem to find a way of inserting themselves straight into the middle of Nicks' life.

No slight against Pree, he wished Nick was with him. He knew he could trust him. Pree, he felt like he could trust, yet there was something between them. An invisible wedge warning him that they weren't equals. Not as partners. Not as humans. He was being ridiculous, he knew that. Pree was a fully minted Unisco agent, she had an impressive number of successful operations on her record. They didn't nickname her the Spectre for nothing. Get in, do the job, get out before anyone knew she was there. Statistically, you couldn't ask for a better person to have your back.

She didn't normally work with partners, despite Unisco doctrine. So why had she asked for him to come on this mission with him?

"Constauri Holdings," Pree said, leaning back in her seat, letting the scope drop into her lap with a dull thump. "Doesn't look like much, does it?"

Wade said nothing, glanced at the timepiece on his wrist. They were entering within the next fifteen minutes, their window was going to present itself, and they needed to be ready. They both were armed, blasters strapped to their legs, dressed in black to mask themselves against the night. Security was not expected to be an issue. Anonymity was Constauri's greatest weapon. He'd seen banks that looked like castles and cathedrals, laced themselves in grandeur and then complained when people tried to rob them, successfully or not. If you felt the need to flaunt it, you couldn't complain when someone tried to take it from you. Always there would be those without to be jealous of those that had. Crime was a fast-growing business sometimes. There'd never be a limit on the number of applicants.

He said as much, Pree shrugged. "I'd still want something grander, but I know what you mean. Sometimes you want to balance image against security."

Wade glanced at her. "I never figured you to be the grand gesture type."

"Darling, they nicknamed me the fucking Spectre. You can't get much more of a grand gesture than that."

He laughed, let it die away as he glanced at the bag down at his feet. Everything they'd need for the mission. He was starting to jitter now, nothing unusual. Sometimes you got like this. Pre-mission nerves. They were good, he guessed. Reminded you to be sharp. You started to think you were invincible, you very quickly realised that you weren't when the first blast hit you. Nerves made you move that bit faster, made you react a little quicker, allowed you to live longer. A bonus in his book.

"True," he said. "As nicknames go, it's a good one."

"Never chose it," she said. "Never unwelcomed it. Think it was meant to be mean, it never quite worked out that way. You throw enough people together at the academy and some of them'll be assholes." Pree's face lit up in a smile. "That's the mark of success.

Taking that with which they'd like to beat you, what they perceive to be a weakness and making it a strength."

He couldn't argue with that. Glanced at his timepiece again, moved to tap a finger against it.

"It's not going to move any faster the more you look at it, you know," she said. "Relax. I can hear your heartbeat from here."

She didn't look worried, he noticed. She looked calmness personified, typical Prideaux Khan. Unfazed. Unworried. Maybe she was doing a better job of hiding it than he was. A lot better job.

"I'm not worried," he said quietly. "Just trying to think of anything we missed. There's the potential for a lot to go wrong."

"Relax," she said again. "I've got a good feeling about this. It's going to be a cinch." She cleared her throat, glanced out the window towards the building. Looked more like a warehouse than a bank, Wade thought. He couldn't see the wealthy rocking up here to make their deposits. Had to be more than met the eye when you got inside. He remembered it was more about storage than moving funds. That made sense.

His summoner beeped, Pree's did the same. He flipped it over, glanced at the screen. Two words but their impact bore deep.

Sixty seconds.

Nerves fading, he pushed the door open and scooped the bag up over his shoulder. Pree did the same, they slammed the doors shut behind them and started to run.

This sort of job required split-second timing. Somewhere high above them, a satellite had traced out their position in relation to the front doors of the building. They'd had their running time estimated from speeder to door, been given appropriate warning. Neither of them had dared park too close, just in case someone in there was suspicious of the vehicle. They'd agreed that they wanted to spend as little time exposed as possible.

A window had been fashioned, someone on Okocha's department had been set to hack Constauri's security system, illegal under normal circumstances. Again, desperate times led to rules being relaxed. Sixty seconds to get to the door. At the end of those sixty seconds, there'd be a five second window in which the locks would be temporarily disabled. Any longer, suspicion would be aroused. Anything less would look like a glitch in the system.

What wouldn't be a glitch would be the subtle disability of all electronic surveillance within the building. There was a lot of it, they'd both been informed, as they'd expected there would be. Leaving property with a bank was buying into the belief that it'd be well protected, and their security would pass muster if needed. Videocams would be the very minimum, they weren't a worry. Unisco techs had had years of practicing removing the activities of their agents from footage to preserve their identities. Most of them could do it in their sleep.

They made the run, a mad dash across two hundred feet of bare sidewalk in time to hear the lock click open. Pree grabbed the door, pulled it and they were inside. The lobby was dark, lights flashed on as they entered. Hands went for blasters, refrained from pulling them. Nobody. They were alone.

Better to be safe than sorry, Wade thought. Being jumpy might be embarrassing but you'd rather pull a weapon in surprise and not need it than the alternative.

Looking around, the realisation that it was a stark contrast to what they'd seen outside quickly dawned. This was more like it, he thought, checking out the black and white marbled floor, the huge desk towards the back of the room, a waiting area twice the size of his first apartment and probably better furnished. It had that look of wealth about it that the puritan in him found distasteful.

"Let's do this then," Pree said, adjusting the bag across her shoulders. Neither of them was happy about carrying them but it was a necessity. Sensor masking equipment wasn't small, it couldn't be hidden in a pocket, it was heavier than initially realised but the benefits were there for all to see. Complete biological concealment from all forms of surveillance. Last thing that they wanted to do was set an alarm off with their heat signature.

The summoner on the desk trilled and he trailed a hand out to snatch it up. "Yes?" He tried to keep the irritation out of his voice, only partially succeeded. He didn't like being disturbed at amidst his meditations. This time was his. A time to refocus, to dwell on his knowledge and to build on it. The best insights came during time alone with thoughts.

"Sir, there's been an incident at the Holdings."

His eye twitched, he closed it and felt the throb behind his eyelid. "Explain?"

"Only a brief one, but not like any we've seen before."

He employed good people. He made sure of that. Retained his anonymity when he did it, just like his building, but they reported to him when they needed to.

"Unusual," he said. If they'd not seen anything like it before, it could mean a great number of things. Some were troubling. Others were downright unsettling.

He reached out, grabbed his weapon and hooked it onto his belt. "Do you wish for us to alert local police, sir?"

"No," he said. Glancing around, his eyes fell on his mask. The skull burning in the sun, his mark of office stared at him in silence. "That won't be necessary. Thank you for informing me. I'll deal with it from here."

"Of course, sir. Good night."

Things felt disturbing, a shifting of the signs he sought. His instincts told him danger was afoot. Checking it wouldn't be a terrible idea. He never ignored his instincts and he'd never run from danger.

He wasn't about to start now. He reached for the mask, slid it in his coat and made for the exit.

They didn't talk as they made their way downstairs, a stairwell behind the main desk had been their point of egress. All good vaults were below ground, their intelligence had told them the same was true here. Part of the data packet that had been included in their brief showed them a floor plan, stolen off the Constauri mainframe. Not for the first time, Wade found himself truly indebted to the hackers working for Unisco. They did their job well, they'd be limited without them.

What they didn't have was the occupiers of each vault, although they'd found them easily enough, a series of eight numbered doors with each of them twice as tall as Wade, three times the size of Pree. The data packet hadn't mentioned who rented out which vault, that information beyond even their guys at short notice. Worse, they'd been told that the vault doors ran under a different system to the rest of the security, leaving it impossible to open them remotely.

Things could only get so easy, Wade thought, the two of them stood amidst the eight doors. One, two, three, four, five, six, seven, eight. He glanced back and forth, gauged each one. Maybe there was some sort of clue or crest. Nothing. Each sheet of steel was as blandly unidentifiable as the other, nothing to distinguish them from the other barring the numbers, hugely hewn copper shapes twisted into digits.

He looked at Pree. She shrugged. "I got nothing if you're expecting me to have some answers," she said. Each vault had a keypad and a fingerprint scanner next to them, those weren't too much of an issue. They had the technology that could beat them, with time, a scanner that could scan the keypads, pick residue off each key and work out which ones were used the most. It could duplicate the fingerprints as well, once the correct one had been found to operate the fingerprint verifier.

Time. It was going to be their problem. They didn't have an unlimited amount of it, certainly not enough to open every vault and check it manually. If they were still here when the staff started to arrive in the morning, there'd be trouble. At the very least, the mission would be jeopardised. Secrecy was their best ally here.

"Maybe it went in order of whomever got here first," Wade said. "First investor got vault one, second one got vault two…" He tailed off. They still didn't know who had signed up first. He closed his eyes, let his head hang. He let them slide open again, saw Pree smile at him.

"Keep them closed," she said. "If it helps. Just… Wade, just listen. Close your eyes and let your mind wander. Think about it all, see if any of them call to you. Use your instincts, and we'll try and work it out."

He tried to avoid scoffing too loudly. "That's terrible advice, Pree. I could do that and still get it wrong."

"You could," she said. "You know what isn't going to help? Standing here wringing our hands. Might as well at least try it. I trust my instincts. You should trust yours too."

Inwardly, she cursed him. Damnit Wade, why must you be so stubborn? Just go with what I say, we can do this. She'd already done it, she knew which one she was going for. One vault called to her, piqued her curiosity and she was going to push for it. Especially if Wade picked out the same one.

Baxter believed in him. She'd seen Wade's eyes when Coppinger had attacked him on Carcaradis Island, she'd heard the tales about how Baxter had taught him to heal himself. He had the gift. It was part of the reason she'd wanted him here. She wanted to see how much and how capable he was. So far, the results had been mixed. He had so much potential but all he wanted to do was shut himself away from it.

He'd closed his eyes again, she was relieved to see that. "Concentrate," she said, deliberately keeping her voice under her breath. She didn't want to distract him. "Just reach out. Feel, don't think."

"You sound like you know a lot about this," he said, keeping his eyes closed. "You want to try it if you're that damn good?"

She ignored that. Not least because she didn't have anything that wouldn't lead to questions she couldn't answer. "Don't listen to my words, listen to yourself," she said. "Hear what your heart has to say."

For the longest time, he didn't say anything, was so still that the only sign of life was the gentle fall and rise of his chest. At least he had control of his breathing, pointing that out to him would have led to even more questions.

Pree had made her choice, had already moved to get the scanner out of the bag. If Wade said door number five, she'd know for sure. Something screamed out at her about that door, might not be the one they wanted, but she got the impression it was worth seeing inside. Maybe she was imagining things. Maybe it'd be easier if she was.

His eyes opened, he turned on the spot until he came to rest against the fifth vault. She couldn't help noticing how proud he looked with himself "That one," he said.

Interesting.

Chapter Sixteen. The Trove.

"Ascension through the ranks of the Cavanda has always come from a position of strength, if you prove you are better than one currently incumbent, then you deserve their place. And of those you displace? Well, we have no need for weakness."

Lord Amalfus to Kyra Sinclair and Gideon Cobb some time ago.

She'd handed him the scanner under the proviso that since it was his choice, he could open it up. He'd not argued, she'd conveniently not mentioned she also thought there was something about that door, just watched him as he ran the scanner across the keypad. The system might be on a different network to the rest of the security, it didn't mean that they'd not been able to find out anything about it. The keypads operated under an eight-digit code, the scanner would find the most pressed eight buttons and feed them into a code cycler which Wade had already plugged in. It'd run through every feasible combination. Even at the speeds it processed, it'd still take too many minutes to check all eight vaults.

"Fingerprints occupying this vault are unknown," Wade said. "Not in the Unisco database."

That by itself wasn't something that disproved the theory one way or another. Unisco didn't have records of every single fingerprint in the kingdoms. Just those of the people who'd caused trouble and been caught. People who owned vaults like this were notorious for not getting caught. If it was Coppinger's vault, records showed she'd never been caught, never been fingerprinted.

Several long minutes passed. She looked at her timepiece, wondered how many they'd have to break into before they found the right one. Wade stood crouched across from her, tossing the scanner back and forth from one hand to the other. He'd gotten the fingerprints long ago for the scanner, just needed to break the code. On the readout, it showed that six out of eight digits had been secured in their rightful position. She tapped her foot, fiddled with the butt of her weapon in its holster, chose to unstrap it just in case. She really hoped she wouldn't need it.

When the beep came through that the code had been cracked, she let go of the sigh she'd been holding in, relief flooding out through her. Already Wade was punching in the code and scanning the fingerprints in. Nothing happened at first, then she saw the faintest traces of movement as the gears inside spun and the vault door gradually began its movement, swinging open with a final decisive thump.

He looked at her. "Ladies first?"

She decided to ignore that, strode in like she owned the place. Might as well start as she meant to go on. He trailed after her like a shadow, a light already flickering on in the vault at their arrival.

Not what she'd been expecting, but at the same time, she wasn't entirely sure what she might have found in the vault. If it did belong to Coppinger, at the very least, there could be a huge pile of credits in there, more than she or Wade would ever see in their lifetime. None of that though.

Crates though, there were plenty of them, sealed up wooden boxes stacked as high as the eye could see. Lots of statues and stonework, most of them figures that looked somewhat familiar but that she couldn't even hope to name. Curiosities and mementos lined the shelves, some of them useless, some of them attractive and some of them radiated power. Slowly the two of them advanced into the room, looking at each other.

"What is this stuff?" Wade asked, wonder in his voice. She couldn't blame him. Based on an initial speculation, she'd guess that a third of the stuff was crap, a third was valuable and the final third was really bloody dangerous in the wrong hands. Some of it was spirit caller stuff, some of it looked like weapons that hadn't been seen for decades.

"Hells if I know," she murmured, trying to shake the horrible feeling of suspicion starting to cast a pall over her. More and more, she was starting to feel the impression that they weren't in the right place. Beyond that, they were in trouble just by walking in here. Every instinct was screaming at her to get out of here, to leave the building before something bad happened to them. "Wade…"

He ignored her, strode into the centre of the room, he looked like a child in a candy store, trying to take in every sight and sensation as fast as he could.

"Wade!"

She couldn't blame him, there was power in this room. Seductive, alluring power that called out to be touched. It wanted to be used, to reach its inky tendrils around you and take everything that you were. Power whispering to you, urging silently to come forth and take it, to realise your dreams and make your enemies nightmares come to fruition. She could feel its influence, she had enough sense to ignore it. Temptation held no dangers for her, she'd wanted for more in the past and let it be.

"Wade!"

Still nothing, she watched as he reached out and put a hand on one of the crates, his face contorted into concentration. She made her choice, hurried after him, a hand on his shoulder.

"Ignore it!" she said, whispering it into his ear. "Whatever it's offering you, it'll not be what you think."

He tried to pull away from her, she tightened her grip, turned him to face her, fingers digging into pressure points on his shoulder. "It's not a price you want to pay!" she said. She saw his eyes narrow, fought the urge to slap him out of it. Anger seared through his pupils, she could feel his muscles tighten.

"Wade!"

Something changed, his eyes softened, and the anger retreated, a long breath slid from him. She could feel the relaxation of his muscles.

"Damn," he said. "That was…"

"It wasn't true," she said, moving to cut him off. "Whatever it was whispering to you, it wasn't true. I don't think we're in the right place, let's go find another vault."

Pree made to turn, heard the burst of sarcastic laughter from behind her and her heart fell. She knew then that they were in trouble, saw the tall frame at the door, the hair framing the scarlet and yellow that made up his face. It was a skull, not like any that Wade would have seen before.

She had, too many times and it never ended well when it did. Darkness swirled around him like a cape, a malignant smell of sulphur and rot heavy in the air.

Shit!

Suddenly she wished she'd brought a different weapon with her. The blaster felt painfully inadequate for the situation at hand.

Wade didn't hesitate, he knew that the guy was bad news and they had to put him down quickly. Lingering would cost them. He gripped his blaster tight, saw Pree react just too late… "Don't!" … he rose, aimed and fired. His aim was good, his eyes were better than they'd ever been before, meant to send it straight through the forehead.

That had been the target. Somewhere between blaster and skull, the bolt had stopped, stuck frozen between them. The ground beneath it shone with its effervescence, he could feel the heat from across the room.

The masked man looked at him, a hand outstretched in front of him. Dark gloves coated his fingers, fingers that he waved lazily in the air at Wade. Gradually, the bolt started to retreat from him, inching backwards to whence it had come. Wade's eyes widened, he went to drop, found his legs wouldn't move. His fingers slid open, the X9S fell through them and bounced away into the shadows.

"You had one free shot," the man said, his voice muffled behind his mask. "One shot and you wasted it. Terrible. The price of failure, dear boy, is always the steepest." He took a step forward, the bolt dancing backwards as if it feared him. "That you would even consider facing me with a weapon like that is nothing short of insult."

The hair, the frame... Realisation dawned on Wade, his mind racing as he tried to work a way out of this. He couldn't see Pree, she'd vanished from sight. Maybe she'd made a run for it. He couldn't blame her in these circumstances.

"You're Allison, aren't you?" he said. "The guy who owns this place."

Maybe he blinked behind the mask. If there was any sign of surprise externally, Wade didn't see it. It was like staring into a portrait, whatever he was thinking hidden behind the layers.

"You're smarter than you look," he said. "You know, I didn't think anyone would ever find this place. You both picked the wrong vault to wander into, son, you know that?"

The wrong place at the wrong time. Story of his life. He managed to contort his lips into a bitter grin, tried to force his legs to work. They wouldn't oblige him, refused to follow his commands. His heart pounded in his chest, sweat beaded on his forehead. He didn't want to admit how bad it was right now.

"Right now, I'm holding you in place," the man said. "I'm slowly bringing you to a standstill. First your body becomes unable to move, as your muscles freeze. Then your blood starts to stop flowing as your heart goes with it. You were dead the moment you set foot in here." He sounded almost apologetic. "A shame, but it is what it is. Such is life."

He sniffed the air, head cocked back like he'd heard something, eyes darting across the corners of the black.

"Interesting," he said. "Someone else's in here, aren't they? Not just you." He looked pointedly at Wade. "You're not doing that, are you?"

Doing what? Wade didn't know, couldn't even start to give an answer. Again, he tried to move, made to twitch his frozen fingers. His body screamed with the effort, fought against the invisible force wrapped around him. Nothing. Not a thing. Still he strained, felt the tips of his fingers twitch before the effort overwhelmed him. A grunt slipped out, he couldn't feel his tongue any longer, the taste of copper flooded his mouth as teeth met muscle.

Pree had known and she'd bolted. Not a chance she was going to get caught up like Wade. That man was trouble, she wanted to face him on her own terms, from a position of strength rather than one of weakness. Right now, they were both in the latter position. She wanted the former.

Shadows leant their cover to her, she slipped into them like a fine cloak, creeping around the boxes. Somewhere here, there had to be something. Come on, please! Anything! Blasters weren't going to be much use against the figure, she might as well go throw rocks at him. It'd likely be marginally more effective.

She heard his voice, exactly how she remembered. A wind across dry leaves on a stormy day. Those had been her impressions, and nothing had changed.

"I know you're there, little mouse."

He wasn't referring to her directly. He didn't know what she was, just that she was amidst the shadows. He might not even know for sure, merely suspect. Suspicion was just as bad as confirmation though. Worse perhaps. With suspicion, the feeling only grew and grew. Suspicious people did stupid things. Both trains of influence in her life had taught her that. It's better to be suspicious than dead.

She saw the light before she heard it, felt it streak towards her and she was up and running, diving behind a crate as the orb struck the spot where she'd hidden. She watched it bounce, shielded her eyes as the flames exploded out into dusty air, as bright as a miniature supernova. She could feel the heat searing across her forearms and screwed up her face at the pain. Another came her way, struck a crate above her head and tore a chunk through the wood, showering her with the contents. Various debris rained around her, bits and pieces of flotsam she couldn't even start to guess the purpose at.

All bar one. She looked at the cylinder in front of her, took in the metal and her heart leaped. Yes!

She brought it into her grasp, twisted one end of it open to check the crystal inside. One was present, she tipped it out into the palm of her hand and felt the weight. It danced with energy, she knew that much. It was alive and ready, filled with the eager presence of something so long locked away.

Okay. This was good. Her heart danced with relief. This she could work with. It gave her a fighting chance at least, all she'd ever wanted. She locked the cylinder back into place, ran a final examination to ensure it wouldn't blow up in her hand.

Maybe this was a stupid thing to do, some part of her cautioned. Either way, she'd die if she failed. Better to go out on your feet than cowering in the corner.

She didn't know who had trained her to think that way, maybe the two fields of influence converged on that point. Live for nothing. Die for something.

"She runs," the masked man said, his attention slipping back to Wade. "Your conspirator has abandoned you, she saves her own skin. No matter, for I will sluice it from her body, she will suffer. You both will. This place is mine. Mine!"

He didn't hear the words, still too busy trying to wrap his reeling mind around what he'd just witnessed. Those orbs, they'd not been natural. He'd known that in an instant, had felt them more than he'd seen them. They left a very distinct impression in his mind, tingling and gleeful. The corners of his mouth twitched up into a grin, he was aware of how much a buffoon he looked.

They weren't grenades, he'd summoned them out of nothing and pitched them out in the darkness. He'd seen her run in the flash, had heard her yell out. Then nothing. Silence.

He hoped Pree had gotten away. She'd tried to stop him, he'd ignored it, and this was where he'd ended up.

That confidence in himself that he was going to win. It had been there, flooded through him, only to be wiped away in an instant. The price of his own hubris, he guessed. He mentally kicked himself.

"Wherever she will run, I will find her. Be sure of that."

He heard her throat clearing before he saw her step out of the darkness, hands behind her back. The look on her face was a thing of sheer beauty, powerful determination etched into her features. Right there, Prideaux Khan was the most gorgeous thing he'd ever seen, he could feel the radiance from her like he never had before. Normally, he got the impression from her that something was being held back, like she was deliberately making herself out to be less than before. A curious mind might have wondered about it, he'd chosen to accept her choice. If that was what she wanted to do, she could. It made her more effective, was the reason she'd been nicknamed the Spectre.

Now though, all of that had been cast away and her full terrible glory apparent, brought to the forefront of her being.

"Who's running," she said, her voice playful and deadly. "I'm right here."

He gave her barely a glance at first, saw her and reconsidered, his head bobbing back and forth between the magic man and the partner he didn't recognise. Ignoring a woman who gave off impressions like that could either be your worst mistake or your greatest triumph.

"Nice mask," she said. "I name you Tarene, if I'm not mistaken. Lowest of the Lords, the Keeper of Curiosities. I'm sure you have others as well, but those two are the only ones I could ever be bothered to remember."

That shook him, Wade noticed, more than getting shot at. He went stiff, his body arched back like she'd slapped him.

"You'd do well to show some respect to your betters, girl," he growled. "Or do you wish to spend your last minutes of life learning the error of your ways."

Pree smiled at him, her grin growing and growing. "Oh, teach me, teach me!" she said. "Please! I've always been a slow learner." He could hear the sarcasm in her voice, could read the way she was coiled like a spring. She had a plan, he hoped. Otherwise this was going to end very badly for them both. Bravado only took you so far unless you had the capabilities to back it up.

The sudden return of movement to his body took him by surprise, everything came back to him in a heartbeat, he fell to his knees as Tarene turned on her. Pree held both hands up, glanced past the masked man and winked at him.

"Okay, okay," she said. "I didn't expect that to work. But since it did…" She thrust both hands out in front of her, locked together at the wrists, fingers outstretched. He felt the effect rippling in the air, and then Tarene was airborne. Wade watched as he flew off his feet, hit the far wall and bounced, hitting the ground in an untidy heap. He didn't look so threatening suddenly. Seeing someone get tossed around like a ragdoll tended to decrease their threat impact.

Down but not out, Tarene rose to his feet, shaking himself like a dog. Gloved hands came up to adjust his mask, the eyeholes out of kilter with the glittering orbs of malice. "You're an insolent little bitch!" he snarled. "I'll tear your head off!"

"Head, skin, you're all talk," Pree said. There was no anger in her voice, just calm detachment. If she was intimidated, she did an outstanding job of hiding it. "Threats of violence aren't anywhere near as effective as violence itself. If you want to regain some dignity, you know where I am."

Tarene's hands moved, fingertips stretched out in front of him, Wade saw the steam rise from them before the liquid blasted out, streaking towards his partner, drenching the ground beneath its path. One moment she was there, the next she wasn't, stepped aside and raised an eyebrow. He hadn't even seen her move. Scalding water struck the space where she'd stood, splashed harmlessly to the stone floor.

"You're a blade," he said. "That cocky disregard, the lack of subtlety. I see it all now. The princes and the Dark King will have your head for your betrayal. You have attacked one of their lords and they will cut you down for it. Your name will be mud, your deeds and your possessions forfeit for the glorious cause."

She giggled, a strange sound seeping out the darkness. "Only if I lose. The dead lose everything, and the living take it all. You know the rules, my lord." The last word should have sounded respectful, Wade guessed, she made it sound so mocking.

Not for the first time, he wondered exactly what he'd gotten himself into here.

She hadn't been lying. She remembered Lord Tarene, had recognised him the moment she'd seen the mask. Of the eight lords, he was the lowest, the one recognised to be most likely knocked off his perch, though saying it and doing it were different things. Not for nothing had he ascended to the rank of lord. The scalding water was a nice trick though, as ineffective as it might have been.

Blade and proud, that was her. She'd hit him with one of her best, he'd shaken it off quickly enough. She wasn't going to beat him in a throw-down over their mastery of the Kjarn. Lords knew secrets. Secrets only the princes and the Dark King would share with them when their loyalty was assured. The only way to ascend to lord was to prove yourself by removing the previous figure in the role, without arousing suspicion until after the fact.

If they were killed, they were weak. They prized power and strength alongside the will to use it. If they were killed, there was someone more deserving of the place.

"You challenge me then?" Tarene asked, the anger gone from his voice. Perhaps now he considered her a threat, she might have overplayed her hand. The cause of death in ninety-five percent of cases where lords had been overthrown, killed and succeeded by their murderer was overconfidence. For him to take her seriously might have damaged her chances of success.

"I do," she said. "In this place, at this time, I challenge you for everything that you have and everything that could be mine, as is my right."

"Grant me your name, Child," he said, his voice not free of condescension. He was doing it deliberately, she knew that, trying to get inside her head and rattle her. She'd seen too many of these exchanges between lord and blade before to let it fool her. Psychology only took you so far. By ignoring her hard-earned title, he diminished her as a warrior and hope to force her into rash decisions.

Since it was going to be her last fight as a blade, she smiled and threw caution to the wind. Leave nothing behind "My name is Prideaux Agnes Khan, Agent of Unisco. Yet you can call me Blade Telles, the name that was bestowed upon me by my master upon cessation of being his apprentice."

He wasn't impressed, she could tell with his body language, stood languid with his hands at his side. That was her first impression, until she looked closer at him. His fingers twitched like an old-time gunslinger. If he did have a blaster, she wouldn't feel the worry flooding through her. Blasters she could deal with, no problem. She'd been shot before, more than once. Underneath her clothes, her body was pocked with the scars of a hard life.

She'd seen his weapon before, he brought it out from behind his back, activated the blade with a push of the switch. A brilliant crimson-blue blade, almost purple where the colours met, erupted into existence and she could have sworn she saw the mask twist into a smile. The hilt of his weapon was unusual in that he'd designed it with a twist in it, like he'd started with a cylinder of metal and then bent it with the power of the Kjarn until it looked mangled and misshapen. Didn't diminish the power, just added a quirk that hinted towards too much of the man's ego. He wanted to be unique, he wanted to stand out from the shadow of the others.

He wasn't considered the lowest of the lords for nothing. His ego had held him back, her old master had once confided in her. The other lords didn't trust him. The princes certainly didn't. A man who wouldn't be missed should he be overthrown…

She couldn't think about that right now. Her concentration was needed to be at its purest, she couldn't afford to think about the risks or the rewards or the potential retribution. She didn't even want to think about Wade and how she was going to explain this to him.

He was a big boy. He knew how the world worked. He'd understand. He'd trust her, she hoped.

Pree brought the cylinder she'd found in the crate out in front of her, held it up with both hands. If it didn't work after all this, she probably wouldn't live long enough to be able to regret it. Big grin to make it look like she had no fear. It had to work. Her thumb met the switch, she pushed it up, breathed the sigh of relief as the green-white blade emerged. Green wasn't her colour, but it would do. She twisted her wrists, flexed her arms, spun the blade in a little salute that her master had taught her back in the day. She might be rusty, she knew that much. They didn't duel much anymore. That might change with the return of the Vedo, but it was irrelevant now.

Wade's eyes widened as the blade flickered into existence out of Pree's hand, saw her do the contactless flurry. What the actual hells? He wondered if he'd taken a bang on the head, his eyes had to be deceiving him. It wasn't possible? Was it?

The thoughts were starting to slide together, half-stories heard second-hand from Baxter, throwaway comments Pree had made while they'd been on the road together.

Oh my...

She studied him. He watched her with cool detachment, his weapon hung down at his side. He let it fall, rest the blade in the ground. She could see the molten furrow left behind by its touch, sword cutting through stone without difficulty, leaving a glowing tear behind its kiss. Neither of them wanted to make the first move, instead choosing to stare the other out. She knew what would happen if she charged in, he'd move the blade and hurl the discarded chunks of stone towards her in hopes of doing her some damage. That was his plan, she was certain of it.

Disrupt then. Her lips played into a smile, she made to look like she was about to move and saw his muscles twitch as kjarnblade ripped through stone. Her foot hit the ground and she moved, enhancing her speed. She was no Enhancile, but she could move when she needed to. It wasn't a long-term solution, it might give her the edge she needed here. She found herself almost on him when shattered stones finally met air, she kicked herself to the side to evade, spat out a yell as rock met her leg, tore hard into the skin. She stumbled, fell to her knees and his blade would have taken her head off had she not used her momentum to keep going, hurled herself under the slash, felt it sweep above her head. She was back on her feet in an instant, caught his blade on hers as he tried to slash her open from behind. He was strong, the effort drove her back, she could see the teeth ground together beneath the mouth slit in his mask.

Pree grunted with the effort, both hands clasped firmly on her sword as she attempted to break the lock between the weapons, tried to stand her ground and force him back, fight for every second of life left to her. Only the final option was the one that gave her any success, she pushed back hard, kept it from going near her face. A wound like that on her skin, it might not have been fatal, but it would hurt like a bitch, as well as leaving a mark nobody would be able to ignore.

She'd kept her face clean of major scarring. That wasn't about to change here.

Outpowered, she did what Unisco had taught her, forgetting the training that had come before. If you can't win with the rules as they are, cheat and take the spoils your own way. She threw a kick out, caught him across the back of the knee and he let out a snarl of pain, his strength wavering for a crucial moment and she broke the lock, thrust out a fist towards his centre mass and watched the invisible force of the

Kjarn blast him back from her. Not the most powerful hit but the job would do. She raised her kjarnblade, went on the offensive, hacking and slashing at him. Most landed on the weapon, one strike burning through Tarene's sleeve, shearing it away. He hissed, continued to block her. He wasn't struggling but neither was he having it all his own way. Her confidence might be rising but she couldn't forget there was a gap in knowledge between him and her, the sort not easily surrendered. To know was to have power and to have power was to bear dominion.

He scooted back, danced out the way of her blade, spry for an older man. Not that it surprised her. Appearances could be deceptive and the Kjarn sustained a vitality that might otherwise be betrayed by an ageing frame. She went for him again, determined not to let him have that respite. He flung out a hand, she twisted to the side before the scalding water could hit her, felt it sear the air near her. A finger twitched, she sensed movement to her left and spun her blade up to cut through the crate. It wasn't empty, she realised that as her weapon sheared through the wood and showered her in the contents. She hoped it was sand, a thousand little flecks of something covering her. Given this was Tarene's vault, she didn't like to think about the sort of stuff he might have locked up here.

Her blade span back, came to meet his inches from her throat. Her muscles screamed with the effort, she pushed back hard enough to force him away and slammed her weapon towards his face. Kjarnblade to the brain was fatal, she knew that. He'd know it too. He moved to block, she feinted, halted her swing and reversed down towards his sword arm. Cutting bits of him would do just as well for her. It was hard to be defensively solid when someone had just hacked one of your limbs off.

Whatever else she might think of him, he wasn't stupid, jumped back out of range and suddenly she'd overreached herself, struggling for balance and a hammer blow struck her on the back. She hit the ground, chin crashing into the stone, her head going fuzzy. Her kjarnblade hissed out, died and then he was on her, snatched her up by the throat in one hand. She struggled, kicked out, didn't come close to bothering him. Beneath the mask, his eyes didn't change, locked onto her in detached disgust. Rather than acknowledge her efforts with words, he chose to squeeze.

"I hope this little outburst was worth the price," he said. "You've failed, Ms Khan. Utterly. I fear Unisco is going to lose another agent today. Two, perhaps when I get your fellow thief and gut him."

She couldn't breathe, little gasps slipping out of her, the corners of her vision starting to darken. Harder and harder she tried to kick out at him, heard the laughter in his voice. Rage swept through her, powerful but impotent. She'd be unconscious in a moment, Wade didn't stand a chance against him. Tarene was powerful, stronger than she'd given him credit for. She'd underestimated him, just as she'd hoped he'd underestimate her.

One does not rise to the rank of Lord without having something about them. Those words felt hollow consolation. In a fair fight, he'd demolish her.

A fair fight. The lights went on, the mention of Unisco had started to stir something and she knew she was going to win after all. Rather than claw at his fingers, she dropped her hand to her waist, snapped the holster open and she saw the look of surprise on his face as she jammed the muzzle of the X9S against his centre mass. Largest target imaginable. So many vital organs.

Just a little squeeze, she felt the vibration through her wrist and into her arm, but it was in Tarene that she saw the biggest reaction. The blast tore through one side of him and out the other, his eyes widened in pain and a scream ripped from his lungs. He dropped her, she hit the ground and was already drawing her kjarnblade back towards her, her lungs gratefully sucking in every bit of air she could take. Everything spun around her, nothing would keep still for her, the world a whirlwind of motion. Regardless, she still had a fight for her survival and her will to live hadn't faded simply because her head felt like someone had taken a hammer to it.

He hadn't fallen, just doubled over in agony. When he rose, she could see straight through the hole in his stomach, ragged and oozing. It would leave one hells of a scar if it was left untended. His mask had fallen away, she could see the enraged face of Robert Allison now.

"You bitch!" he growled. "You're going to die!"

"We're all going to die," she said. Her voice sounded like she'd been gargling saltwater and glass. Her kjarnblade hissed into life. Incredibly, he stood up straight, despite his injuries and stared at her, hatred hard on his face. She tried to keep the dismay off her own, she hoped that blast would have put him down. Her best guess, the Kjarn had to be keeping him on his feet, fuelled by his own pure rage.

Not the worst news she'd ever heard. Ignoring the pain or not, if she could keep him on the move, he'd really fuck himself up. Those injuries were fatal unless he got medical help or the respite to heal.

"Some of us sooner than others," he said. She saw him coming at her a split-second before he did, had to move to stop him from bisecting her. Their blades sang as they met, crackles of energy bursting from their kiss. He'd abandoned finesse now in favour of force, his movements speeding up as he hammered at her, both hands on the hilt of his blade. With ever motion, fresh blood burst from his wound, she chose to retreat and defend for her life. Stand her ground. Forget about winning, focus on surviving. Even with the Kjarn holding him up, he had to be blocking out the pain, he wouldn't last forever. His breathing was laboured, his face losing colour. Each blow he flung at her, she could sense a little less strength in it, each weaker and slower than the last.

Pree smiled, made sure he saw it. Beneath their feet, the floor was slick with his blood. His body was betraying him, they both knew it. As quickly as he'd engaged it, she made the switch, went from defence to attack. He got his blade up to block hers, just barely. She could feel him pushing back, his breath coming out in gasps. She forced him back, took a wild swipe out at his midriff with her foot. He tried to dodge back, couldn't move fast enough, his legs unresponsive and he slipped, landed on his ass almost comically. His sword went flying, she threw out a hand and summoned it to her grip. The twisted hilt felt alien beneath her grasp, unusual but no less effective. He managed to scramble up, tried to reach for it and failed.

"You're right," she said. "Some of us do die sooner than others."

She took his head off without thinking, saw it fly away through the air as it left his shoulders, bounce off somewhere in the shadows. His body fell, no longer a concern.

Wade couldn't believe what he'd just seen. He'd hidden through the entire thing, gotten a good sight of it but decided not to interfere. No way he was getting caught in the middle of those two. There was something going on there he wasn't going to be party to. If he'd interfered, he'd have died. That much he knew.

He looked at the headless body. Someone had died. A suspect. Someone they probably should have talked to. That was gone now. His partner looked a mess, coated in dirt and iron and blood, almost like she'd gone feral. It felt like he was seeing her for the first time, looking at her and realising what she was truly capable of. He'd never known. He'd never even suspected.

Pree deactivated the weapon, gave him an uneasy glance. Just for a moment, the fearsome woman he'd seen before was gone and the one he'd called a friend was back. It wasn't even like there was anything physical about the difference. Just the impressions. One woman you couldn't help but notice and one that just faded into the background. "Guess I've got some explaining to do, huh?"

"You... You're a Vedo?" The words fell out of him. That was impossible, wasn't it? He hadn't heard anything about it. Clara had never mentioned it. Ruud had never mentioned it. As far as he knew, before all this, there hadn't been any Vedo in Unisco ranks.

"No," she said. "Not a Vedo."

Chapter Seventeen. A Prelude to a Hunt.

"I'm personally not a big fan of that final examination. I know it has its merits, I know we all did it, but I think that it's had its day. The way we're going with technology developing the way it is, I think it's getting harder to keep quiet that we're doing it. If our enemies know that we do it, then it's easier to pick off a field of unqualified cadets than a group of seasoned Unisco agents. I can't dispute it as a test, but the logistics of performing it are becoming unreasonable. We're already looking into alternative processes to deal with it. Something perhaps a little more balanced than cadet versus cadet."

Tod Brumley on the final examination all Unisco academy trainees must complete before being permitted to graduate.

Present Day.

That damn simulation!

Theo wasn't impressed, not an unusual state of mind for him, but his feedback had been less than satisfactory. They'd dropped it off for him the night, he'd found it in the morning, woken up to it on the footlocker at the base of his bed. Of course, he'd had to read it through. He thought he'd done rather well with the whole damn thing, to find out that they disagreed…

Too focused on revenge. That comment stung. The whole thing had been a simulation of being invaded, his focus had been on removing the threats. Who the hells did Konda think that he was?

An inquisitor, that was who. They'd been told all about them, how they had the belief that they were always right and everyone else was wrong, even when the evidence proved otherwise.

Liability to himself and those around him. Even harsher. They were being trained to be killers at the end of the day. They might talk about law and order, upholding justice but that was bullshit. When they taught them unarmed combat, when they'd given them blasters and told them how to shoot, they didn't say shoot to wound. They made you hit the head and the heart. Not arms and legs. Everyone here got the same training. The sort you walked away from.

"How'd you do?"

He looked up at Roberts, scowled. He didn't need the pity which would no doubt come his way. That might just lead to him throwing punches and then he'd be in further trouble. Jacobs had aced the damn thing by all accounts, of course he had, golden boy. Roberts, Tamale, Hill, they'd all run through it and had similar accounts. Only his way had been criticised.

He couldn't appreciate the irony of it. He'd taken out every single enemy in the simulation, beaten them, killed them, crushed them. They'd had to generate more just to bring him down, had thrown fifty of them at him. He'd been pinned down in the end, ran out of shots in his blaster.

He rubbed his stomach. They might not be real, but those things stung when they hit you. He'd long worked out that the academy operated under the principle that stupidity should be painful. If it hurt, you remembered it. He'd never subscribed to that theory. Memories of pain faded. It didn't linger, as the body healed, so did the mind.

Not everything was a criticism of his methods, he'd been relieved to say. They'd praised his tenacity, if not his judgement. They'd admired his skill, not in so many words but enough that he got the message, though they questioned his applications of it.

More than that, they'd wondered if he'd realised the point of it at the end. The whole 'you-can't-always-win' thing. He'd not held much stock by that. What was the point if you couldn't win? And he didn't buy that it was so that you learned to accept defeat gracefully, that sounded like a crock of shit to him.

Paddington, Konda, even Stenner as she'd examined his burns from the blasts, he'd said the same thing to all of them. If you couldn't always win, what was the point?

He didn't want to talk to anyone, just pulled on his trousers and shoved the results in a pocket. Dom Hill glanced at him, smirked to himself. If he said anything, Theo thought, he might just go for him. Smug bearded bastard. He'd always wanted to punch him, despite him being easily a head and shoulders taller than Theo. He got the feeling the instructors knew it as well, probably the reason they'd never been paired up in training.

Some of them were eerie like that. He supposed they'd seen it all before, they knew what to look for. Once you'd seen one sign, you'd seen them all. And he doubted he was the first cadet who wanted to hit another.

Dom Hill wasn't actually a bad guy, as far as he could tell. No better or worse than any of them here. There was just something about him that couldn't reconciliate with. Might be the beard. He didn't trust beards.

He tried to sit alone as much as possible in the mess hall, he didn't like company. He worked best as a solitary man, did what he could alone and only asked for help when he recognised that he needed it. Of course, realising when you needed it was a subjective thing. Stubbornness ran in the family, as much as he hated it, there wasn't a lot he could do about that. He might get it from his father, he wasn't willing to change it. People who spoke of wanting to change were deluded idiots. For better or for worse, people were who they were. They might talk a good game, they often didn't play one. To change something about yourself was to deny your true nature.

He'd never wanted to do that. He'd accepted that there were things he could work on, Anne had told him as much. She'd shown him that his strategies were inherently flawed, she was the first person he'd ever been truly close to. Maybe he'd misread her intentions, maybe he'd built her up too much in his head because of that. She was attractive, something about her he couldn't quite place. Didn't help that she was so bloody nice, he didn't get the impression that it was an act either. When he'd found out she was with Unisco, more than that, a sniper, it had made him question his judgement. A sniper's entire purpose was to eliminate targets, that took a certain cold rationale and yet he'd found her to be the friendliest of them lot.

He wanted to be alone with his salted porridge, he didn't think that he was going to get it. Jacobs slid himself into the bench across from him, gave him that curiously eager look which scratched at his brain like a feral kitten. Divines save him from curious people looking into that which wasn't their business.

"How'd you do on your sim?" he asked. "Seriously, come on, talk to me. You looked pissed this morning."

"I can't see that it's any of your…"

Jacobs cut him off. "Yeah, we can do this dance, you can tell me it isn't any of my business, I can tell you to come-on-talk-to-me, we can back-and-forth for a while or we can skip all that and get down to it like actual human beings."

That made him smirk. Jacobs might be an idiot at times, but he wasn't entirely stupid. That situation was entirely what would likely have happened. Apparently, he was that easy to read.

"Weren't complimentary," he said eventually. "Put it that way."

"What did you fail on?"

"Apparently I tried to kill everyone. Succeeded as well. They changed the game to beat me." He couldn't keep the bitterness out of his voice. "With everyone dead, they brought in reinforcements. Too damn many of them."

Jacobs whistled. "Wow. That's impressive."

"I thought so too." Unbelievable. Was he really agreeing with another cadet? He must be tired. "I'll tell you, those blasts hurt."

The look he got was one of surprise. "What do you mean?"

"Getting shot with those blasters in the simulation hurt." He rubbed his side, saw the look of confusion on Jacobs' face. Divines, could he really be that dense? Theo had always assumed you needed a relative amount of intelligence to work for Unisco.

"Oh, right." Jacobs shrugged. "I didn't get shot."

He felt his eye twitching again, tried to ignore it. "You didn't?"

"No. When they overwhelmed me, I surrendered." He actually looked smug about it. Theo felt the urge to smash his head against the table. Feeble, little… Something was digging into his hand, he opened it up, let the spoon clatter to the table. Spatters of porridge fell everywhere, he didn't register it.

"You surrendered?" He couldn't keep the disbelief out of his voice. "Things got a little tough and you gave up?!"

"There were loads of them around me…" Jacobs was on the defensive now, had his hands up in front of him, Theo had already decided he wasn't letting him off the hook.

"You should have fought. You didn't know it was a damn simulation at the time! They could have killed you!" Anger laced his voice, he wasn't shouting but he felt like it. Best not to cause too much of a scene. A few people were looking around at the two of them.

"And what did they do to you? Pat you on the head for effort and send you away for milk and cookies? They did kill you."

"Only when they changed the game!" Part of him was dangerously close to conceding that Jacobs had a point and that unsettled him. Coming close to seeing his point of view was worrying. If he admitted his way was wrong, it'd bring a lot of his flaws up to the surface, he didn't want it to come to that. He'd softened his stances once, for Anne, and despite the results, he regretted it had had to come to that.

"They can do that! Life's a game that's always going to hold all the cards against you."

"I refuse to accept that!"

He slumped forward in his seat, folded his arms in front of him, rested his chin on his wrists. The sigh escaped him, he gave Jacobs a weary smile. By his standards, it was a smile. It probably looked like a stomach pain on anyone else. Spilt porridge stained his sleeves, he'd worry about that later. They were old clothes, not any part of an official uniform. Probably ready for the trash anyway.

"You know why I became a spirit caller?" he asked. He couldn't keep the fatigue out of his voice. He hadn't slept well since the simulation, the burns on his side keeping him awake. More than that, the failure haunted him. He'd done everything he could, he'd used every inch of his willpower, the skills they'd taught him, and it hadn't even been enough. He'd been overwhelmed, plain and simple. No other way of describing it.

"The credits, the women, the prestige, the glory?" Jacobs asked. A perfectly inane answer, exactly what he'd have expected from him. Credits didn't motivate him, they were a means to an end. Women, he could care less about, barring one. The glory was a fleeting sensation, a temporary fix for sure, a tiny bit would leave you wanting more and more if it was your choice of high. He liked the feeling, he didn't think he was dependent on it for his ego.

Prestige was an interesting choice though, now he thought about it. Not a million miles away from the truth yet still so far.

"I wanted to prove I was the best," he said. "I wanted to prove I was better than my father, I wanted to prove that there was nobody who could touch me."

Jacobs said nothing, miracles did apparently occur and for that, he was grateful. John Cyris had never been a renowned spirit caller, he'd dabbled in the sport, but his talents had lay in other areas on the murky side of the law. He'd gone with the name Jameson from his mother, didn't want to be associated with the bastard. If he'd gone by Theobald Cyris, people would have talked. They'd have detracted from his achievements and he didn't want that. He wanted them to be recognised as truly great records.

"I nearly did that, you know," he continued. "I nearly proved I was the best in the kingdoms. I beat your sister. I overcame Katherine Sommer. Would have beaten your idiot best friend for sure…" He saw the flush in Jacobs' cheeks. "I genuinely have no idea how he got to that final. Not a chance he was even close to that good before."

"Some people grow into a tournament," Jacobs shrugged. "It's not a bad thing to be able to do, start off poorly and get better as you go along."

Again, he had to concede Jacobs was right there. His start had been okay, enter Anne and her tutelage. She'd taught him that while his techniques served him well to a point, they were predictable and lacked subtlety. He'd accepted her help because he'd seen what she could do, and he wanted a piece of it.

"So, you're telling me that you knew he'd get there?"

"I just thought I'd be fighting him in the final." Jacobs' grin was beyond ridiculous, so proud and yet so naïve. Theo wondered what effect it'd have if he slapped it away, just reached over and cracked him. As satisfying as it might be, it'd serve no purpose beyond brief gratification and the trouble that would follow outweighed that. "Anyway, you didn't beat him. We'll never know what might have happened there if the bout had been allowed to come to a natural conclusion."

Another point where he was correct. Theo knew he'd been on the up when Coppinger had interrupted. It wasn't impossible he might have won. It wasn't impossible he could have let it all go and lost. Nobody would ever know.

"Anyway, I nearly made it. I'd have done it, made it to the top. I'd have been recognised as the best in the kingdoms. More than the best, I'd have been superior to them all. You. Taylor. Sommer. Roper. Wallerington. None of you would have done what I did."

"I presume that you're going somewhere with this," Jacobs said. "Because if you are, I just don't see it."

He ignored him. He wasn't here to make Jacobs' life easier for him. The harder he had to work to figure something out, the better for him.

"I was nearly the best. If I'd won that tournament, nobody would be able to take it away from me. They wouldn't have been able to dispute it. Winner of the Quin-C can claim that title of best caller. I'd have achieved superiority."

"For a while anyway." Jacobs didn't sound like he was buying what he was saying. That didn't matter. He didn't need his validation. "Someone would have knocked you off your perch eventually. Can't win them all. And that's why you failed the sim."

"You're a psychologist now?"

"Nope, but that's what they told me. The point of that exercise was to make you realise that there are some things that you can't beat. No matter how hard you try or how hard you fight, there'll always be a tipping point. You'll hit a wall you can't climb. It wasn't meant to be beaten, it was to make sure you tasted defeat."

Theo said nothing. Had nothing he could say.

"You get this way after every defeat? Take it so personal?"

"Yep. Those who accept defeat will never taste success."

"And who told you that? Your dear old dad?"

That was a cheap shot, Theo quickly realised. His fists bunched under the table. Deep breath. One. Two. He could feel his heart hammering in his chest, the blood roaring in his ears.

Don't do anything stupid, don't do anything stupid, he repeated to himself mentally.

They were in so much damn trouble, they'd had to be pulled apart in the mess hall. Apparently trying to smash a fellow cadet's head in with a bowl was frowned upon. He'd tried. He really had. That quip had been uncalled for. The only saving grace from the whole thing was the hardness of Jacobs' head and the flimsy nature of the crockery in this place. Anything sturdier and he'd be in the infirmary with a cracked skull. All he bore was a bandage on his forehead. Maybe it'd leave a scar.

Good. It'd serve him right for making that comment. He thought he'd heard all the comments about his father, he didn't realise that they still got to him like that. His own mouth hurt like a bitch, Jacobs had got a few good licks in on him and the bastard could hit. He was a head and a half taller than Theo, twice the size, he should have a punch on him. The taste of blood still lingered in his mouth, bitter and coppery. The urge to spit had been gnawing at him ever since. Testing with his tongue, it felt like one of his teeth had been loosened, every time he poked the offending item, he felt the irritation surge through him.

Not that he was going to likely get the chance to dwell on it. So far, they'd been thrown into an office, someone was on the way down to deal with them. He didn't know who, he could only suspect. No matter who showed up, he got the feeling they were going to get the mother of all bollockings for what had gone down. Violence between cadets was frowned upon outside of training, he'd be amazed if one of them, if not both were still at the academy come the end of the day.

Jacobs hadn't said anything, not since he'd joined him from the infirmary. The look on his face was priceless, Theo would have paid anything to see it more frequently when conjoined with the bliss of silence. He didn't want to talk right now. He didn't have anything to say. Instead he looked around the office, tried to work out who it belonged to. No clues sprang out at him, given they'd had a rudimentary introduction to situational analysis, that didn't bode well for him. The only analysis he'd developed of his current situation was that he was screwed. He didn't know how much it bothered him, he'd wanted to join Unisco, become a minted agent. He'd wanted the prestige of being able to say that, even if it was just to himself.

A smile played across his mouth. Maybe it did all come back down to his father. John Cyris' only son becoming an avatar of justice, a man of law and order. He'd wanted to stick it to him for as long as he could remember, and this'd do it. Cyris had been a criminal, there were stories that he'd gone straight in the last months, he no longer did what it was rumoured he'd spent his life doing. Rather now, he practiced what he preached. Peace. Making the kingdoms a better place. Theo didn't buy it, but since he had no desire to talk to the man to dispute it, he couldn't care less.

The door to the office opened, Takamishi strode in with a face like thunder, Konda following him. Konda looked more amused than anything else, arms folded in front of him. They both rose to their feet, threw a salute to the two of them. It felt, Theo thought, a wholly meagre gesture. They were in the shit, him perhaps more, but following the protocol wasn't going to soften the punishment thrown at them. Still he'd done it though, maybe it might earn them just a few plus points. By them, he meant him. He couldn't care less about Jacobs. That much he'd always tried to make abundantly clear and yet he still tried to be friends.

"Well, well, well," Takamishi said, his voice low and the sarcasm thick with it. "Well, I never. You two have been certainly busy today, haven't you? Brawling in the mess hall. Trips to the infirmary…" Doctor Stenner had looked over him, judged him okay. She'd given him an apologetic smile as she'd sent him on his way. Theo liked Stenner. She knew what she was doing, she didn't take any shit and she told it how it was. In other words, his kind of person. There weren't enough of them about it in today's world. There were people who said nothing and there were people who said too much, with rarely a middle ground. "… and now I have to deal with you!"

Sarcasm had been overwritten by anger, the fury radiated from him. Spittle sprayed the desk in front of him. Theo fought the urge to wipe his cheek. That really wouldn't go down well, he could read the signs enough to realise that. "Because I clearly don't have enough to do with my life." He pointed a finger in between them, let it hover, clearly debating which of them he was going lash out at first. Theo kept his mouth shut, didn't dare move a muscle. Just in case.

Some part of him had known this would come, had been waiting for it in expectation since he'd shattered that bowl against Jacobs' skull. Didn't make it any worse though, he knew that for damn sure.

"You're both lucky I don't throw you out here and now!" Takamishi said. "If it were up to me, I would do. You're both walking a knife edge. Screw up one more time…"

Konda cleared his throat. "Administrator, if I may interject. I've reviewed the footage of the incident. I don't dispute punishment is in order. In fact, I encourage it."

Terrific, Theo thought. The look on the inquisitor's face, he'd thought that Konda was about to speak up for them and get them out of the shit. No such luck, it would appear.

"Because they broke the rules, and if there is one rule of society that is immutable, it is that blatant transgression of the laws needs to be snipped in the bud or those offences will grow and grow."

"You want me to throw them out?" Takamishi looked hopeful suddenly, his face lighting up like he'd stared at the sun and not gotten burned.

Konda snorted. "Hells no, I think it's time to promote both of them to the next stage of their training. I've reviewed the footage, I think I already have recommendations."

The smile on Takamishi's face faded, his composure took a moment to recover. "Go on?" The disappointment in his voice was hard to miss.

"Hitting Cadet Jacobs with the bowl was an inspired bit of improvisation from Cadet Jameson. Any blunt object in a storm, as the saying is paraphrased. We spend a lot of time trying to teach those improvisation skills to combat specialists, this cadet did it naturally. Even looking at his simulation scores, he might have failed it, but it was a spectacular performance in failure. He has potential, he's worked well in unarmed combat and blaster training. Temperament and self-control are lacking but that's not always a negative thing. It can be worked on."

Was he being punished or not now? He couldn't tell. A moment ago, it had sounded like Konda wanted him out the door and now he was praising him.

"Cadet Jacobs on the other hand, was trying to wheedle information of out Cadet Jameson in the build-up to the assault, he was trying to get him to talk. Was succeeding as well, it's a skill you can't teach, reaching people on their own level. He even managed to coax a reaction out of him, that's impressive. Granted his judgement may have been less than sound in doing it while they had a weapon in reach, but you can't have everything."

Konda grinned at Jacobs. "Ever thought about joining the inquisitors, boy?"

Theo snickered. "Well that'd be about right. I heard most Unisco inquisitors couldn't fight worth a damn when it came down to it."

Takamishi's skin had gone a funny red colour, he looked ready to burst a blood vessel in his eyes. If he hadn't been the target of that rage, Theo might have found it funny. What wasn't funny was Konda's reaction.

"Actually, Cadet Jameson, most inquisitors can fight exceptionally well, your information is flawed in that regard. Their duty is to enforce the Unisco regulations. Occasionally an agent needs to be apprehended and interrogated. You've seen the level of training we go through here for the basics. How do you think we bring in combat specialists who don't wish to come quietly? Ask them nicely and pray?"

"He is a talented spirit caller as well," Jacobs offered up. "I mean, he was a Quin-C finalist. You know, if that helps his case for being a combat specialist. Those guys have spirit duels sometimes, don't they?"

"Sometimes," Takamishi said, the anger still creasing his face. Out in front of him, he flexed his fingers, couldn't bring himself to look at them. "It's a handy skill to have in the locker, but when most agents are out in the field and under fire, if they have a blaster in hand, the instinct is to shoot back, not bring out a spirit and do something fancy that might not pay off."

"Doesn't count against him," Konda said. "I'm recommending that following your time here, you both ship off to separate academies to develop yourselves further into your chosen fields…" He paused, let the sentence hang. "Unless you wish to add anything further to it? This is just my opinion, I'm not sure if Administrator Takamishi agrees with me or not."

"One can talk, and one can fight," Takamishi said. He sounded like he rather wouldn't comment but the situation had been forced upon him and he couldn't ignore it out of fear of looking churlish. "We've moved people into specialist positions with less to go on, Nandahar. Might not be stupid ideas on either part."

"Is there someone we can talk to about this?" Jacobs asked. Theo fought the urge to roll his eyes. Typical. He was being handed a great chance, an opportunity that neither of them had thought they would get minutes earlier and he was already trying to pick holes in the offer. He'd already thought it through. Combat specialist. A man of action. It sounded good, like it'd suit him. Granted, he could already tell that it was going to be damn hard. He'd long suspected Nicholas Roper had graduated this academy with skills leaning towards that, he'd seen Roper in action first-hand at the Quin-C final, as well as several other individuals with Unisco training. It had been scary watching them, the way they moved, attacked, and the way they killed. There was something otherworldly about them.

Plus, Jacobs was right. He did have an array of powerful spirits and that'd count in his favour. Could never have too many weapons at your disposal.

"Of course, we'll summon someone in to talk to you. If you want to know more about being an inquisitor, Cadet Jacobs, come see me at some point. I'll give you the rundown. I've been one for too many years now. I thought doing my part in running this academy would be a nice change of pace." He grinned as he said it. "How wrong was I, it turned out."

His attention turned to Theo. "Cadet Jameson, should you wish to talk to a combat specialist, I can arrange for one to make an appearance at some point."

He considered it. Might not be the dumbest thing ever, providing it wasn't Roper. He still had some unresolved irritation towards the man, didn't want to spend more time with his company than he had to.

"I'd like that," he said. "I'm sure it'll be enlightening."

"He'll not be showing you how to set fire to things," Konda smiled. "Be sure of that. Now, anyway. About your punishment…"

It was probably fair, he had to admit. Fair and didn't lack for any sort of irony. Konda had been swift with his judgement and set them straight to it. As much as he wanted to promote them, he had tossed them back into the mess hall with a warning about what would happen if they stepped out of line again.

"You won't like the consequences," had been his choice of words. "Now clean this shit up!"

Shit summed it up right. It looked worse than when they'd been here last, the normally spotless room gave the impression it had been party to a vicious explosion in a food factory. It was everywhere, up the walls, on the floor, he could even see some pudding on the ceiling, a brown stain several hands wide dripping to the floor. At least, he hoped it was pudding and not something else.

"Seriously?!" Jacobs said. "What did they do, just tell everyone to throw it everywhere to give us more of a job?"

"Probably." It was all he felt like saying on the matter. Still didn't want to talk to him, not after he'd wound them up into this situation. Jacobs could go and work in silence in his own damn corner, he'd start over here and they'd meet somewhere in the middle. He'd like that very much.

"It'd have just been easier for you not to start a fight," he offered. "Rather than us having to do this."

"It'd have been easier for them to kick us out rather than making us do this," Theo said, having to fight the urge to keep the snarl out of his voice. Hearing Jacobs whine about it was already starting to grate and they'd been here all of a minute.

"It's not my fault you've got breath-taking anger issues," he offered. "I mean, who the hells hits someone with a bowl for offering a helpful suggestion?"

"Why offer a helpful suggestion when someone doesn't damn need it?" Theo shot back. There were mops and buckets towards the back next to the kitchen door, he genuinely hoped they didn't have to clean in there as well. There was punishment and then there was sadism. He'd lived with John Cyris for sixteen years, he knew how to tell one from the other. Some found it hard. He didn't. In his experience, punishment came with an emotional detachment. Sadism had something in it that resembled love, although not the sort of love that any normal person would recognise.

Sometimes he saw the way two people were in the street, he'd wonder why he never felt that way about anyone. It just looked something so alien to him, he'd never understand it. He'd tried comparing it to the way he felt about Anne, but those waters were so unchartered, he didn't want to consider them. Anne was an incredible woman, she'd taken the time out to help him when she'd thought that he needed it, despite his protests. It took a lot to do that, not just to offer him something, but to stick at it when he made his automatic refusal. She'd put in the time, she'd brushed off the attempts to get rid of her and she'd gotten in under his defences.

Friendship? He'd never really had one before, friends were weakness, his father had always told him. As much as he hated what the old man had imparted to him, some of the lessons had stuck hard to him.

Fling enough shit at any given situation and some of it will stick, he thought, trying not to look too unhappy. If Jacobs thought he was suffering here, he'd have won and hitting him would have been for nothing. He wanted him to be as miserable as he was.

Divines, what was wrong with him?! He shook his head, went to fill the bucket. Trying to psychologically outdo Jacobs in a bout he likely didn't even know he was competing in? That had to be the definition of insanity, surely.

"Hey!"

He'd surprised himself by speaking up, hadn't thought that he'd have it in him right now. He wanted silence, it appeared that his mouth had different ideas. Maybe the situation had gotten to him.

Jacobs looked at him, his expression unmistakeable sour. He couldn't blame him. He had given him a beauty of a mark on his head. Might even leave a scar. "What?!" That level of irascibility sounded familiar to him. It was how he imagined his own voice sounded whenever some idiot tried talking to him when he didn't want them to.

"For what it's worth, sorry about hitting you. Probably shouldn't have done that. It was uncalled for."

It sounded even dumber as he said it out loud, he could already feel the regret flooding through him for opening his mouth. Should have just stayed silent.

"You don't apologise much, do you?" Jacobs eventually said.

"Try not to," Theo said. "Never feel like I've got much to apologise for. That's like admitting that you're wrong."

"Well, sometimes you have to do that in life unfortunately," Jacobs said. "The kingdoms'd be a messed-up place if everyone was right every single time. It can't happen. Too many opinions. Too many assholes." He gave him a pointed look. Theo smirked back.

"You know, I apologised for hitting you before. Doesn't mean I won't do it again."

"Yeah, like you'd get the chance," Jacobs said. "You took me by surprise before."

"I think you'll find that's the point in a fight," Theo retorted. "Wouldn't be very fair if I stood up and declared I was going to punch you ten seconds before I actually do."

"Oh ha-ha," Jacobs said. He didn't sound amused. "So why apologise now?"

A good question and he wasn't entirely sure that he had the answer to it. "Not sure." He regretted it the moment he said it, quickly moved to follow it up. "I mean, I think we've probably got a good few days of this, maybe weeks. Just figure it might be the best thing to bury the hatchet before it all boils over."

"Hey, I'm supposed to be the diplomatic one," Jacobs said. Theo fought to narrow his eyes at the stupid grin he wore. "You're supposed to be the one who does stuff without thinking about it."

"I think we all have the potential to grow as people."

Just a week later, their punishment duty over and everything apparently forgotten, Theo had found himself on his way to his meeting with the combat specialist when he'd found himself thinking about his past even more. He'd turned the corner, come face-to-face with a woman he hadn't thought about for years, more than that he hadn't expected to see her here given the circumstances of their last meeting.

It had been a long time ago now, maybe a few days before he'd finally walked out of Cyris' life and his three lieutenants in Cyria had come to the house, a dangerous play at the best of times given the way that everyone wanted to get their hands on the four of them at the time. Remove them, and Cyria would have fallen. He'd toyed idle plenty of times with the idea of finding something incriminating that would have gotten rid of them and posting it anonymously to the authorities.

That'd show his father. Shatter his organisation. Silas had been there, Theo had never liked him. There'd been something tremendously off-putting about him, a man just as cruel as his father and who Cyris had liked to proclaim as 'his true son'. That was okay, Theo had always wanted to reciprocate that feeling and never consider Cyris 'his true father'.

Jenghis, the tall woman who'd never even bothered to acknowledge him was there as well, he'd never heard her, or Mara be referred to as Cyris' children and that came in some small part, a relief.

He was grateful that he'd never had a sibling, Divines knew what sort of mess they'd be in given his father's attitude to parenting.

At least Mara had always tried to be the nice one out of the three, she'd always stopped to engage him in chat he'd found uncomfortable even back then. If she thought that being nice to his only blood son was going to win her points with his father, then she had been sorely mistaken. Even back then, he'd never got the impression that she was the favoured of the three.

"Mara?" he said. That shock of red hair was immediately recognisable, she'd grown it out in the years since he'd seen her last, years that hadn't been as kind to her. She looked tired, dark circles around her eyes, a mad contrast to the tan of her skin. Weight had dropped off her, she'd never been fat all those years ago, but there'd been a fullness to her. Her uniform hung off her almost, made her look emaciated.

For a moment, he thought she didn't remember him. He didn't care if she did or not, he was more interested to find out what she was doing here, and why one of his father's former top lieutenants was wandering around a Unisco academy like she owned the place.

"Little Theobald Cyris," she said, not even bothering to hide her amusement. "Or, is it Jameson now? You grew up."

"You grew inwards," Theo said, the irritation sparking at the back of his consciousness. He wasn't going to be talked down to her, not by someone who should be in a jail cell by any reasonable definition of the idea. "What the hells are you doing here?"

"About to talk to someone," she said. The amusement had faded, replaced with aggravation on her head. He'd touched a nerve there.

"Shouldn't they be arresting you at a more conventional facility? Not an academy?" It sounded petulant and dumb the moment the words left his lips. Of course, she wasn't under arrest. If she was, she'd be in cuffs and she'd have escorts and she wouldn't be wearing a Unisco jumpsuit. There'd be a lot of things that would be different about this scene. He gulped. "Crap! You were working for Unisco, weren't you? All that time with my dad, you were reporting back on him."

She smiled at him. "No, actually, I wasn't. But the past is in the past and it is what it is. I was nobody's first choice to come work for Unisco. But they offered me a deal, it was a better shot than I was going to get anywhere else. Not that it's any of your business." She gave him a hard look." And if you go running to your father to tell him…"

"If I do any running involving my dad, it'll be in the opposite direction," Theo said. "Don't worry on that. I'll not tell him that you're working for his enemies. He can find out on his own, preferably in as crippling a manner as possible." Maybe she'd be the one to slap the cuffs on him. Wouldn't that just be the cherry atop a very succulent cake?

"Sorry to break it to you, your dad is yesterday's news. Nobody wants to catch him anymore. He had his record wiped for services to the kingdoms. If he keeps his nose clean, Unisco aren't going to chase him. There's bigger fish in the ocean to worry about."

"Coppinger?"

"Bang on," she said. "Cyris was an amateur compared to some of the shit she's been involved in, I probably don't have to tell you. Nobody else ever gave Unisco this much trouble, not like she's been doing for the last few months."

A lot of people had been saying that, he'd overheard some of the instructors come out with the same thing when they'd thought they'd been alone with each other. For a super-secret spy academy, it could be amazingly difficult to find a moment of privacy.

He didn't know how he felt about Unisco not hunting for his dad anymore. He'd always dreamed of seeing Cyris languishing in a prison cell. Services to the kingdoms? What the hells did that even mean anyway? He'd always thought of Cyris on the taking side of the deal rather than the giving.

She reached out, patted him in the shoulder, gave his arm a squeeze. It might have been meant to be reassuring, it just felt condescending like she was throwing him a treat for getting something wrong anyway. "Cheer up, Theo. You know what your dad's like. He'll screw up again eventually. He's a greedy bastard. Someone like him can't stay innocent forever, they'll have a moment where they throw it all away."

That was moderately reassuring. Not a lot but some. He wondered how much she actually knew Cyris. He was smarter than she was giving him credit for here, a lot smarter. His idea of passion was to be a little less cold, a lot more emotionless. No wonder he was like he was. He'd had no chance.

"I'll see you around, anyway," Mara said. She offered him a hand. "Nice to see you again, Cadet Jameson. I've got an appointment. Talking to someone about being an undercover asset."

Yep. Traitorous bitch probably sums up your skillset, he thought.

"If you ever want to talk though," she dug into her pocket, produced a card. "Give me a call. It's good to talk to others who survived... Well, your dad."

"You seem to have done okay out of it," he said. Regardless, he took it, glanced at the name embossed on it. Maria Estrella. Unisco. "Take it you don't go by Mara anymore then?"

"I never was her," she said. "Not wholly. That was only who your father tried to make me into." She lowered her voice, leaned in close to him. "I don't regret getting out the way I did. Jenghis died. Last I heard, he'd beaten Silas into a coma, they didn't expect him to live. Your dad is a monster and if you ever want to get revenge on him, just wait. When Unisco do try to hunt him down, I'll be the first in the queue to go on that mission. You might be qualified as… They spoke to you about your speciality yet?"

"Combat, they reckon."

"Well, it's a noble thing. Always going to need those guys. These days more than ever. Someone who can shoot, and fight is always going to have work. The kingdoms aren't getting any safer unfortunately. We'd all be out of work if they were."

Finally, he took her offered hand, squeezed it and pumped. Her skin was warm, her fingers bearing calluses. Years of pulling triggers for one cause or another?

"Nice to meet you, Agent Estrella," he said. "Stay healthy."

If she took offence at the comment, she didn't show it, just gave him a wry smile. "You too, Theobald. You too."

The past had too many ways of catching up with you when you least expected it, he was starting to think. Even when you thought that it was away from you, little things crept in that you hadn't even considered to be a possibility.

"As you all know," Bruno Hans said, casting his gaze across the room. "Or you might not, it is possible that you may not have picked up on it, before we set you onto the next level and break you all up, we like to administer one final class test to see how ready you all are. Consider it your final examination for the Iaku academy. You guys have been here for six months. We've rushed it all in, your basic training, everything that you need to graduate as a field agent. Normally it takes two years, but circumstances are what they are. You've taken it all in well, but it is time for you to put those skills to a practical use."

They'd all been summoned to the main hall of the academy, been told to pack their things together. Most of them hadn't brought much and they'd accumulated even less, it hadn't taken long to pack. Their cadet uniforms had been returned to the academy for a thorough cleaning, the clothes they'd spent the last six months living in until they'd become like second skins had been stripped from them. Now they were back in civilian gear and Theo didn't know if it felt strange or not. It was unusual. Felt alien putting his old clothes back on. They didn't feel the same.

Maybe he wasn't the same. He felt like his body hadn't changed. Hadn't been thin before, hadn't been fat. Just probably what they'd call average. Now they felt tight about the arms and the legs, he'd been surprised at first until he realised how dumb that shock was. He'd been training physically at least once a day, sometimes twice for the last six months. Muscular development was about the least that he could have expected out of this situation. He was probably in better shape now than he had been at any time in his life. They all were. Jacobs actually looked dangerous now, he'd been big before but now the muscles looked like they'd been forged through use, rather than to look pretty. Tamale, quite curvy before but now looking lean and renewed stood at the end of the line, the muscles in her legs pronounced under her shorts.

"Your final test is the same as it always has been in the finest traditions of the academy. Everything you have learned is something that you will be forced to use in order to pass the field test. Even should your future not lay in the field..." Hans' eyes moved towards Dom Hill as he said it, Theo noticed. Rumour had been flying around that Hill was being groomed for a technician position. A bit of a waste, in his opinion, but he was starting to concede that the instructors probably knew their job better than he did. Maybe he was growing as a person after all.

He wouldn't have liked the job. Not a chance. His interview with the combat specialist had been enlightening, it looked like that was the direction in which any future Unisco career was going to be driven. Not that he was especially unhappy about it. Like Mara had said, it was a fine position, if one where the life-expectancy was a lot shorter than expected. He didn't care about that. You could have ten good years, even that might be a generous estimate he'd been warned, or you could have fifty dull ones.

"You shall all be split into two teams and placed in an urban environment. One team shall be the hunted, it is your job to work together to evade the other team for as long as possible who are tracking you. The other team are to take the job of the hunters, you are required to find them and catch them as quickly as you can. The test is over when all the hunted have been found or the hunters are no longer able to complete their mission."

Well, this had the potential to be interesting, Theo thought. The idea of teamwork sat sour with him but that was something he'd have to suffer through. If you couldn't work as a team, you died very quickly in the field. Just one of the lessons they'd forced into them and it had stuck, as much as he didn't want to have to admit it.

"To make the challenge fair, neither team is permitted to leave the boundaries of the city, meaning instant failure for any cadet who sets both feet outside of the lines. We will know, we will watch you. Just keep that in mind. Graduating the class is not dependent on winning or losing, rather your general approach to the task. You will be graded accordingly to how you go about your mission, your sense of teamwork, any skills you show. In short, you get to put on an audition for how you would perform in the field. I advise you not to blow it."

This really had the potential to get interesting. His curiosity had been raised, Hans looked around to Konda and Takamishi. Konda stepped forward, craned onto his toes and whispered something in Hans' ear.

Curious. Now what were they saying? He tilted his head forward, some part of him knew there was little chance of hearing it, even so. Still he had to try. Curiosity was a dangerous thing. Cyris had discouraged it. The sort of thing he liked to punish with a clip around the ear.

Konda stepped back, Hans didn't look happy, but he swallowed the look down and cleared his throat, the attention back to the crowd.

"Inquisitor Konda," he said. "Has just proffered an unusual suggestion to me, one highly unorthodox but in these dangerous times, I feel they may be more of use. In past trials, we have preferred to have even teams to make the contest a fairer one." He looked like he wanted to swallow the words down, never have them see the light of day. "However, it is prudent for me to remind you all that life is never fair. Sometimes it works for you, sometimes it works against you. Inquisitor Konda's decision is that only two will run, the rest will hunt."

He must have been imagining things. He was sure Konda was looking at him as Hans spoke out, the inquisitor's eyes burning into him. In that moment, Theobald Jameson had a horrible feeling rush through him, the knowledge of certainty that this wasn't going to go well for him.

"Cadet Jacobs. Cadet Jameson," Hans said. "I'm afraid to tell you that by the choice of Inquisitor Konda, you will be the two running. The trial begins tomorrow morning at dawn, we are to meet outside for transport two hours before. Anyone who is late will automatically fail and face expulsion. This test is the most important of your meagre lives so far, treat it as such."

Konda had collared the two of them, given them both a big smile. "Looking forward to your challenge, boys?"

"Why?" Jacobs had asked the question, Theo found himself in agreement with him for what had to be a first time. It was the fifty thousand credit question. Why? Why? Why?

That smile had only grown. "I think you're both capable. I think you're both holding yourselves back in so many ways. Cadet Jameson, you're a ruthless son of a bitch, you lack control and composure without a voice to guide you. Cadet Jacobs, you're arguably not ruthless enough. You need a nastier streak if you'll hope to survive. I think Cadet Jameson can bring that out in you. That's what this test is truly about. Smoothing over rough edges before the next stage."

"Does it help that I'd quite like to strangle him?" Jacobs asked. Theo gave him a dirty look, clenched his fists, felt the muscles in his hands tense up. Just in case. Punching him would be a stupid thing to do now. Not when he'd gotten away with the last blow he'd thrown.

"Well, it's a start." Konda smiled as he said it. "And all great achievements must begin somewhere. Remember, you both must succeed together to avoid failure. You're responsible for each other when this test starts. Treat each other like it."

Son of a bitch!

"I think this experience will be good for the pair of you. After tomorrow, you may never see each other again, should you pass. You will go on to be parts of the whole, a sum greater than its parts. Unisco needs people like you and I suggest you don't disappoint." He clapped them both on their shoulders. "Right, I think Hans mentioned it, but the rest of the day is yours to prepare however you wish. I advise you not to worry too much, not to try and prepare for it beyond the rudimentary. Just relax. You've had your basic training, there is nothing in this test that shouldn't be beyond you. And remember, those hunting you have had the same training."

He smiled at them, the expression grandfatherly. The pride was there in his face, emblazoned for all to see. "That's why the inquisitors exist, I feel the need to tell you. Different training, different approach to the rest of Unisco. When we want someone, we find them. It's not even a contest. Not like this. This is going to be an entertaining challenge, I feel, and I am looking forward to watching what happens."

Chapter Eighteen. The River Runs Deep.

*"Three dead men and a jungle beat.
Three dead men rose to their feet
Skin as white as a sheet
Soon burned brown from the sunny heat
Sizzle, sizzle, cook that meat.
Three dead men and a jungle beat."*
Song sung by Vazaran children in the days following the emergence of the Green.

They'd been in the Green for days now, hadn't seen another living soul for miles. Not a man, nor animal. Even the beasts were avoiding the accursed place, the ground even picked clean of any sort of remains. Wilsin didn't like it, couldn't shake the bad feeling stagnating in the pit of his stomach, aware it had started to slowly snake its way through the rest of his body until unease weighed heavily on every limb. He'd tried to ignore it, tried to offer another explanation to himself.

None had come, not easily and not feasibly. The point had come where he had to maybe admit this trip had been a bad idea. In the days that had passed, he'd come to realise that he wasn't the only one with those feelings. The others on the trip looked as bad as he felt, Brendan's moods growing almost as dark as the tan across his weathered features. The heat was unbearable, the humidity stifling and the water they managed to salvage from the river felt painfully meagre. They'd brought enough purity tablets, for cleansing the water, to last a year yet he hoped it didn't come to that. A year here would probably feel like ten elsewhere. A year with no communication with the outside world. They'd already tried. Summoners still worked here, though access to the CallerNet didn't exist. Maybe they'd leave, and the war would've concluded in their absence. That would be nice, even if he knew he was deluding himself. What could happen wasn't worth contemplating. All they could do was focus on their own situation and hope they made it through unscathed.

He was getting sick of the boat. The few hours a day they spent on solid land were starting to become welcome distractions. Every day brought its own trip to the shoreline, either because Brendan wanted some information from their position. Or Bryce did. Or Fazarn did. Always someone needed something. He couldn't complain at the chance to stretch his legs. The boat wasn't uncomfortable but being trapped aboard it with seven other people for long stretches was becoming unbearable. Their number had started with nine. Already the chemist from Premesoir, Ballard Brown had failed to make it to the end.

Their first night, they'd slept on the shore and he'd woken up screaming, covered in large red-and-silver ants, all biting away at exposed skin. Wilsin and Reeves had tried to get them off him, Wilsin had snatched one away, felt its jaws snap into his finger and he'd sworn as his entire hand had gone numb. For each one they ripped away, a dozen more swarmed over the bleeding man, snapping and biting away. Finally, Reeves had acted decisively, smacked his palms together with a thunderclap and the resulting shockwave had thrown dozens of the biting little bastards off. Wilsin had felt the hairs on the back of his arm and his chest stand up at the proximity to the blast. Too little too late for the bleeding Ballard, they'd buried him an hour later. He hadn't so much resembled a human being come the end of it, more a giant bloody bruise, swollen and misshapen by thousands of bites, mangled his flesh. Fazarn had said a few words, Bryce had passed around alcohol and Reeves had offered a few words of his own. It had taken a day or two for the numbness to recede in his hand. He'd been worried about poison, he'd taken Nordin Nmecha's advice as best he could, had done the best with their meagre supply of drugs. They'd slept on the boat every night since then. Maybe the ants only came out at night, discomfort was certainly to be favoured over death. None of them were going to forget Ballard's screams as the ants had devoured his flesh.

An increasingly grumpy-looking Alex Fazarn had explained later to them that the ants looked like a much larger cousin of the Vazaran Fire-Eater, one of the largest species of ant in the kingdom. The damn things had been the size of one of Wilsin's fingers, he wondered if that was as big as they got. Fazarn had christened them the Vazaran Warrior-Eater Ant. A little strange, Wilsin thought, given Ballard hadn't been a warrior. He supposed it sounded better than calling them the Doctor-Eater. He'd let it go. Moral was already low in the camp without adding excess fuel to a simmering fire. Fazarn gave the impression he was regretting the whole damn thing. Bryce had spent more time with his hip-flask than he had with most other members of the expedition. Reeves had retreated within himself, spending the days sat atop the bow of the boat, eyes closed, deep in silent meditation. Suniro Suchiga was notable by his silence, Tiana Aubemaya did her best to keep up with Fazarn's every whim and mood swing, but Wilsin could see she was losing patience He'd seen that look before, usually before a spouse flipped out and started whaling on their partner. As much as he might support that decision if she suddenly shoved Fazarn overboard, he couldn't see it doing the expedition any good.

The doctor was the only one unfazed by the circumstances they found themselves in, Nmecha in consistent good spirits so far. Maybe he anticipated a lot of business shortly. The way things had gone so far, Wilsin wouldn't be surprised. Nordin Nmecha sang through the days, he had quite a good voice for someone who looked like they'd been a bandit in a previous life. He wasn't exactly sure where he'd gotten his medical qualifications, but he knew what he was doing. In previous days, he might have thought singing would have gotten tiresome but Nmecha had worked his way through the catalogue of songs he knew, just enough of a variety to keep them all entertained.

Maybe he'd been sneaking some of Bryce's special brew. It hadn't taken Wilsin long to work out exactly how the botanist was pickling himself, he'd seen him adding powder to his water rations. Funny, they spent the time cleaning the water of poisons and parasites, only for Bryce to add his own poison back to it.

He'd tried to bring it up to Brendan about why Fazarn had brought Bryce along, surely having a rampant alcoholic on the expedition would end badly for them all. His queries had fallen on deaf ears, Brendan still pissed with him over the way he'd put that blast through the endroid's head. Subtlety had apparently gone out of the window when he'd done that, listening to the way his boss had gone on about it. He'd been given the mother of all dressing downs over it, had been annoyed by it but ultimately gotten on with everything. Bearing a grudge out here was pointless. It might just be the sort of childish act that got them all killed.

The sun was lowering in the distance, crawling towards the horizon and he found himself sat next to Nmecha at the back of the boat, watching the doctor go through his medical pack. For once, he wasn't singing, his concentration focused on the drugs in front of him.

"Doc," he said. He didn't get an immediate reply, Nmecha still focused on his wares. He'd only offered the greeting to be polite. He didn't think he was being ignorant, far from it. Despite the fearsome appearance, he'd found the company doctor to be the most pleasant member of the expedition, maybe barring Aubemaya but even her patience appeared to be reaching its limits. He wondered how she'd wound up working for a dick like Fazarn, no doubt there'd be a story of how he was one of the greats in his field and she wanted to learn from the best. If he had to work for Fazarn, he'd probably have bought a blaster and shot him long ago.

Different strokes for different people, he thought. Couldn't change the kingdoms, no matter how much you might want to. Sometimes you just had to take people as what they were, not what you wanted them to be.

"Wilsin," Nmecha finally said. "Thank you for allowing me those moments to check our supplies."

"Be honest," Wilsin said. "How bad is it?" He felt partially responsible for it, given the mostly-healed bite on his hand. "Are we going to run out of medicine before the end of the trip?"

"Depends," the doctor said. "There are always situations out there we can never foresee. If we avoid any stupidity, then perhaps we will be okay. A few random accidents, we might muddle through. A catastrophe though, that is something we will not survive. I would have liked to have brought a full medical suite but alas, they wouldn't go for that."

"How did you wind up on this trip?" Wilsin asked. He'd wondered for a while, Nmecha looked so out of kilter with the rest of the academics that Fazarn had plumped for, there was something about him that suggested he didn't spend most of the time living in his own head. They all looked like they'd spent most of their time in the classroom, despite their actions on the trip suggesting they'd roughed it before. Nmecha gave the impression he'd lived an interesting life. Might have been the eyepatch.

"Credits," Nmecha said. "They wanted a doctor, I needed to get out of town for a while and get some credits together. Felt like a good marriage."

"Uh-huh?" Wilsin rubbed the back of his head. He didn't like the sound of what he'd heard. People who needed to get out of town for a while and put together credits usually had some sort of skeleton in their cupboard and he didn't know whether this was going to be a good thing for the expedition or not. It inferred problems and problems were not what this whole endeavour needed right now. They didn't need Vazaran gangsters showing up demanding payment for gambling debts. He assumed it was gambling, as good a theory as any. "And how did you meet Fazarn?"

"Is this an interrogation, Mister Wilsin?"

"I'm curious as to how you met up with these guys. You seem a bit like the sort of company that they wouldn't keep."

Nmecha laughed. "I get that a lot. I'm an old friend of Bryce. We went to college together, took different paths through life." Wilsin looked at Nmecha and then at Bryce. He wouldn't have had them as the same age. Bryce looked to have had a lot harder life than Nmecha, remarkable when he considered that Bryce packed a full complement of eyes. "But there was supposed to be another doctor coming on the expedition, he had to pull out. Bryce recommended me to Fazarn. He has friends everywhere, does Shane Bryce."

Wilsin glanced back towards Bryce. He had that glazed look he'd come to associate with him, staring unseeing towards the sun as he sat with his back to the mast of the boat, his flask in front of him, wobbling with every kiss of the water beneath.

"Is he okay?" Wilsin asked. "Bryce, I mean. He often doesn't look it."

"He took a bad injury in his youth," Nmecha said. "Never really recovered from it. Surgery was botched, I saw the x-rays of it. Lives in constant bloody pain. I'd drink too if I were in his position." He laughed bitterly, zipped up his medical kit. "I'd drink more than he does, I think he does well in my professional opinion."

"It's not a criticism," Wilsin said. "You just wonder about these things."

Again, Nmecha laughed. "Don't you worry about Shane. He's a lot better at what he does while inebriated than most are while sober. He'll get the job done, he's a brilliant man. I think he'd have been wasted as a shadow fighter."

He's perennially wasted as a botanist, Wilsin wanted to say. He chose not to. "So, do you regret it yet? Coming out here?" He threw out an arm to the length of beyond around them, nothing but trees and water. Up ahead there was a clearing in between the trees. These trees that should have taken decades to grow but instead had reached maturity within months. More proof that everything wasn't right within this place. He'd seen the initial aerial photos, it had started out as grass, a fine dusting of it from the centre of Vazara. That wouldn't have been too bad. At least they could have walked it. The grass had been just the start. Nothing had been able to prepare him for the sight of the rainforest greeting their arrival. He got the impression Brendan had been surprised as well, even if he hadn't outwardly shown it.

Bryce on the other hand had lost his shit, pointing excitedly and going off on a stream of slurred mumbo-jumbo that probably meant more to the scientists amongst them than it did to him. Wilsin didn't care about the science. He was here as protection.

Nmecha shook his head. "It's not good to have regrets in life. For better or worse, we all make choices and it's best to live with them while you can. Whatever we do, it changes us, grants us new experiences. We can learn from that, it's never wasted." He smiled at him. "Why a spirit caller like you came along, that's the mystery here. There's no glory in what they're going to do here, no prize at the end of the game."

"Maybe I was curious," Wilsin said, baring his teeth in a grin. "Maybe I made a choice to get a new experience."

"Very funny, Mister Wilsin." For the first time, Nmecha didn't look amused. "I ain't never seen a spirit caller carry a blaster like that either. I saw you shoot that endroid. Didn't hesitate. It's not a weapon for a novice, your average novice might think the blaster looks cool, but it'd break their wrist the first time they pulled the trigger. Bust all the bones up there with one discharge. I've seen it before, you know. You got more than a rudimentary knowledge of blasters."

"Maybe I'm a weekend enthusiast," Wilsin said. He didn't like where this conversation was going, made the conscious effort to try and divert it. Given it had reached this point, he doubted Nmecha would be fooled, but he had to try. Keep talking until you talk your way out of it. That little nugget had been sound advice he'd once been given, at least he'd thought so at the time. Unfortunately, the more you talked, the more chance you had of tripping over the lies.

"And maybe I'm just your average scalpel jockey."

"I've never heard that term before," Wilsin said. "It sounds derogatory."

"And I ain't never heard of no weekend enthusiast carrying a blaster like that neither so it might sound derogatory when I accuse you of talking a whorl of shit."

"What exactly do you think I am, Nordin?"

"More than meets the eye, perhaps," the doctor said thoughtfully. "I'd say maybe you're not just a spirit caller, but you never know who be listening, even out here and this place ain't healthy for people like that at this time. Think you can appreciate that."

Wilsin could and he did. The pallor of suspicion ran deep, and he didn't need it cast on him at this time.

"I think we're all more than we seem," he said. "And some of us do have secrets. Some secrets are greater than others though, I think you understand that."

"I reckon I do." Nmecha clapped him on the arm. "Good talk. Now if you'll excuse me…"

Wilsin stood up, moved away from the doctor, towards the edge of the boat. The clearing loomed ahead, he fixed his gaze on it…

Huh!

He blinked, focused on the gap between the trees. He'd only glanced fleetingly at it, suddenly sure he'd seen something there, something man-shaped but not a man. He continued to stare, curious but nothing came to sight. Maybe he'd imagined it. Maybe. He would've appreciated longer, yet the boat continued, and the clearing was lost to sight. He rubbed his eyes, mopped the sweat out of them. He'd like to think that he was seeing things. That thing had stood like a man, but it didn't look like no man he'd ever seen. Green-skinned, covered in protrusions, naked otherwise.

Seeing things. Had to be. He glanced back to the passengers of the boat, he didn't know much about boats and little about this one really, other than it was big enough for them to all be on deck and not all up in each other's space. That was a relief. Nothing worse than working while someone was all up over your shoulder and able to see what you were doing. It was okay for them. All the academics had stuff to do, journals and reports to fill out, samples to analyse. They were all busy in their own little worlds, Brendan pouring over a data pad. Fazarn and Aubemaya in conversation as they compared notes, Suchiga and Bryce studying plant samples they'd acquired in previous days. Wilsin watched them examining the beakers. One of them had poured a purple solution into each container, both watching the way that the plants reacted. Within seconds, tiny little flowers had started to spring to life, cracking open the stems in the jar, forcing their way out into the world, hungrily ingesting the purple stuff. Whatever it was, he didn't know, but they liked it. Not quite as much however as Suchiga and Bryce, they both looked like they were about to lose their shit over the revelation.

He was no botanist, but he had to admit it was something impressive to see life created where it shouldn't be able to thrive. That was like the first basic rule of plant-life, once it was cut out of its natural environment, it should start the slow process of death. This was doing the exact opposite. He wasn't an expert and he recognised it immediately. Divines alone knew what Bryce and Suchiga would make of it.

He stepped over to the front of the boat, dropped down next to Reeves. Maybe he should have come up with something to do during the long hours on the boat between their excursions to the shoreline. He should have followed Perrit's example, written a book about their journey. Too late to start now, he could have recalled every event in crystal clarity at the time of writing, but now those early days felt hazy. His own contribution felt like it had been solely to shoot that damn endroid. Even then, they could have done without it. The owner of that yard had freaked out, almost shot back. Way to go Wilsin, Brendan had said. You just nearly caused an international incident. What part of keeping a low profile don't you understand?

Reeves probably understood where he was coming from. Brendan had fought to get a Vedo on the expedition with them, that told Wilsin that he'd expected trouble and though it hadn't been apparent so far, it didn't mean it wasn't around the corner. He could remember the stories he'd heard about this place, roughly translated from what the scrap man had said. People came in here and didn't come out. He'd already made a point of keeping his T6 on him when they went ashore, if that apparition was anything to go by, he might start taking a blaster rifle with him. Reeves was posing as one of Brendan's students, the ruse had already started to fall away. He'd made best efforts but anyone with even a little intelligence could see the lie, although they'd kept quiet. Maybe he was being overtly critical because he knew the truth and he could see through the efforts the Vedo was making. Whatever other qualities Reeves might have, subterfuge wasn't one of them. He didn't look like a student. He didn't look like anything, quiet, unassuming and polite. When he'd used the Kjarn to throw those ants off Ballard Brown, that should have been a clue for the rest of the expedition as to his true nature, yet even that was up for debate. Wilsin didn't know how much they'd seen in that moment, and nobody really wanted to talk about that night, a curious juxtaposition between human curiosity and respect for the dead.

"Something bothering you, David?" Reeves asked without opening his eyes. "You feel troubled."

"Just thought I saw something," Wilsin said, rubbing the back of his head, scratching at sweat-soaked hair with his nails. He'd been bitten somewhere there, and it was starting to aggravate him, little bastard mosquito. Even the little bloodsuckers seemed to want to avoid this place, which was about the worst omen he could think of. "Out there in the clearing a while back. Unsettling. Maybe I was seeing things." I hope, he wanted to add. "Only for a moment and then it was gone."

"It is an unfashionably hot day," Reeves said. This from a man who didn't have a single drop of sweat on him, he looked like he'd spent his day sat in the shade sipping iced water in a tall glass through a straw. If it hadn't been inappropriate, Wilsin would have touched him just to check that he wasn't imagining things. He was putting it down to Vedo powers. "The heat does befuddle the mind and play tricks with your eyes."

"Did you sense anything out there?" he asked. It felt a ridiculous question to ask, yet he'd seen what Reeves could do. Reeves had been one of the Vedo at the Quin-C, Wilsin had seen him cut through a dozen Coppinger soldiers on the viewing screen in half as many seconds without so much as flinching. His speed and coordination had been incredible, if he hadn't seen it, he wouldn't have believed it. Just because something was beyond your comprehension didn't make it impossible. Impossible was becoming something of a difficult term these days, it didn't mean what it once did.

"I sense a lot of things," Reeves said. "Mainly from this boat. There's an incredible melting pot of emotions out here. You feel frustrated. You're not the only one. I feel incredible desire, I feel sadness and pain, sorrow and pity. I feel jealousy and rage, though nothing beyond what you'd expect." He straightened up, opened his eyes. "It's not a pleasant thing, David. Being able to sense other people's emotions."

"Anne said that," Wilsin said. He'd never believed the stories about Anne Sullivan and what she'd been able to do. Half of Unisco had believed her, half had thought she was deluded and in the current climate, that half had felt chastened by revelations. "I always thought she was…"

"It is only natural to disbelieve what you cannot understand," Reeves said. "It makes things easier, for one thing. An easy lie is always better to swallow than a hard truth."

"Some people like the truth though."

"Those are usually the people who don't know what the truth means and wouldn't choose it if they knew the consequences," Reeves smiled. "I know what you're thinking. Wisdom from a man younger than yourself."

"Not that much younger," Wilsin said. "And I've always been under the impression that although wisdom comes with age, some people pick it up a lot faster than others."

Reeves laughed at that. "Well that's more or less true, I'll give you that. Attitude takes you a long way. I imagine you didn't become what you are overnight and neither did I. Training. Knowledge. Education. They're all what you need to get ahead. And wisdom earned is always at a price. You won't win a debate with me on the subject."

"I don't know how it did turn into a debate," Wilsin smiled. "So, you didn't sense anything out there in the trees?"

"I sense something," Reeves said. "There is some form of life out there. Whatever it is, it's not life like anything we know."

"You know, I came over hoping you'd make me feel better," Wilsin said, half-joking. "You've not exactly reassured me."

"Well I can't help you then. Reassurance is not something you should ever come to a Vedo for. We deal in truths, the sort of honesty that you don't want to hear. Such is the word of Baxter." Reeves shrugged. "We do apologies though. Sorry."

They left the boat shortly after for their nightly meal. Cooking on board the boat wasn't something any of them were willing to try, Brendan had regaled them with a tale from his youth the first night in which they'd made those very efforts and the whole event had wound up in disaster. Mistakes, he'd said in his deep baritone, are all well and good provided you need never repeat them. A mistake is nature's way of telling you to not be such a pillock ever again.

Wilsin had had to smirk at that. It was something he found hard to do, imagining Brendan King as a young man, making a young man's mistakes. He always got the impression that even when he'd been a child, he'd been serious and studious, his hair that same shade of dirty steel that it was now.

Either way, young man or ageless child, he'd had a point and they'd not had their evening meal on the boat ever since. Always the process became the same, they'd disembark and tie up for a few hours, stretch their legs while the scientists did their thing. Inevitably it ended up being him and Reeves who made up the fire, two spare parts amidst a well-oiled machine, left searching for a purpose. Between them, it wasn't as hard as it might have been. Wilsin had used his machete to cut down the best branches he could find, not hard in the conditions. Every bit of moisture felt like it had been sucked from the trees, the bark brittle to his touch. The crack as metal bit into it was satisfying, the crack giving way to the snap and tear as bark shattered under the unbreakable blade. He cut, Reeves carried, taking armfuls of the timber back towards the clearing.

The first time he'd seen it, he'd inquired as to if Reeves ever considered carrying them back using his powers. The answer had been a resounding shake of the head, Reeves giving him a look as if he were crazy.

"Not the best use of it though, is it?" he said. The tone in his voice suggested that the notion was genuinely alien to him, that he could no more do it than grow a pair of wings and take to the sky. "A tremendous waste."

"You have it. Why not use it?" He wasn't letting this go, he was determined that an answer was going to come his way, no matter how hard it might be.

"Master Baxter taught us all that to use the power with frivolity is to betray the nature of it. We do not control the power, it resides in all of us, we are partners above all else. To use the primordial forces for selfish gain, nay, for menial tasks we are capable of carrying out ourselves will do us more harm than good." He cleared his throat, threw the last few twigs down onto the fire, stretched out his arms. "It never does too much to become reliant on power either. Rely on yourself first, what you might be able to do second. Because the self is always the first port of ingenuity."

Wilsin smirked. He'd heard that before, some variant of it. "That's a Unisco saying, he got it from us back in the day."

"Yes, I forget about Master Baxter's colourful history," Reeves said. "Always find it hard to believe that he managed to balance three different lives."

"He's a special man," Wilsin said, surprised to find that he meant it. "He's a legend at Unisco. Had a knack of surviving, although given what we know now about him, it's hardly surprising."

"For all his powers, he tried to teach us self-reliance. Just because something is easy, doesn't make it right." Reeves held out his hand in front of him, Wilsin saw the glow emanating from his palms, moved to shield his eyes. The twin fireballs that fell from his skin hit the twigs and the branches, tore into them with hungry determination. Within seconds, the flames were flickering merrily, a beacon amidst the dropping darkness. Wilsin looked across at the Vedo, not sure whether to call him out on what had just happened. Apparently, he didn't like criticism.

"But he did always knock into us that time is something we don't always have," Reeves said, inclining his head towards the flames. "And that if we need to do something quick, then it is worth doing. Easier than scrabbling up a fire, wouldn't you say?"

"I would," Wilsin said. "I would say that."

Their evening meal hadn't been spectacular, the food supplies weren't close to being exhausted but most of the tastiest morsels had already been snapped up. Even with Ballard Brown's portion no longer needed, their supplies weren't limitless. Sooner or later they would run out. Wilsin wondered where the next meal would come from when they reached that point. He didn't want to dwell on it, hadn't seen much edible within these trees, not unless they fancied trying to lure more of those ants out into the open and they didn't look the tastiest things he'd ever tried to force down his throat. It might come down to it. Better discomfort than starvation. He'd seen the latter and it wasn't pretty. Seeing the human body waste away because it wasn't getting enough of what it needed, emaciation in process, was a sobering thought.

Although the meat they'd cooked over the fire had long lost any sort of identity, he'd found it well worth the wait. Wilsin hadn't realised how hungry he was going into the meal, his stomach giving little sounds of appreciation at the burnt offerings he'd found himself tucking into. The taste was smoky, a little burned, the spices scorched away by the heat of the fire leaving only a lingering essence in the back of the mouth. The spices kept the flies away, kept it preserved, not the worst taste imaginable but he couldn't imagine finding anything like it outside of Vazara. Their conditions left them resourceful, more than most would be willing to admit. Not everyone could survive in a place like this, natural selection meant not everyone did. Only the strong and the smart rose to the top, the weak and the stupid died.

He could see why people fell in love with the kingdom. There was a sense of raw beauty about it, even here sweating himself to death in a jungle which shouldn't even exist by any law of nature or logic. A jungle claimed to have sprung from the will of a madwoman. Even amidst what should have been ugly, something pure felt like it was on the verge of slipping through the cracks.

Halfway through the meal, Brendan cleared his throat. "Feels like we do this every night, just sit here and eat in silence like strangers," he said. "Yet are we not comrades in an expedition to change the future and bring knowledge to those who have none? What we do here could have consequences for the kingdoms, it is only perhaps for the best that we do not consider each other strangers. Our number has been reduced, Divines care for Professor Brown's soul and I think now perhaps we consider the danger in our undertaking more than ever. We might come to rely on each other to survive."

Nobody immediately said anything. Wilsin continued to chew on his spiced meat, mulled over what his boss had just said. He wasn't proffering anything.

"Come on now," he said. "From each of you, one story. We talk over this meal. No backing out. No lies. Just the truth." Did Brendan's eyes dwell on him for a moment, Wilsin wondered. Maybe his way of warning him that the truth didn't necessarily mean the truth as it was. A casual deception. "I'll go first, if you like."

Nobody moved to stop him as Brendan cleared his throat.

Chapter Nineteen. Campfire Tales.

"Attack can come at any time. Always be aware of your surroundings, especially when alone in enemy territory. Those who know the environment ultimately don't get caught with their pants down. And we all know there's little more embarrassing than being caught unawares by those who want to kill you. At least you won't live with the shame, but you'll sully Unisco's name with your piss-poor performance and I won't have that."

One of Tod Brumley's former rallying speeches while a Unisco instructor.

"I always wanted to be an explorer, you know. I got it from my father. He didn't go anywhere much, not least after I was born, he was the sort of man who read about places rather than experiencing them for himself. He used to talk about them like he'd been there. Don't get me wrong, I think books have a place in the kingdoms. The knowledge of the past should never be ignored. Believing something at the time you felt you had all the facts about, no matter how ridiculous it might seem today, it can offer up perspective. That's the one thing that comes with time.

There you have it. I loved my father, but I found his attitude a little lacking as I got older. Mind you, he did as well. The older he got, the more excuses he found. He got settled within a life and didn't do much to change it. He ended up living vicariously through his friends, I'll never forget the times Brennan Frewster used to show up unannounced at my home growing up. He and my father were good friends, he named me for him. Not well, admittedly, but still. As he got older, his health faded, I've been lucky in that regard, my mother had a constitution of iron whereas my father wilted away.

That first time I stepped out into the world away from home, it was when I went to get my caller's licence, we lived in a small town and I had to go to the nearest city. I stepped out on the road, walked down it like I owned it. I was a scrawny sixteen-year-old back then, but a cocky little shit. For the first time, I was out on my own, ready to take on the world. I felt like I could have beaten it as well. That feeling is unmistakeable, you know. Beholden to nobody and no one else. I took the long way, ignored the warnings to stay close to the road. You all know what it's like when you're young, you always think the sun is going to shine, that your parents can't possibly know what they're talking about and nothing bad can possibly happen.

Anyway, I got lost. Bound to happen, right? Got lost, what should have been a three-hour walk ended up being a two-day trek in the wilderness. I know you're wondering how much of a wilderness Canterage can be, but this was forty-odd years ago. It wasn't then what it is now. I was sure that if I kept on walking, I'd hit a city sooner or later. My supplies were meagre, but I resolved to carry on going. Stopping and complaining about it wouldn't have done me a damn bit of good so I did what I could. One foot before another and eventually I hit civilisation. Well that's what I thought it was.

The only good thing about hitting the Montaigne house was that it gave me a starting point, I knew where I was in relation to the rest of the road. That said, it was the only good thing. For those of you who don't know local Canterage legend from some hundred odd years ago, and I imagine that's most if not all of you, Albert Montaigne was an inventor who built a house outside Dalphan. Nothing happens by accident, I think you'll find. I wandered into the shadow of the house, remembered the stories.

Montaigne made some great discoveries back in the day, had some theories but the common consensus that followed him into history is his complete lack of personal sense. I think any inventor needs to lack a certain sense of self-preservation, but this man was notorious for doing what any garden-variety lunatic would have considered over the top. Nobody knew exactly what he was working on back in the day, only that without warning, it caught fire and took most of the house with it. The stories go that it lit the damn thing up like a bonfire, killed Montaigne, killed his wife and their two children. Some legends say that one of the children was already disfigured after an acid mishap, but I investigated thoroughly some years ago, curious you see, found nothing to back it up."

Imagine my youthful excitement at discovering this, something I'd heard about but never seen for myself. Even in my weakened state, I rushed towards it, determined to look around. Maybe, just maybe, there was some food left. Looking back makes it seem ridiculous, but back then I was ready to believe anything. It wasn't impossible. It was very likely I was going delirious with hunger, but the idea that Montaigne had invented a fireproof refrigerator stocked with dateless sandwiches was a real boon to me. Besides, I was a curious lad and how often do you actually get to explore an actual haunted house?"

Brendan looked around at them all ruefully. "Well, it was haunted to a fashion. I pushed the door open, heard the creak as it swung on rusty hinges, daylight followed me in there like a faithful companion. Rumours said Montaigne created electrical lighting before anyone else in Canterage, but it didn't survive the fire. Might even have been what caused it. Nobody wanted to go on record and say for sure, couldn't blame them really, it was a bit of a shitstorm that one of the kingdom's most famous sons had killed himself in an accident. I pushed the door open, in went the light and about a hundred bats that were sleeping in there decided to wake up and greet me. That scared me, I had to admit. Ran a mile, beat my personal best record for running in fear."

Wilsin fought the urge to smile. Montaigne he'd heard of, nothing about how he'd died though. Interesting story. He'd heard Alvin Noorland talk about Montaigne a couple of times, mention him as an influence.

"The house isn't there anymore," Brendan said. "I went back about twenty years ago, and they'd knocked it down to build a shopping centre. Absolute travesty. It's also the reason I don't like bats. Just saying. I can remember them clawing at my face, their wings scratching my skin…" He tailed off, shuddered. "Just one of those mornings."

He glanced around the fire, from Suchiga to Bryce to Aubemaya to Fazarn who stood up, stretched his arms out and grinned.

"I'll tell you a story," he said. "One of my favourites of all time and what it means to me. You may have heard it before."

"One of the first stories I ever heard in my life was one of Melarius and Gilgarus. I happen to think most stories descend from stories about the Divines because I don't think anyone knows what humanity did before then. It was a different time, a darker age. War and savagery raged across the land, kings sprang up and were knocked down, warlords had the time of their lives, keeping themselves fresh for the rigours of battle between skirmishes.

I am a proud Vazaran, you know. Always have been, always will, they can't take that from me. The story goes that those that would become Divines, the twenty, they walked the kingdoms for years, surveying all that would one day be theirs. That it did not yet belong to them was just a minor detail. Gilgarus and Melarius towards the front of their legion, they strode across the sand plains of Vazara in front of a mountain known as Cradle Rock after translation. Some stories say that it looked like a cradle, it's from where they all take their shape, but I've always found that part of the tale too apocryphal for my liking.

With them to Cradle Rock, they brought two armies, one in favour of what they were doing and one against. Remember, they'd walked the kingdoms for years by this point and people had heard their names. Belief is a powerful thing. They'd walked the kingdoms, made declarations of what they were going to do, displayed their power for all to see… Don't interrupt me, Mister Reeves, I know what you're going to say, I've heard the theory before that they utilised the ways of the Kjarn. It's not an unreasonable theory, but utterly unprovable. Some people followed them, they worshipped them like the Divines they would become, others hated and feared them as only one can hold such emotion for the gods themselves. Nothing polarises us more than religion. It can unite, and it can divide, it can create, and it can destroy, it is a force of love and one of hate.

So yes, they are stood on top of this rock in the middle of the Vazaran desert, one army on one side and another on the other and Gilgarus steps to the highest point of the rock, surveys all around him and makes his proclamation with his wife and his children and his lover and his peers stood there up with him. Some stories dispute what he said in his entirety, translation variations and all that but my favourite version goes like this:

"You have all been summoned here today to bear witness to the end of the old and the start of the new. The old order has ended and today starts the first day of forever. Today we circumvent the flesh of mortality and we embrace the sweet bonds of eternity. We have walked these kingdoms and throughout them, we have discovered the truth of immortality. With eternal life comes a stand apart, we know this secret and thus we can never truly be one with you all again. As King of the Dei, I make the decision to withdraw. As part of the human tribe, our time has ended. We only watch from afar, we may judge you, we may favour you, we may punish you as our whims take us but our time among you is over. Always you have feared our retribution and sought our aid in life, thus the same shall be in death."

A stunned silence fell over the crowd, they tried to work out what Gilgarus was saying as he made that proclamation. Warriors were there, they're not renowned for being the strongest in the head and that much double talk had left them confused. Scholars and acolytes, they could understand what he'd said but the implications had left them silent. How else do you comprehend a time like this? We can't, you know. Nothing like it has ever happened since. The area around Cradle Rock was as silent as a grave, nobody has ever heard two armies and everyone between go silent like that. Perhaps the Dei's greatest ever feat, bringing silence to a legion.

Of course, we can never know truly for sure what happened next. We have stories and we have hearsay and we have supposition. The believers believe, the sceptics question and I think everyone else stands somewhere between. They'd like to believe but there's no way of knowing for sure.

Above them all, the sky started to glow and shake, as if it were being torn apart. The Dei all looked to it, their lips moving in silent chant as a hairline crack started above the watching masses, worked longer and longer as if something was forcing its way into it.

"Always remember," Gilgarus said. "We are watching, and we wait. For those who believe, we will see you again. For those who don't, we're looking forward to seeing you even more." His smile was sinister as he said it, as the crack continued to expand until it could have swallowed the entire rock and everyone on it. Those towards the front of the watching crowd had to scramble to get back, lest they be sucked in. "Divinity will always be within reach for those who cherish us."

With those final words, Gilgarus stepped into the crack, his body bathed in the light. Melarius and his children, Garvais, Kalqus and Griselle following him, as did the rest, one by one. As the last of them, Ferros and Leria stepped through, the door shut behind them and the sky was silent as if it had never been disturbed.

They always say that Cradle Rock crumbled immediately in the aftermath, no longer looked like it had. Maybe their power had been too great for it, the release had shattered it to pieces, maybe nobody has just ever been able to find it since. Maybe time wore it down. So much supposition and yet nobody has ever been able to say for sure. I always wanted to find it. See it for myself. That's been a dream and it all sprang from that story my mama told me when I was a boy."

Fazarn paused, smiled at them all. Wilsin didn't know what to say. He'd heard the story before, it was quite a famous one. It wasn't even the best version of it he'd ever heard, there were much more erudite and vocally fascinating telling's of it. They'd even made multiple cinematic versions of it, some worth seeing, others not so.

"You know though, an old friend of mine discovered some writings on the subject that nobody else had, he found evidence to claim an addendum to that story. He offered it up, but nobody took it professionally seriously. Didn't best impress him. He knew a lot about the Divines and people not listening to him on the subject infuriated him."

Another cough, he cleared his throat with a sound like ice being torn off a windshield. "Allegedly, there was talk that when Leria and Ferros were walking through the portal, a believer braved the danger and flung himself at them to ask tearfully when they would return to the kingdoms. Leria, the Divine of Knowledge, took pity on his state, stopped next to him and said something to him very few people have ever heard. It was only passed down through a select few over the ages, through journals and notes. They called it prophecy, hence the reason why few take it seriously. I personally think if it comes from a proclaimed Divine of Knowledge, it's probably a good idea to listen. Let me see if I remember this right…"

He paused, made a face of concentration that looked just a little too forced for Wilsin's liking, like he was making it for effect and then he spoke aloud. Wilsin couldn't help but notice the look of surprise on Brendan's face as he heard the words.

"What was once shall be again.
First there was chaos
As order became unrestrained.
A champion falls and inferno rises,
And sacrifice is its name.
A new rising, an age gone since the last.
The three pillars shall fall in their wake
The cherished will be united.
Courage. Hope. Compassion.
Anger. Fear. Love. Greed.
All will form the chain of fate
That will shackle the beast beyond.
And the Green will overcome."

"And what the hells does that mean?" Nmecha said. He'd gone silent during it all, sat next to Bryce at the back of the fire.

"Like anything, it's subject to interpretation," Fazarn said. "To different people, it means different things. My friend Jerry believed that it meant that one day divinity would return to the kingdom. Order would fall, chaos would rise, a champion would die, an inferno would bring sacrifice and with it would come the new order."

Something horrible twitched in the back of Wilsin's head, an uneasy feeling he couldn't place no matter how much he worked at it.

"The three pillars, I don't know. The cherished, well I think that's something to do with the myth of the Divine-born, Jerry didn't know much about that. The chain of fate, well that's a name that you don't really find in history. Beast beyond, don't know, the Green…" He threw out a hand. "I think you can't get much more divine Green than this."

"Jerry?" Brendan said, his voice like a whip crack in the silence.

"Jeremiah really," Fazarn said. "Blut. Jeremiah Blut. Not heard from him for months now."

Oh, Wilsin thought. Brendan must have thought the same thing because he shot him a warning look and spoke up. "An interesting tale," he said. "Mister Reeves, what about you."

Wilsin dreaded telling his own tale here, something from his past that wouldn't compromise his actions as a Unisco agent while at the same time being a tale to capture their imagination.

Maybe, just to see the reaction on Fazarn's face, he'd mention his one and only encounter with Jeremiah Blut. That'd be an interesting result, given way it had played out. Now though, if Reeves had heard Brendan, he didn't show it. He'd cocked his head to the side, tilted it as if listening in the darkness for something only he could hear. His eye shimmered in the dusky half-light, one hand went to his waist for the kjarnblade he wore there.

"Ben?" Brendan said. "What do you sense?" His voice sounded outwardly calm, composed and measured but Wilsin had heard the tone before and he knew the warning sounds. He knew the secrets, that when Brendan sounded calm like this, he was worried, and he wanted to hide it. Only with experience came such a read of a man.

"Something's out there," Reeves said. "Watching us. Lurking." His own voice was low, quiet but urgent and he'd removed his kjarnblade from the hook on his belt. Both hands had wrapped around the hilt, his finger centimetres from the activation switch.

"You can't be serious," Fazarn said, his voice disbelieving. He rose to his feet, stepped to the edge of their camp, just outside the firelight. "Mister Reeves, it is pitch black out there…"

"And the Kjarn needs no light for it is its own sense of illumination, it is its own darkness and shadow, its own bright illumination," Reeves said, the faintest trace of a smirk on his face before it fell away, replaced with horror. He'd seen something, Wilsin could see it in his eyes, the Vedo pushed himself forward towards Fazarn. "Get down!" Even with his legs carrying him faster than the eye could follow, he just wasn't fast enough.

Something whistled through the night air, struck Fazarn in the centre of the chest. He coughed once, clapped both hands to his breast where he'd been struck. Bemusement spread across his face. In the firelight, Wilsin saw the crimson spread across his shirt, dribbling from his mouth. Fazarn blinked several times, not quite able to believe what had just happened His mouth twitched, Wilsin knew he wouldn't ever forget what he saw next.

Something hit the ground at his feet, a shower of blood exploding into the air and striking the fire. He had to look, his body numb with realisation at the sight, a flesh-covered jawbone kissing his foot. He couldn't help it, punted it away involuntarily with the toe of his boot, heard the splash as it hit the water. Reeves had Fazarn in his arms, something long and wavy protruding from his ruined face, wriggling in the dusk. He could hear movement around them, not footsteps but rustling, like leaves in the wind.

Wilsin went for his blaster, the first one lurched into the clearing, he heard Aubemaya scream and Bryce curse. Something long and green protruded from its body, its skin the same shade of emerald, flecked with mud and something crimson that could have been blood. He followed the protrusion, watched it give the fire a wide berth, all the way to the burbling Fazarn and he pulled the trigger twice. The first shot blew the protrusion away, the second punched through the area where its face would be if it had a head.

It didn't have a head. That thought hit him like one of his shots, he'd aimed and pulled the trigger, saw the area cave in and the realisation had swept across him. They were human-shaped but not human, he could count limbs and a torso but that was where the similarity ended. They were naked and sexless, fauna and foliage rustling across their bodies as they moved on stiff legs that had the consistency of tree bark, root-like feet tearing into the earth beneath.

Behind the one he'd just shot, the one that had murdered Fazarn, another lurched into view. And another. And another. How many of them were there? He didn't want to know but he felt the dread rush through him.

The Tebbit didn't hold as many shots as an X7 or an X9S, he burned through them as quickly as he could, putting fresh holes through bodies not showing any signs of distress. He gulped, slammed his weapon back into its holster and went for the rifle across his back. Brendan was on his feet, firing into the crowd, his blaster jumping in his hands as shots found their mark. One of them got too close to Suchiga, wrapped its arms around him despite his struggles, thin tendril-like ropes grabbing him tight. He let out a scream, fought against them, his struggles in vain. Wilsin could see them tightening against his body, the sound of cracking bone erupting over Aubemaya's screams as one of them went for her. He continued to fire into the crowd, not sure where to shoot them, just determined to blow them apart if it came to it, the blaster rifle hammering against his shoulder. Suchiga went down with a whimper, vanished from sight, Aubemaya was silenced, did the same. Nmecha howled as a vine grabbed him by the throat and twisted hard, the snap cutting off any other sounds he'd ever make. Finally, he heard the familiar sound as Reeves' kjarnblade snapped into life and the Vedo was past him, ducked under a vine and cut it away with a deft flick of his twist. The serrated limb hit the dirt with a plop, twitched into stillness. He saw Reeves dance amid them, blade hacking through bodies with little resistance but always there were more, he'd be surrounded in moments. Reeves looked like he'd had the same thought, tensed his legs into a crouch and sprang a dozen feet into the air, landed next to the fire.

His rifle clicked on empty, he fumbled for another charge pack, heard Brendan let out a yell of pain mingled with fear and his boss went down. He slammed in the pack, raced forward to join Reeves in the fray, saw the three of them still alive being dragged into the darkness. Still more of them remained between him and them, he brought his weapon up and targeted the central one. Deep breath, fire on the exhale…

"Move!" Reeves shouted, the urgency present in his voice and Wilsin dropped, heard the roar above his head, felt heat wash over him. The jungle was suddenly alight, flames covering the plant-things. Out the corner of his eye, he saw Reeves blowing on his palm, his blade still lit in his other. Finally, they made a dismayed shriek that sounded like metal being shredded as they burned, their bodies collapsing into piles of charcoal briquette.

He lowered his weapon, glanced around. Nmecha and Fazarn were down and dead, he could tell that immediately. Nobody survived having their neck broken the way Nmecha did, his face almost a complete opposite to the direction it should face, his one eye showing surprise. Ditto Bryce laid on his back, a thorn-like branch poking from of his abdomen, final breaths already coming out ragged and broken. Blood stained the ground beneath him in the firelight, an eerie colour in the flicker of the flames.

Ahead of him, Reeves deactivated his kjarnblade and let out a violent curse into the night, a language Wilsin had never heard before. The venom in the words left no doubt as to their meaning. He dropped to his knees, Wilsin paid little attention, was already crouched down by Bryce. They had to try and save him, no matter how futile it might look. Bryce's shirt had torn, Wilsin finished removing it. He ripped his own shirt off, wrapped it around the wound.

"Reeves get your arse over here!" he shouted, pressing it down. Staunching the bleeding at this point might be too little too late. He didn't even know when Bryce had been hit, couldn't say but it didn't matter. "Reeves!"

He came, his face pale in the firelight. He'd seen that look before, the expression of someone who'd just seen combat and hadn't taken it well. Normally he might have tried to reassure him. These were about as far from normal circumstances as one could get. Those things weren't human, they didn't look animal either and he'd no idea what they were. If Reeves wanted to freak out, he could do it on his own damn time when a man's life was at stake. This was in no way worse than the Quin-C final had been and Reeves had survived that with flying colours.

"If you can do that fancy Vedo healing, you best do it and fast," Wilsin said, giving him a hard look. He needed to snap out of it and fast, strong words and work would help. Something to focus on would help him forget his shock. That was his theory, he couldn't let Bryce die while he worked out a better one. This had to work, and it had to work now. Worst came to the worst, he'd slap him and hope that brought him around. Slapping a Vedo. That had the potential to go badly. The way he'd burned those things was still branded into his memory, a sensation he couldn't shake. It was one thing to hear about that power, it was quite another to see it flourished in front of you. The power in this instance was something that he couldn't even start to comprehend, he couldn't touch it, he couldn't feel it, he could just see the way that it affected the world around him.

Reeves came at last, a hand already snaking up across Bryce's skin, the faintest glimmer of light creeping from them and into the wound. Bryce let out a shudder as the shimmering forced its way in, his mouth opening and closing in tiny whimpers. Once Wilsin had had a dog that'd gotten one of his furry little legs caught in a bear trap, he'd heard it make a sound like that. It had broken his heart. He didn't care about Bryce like he had that dog, but it didn't mean he wanted him to die. Gullit. He missed him. He'd always wanted that dog to be his first spirit, hadn't happened and Gullit had had to be put down after that trap. The circumstances for survival just hadn't been there.

First rule of life. Shit happens. Can't do a damn thing about it.

He continued to apply pressure to the wound, saw the glow intensify within Reeves' grip. Bryce's body contorted, writhed in agony, hands scrabbled at mud and dirt. His skin felt so cold, like all the warmth had been sucked out of him. The fire was dying, Reeves had killed it in the attempt to save them all.

If it went out… A chill rushed through his body, one he tried to ignore. Thinking about what might happen if it died on them didn't bear thinking about it. The fire had killed them a whole damn lot more effectively than any other weapon barring Reeves' kjarnblade and maybe it'd made them wary. No fire though...

In front of him, Reeves groaned, sounds of pain slipping from him. When he looked at Wilsin, their eyes met, and he saw the blood running from Reeves' gaze. He flinched a little, tried not to think about how much that had to hurt. Pain lingered in his smile, Reeves dropped from his haunches to sitting, leaned even further over Bryce, concentration triumphing over the discomfort for a moment. Still Bryce whimpered in agony, Wilsin reached to squeeze his hand. Hold on!

Hold on. He repeated it again and again under his breath, determined that the words wouldn't be in vain.

When it came, death was quick and sudden. He saw Reeves' eyes widen and he fell onto his back, hand coming away from Bryce's skin with a faint pop. Where the Kjarn was involved, he'd come to expect big and dramatic, but that pop was a much more final sound than he ever could have imagined. Bryce's final breath came out long and laboured, death rattling in his throat before he went still. His chest would never rise again.

They'd moved the bodies of their comrades, wrapped them and secured them before returning to the boat. Neither of them was willing to share the deck with the corpses, they'd put them below deck and they'd remained up top. Neither of them felt like sleeping, though the first thing they'd done was move the boat away from the shore and drop anchor bang in the middle of the river, furthest point between two shorelines.

Wilsin stared into the jungle, a prisoner of his own thoughts. He wondered how things had gone wrong so quickly. Just an hour earlier, Brendan had been making them tell those stupid stories to each other, all so that they could get to know each other. Wasted effort, but it left them something to mourn. Wasted lives. Unfulfilled futures. Something like that. He didn't know. A lot of those epitaphs might be bandied around the group in front of him, people did like their twee little moments of nonsense, fluff designed to distract from more serious issues.

He didn't mean that. Bitterness and anger didn't feel far apart from each other lately, he didn't know whether to scream or cry. Neither of them felt like his style, but Divines, this mission had gone so badly so quickly. It couldn't have been true. He wanted to believe he'd fallen asleep around the campfire and this was a dream, he'd get up and tell his story shortly.

He knew it wasn't a dream. He knew too many had died, and Aubemaya and Suchiga and Brendan were still out there alive. Somewhere.

Wilsin also remembered what it was that Brendan had said if something went wrong like this. Get out. Get home. Leave. Don't come after us. Granted, it had been more if they were captured by Vazaran security forces, but the message remained the same. Vazaran security forces, man-plant things that rustled as they walked. What was the difference? They both had it in for them.

He made his choice, got up and headed over to where Brendan had left his bag. Maybe it was possible to do both. Maybe.

Reeves watched him get up, a bemused look on his face. "What are you doing?"

He didn't have an answer, just started to go through the bag. It had to be somewhere. He'd already wiped down and reloaded his weapons just in case. He'd helped himself to the spare charge packs in Brendan's bag, rooting down to the bottom until he found what he was looking for.

It didn't look like much, a dull thick disc of metal with a crimson button supplanted in the middle of it. The very picture of temptation, he had to fight the urge to reach out and touch it, press it down until activation.

"What's that?"

He tried to cut all negative thoughts, ignore what he'd been told to do and think about what was right. He'd come on this mission to watch Brendan's back, make sure he got through it uninjured and unhindered. He'd failed in that. Looking at the emergency beacon rammed it all home. Wilsin smiled, with his face still covered in the dried blood from Bryce, it must have made for a terrifying sight. He continued to smile as he looked at Reeves.

"Beacon," he said. "Brendan brought it with him in case of emergency. Push it down and we'll get an evac to its position."

"I think this qualifies as an emergency," Reeves said. "Push it. We need to get out of here before those things find a way to cross the water."

Was that fear in his voice? Wilsin didn't know whether to worry or feel disgusted. All that power and he wanted to run and hide.

"No," he said quietly. "I'll push this beacon when I'm damn ready. You know what we're going to do first, Ben?"

Reeves shook his head, but his face betrayed him, gave the impression that he at least had the inkling of an idea. The corners of his mouth curled up in a smile. Maybe he'd read his thoughts, Wilsin thought. Some Vedo could do that, he'd heard.

"We're going to go find the rest of our expedition. We don't leave anyone behind. Not now, not ever. More than that, we're going to find where these damn things came from and we're going to make sure they don't come back. You in?"

It took only a fraction of a second for Reeves to grin at him, offer him a hand which Wilsin slapped his palm into. "Partners," Reeves said. "Let's get this shit done."

Chapter Twenty. Last Rites.

"Without the Kjarn, there is only chaos. Where only there is chaos, there can be no order. Without order, there cannot be the Kjarn. We are the servants and the masters, we cast the shadows that we might bathe our ignorance in. Without the Kjarn, there cannot be light. Without light, there can only be dark, and with the dark comes death."
Mantra of the Vedo old and new, according to Benjamin Reeves.

They'd slept on the boat the previous night, uneasily for the dead bodies of their companions stared sightlessly at them through the burial wrappings they'd fashioned out of their clothes. Neither of them had relished the task yet it needed to be done. The first thing Wilsin had insisted on was moving the boat out into the middle of the river and dropping anchor at the furthest equal point from the two banks. If more of those things were out there, he didn't want to make it easy for them to come aboard and murder them in their sleep. Or abduct them. He could remember the way they'd dragged off Brendan, Aubemaya and Suchiga. Better not to take chances that you didn't have to. Common sense wasn't something he'd always found in mass supply across the kingdoms, but it was amazing how much it put your mind at ease when applied to a situation. Maybe the plants could cross water. If that was the case, they were dead.

Reeves didn't look like he'd slept, his eyes black and his words a mumble. Wilsin's response had been to go and look through Bryce's pack, see if he had any alcohol left. Anything to pep him up. Might not be the most responsible thing heading into combat, but you did what you had to do. Besides, Reeves wasn't a Unisco agent. He was a Vedo. Different rules. Different abilities. His metabolism could cope with it, Wilsin hoped.

Hope. It was about the only thing getting him through the motions. Hope that they could pull this off. Hope that they could survive. Hope that they'd get there, and it wouldn't be too late. Too much to hope for. Not all of it would be enough, too little might come to pass, and failure would reign.

"You're blaming yourself," Reeves said, glancing at him. Neither of them had been in favour of chasing the rustlers off into the darkness. Good night's rest, full stomach and they'd be in much better shape for it. Best possible chance. How far could they get with prisoners across rough ground in the dark? He didn't know. Too many variables, but he'd made his decision. Wait until daylight. He supposed he outranked Reeves, though quibbling over the chain of command wasn't going to be a helpful thing. Brendan had given him the orders of what to do in the crisis and he'd already made the choice to ignore it. A hard choice but the obvious one. He could no more have abandoned them than he'd hoped they could have abandoned him. "You think we should have done more already."

He wasn't entirely right, but nor was he entirely wrong. Whatever decision he made, he'd have berated himself for its implications. Wilsin looked at him across the can of cold beans, boiled in their own sauce two days ago, tomato and muscardo mushrooms. He couldn't enjoy it. They weren't meant to be eaten cold and it was reflected in the taste. Still, any sort of sustenance. He'd eaten worse. These weren't gourmet times.

"Not that at all," Wilsin said. "They took them alive for a reason. I've got to hope that that reason involves them being kept alive for long enough to catch up with them." As gambits went, it was the only one he had to play. He didn't have enough information to their motivations. The things looked like plants, it didn't necessarily mean that they were. There were carnivorous plants. Maybe they wanted them for food. At the same time, they'd taken them alive and run. They'd left dead bodies behind. Maybe they liked living flesh more than dead. There'd been a lot of them, Reeves had burned a whole bunch of them, but he couldn't have kept it up. If they'd desired, they could have overwhelmed the two of them and then they'd have even more bodies to feed on.

It was a conundrum, he realised. Without studying them and their habits, he couldn't hope to understand them. He just had to treat them as he would any other enemy and hope that he could improvise enough on the fly when the fighting started to get them out of trouble. Yet with that came the knowledge that they surely weren't like any other enemy. He'd never faced anything like this. Their tactics might not even be tactics he recognised. He and Reeves could be running into a trap.

"They'll have a good start on us," Reeves said. "I hope you're right."

"Reeves," Wilsin said. He'd had enough of the thoughts whistling through his head, doubts clawing at him. "You ever seen anything like those things last night before? Because I'm trying to work out what they are and I'm coming up empty."

The Vedo shook his head. "In all my time in these kingdoms, with all I've learned, they remain a mystery to me. They were even alien to the Kjarn. They didn't register as a threat. Not until they were on us."

"I don't know what to say to that," Wilsin admitted. He didn't either. The Kjarn remained as much a mystery to him as the workings of the minds of women in most of the relationships he'd ever entered into.

"I mean, the good news is that they can't fool me again. Not like that. Before they gang up on us again and murder us, I'll at least get us a warning."

"Not loving the optimism," Wilsin said. "But that's good. Any crumb of comfort, right? Anyway, they're not going to ambush us."

"How do you work that out?"

"Because of my plan," Wilsin said, rubbing his hands together. "Rest assured, Ben, I do have one."

Reeves smiled at him. "You know, I figured you were cooking something up. Do I want to know what it is?"

"Well they've got a good eight hours head start on us," Wilsin said. "Across ground. We're going by air."

"We don't have any gliders, speeders or aeroships," Reeves quickly said. "Doesn't that pose a bit of a problem?"

It was Wilsin's turn to smile at him. "The only limits we have are the ones we make ourselves. You're a Vedo, you should acknowledge that. It's good advice."

"Master Baxter has a similar saying," Reeves offered. "Whether you think you will, or you won't, you're probably right."

"Master Baxter is a wise man," Wilsin said, fingering his summoner. He looked around the boat, took a quick mental count of the inventory they had here. Too many things to take. Not all of them important. "You know, we're probably not going to get back to the boat. Soon as we hit the air, I'm activating the beacon, calling for reinforcements. They get the signal, they'll scramble a transport to pick us up. A neutral transport." He hoped that was the case. A Unisco vehicle would be shot down long before it got this far inland. All the negotiation in the kingdoms wouldn't save it. Mazoud had made that all too clear. He didn't want interference. He didn't want Unisco entering his kingdom. He knew they were there, he knew they were hiding and that there was little he could do about it until they showed their faces, but an overt act would be too big a target for his ire to ignore. He could either act and prove himself a man of his words or he could fail to do so and prove his threats ineffective. He couldn't afford to do the latter, yet the former would bring down all manner of unpleasantness on him. A war with Unisco would do Mazoud little favours, hence his reluctance to start one. The organisation might be split across all directions trying to counter the Coppinger threat, but a few more eyes on him might prove difficult for Mazoud to come away from.

Screw thinking like this. The politics of the kingdoms was a million miles away from their situation. They'd get someone out to them to pick them up if they needed an emergency evacuation. Brendan had made it clear he'd arranged it. Brendan didn't make mistakes of that magnitude. Wilsin had faith in him. He slapped his container crystal into his summoner, pushed the button.

"We're not going to walk," he said simply. "We're going to fly. Ever ride a dragon before, Ben?" He didn't look at Reeves to see the expression on his face. Few people could hide their emotions about riding a dragon. The species was dying out. Fewer and fewer were being born in the wild. Callers had claimed too many in the distant past and now those selfish acts were taking their toll. The Senate had introduced legislation to stop the rampant claiming of creatures, but too little far too late. Wilsin looked at his own dragon, Aroon, realised he'd been damned lucky. Most dragons lived on preserves, far away from easy access to the general population. They were a protected species. He recalled something about a dragon that had been claimed in Premesoir a few years back and there'd been a national uproar about the town of Threll that their symbol had been taken.

Aroon was a special dragon, he'd claimed as much before and he would continue to until the day he died. Lean and muscular beneath a coat of soot-black and acid-orange scales, Aroon's wings flared out behind him, the size of paddle boats and coloured the musty green of leather. Six powerful limbs emerged from his body, four of them digging six spike-like claws into the deck, two developed forearms towards the front of his body, one of them clawing at an itchy point up across his serpentine neck, digging between the scales with abandon. The powerful tail thumped happily against the deck, tearing cracks in the wood.

"Good boy, Aroon," he cooed, striding over to pat the spirit on the neck. Aroon's triangle-shaped face turned to look at him through beadily alert eyes, pointed jaws showing an impressive number of fangs as the dragon yawned. Touching a dragon was always like touching a warm piece of coal in his experience, the threat of the heat was there yet it wasn't enough to burn. Unlike most dragons, Aroon didn't have horns. He'd never seen the need for them. The lizard-like tongue slipped out between the mouth, licked at his hand. He tried not to wince, it was like being slathered with sandpaper.

"A fine specimen," Reeves said. "Do you object if I show him some attention?"

"We'd both be insulted if you didn't," Wilsin smiled. "Aroon's my buddy, aren't you buddy?" He spoke directly to the dragon who growled in response, not a threat but almost akin to a purring sound.

Like a giant cat. A ludicrous image came to his mind, he had to admit, one of Aroon curling up around him like a giant snoring tabby.

Reeves reached up a hand, Wilsin coughed out the side of his mouth. "Careful! Take it slow. Don't startle him. And for Divines sake, don't touch the top of his head, he doesn't like it."

Wouldn't do if Aroon bit one of Reeves' hands off. That would officially kick this rescue mission off to a bad start. Might not be the worst one ever but there was a chance it would be up there with the contenders if it did.

"Hello there, drake," Reeves said. Wilsin had heard the term before, an old word for dragon, some old tongue. Ancient Sidorovan, he thought. "You're a fine fellow, aren't you? Big and powerful and your wings are so majestic. I bet you can fly for miles with them, can't you?"

Reeves had done his research, Wilsin had to admit. Dragons were smart, some of them just as smart as some people and they knew immediately whether they liked you or not. If you irked them, they'd burn you. If you pleased them, there was no distance they wouldn't go to accommodate you. Legends had them as jealous, greedy creatures filled with capriciousness. He'd never found that to be further from the truth. Always there would be those with a negative opinion and the need to shout it.

Aroon might need to fly them for miles. Reeves had a point. Best to make sure he was up to it. The boat shook beneath their feet as the giant lizard stepped away from them, moved towards the river and started to lap at the surface of the water, slowly at first before the sound got more powerful and more frequent.

"Didn't answer my question," Wilsin said. "You ever ridden a dragon before?" He couldn't keep the smile off his face. Personally, he loved this part. It was like every childhood dream he'd ever had come to life right in front of his eyes.

"I've ridden spirits before," Reeves admitted. "I rode Master Baxter's armoured bird. That, I didn't like. Not very comfortable. How fast can he fly? Aroon?" The dragon looked up from the surface of the river at the mention of his name, eyes blinking in the morning sun. He was listening, Wilsin could tell that.

"Clocked at least as fast as the average mag-rail," Wilsin said nonchalantly. "Powerful as well. He can keep going and going, at least with one passenger. With two, it might be tricky. We'd need to make frequent stops. I don't want to burn him out. I don't want them to get too far ahead of us."

"Can't have everything, David. You'll spread yourself all over the place if you don't stop trying to control everything. If we're going to get there in time, the Kjarn's will shall make it so. We can run, or we can walk, we may never make it there at all. What won't help is worrying." Reeves put a hand on his arm. "It doesn't suit you. Come on, give me a smile."

Wilsin grinned, he couldn't help but oblige despite the reluctance flooding through him. He gave it everything he could. Strangely, he felt better for it. Weird. Reeves seemed halfway convinced. "That's better."

There'd been a knot in the pit of his stomach, a knot he'd been worried would only grow and grow and grow until he choked on it, wanted to hurl it up with the contents of his breakfast, yet now it felt like all was well. The stress had faded, the unease was moving to the back of his mind and he stretched his arms out in front of him, testing the dexterity of his fingers as muscles strained under the efforts.

"Right," he said. "We might not see this boat again. Maybe we'll get the chance to come back for it, but I doubt it. Our team is gone, they took most of their research to the grave with them and there's nothing we can do about that. Frankly, I don't care either. This always was a dumb venture under the circumstances. Search through every pack you can, find anything that will be immediately useful. If you think it's useful, throw it into the middle of the deck. We need everything scavenged as quickly as we can manage. We're burning daylight and our friends are out there." He didn't much care for any of them bar Brendan but that didn't mean that they deserved to die. "Come on, Ben. Chop-chop! We move out in twenty."

Aroon had lazily taken to the skies, stretching his wings while they searched. It was important for a human not to go into a great period of exercise cold, the same went double for a dragon nearly four times the size of an average human. Wilsin kept an eye on him out the corner of his eye, watched as Aroon swooped down, body barely inches above the water and continued to follow the length of the waterway until almost out of sight before he swept into a powerful loop, wings flaring at the top of his ascension. A strangely beautiful sight, one soon be lost to the kingdoms.

Not in his lifetime. He was certain of that. He finished rooting through the bags, focusing on food and weaponry and any sort of technology that could come in handy. Medicine too. He'd gone for Nmecha's bag first, pulled out whatever pills and ointments he could find. Suchiga had sounded like he'd been injured in the commotion, he could still remember the sounds of bones cracking and screams as he'd been dragged away. Bandages, medical webbing, he secreted it all into his pack, moving the stuff around. He'd come to like the one-eyed doctor, going through his things like this felt disrespectful but what could he do? Nmecha, Bryce, Fazarn, they were all dead. The rest of them weren't. They had to keep on living and if that meant looting what they'd left behind, so be it.

He debated what to do with the bodies. They'd left them on the deck, out of the sun and wrapped but if they were to abandon the boat as his plan was, it might be stood here for quite some time on the river, exposed to the elements. The implications of discovering it might be terrible for all. He wouldn't want to be one of a boarding party who set foot aboard this abandoned boat and discovered sun-spoiled corpses. That sort of thing could traumatise a man. The stench alone would haunt you.

Dumping them in the river felt even more disrespectful than stealing their possessions but it was probably the best option. He'd get Reeves to help him. If the Vedo thought it was wrong, it was almost certainly wrong but that didn't make it any less necessary. The necessary things were often the hardest.

He'd found all of Brendan's spare charge packs for the weapons, the blaster rifles hadn't been effective against them before, but they were better than nothing. Besides, before he'd been treating them like they were human. They weren't. Their weak spots had to be different. He'd reloaded and wiped down the Tebbit in his hip holster, tucked the charge packs into a bandolier across his chest for easy access. He looked like he was ready to go to war. Both lukonium machetes hung across his back. They might be a better option if things got hairy, better than blasters in close.

He felt laden down, like a camel, with weaponry when he saw Reeves. The Vedo just had his kjarnblade hung from his belt, hilt glinting in the sunlight. He'd gotten a pack together, clipped it around his waist on the other hip.

"We need to move the bodies," Wilsin said. He hadn't been wrong when he'd expected the look of distaste on Reeves' face. He might well have asked him to murder his mother or give away the secret location of his order's greatest secrets. "Can't leave them here."

"But... But..." He was struggling for an answer, Wilsin saw, he didn't have one. He couldn't blame him, he felt a bit sorry for him. All the training he'd gone through and he'd never thought he'd wind up in a situation like this, a sorry shit-show of a time.

Welcome to working with Unisco, son, he thought. Shit happens, sometimes you can't do a damn thing about it no matter how much you want to. You can't control it. You just survive it.

"What about their families?" Reeves asked, grunting with the effort as they humped Bryce's body up against the railing, a few sparse droplets spraying them as the corpse hit the water. It floated for a moment before starting to sink, before their eyes.

"What about them?" Wilsin said. He hated sounding like this, made out to be the bastard, but he couldn't help it. The dead were the dead and the living had to be the priority. At least this way, their bodies would serve a purpose, would provide food for whatever lived in the river. He didn't want to think about whatever that might be. This hadn't even been a river a year ago, just a scar in the ground, and look now. "We'll let them know that they died on the expedition. Tell them the truth. Their bodies are unrecoverable. It happens. They had to know this was a risk."

Didn't mean that they'd like it. He also couldn't bring himself to entirely care, as they went for Fazarn, dragged him to the railings and did the same. He was heavier in death than Bryce had been, the two of them were covered in sweat by the time they'd finished.

"Seems a little impersonal," Reeves said. "I mean, I'd want some sort of closure."

"Nature of the kingdoms these days, Ben," Wilsin said. "We don't always get what we want no matter how much we think we need it."

Surely Reeves should be putting this sort of practical non-sequitur out there. He'd always gotten the impression that might be the purview of the Vedo. Semi-mystic wisdom offered up even when you had no need for it. Baxter had given him that impression.

"Look, if it bothers you that much, you can tell them what really happened," he said. "But they won't thank you for it. Trust me on that. They might tell you that knowing what happened is really the best thing. They're wrong. Trust me. Ignorance is bliss, they say that for a reason."

"They also say knowing gives you closure."

"Okay then you give them a middle ground. Confirm they died. Tell them they died as heroes. Nothing you could do. There wasn't, was there? You tried to save Bryce and you failed miserably."

That got a reaction as they lifted Nmecha. "I tried to save Bryce, I never could. He was too far gone and I'm not a Restorer. That's just an unfair criticism."

"A Restorer?" Wilsin had never heard the term before, he raised an eyebrow with interest.

"What you'd call a healer, I guess. That's our word for them. Restorers can heal themselves and others of almost any wound, bring someone back from the brink of death if they're fast enough. It's never easy."

"You can't all heal?"

"It depends," Reeves said. "I mean you people who can't touch the Kjarn, you're all good at different things, right? Why would this be any different?"

He didn't know, shrugged as his muscles complained under Nmecha's dead weight.

"There's seven different fields to Kjarn manipulation," Reeves said. "I don't like using that term because it implies that we're in control, but it's the best word to explain." The silent 'damn you' didn't even have to be said aloud, Wilsin saw it in his face as clear as the sun above. "Each Vedo has a natural inclination towards one of them. It's never obvious but you come into it as you train and start to understand more of the mysteries of the Kjarn."

"Why has nobody ever heard this before?" Wilsin wondered.

"Because it's a trade secret and how many Vedo have you ever had this level of conversation with?" Reeves asked. "David, we're moving bodies together, I think we can speak candidly to each other."

Point, Wilsin had to concede. If doing something like this didn't bring you closer to another person, then he didn't know what would.

"Anyway, seven specialities. Six of them can learn other basic skills from other fields but more complex ones remain out of reach. You could train for years and all you'd do is waste your time if you get me. So yeah, I can heal cuts and bruises, maybe a broken bone if it's not too bad but what happened to Bryce was well beyond me."

"Yet you tried anyway?"

"You told me to!" Reeves said, more than a little defensive. "I had to try. Maybe it wasn't as bad as it looked. I had to hope that things would work out. Maybe it'd have kept him alive long enough for us to try other methods. I don't like blood, I think I did okay all things considered."

Wilsin sighed inwardly. Not Reeves fault then. He didn't pretend to understand the Kjarn, but the explanation made sense. "So, what is your speciality then? Tell me it's at least something useful for the situation up ahead. I saw you throw that fire at them. Can you do that again?"

Reeves face fell. "Not like I did before. That was something else entirely. That's the purview of Elementalists. Master Baxter does that. The showy stuff with fire and lightning, that's what they do. Again, rest of us can conjure up a flame or a spark if we want but it's not something we can really make a point of doing. It'll never be as powerful or as potently sustained. What I did with the fire was transference."

"That another field?"

"An element of mine," he admitted. "I'm an Alchemite."

"What the bloody hells is one of those, then?"

"What you saw. I can alter things. Transfer properties of one thing to another. That wood we cut up to make the fire? It was inorganic matter aflame. I transferred the properties from one of them to another. They might be alive but parts of them weren't and that was enough. I didn't even know if it'd work or not. Doesn't on man or beast. Can't directly influence them, I'm not a Manifold. Good job for us it worked, huh?"

"Yeah," Wilsin had to concede. He was right there. It was luck. It was more than lucky. They'd caught a break there. "What else can you do?"

"I turned gold into lead once."

"Yeah?" Wilsin tried to keep the incredulity out of his voice, failed miserably. "Why?"

"Just to see if I could," Reeves said with a shrug. "I mean, I know it's not a valuable skill, not like the reverse. But I think understanding the theory helps sometimes. Look at it this way. Lead is worthless, and gold is precious. Yet they're linked. At their heart, they're both metals. Neither of them is alive. If you can find the link, it's the easiest thing in the kingdoms to alter an element here, a twitch here and... I can't really explain this as well as I'd like."

He placed a hand on the deck of the boat. "Pick me something. Anything. Something rare. Something precious. That's what everyone inevitably wants to see."

"Okay," Wilsin said. He thought about it for a minute, gave Reeves a smile. "Sapphires. Show me sapphires." He didn't doubt for a moment that the Vedo could pull it off if he desired to, but he seemed to want to prove himself. He'd let him have his moment in the sun. Trust him to end up partnered with a Vedo who wasn't skilled with the fire and brimstone type of wrath they'd need. Reeves might need to feel validated, though he wasn't sure. Confidence wasn't one of the things he lacked for.

"I'll give you points for originality."

"Don't get that request a lot?"

"Most people say gold when they hear what I can do. Sometimes diamonds. Never sapphires. First time truly for everything, I suppose."

Wilsin had stopped listening, tuned out as he studied the last of the equipment. He might be about to take back what he'd thought earlier. Those tendrils on the rustlers, he'd seen the way they'd torn through Fazarn and Nmecha with ease. They'd been unprotected, the fabric of their jungle gear providing little defence against them. He and

Brendan had been here covertly, neither of them had sought to bring body armour.

He glanced back towards Reeves, did a double take as he saw the deck. Once it had been pristine white, wood glossed to avoid rotting against the water, aged but the sort of sturdy that came with a long life. Now though, he saw a sea of blue spreading out across it all, a thousand little shimmers in the sunlight. The sapphires were almost the same colour as the water beneath them, he didn't want to even think about how much wealth he was stood on. Slowly his eyes came towards Reeves who grinned at him, lifted a hand and waggled his fingers.

"Impressive," Wilsin said, he found he meant it as well. "If the Vedo thing doesn't work out, you can retire an incredibly wealthy man."

Reeves smiled, though it was an expression devoid of happiness. "You know, you're not the first one to say that to me, David. It's not a funny joke. Worse, some people aren't even joking about it. Might not be a Cognivite but I can tell when they're sincere or not."

"You need to make notes about these things," Wilsin grumbled. "Can't keep track of them." He straightened up, cut across to the bags of clothes he'd decided to abandon. None of it was any use.

Wilsin saw the bag filled with food and water Reeves had prepped, he approved of that choice. He'd thought of suggesting it, had decided against it. The Vedo wasn't stupid, the food had been stored in his half of the boat, only would he have brought it up if forgotten. He split the rucksack open, pulled out on of Brendan's padded vests, lightweight and cool against the heat. Plenty of pockets.

Before, he wouldn't have bothered. The protection on offer would have been minimal, worse than nothing. It had layers within it. Thin layers of fabric, weak cotton, thin on their own but when they were stacked on top of each other, a respectable depth.

"Ben," he said. "You think you can do something for me?"

Chapter Twenty-One. Jungles and Dragons.

"I do not fear the unknown."
The five words written on the tomb of famed explorer, Gin Farwalker.

He was going to miss the boat. It'd been their home for days now, they'd become close aboard it as people did in circumstances like theirs. In the end though, it had never been a home. It had been a means to an end and now that end had come. Maybe one day, someone would find the boat with the mysterious sapphire deck and go home with some hells of a story and untold riches from it. Maybe it'd be lost to time. He didn't know. Reeves had assured him the changes to the deck were as permanent as could be unless another Alchemite came along and changed it back. He'd shown no inclination to do it himself. Wilsin couldn't blame it. An effort like that, he'd be proud of it too.

What he hadn't admitted to Reeves was it had been too long since he'd ridden Aroon, since anyone had straddled the back of the dragon. Credit to Aroon, he took it with a sense of mild bemusement as the two of them fixed on their packs, Wilsin wearing his new vest. If he fell off, it wouldn't do much good, but it might give him an edge. He didn't have fancy powers or a laser sword. What he had was his wits and his reflexes, an ability to plan and improvise. He meant to damn well use it.

As the caller to Aroon, he felt the duty to get on first, silently ordering the dragon to fall to his stomach. The boat dipped as Aroon landed on his four legs, spikes leaving cracks across the sapphires, he gave Wilsin a grin that probably would have terrified someone who didn't know better, before dropping to a prone position. He raised his leg, stepped over the neck. Inside he was pleading Aroon not to suddenly rise in surprise. Best case scenario there, he ended up sore and Reeves killed himself laughing while he tried to rearrange his groin into something resembling a regular shape.

How best to do this? His first thought had been to straddle the base of the neck, he quickly realised that wasn't a viable option. The wings would chafe him quickly, Aroon would probably get fed up with his weight on his neck and might even look to dislodge him. A spirit couldn't directly hurt a caller, didn't mean that they couldn't accidentally knock you off in mid-air.

He stepped back further, looked under the wings, the lower back area. Might be a tight fit between him and Reeves, they'd have to get up close and personal with each other but wasn't like they had too much of a real option. The back was broad, but not enough for them to spread out. He gestured to the Vedo. They were both adult enough to get on with this.

"Ready to get out of here?" he asked. "They had to go somewhere. Let's get following them. You sense anything, give me a shout."

Pilot and navigator, like none the jungle had ever seen before. Reeves had said he could hone in on them now he'd felt them. He could bloody track them if it came down to it, even if he didn't know that was what he was going to be doing yet. The Vedo took his hand, stepped behind him and Aroon rose up, pushing them both into a seated position across his broad back. Wilsin's legs just about made it to the scaled belly. Reeves wrapped his arms around Wilsin's stomach, his hands found loose scales he'd modified into Aroon's back to serve as handholds for a situation like this.

"We got everything?" he asked. No harm in one final check. It'd be prudent, above anything else. Once they left, they weren't coming back. Weapons, he knew were there. He wasn't leaving them behind. Food, water, medicine. All there, split between the two of them. Hopefully they could catch up with them before night fell. He didn't fancy sleeping on the jungle floor, not after what had happened to Ballard Brown the first night. They were to travel light, and he wasn't sure about taking camping gear with them. He'd declined. They'd fly all day, ride all night if they had to. Once they started, there was no stopping them.

"I can tell by your growing sense of certainty you're starting to come around to the idea that we have," Reeves said from over his shoulder. He could feel his breath on the back of his neck. He wasn't going to lie, he felt a little uncomfortable, shifted to make himself more secure. That might be quite important. They'd be on here for quite a while, he guessed. "You ready to kick this off?"

He nodded. "Yeah. Yeah, I guess I am." His voice was strong, he sounded convinced. He couldn't fear the unknown. The unknown was there to be conquered, just another one of life's mysteries which only gave an answer to if you took the plunge. Wilsin patted Aroon on the neck, returned his grasp to the scales. The dragon let out a snort, twin streams of smoke breaking from his nostrils, studied the sky.

"Let's go, Aroon."

Wilsin didn't need to say it out loud, he did regardless. The dragon flared his wings, gave them a first flap to test them. Brought back his head and roared proudly, one step forward and they were off, airborne.

Those first few seconds had been absolute hells, Wilsin had been glad for the handholds, he'd almost been torn off by Reeves, felt the drag back, heard the screech as hands scrabbled at his waist. He'd not been expecting it, fingers dug into his side, searching out any sort of grip. He winced, felt the vest almost tear before Reeves gave him a reassuring pat on the stomach.

"I got it!" he shouted. "Sorry. Took me by surprise."

"Thought you were supposed to be able to see the future!" Wilsin shouted back. It was petty, but he didn't care, he thought it was a valid point. Reeves either didn't hear him or didn't dignify him with a reply. He'd bet the latter. Behind them, the gleaming blue deck of the boat was already turning into a speck as they crossed into the mainland, he could see the previous night's campsite below. He guided Aroon to a hovering halt for a moment, considered the direction they'd taken Brendan and the others the previous night. From a dozen feet above the treeline, he could see the outline on the ground where they'd been initially dragged before the tracks had vanished. Maybe they'd been hefted onto backs. Worse, the rustlers didn't leave any sort of trail. They'd just melded into the fauna.

Terrific. He shot a glance back to Reeves. "You get any sort of hint on where they went? Psychically?"

Reeves' look gave nothing away. "Think so. They went..." He freed a hand from locked around Wilsin's waist, stuck a finger in his mouth and held it up to the sky. His eyes glanced back and forth across the jungle, the electric blue around one orb flickering. All Vedo he'd ever met had that, it'd surprised him at first and yet it was eerie how quickly he'd gotten used to it. "That way. I think." He pointed out across the tops of the trees, gestured through dozens of miles of jungle. "Yeah, that way. They're in that direction."

"You sure? We get this wrong..." Wilsin didn't have to finish the sentence. He hoped Reeves got how important it was.

"I'm sure." He didn't sound impressed at being questioned. Yet Wilsin had to be sure. "I've been combining psychic traces of those plant things, the energy signature they left behind, I can feel them, but it's faint." He exhaled sharply. "Just as I can also feel traces of the group from last night. It's fading but hopefully it'll get stronger the closer we get."

He couldn't argue with that. He made a good case for having done due diligence. He shot Reeves a grin. "Sorry for doubting you. Look, we need to get them back."

"It's okay." He didn't sound okay with it, but he looked like he understood. Wilsin freed one of his hands from Aroon's neck, reached into his pocket and found the beacon. It didn't look like much. A white plastic disc with a button and a bulb. Very simple. Only meant to be used in an emergency. If this didn't qualify, he didn't know what did.

Sorry, Brendan for the final time. I know what you told me to do and I just can't do it.

He hoped that being rescued would soften the old man's heart. He was in a world of trouble if it didn't. Unisco didn't take kindly to disobeying of orders, even when intentions were good.

Mentally, he gave Aroon the command to go and the dragon started flying again, powerful wings breaking great strides through the air. He'd delayed because of this, his faith in the speed and power of his dragon, Aroon could keep pace with a few damn rustlers. Finding them at night would have been impossible. Defeating them in the dark would have been even harder without the fire.

"What the hells is that?"
They'd been flying for what had to have been hours, time felt like it had melted away into one long unending sequence, the land beneath them one continuous blur of dark green ocean as he, Reeves and Aroon had flown. He didn't want to think about how many miles had passed, how far they were from the river. He'd glanced back more than once wondering if he could hear sounds of their evac in the distance. If it had been hours, they had to be in the air now. They'd likely have to scramble from Serran, getting airspace permission would have been tricky. If all had gone to plan, they'd have already had the flight plan in place, awaiting clearance to transmit. If the Vazaran authorities suspected anything, they'd delay them even if they couldn't refuse outright. Just to be contrary.

Wilsin heard the shout, raised his eyes and started in surprise. He'd only let his head sag for a few moments, focused on his own thoughts and the pattern of the scales on Aroon's back, he looked up and the entire landscape had changed.

"Great Divine shitballs!" he exclaimed.

The sea of green had only intensified, thicker and brighter below them than it had been before, he looked back and there was a very clear point where it changed, went from one colour to the other. Before, there'd been the occasional gap between the trees, offering sight of a patch of brown below, now it was a continuous desert of foliage. All the way to the clearing ahead, the size of a dozen stadiums where nothing grew from the ground but a huge stone structure which looked anything but congruous to its surroundings.

"Great Divine shitballs is right," Reeves said. Wilsin said nothing, kept his eyes on the contours and crevices of the stone structure, mentally examining every protrusion and buttress, trying to take in the shape of the whole thing. He knew what it looked like, he knew exactly what it was, but he also knew it was impossible. Fazarn's story from the previous night nibbled at his mind. Before, he wouldn't have had a bloody clue. Now though, there was only one thing in his mind as to what it looked like.

The rock was shaped like a damn cradle, curved in all the right places, giving the impression that the only thing missing was a giant stone baby to curl up inside it. Maybe a giant stone blanket and a giant stone teddy bear. The image made him smile briefly.

Cradle Rock.

They'd found the one thing people had been looking for over the centuries the way Fazarn had told the story, searching for it without success and yet they'd happened across it. The two of them entirely by accident had found it.

Impossible meant something different these days to what it used to, it felt. He wasn't sure he was secure in that knowledge. He liked the times he remembered when impossible meant impossible, not merely improbable.

"David."

"I know," he said. Two words which simply couldn't sum up the depth of feeling rushing through him. All the while he could remember an old riddle about the man who doesn't need something finding it while the man who was desperate for it not being able to get it. He felt a little that way. When Fazarn had told the story, he'd given the impression that Cradle Rock had been lost in the ravages of time, it had been shattered by unknowable forces and left broken out of shape by them all. This rock looked as new as a formation like that could look. His initial assessment had been right. It looked manmade, as impossible as that thought was.

There was that word again. Impossible.

He sighed, gave the mental command for Aroon to start his descent. He'd mull this over when they got there. Approaching from the sky was risky, all it'd take was for one of those things to look up and they'd be visible. Not another beast or bird in the sky around them for miles. The closer they got to landing, the more the trees started to bear in on them, the more the heat started to intensify. He could hear the chatter of insects in the distance, very distant at his guess, like listening through a jar.

"Something isn't right here," Reeves said. "The entire area feels off."

Wilsin glanced at him. "Off how?"

"Just a feeling." He shrugged his shoulders, gave the area around him a furtive glance like he was worried they were being watched. Maybe they were. This entire situation was filled with variables he couldn't start to comprehend. All he could do was deal with it in the manner with which he'd been trained. "Like sometimes, you go somewhere something bad happened, you get a bad feeling. It's not a quantifiable. It's just there. I can feel it growing in the pit of my stomach, it wants attention."

"You know what they say?" Wilsin asked. "Listen to your gut. It's usually right. Something feels off, it's probably off. I sort of get what you're saying." Reeves nodded at him, he looked grateful he didn't have to explain things further.

"You knew though, didn't you?" he said. Not accusing but just a simple statement of fact seasoned with a hint of suspicion.

"Knew what?" Wilsin was nonplussed, didn't know what he meant. The look of confusion crawling across his face wasn't an act.

"You knew something like this was going to be the case, didn't you? I mean, you were talking about us possibly flying for hours. We've not even done a fraction of that."

Wilsin nodded slowly. No harm in building some credibility. Suspicion was all it had been, it didn't mean he hadn't considered the possibility. Whatever these things were, the rustlers, they hadn't walked for miles to ambush them. Now he thought more about it, he was sure he'd seen one earlier in the day yesterday at the riverbank. Maybe a sentry. Whatever else they might be, they didn't lack for organisation which he found troubling. They'd showed some effort of planning their attack, they'd waited until they were settled around the fire and distracted with the stories which hinted at intelligent coordination. Most animals couldn't plan like this, not without modification and enhancement, so they were above the beasts in the food chain in that regard.

Part of every successful attack was an escape. No point in trying if you were going to get killed while leaving. Always have a way out, Wilsin remembered that was a lesson that they'd made sure to drum into them at the academy. Sometimes, it was even best to have more than one possible exit from a situation. Things went awry given half a chance. More words to live by from the academy. In his time as a Unisco agent, he'd discovered the truth in that statement more than once. Things didn't only have the chance to go awry, they'd jump at them if they could. Situations hated people who tried to plan for them in his opinion.

Anything could have happened. They'd not planned for a Vedo to attack them, they'd not expected the fire to come at them. The blasters yet, but not the Kjarn. Now they knew, would they adjust their tactics accordingly next time? Were they smart enough or was he trying to outthink them a little too hard?

Yes, he and Reeves could have chased them into the jungle at night. Anything could have happened but wasn't a guarantee all would have survived. They'd had to have come from somewhere. It wasn't an army they'd encountered last night, it was a raiding party, a group chancing their success and they'd gotten it. They'd routed them. Three dead. Three captured. Only him and Reeves left on the table. If this was a raiding party, the main bulk of them had to be somewhere. If the sentry had summoned a raiding party, they had to be relatively close. They had no signs of communication Wilsin had seen, then again who knew how walking plants spoke to each other in the first place.

"I suspected," he said eventually. "Let's leave it there. I don't pretend to understand how these things exist, but they do and that's the end of it. Let's just get this done. We approach on foot. Anything we come across…" He slid one of the machetes out of its sheath. "We kill. Try to get the lay of the land and then we…"

"Wouldn't we have been better aboard the dragon for that?" Reeves asked. "Just asking."

Wilsin ignored him. "We see if our friends are still alive, try to get them out." He fought the urge to look at the beacon, knew it wouldn't do much good, how long they'd be. Wouldn't even tell them if they'd got the message. For all he knew, this might be a futile effort and they were truly alone out here. If the evac didn't show up, they'd be dead. Not a chance there was another outcome. Nobody would ever know what happened to them.

He'd killed his first rustler less than five minutes after setting out from their landing point, had seen it stood in silence amidst the trees, the browns and greens of its body doing a job camouflaging it against the foliage. Not good enough to hide it from Reeves though, Wilsin had felt the tap from the Vedo on his shoulder, seen him point towards it. He'd followed the gesture, nodded in silent agreement. Once you knew it was there, it didn't take much to make out the misshapen body amidst the trees, to realise that it wasn't bark but an actual living creature. It was eerie watching it stand there, alone and uncaring, didn't deviate from staring ahead, didn't fidget or move, just impassive like the trees it was hiding amidst.

No hesitation. Reeves had confirmed it was alone, had examined the scene for another few moments and then held up a single finger. Mouthed the word 'one' to him. Wilsin would have appreciated the kjarnblade to do the job with, his machetes would have to suffice. He broke out the bushes, on the thing before it could react. Up close, it was hard to miss just how big the rustlers were, Wilsin wasn't the shortest but it towered over him by a head. Both arms came up, tendrils snapping like whips, cutting into the dirt beneath their feet, churning earth and fallen leaves up.

Big but not the biggest opponent he'd ever faced in combat and probably not the most dangerous either. Memories of his fight months ago with Domis Di Carmine rushed through his head, he felt his adrenaline spike and he rushed forward, spinning the machetes in his grip. He leaped at it, whips an unhelpful weapon in close if you could keep inside their range. One machete flashed up, cut a tendril away as it came towards him. A squeal broke from somewhere, not that he could see a mouth. Green stained the blade, not blood but something else. The cut tendril hit the ground, twitched like a serpent for a few moments before going still. The shrieks were already threatening to grow louder and louder, Wilsin made his choice, dropped into a crouch and swung the other machete low. The blade met only token resistance as it tore through woody flesh, a spray of green gushing out. It vaguely reminded him of plant food, his mother had always loved flowers and she'd insisted on putting that bloody stuff in the water with it, all so they'd grow. Their home had resembled a greenhouse at times, she'd filled every room with them where she could. There'd been more life in that house than the people who'd lived there.

He wondered what his mother would say if she could see him fighting a huge walking plant. She'd probably be unimpressed at the way he was hacking at it, he could see her with her hands on her hips and an exasperated look on her face.

The blow had been good, the rustler fell to ruined knees, he took its head off with a third swipe and watched it bounce into the trees. Still its body twitched, he gave it a kick in hopes of subsiding it. Nothing, one of the arms even tried to move towards him, might have grabbed him had he not driven both machetes down into its exposed back, tearing deep through flesh.

It wasn't pretty, but he'd done the job. He looked at Reeves. "Next time, you get them."

The Vedo only gave him a smile. "Of course. As you wish. I can't kill them all though, I want to leave some for you." His grin grew. "Ooh are we having Unisco banter. I always heard it was the height of wit."

Wilsin said nothing, just wiped down his blades and carried on walking.

Maybe he'd misinterpreted the situation, he thought, the closer they got to Cradle Rock. He could see it rising into the sky, a beacon to the heavens. No wonder the people of the past had flocked to this place, there was a certain sense of majesty here. The jungle couldn't have been there back then, Fazarn had never mentioned a jungle. He was sure that he'd said it was all desert. Maybe it was one of those many inconsistencies that seemed to operate within tales of the Divines.

What was religion without a little debate? If he knew the answer to that question, he felt like he'd know the answers to even more. He stretched his arms, one machete still in his grip, the other back in a sheath. Couldn't be far now, just a little further. When they got to the rock, there had to be answers.

Right then, he heard more shrieks, could hear them. Rustlers. They weren't screwing about. They were hunting, tearing through the jungle, their limbs making the rustling sound he'd named them for as they brushed against their surroundings. Shrieks and cries and catcalls rippled through the jungle. Next to him, Reeves activated his kjarnblade.

"I think we might have some running to do," the Vedo said.

"Ben... Don't talk about it. Just do it."

He was in motion before the words had finished coming from him, machete sheathed. Most sensible people would run away in this circumstance. The two of them had found themselves running towards it, legs pumping and desperately ignoring the heat. Neither of them wanted to die out here.

Please... Please have heard my beacon.

The first one came into sight, the blaster rifle came up from his back, he put a trio of shots straight through its centre mass, watched as Reeves swept into the inside and hacked it into three pieces with minimal effort. More were starting to filter through the trees, shuffling green shapes coming into view, he fired again and again, only when they were in his immediate path and soon his muscles ached from the assault of the rifle thumping against his shoulder, the vibrations reverberating up through his forearms. It clicked on empty and he tossed it aside, pumped his legs again. Sweat poured down him, his palms thick with it. He drew a machete, hacked at the neck of another, gripped the hilt so hard he thought his knuckles were going to crack. Lukonium bit through green-brown skin with a crunch, another head went flying and he shoved past it, felt something sharp catch his arm, something wet and warm dripping down it immediately. He tried to put it out of his mind, ignore the sharp burst of pain.

Behind him, Reeves ducked and dived, wielded his blade like a surgeon as he landed blows that cut anything near him into pieces. Bisecting them didn't appear to kill them instantly but it'd do for now.

Compromise or kill. Either worked.

Reeves could run, he had to give him that, easily keeping pace with him despite the humidity clinging to them. Wilsin's heart kept thumping, he fought for breath and the urge to keep on running.

This had been a bad idea in retrospect. Maybe they should have via the sky. Running and fighting was never as easy as it looked, especially not if they had to fight their way out of here as well, not an unlikely proposition. Death had always been close, he knew he could feel it reaching for him, a bony hand ready to tap him on the shoulder.

Or was it? He could see the edges of the clearing up ahead, could see the light breaking through. Cradle Rock loomed high over their heads, they had to be close now. So close. If he reached out, he might well be able to touch it. Reeves could see it too, Wilsin could hear his breathing, could see the sweat covering his face as he redoubled his pace. Running for your life had never taken on such a succinct meaning as this. Yet, were they? He allowed himself a glance back, saw the rustlers were lingering. Amidst the jumble of his thoughts, he considered it interesting.

Why?

Had he not been so consumed with getting ahead, he might have considered what they were hanging back from. What up ahead was keeping them back? As it were, his thoughts were more preoccupied with relief. Imminent death was no longer an option. He let out a choked gasp of relief, slowed his run to a jog for the last hundred feet and then they were through the last bastion of trees into the clearing.

His first thought was to turn around and sprint back into the jungle, quickly realised the futility of that thought as they turned to look at him. Not one rustler, not a dozen, not even a hundred.

Thousands. Easily. A thousand eyeless faces turned to stare at him and Reeves as one, not really seeing, definitely not blinking but clearly looking at them the way a curious cat idly considered a mouse. They looked at them like they were food. Prey. An inconsequence.

"David," Reeves said, his voice strangely neutral given the circumstances. At least he hadn't screamed. That really would have put a dampener on the situation. "Tell me you had a plan for something like this."

"I had a plan for something like this," Wilsin said. It was what he wanted to hear after all, no point denying someone a crumb of comfort right before they were both horribly killed. "Don't worry about it. It's going to be over very shortly."

"Not comforting."

He smiled weakly, unhooked his second blaster rifle. He'd die with a weapon in his hand, kept it pointed at them with one hand on the grip, the other going to his summoner. Might as well go all out. The spirits might be the turning point. The difference between dying quickly and surviving that little bit longer. When your only choice was dying now or later, it was a pretty sorry shit show.

They hadn't attacked though. Rather the opposite. In front of them, the rustlers were moving out of the way, parting to reveal a single unbroken path of grass ahead, leading out into the midst of their bodies

"I think they want us to go that way," Reeves said, voicing the thought Wilsin had already been considering. "Right into the middle of them."

"Easier to kill us when we can't run," Wilsin said. "When we've got nowhere to go."

"They could easily kill us with this many regardless whether we run or not," Reeves pointed out. "It's not too much of a stretch. They could throw dozens at us; never mind hundreds and we'd be overwhelmed quickly."

He was right, Wilsin had to admit. They were already in the killing field, might as well walk a bit further. The rustlers clearly wanted them to do it for some reason, maybe it would be okay.

Maybe. There was theoretically a chance of that happening. He might as well delay the inevitable for as long as possible.

Wilsin lowered his weapon and took the first step onto the path. The rustlers were barely feet away from him, close enough to smell their pollinated odour. Wild flowers and jungle mud. Reeves had replaced his weapon on his belt, strode along like he didn't have any sort of care. Maybe he had a plan.

He was really starting to hate the word maybe.

About the time he'd started to lose count of how many they'd passed, the path started to widen out into a clearing within the bodies, something very strange already underway as they approached, roots and knots of grass rising from the earth, twisting and contorting into an unusual shape. Wilsin watched them continue to work their form until slowly it took the appearance of something he could recognise, thorns and jungle flowers resting atop a carpet of weeds to add decoration. He'd seen it all now, he figured. Who'd have thought that whatever this whole thing was, it'd form its own damn chair.

Not just any chair admittedly. When you saw the stories about the kings of old, it was like it'd seen all of those and set out to top them. A throne fit for a ruler. All these things looked alike, he didn't know how they considered which of them was the leader. Maybe they didn't have a ruler. Was that so unusual? They looked like plants after all and plants didn't really have leaders. They weren't sentient, the idea was ridiculous.

"Interesting," Reeves said.

"You ever seen the Kjarn manipulated like that?" Wilsin asked out the corner of his mouth, the hope that a positive answer would come his way heavy in his soul. He needed a win. Any win. If they were dealing with some powerful Vedo, that'd be grand. He could put a label on it, maybe not a neat one but he could deal. This... This was too far into the unknown.

He was to be disappointed as Reeves shook his head. "Never. I might be able to do it if I trained for decades. Now though? No chance."

It wasn't a denial. He'd take that.

"I don't think so," the Vedo added, shattering his hopes with four simple words. "It feels off. Weird. Like nothing I've felt before. Sorry," he added, a little limply. "Can't help you."

"You know, it's rude to whisper amongst yourselves."

Wilsin stiffened up, saw the figure move out from the crowd, gliding effortlessly through the rustlers. To say that it was a rustler like them was an understatement, bigger, heavier, greener and with a crown of cherillo berries dangling from the circlet of branches around his head. It was a he, Wilsin realised with surprise, some part of him looked almost human but for the moss-green skin and the cracked bark covering his limbs. Unlike the rest of the rustlers, he had a face, eyes and a nose and a mouth slashed into the wood but moving regardless. Though the eyes were empty, they gave the impression that they could see right through the two of them. He didn't want to lock his gaze on them

Plus, that voice. There was something about it that resonated with him, ever so slightly, and that unsettled him. He couldn't place the face or the voice, he hadn't met many giant plant men in the past so to say he felt unsettled was an understatement.

"That's better," the plant-man said, his lips moving in sync with his words. Wilsin wondered if he had vocal chords, if they were also fashioned of wood. A strange thought but it made him smile and Divines knew he needed some of that. "Now we can have a pleasant chat."

He was taller than the rest of the rustlers, towered a good few feet above the largest of them and they bowed their heads as he passed them by, faces low in deference. He barely gave them a glance, stepped over to his throne and lowered himself into it, the wood and the vines creaking under his weight. Wilsin didn't want to think about how much a body like that might weigh. The strange thing was, he didn't look cumbersome. He looked graceful and lethal at the same time, like an ice panther, floated across the grass rather than walking. His legs were thick, finished at the end into four-taloned feet.

"Dare I ask who you are?" Reeves asked, letting both hands fall to his side. Wilsin saw out the corner of his eye that his fingers were flexing near the hilt of his kjarnblade, he still had his own weapon in hand even if it wasn't levelled at the huge plant-man.

"And yet I know who you both are, Master Benjamin Reeves of the Vedo. You've killed a great number of my people here in this jungle, not a mean feat I admit but a particularly tiresome path that you chose to walk." Reeves looked like he wasn't too fussed by the way it had tossed his name about, yet Wilsin saw the flicker in his eyes. Unisco always wanted you to notice the little things. The little things were the true difference in the kingdoms, pick up enough of the little details and you got a glimpse of the bigger picture.

"Yet your crimes are naught in comparison to that of Unisco Agent David Peter Wilsin next to you," the plant-man said. "Do you know who I am, David? Do you know who I was?"

As familiar as the figure felt to him, Wilsin had to shake his head. He couldn't place him, he said as much and at least the figure looked mollified in part.

"I admire your honesty, much as my heart swings one way to the next in debate over whether to permit you to live or not." The huge rustler leaned forward, Wilsin could have sworn the mouth was contorted into a smile. "I suppose you could say that I'm their king and these are my people." He threw out a bare arm flecked with brown, gestured to the area around them, his smile growing. "Before I was their king, I suppose you could say I'm someone you tried to kill."

Chapter Twenty-Two. King of the Plants.

"Some enemies are easier to vanquish than others. Some deaths you never hear about and always their expiration leaves you wondering. Then there are those you think dead, only for them to reappear when the moment is at its least opportune."
Brendan King in a lecture to the cadets at Iaku academy some years ago.

Wilsin blinked. Those words he hadn't expected, took him moment to wrap his mind around them, consider the full weight behind them and work out their value. The chances were that it could be the truth. He'd been a Unisco agent for a long time and though he'd never actively sought to end a life, triggers had been pulled. People had died. He was still here. If it came to a choice between them and him, he would continue to pull those triggers. Self-preservation might sound like a dirty word, but it was a guiding light for every living thing in the kingdoms. You exist, you carry on, survive before you die.

"I don't remember you," he repeated, not entirely sure whether it was the best approach to take. The plant-man looked impassive, his carved face hard to read. He might be angry, he might be impassive, he might feel nothing at all. "I've seen a lot of faces in this life."

"What you mean is that you've sent a lot of men to their deaths," the plant-man said. "I can emphasise though. That's the nature of being a king. You have their lives in your hands. They are theirs to do what you want with. You can keep them alive, you can send them to their death, you can make them dance or you can maim and mutilate them at your pleasure."

Wilsin glanced around the creatures surrounding them. Mutilation here would probably be what others called horticulture.

"Can with subjects like these anyway. You know, they'd never had a leader until I came along. Just wallowed in the muck for aeons. Never got up, never got out. Never dreamed. Then I found them, I embraced them all and they took me to their hearts. For centuries, it felt like, I lived among them. That place changed me."

Wilsin blinked. That place…

"I mean, humans would never put up with how I rule. But you know what I found? Humanity is massively overrated. You people disgust me now I've moved on. You want so much and you're willing to give so little in exchange. Everything for nothing, entitled and spoiled. You want to change the world, but you don't want to make the effort."

"Are you having a little moment here?" Wilsin asked, finally interrupting. He'd heard enough. He didn't like the way this thing was questioning what he'd ever done for the world. He'd kept it safe. He'd tried to improve things. Wasn't that all anyone could have asked of him? Not everyone went to work for Unisco, he'd done it and those who hadn't couldn't criticise him for it. He knew duty and he knew that his part had been played. "Because if you are, we can come back later with our friends. Where are they, by the way? Some of your people walked off with them earlier and we really need them back."

"Your Grace," Reeves added. Wilsin did his best to avoid rolling his eyes at the subservience.

"One of you knows respect at least," the green king said. He sounded amused, Wilsin couldn't care whether he was or not. "But we have your friends. They're up there." He jerked his head towards the rock. "They're fine. For now, anyway. A means to a purpose, I think you'll find."

"And what purpose is that," Wilsin said, his hands tightening around his weapon. He was amazed he hadn't lifted it and fired yet, something that the green king also wasn't apparently unaware of by the laughter in his voice.

"You might have noticed I've let you keep your weapons. If I had a shred of doubt that they would be able to harm me, do you think I would have done that? You've already seen my people in combat. An army of Vedo might be able to exterminate them..." His voice tailed off, grew menacing. "An army of Vedo did do their best to exterminate them. But their best was not good enough. And I believe that you're fresh out of Vedo to cleanse us."

"There are more of us than you think," Reeves said smoothly. "Be assured of that. The Kjarn is within us all and there are always those who will be able to rise when they hear it. The Kjarn is eternal."

"The Kjarn is what it always has been. A force with which mortals have played with over which they claim their lack of control is down to an inability to dominate. Let me tell you this, Benjamin Reeves. The Cavanda knew different. At least they did back then, whether they still believe or not is another matter entirely. They of the old ways knew the truth, that control comes through dominion, that dominion comes through strength and strength comes to those that earn it."

He likes a speech, doesn't he? Wilsin thought. The green king had some issues, unfortunately he had some knowledge and that made him a dangerous foe. He knew stuff about Reeves and the Kjarn and whatever the hells the Cavanda were. He tried to shoot his partner a glance, see if his face betrayed his thoughts, though he doubted it.

Reeves had a face perfect for cards, he wouldn't show anything he didn't have to. They'd played some nights on the boat, Wilsin had always thought himself a decent enough Ruin player and he'd lost too many credits to the Vedo.

Never play a game with someone who can sense your emotions. It gives them too much of an advantage. Reeves had claimed he wasn't doing it, Wilsin hadn't believed him. More than that, he got the feeling Reeves knew he didn't believe him by the way further denials had come.

"Okay, you hate society, you don't like humans, you don't rate the Kjarn," Wilsin eventually said. "What do you want? You were about to tell us before you decided to try and stick your sense of superiority down our throats, which by the way I'm not swallowing so you might as well put it away."

Reeves snorted with laughter. Wilsin didn't think it'd been that funny, but apparently his expressionless face had its limits. Maybe he was nervous. Maybe he just liked euphemisms.

"Your friends we took for a purpose," the green king repeated. "I needed them. I knew you'd come. After all, I couldn't turn down the chance for an audience with one of my killers now, could I? Or at least one of the ones who attempted it."

"You wanted them as bait? For me?" He didn't know whether to laugh or cry. He knew he wasn't impressed. Still, if he had killed him, or at least tried to, then it was probably justified.

"Bait. Revenge. Those words meant more when I was human. Maybe now I just want you to take back a message."

"Sorry, buddy. Not a courier." He was deliberately ignoring the self-proclaimed position the king had taken, he could feel Reeves' wince from where he stood. He didn't care. "Nor a messenger nor an envoy. You want to deliver a message, you take it yourself."

"David Wilsin," the green king said, voice laced with menace. "I only need one of you to take that message back. Not both. That you should choose to make yourself inconvenient when this is the case makes me wonder if you desire to live when I'm offering you clemency."

"If you're feeling that level of generosity, how about you tell me your name, so I know which of the sorry sacks of shit you really are, rather than hiding behind claims of supremacy and masks."

The green king gestured to his face, looked almost insulted at the suggestion. "Mask? You mistake me for what I am not, David. You still assume me to be man when I have become so much more. When my people move, I see through them. When they kill, I feel the blood on their limbs. When they die, I feel their pain. I'm not a man anymore, hells I may well be a Divine. And where better to proclaim that than at the foot of Cradle Rock. This place is synonymous with it. They know what it meant to the old ones, to the Divines that came before, and they know what it'll mean again. They'll know I mean business."

"What's your message?" Reeves asked. "Your Grace, pardon my associate but his mouth is free and wild. He respects not your position, but I sense your power."

"And how does my power make you feel, little Vedo?" Wilsin heard the condescension in the voice, blaster rifle starting to tremble in his grasp. He found himself clutching it so tightly, he thought it might break.

Just give me an excuse to put a flurry straight through your face!

Even if it wouldn't do any good, it was still something he'd enjoy, baiting this guy further. He'd never had a problem with patience before, now he just wanted to blast a few charge packs into him.

He'd tried to kill him and failed, or he'd been involved in a similar attempt. He didn't know, nothing beyond the vague familiarity in the carved face. Normally he was decent with recognition but seeing a face made of flesh and one made of wood were two entirely different things, especially when it came to facial recollection.

"Honestly?" Reeves asked. "You don't sit right with me. You worry me. I can feel the power radiating off you and it's like standing too close to something that's about to explode."

"Interesting choice of language. I've never felt better in all my centuries."

"The calm often does feel good before the storm hits," Reeves said. "You terrify me. I'd be anywhere else right now if I could. But you claim to be a king and I will show you that respect that I'd hope you'd show to me if our positions were to be reversed."

"Respect is earned, not given freely. I respect what you have learned in your studies as a Vedo, I can't imagine it is a path that was easily walked. The Vedo are all but extinct, the Cavanda silently rule the kingdoms now, worming their way into places of power. The Senate, the ICCC, Unisco, the pillars are falling, you know, you just haven't heard the crash yet!"

What?! That was the first Wilsin was hearing about that and by the look on his face, the same was true of Reeves.

"To be a Vedo now is a very different game as to what it was before they fell. I believe there are those who think the Vedo of old fell because they got complacent. I think the reverse is true, that the kingdoms got complacent that they would always be there in secret. The Kjarn was in balance and everything was in harmony. Now though, the Cavanda outnumber you ten to one and more, you are scattered, lost, hopeless, you align yourselves with men like Agent Wilsin and Agent King in hopes of gaining some succour."

The green king shook his head. "Don't assume that I despise Agent Wilsin there." A thorned green finger came up, levelled at him. "I do have tremendous respect for what he and his partner did the night when the rains came down. I was just a man then, but I nearly washed the entire tournament away."

Something started to stir in the darkest recesses of Wilsin's memory, long forgotten but crawling back to the fore. That night still haunted him.

"Anyone who rises to do what he has done as an agent of Unisco is worthy of respect, if not admiration. To be a killer is not a noble thing, it is to weaken and destabilise not only yourself but the very fabric of a modern society. In a perfect world, Unisco wouldn't exist."

"In a perfect world, we wouldn't need to," Wilsin said. He believed it as well. "We do what we have to. Because nobody else will."

"Nobody else was asked. Instead, the first sign of any sort of trouble, the Senate turns to their own secret police to do it. Their killers and their blackmailers and their thugs. That's what most of you are, you know. You turn everything you touch rotten."

"What's the damn message," Wilsin said. "I don't have all day." He was tired, his body ached, and he was slick with his own sweat, salt stinging his eyes. "Are you going to give it over are just talk us to death?"

"Say my name."

"What?!" Wilsin almost spat the word out. "What did you just say?"

"You want the message, you say my name. Acknowledge what you and Nicholas Roper did without hesitation and I'll let the two of you go. Fail to answer and you die. I won't take any pleasure in killing you… Huh, I never knew that lying was so easy to me now. With people like these…" the king waved an arm out towards the surrounding hoard. Wilsin hadn't forgotten that they were there. "… One never needs to lie or cheat or steal because they'll give if asked. Which society contains the real monsters? Now Agent Wilsin, I command you one more time to say my name!"

Anger had laced the voice, Wilsin smiled, took a step forward and held his arms wide open, pushed his chest out. "You want to kill me? Kill me. I don't know who you are, I won't say your name now stop wasting…"

He didn't see the tendril move, never saw it coming, the first sign he got was the pain in his chest. The weapon was no longer in his hands, he heard it thump to the ground. Looking down, he saw the length of green bursting into his vest, an immense look of satisfaction on the king's face. Suddenly he couldn't speak anymore, lungs on fire. His legs couldn't hold him, and they gave, knees kissed the earth and then his chest met it in embrace. The last thing he heard as the world went dark was the laughter of the green king, his last thought left the man's name emblazoned in his slipping mind.

Oh!

Ben Reeves saw Wilsin go down, his first instinct was to run to him, yet he did not for he knew the chances of Wilsin surviving a blow like that were minimal. He'd seen the power of tendrils like that the previous night, the way they'd torn through flesh and bone, ripped it asunder without pause. That their king might be weaker didn't cross his mind. The world didn't work like that, not the world he knew nor the one he thought he knew. The strong rose to lead, to impose their will on those below. That was the first rule of life. The weak didn't necessarily lack the will to lead, but rather the qualities. Something would be missing from them, something forever dooming them to follow.

Maybe that was wrong. Maybe the ones who ended up leading were the ones who could shout the loudest, could make themselves heard. That itself was a quality admittedly, albeit one only of value if the speaker had something to say worth listening to.

Too often, the ones who spoke the loudest had the least to say, simply desiring to hear their own voices.

He wondered what sort of leader the green king was. What sort of man he'd been before all this. He withdrew that tendril from Wilsin's chest, crimson staining the hole that had been torn in the material, one ragged hole gaping to the crowd. Around them, the rustlers as Wilsin had called them, were going crazy, hissing and squealing through mouthless faces, a sound leaving the hairs on his arms standing up.

He chose not to respond, let his kjarnblade hang from his belt. Getting into a fight wouldn't solve anything. Since Master Baxter had revealed his Vedo to the kingdoms in as public a manner as possible, people had been running with a false sense of knowledge about their capabilities. They believed all manner of things of the Vedo and the Master had insisted on letting them do it. The more they believed, the more their legend would grow. If rumours abounded there were Vedo out there who could grow ten feet tall and lift buildings with the power of their minds, then so be it. That sort of publicity could only be a boon. Those with talent would want to learn how to use it and although the truth might not be as glamorous as the myth, discipline could be instilled within them and they be turned into something greater than the sum of its parts.

More than that, the myth would be a deterrent. Why mess with those that could destroy you on a whim?

"Your Grace," he said. "There was no need for that." Voice calm, level and controlled. Just the way Master Baxter had always told them to if ever they encountered a powerful being with a desire for respect. Reeves could remember that session, even now. The Master had stood at the front of the chamber and solemnly informed them 'it'll happen more than you think'. Reeves hadn't entirely believed him, but he'd still listened. None of them had been there to not listen. All of them had heard what he had to say, it wouldn't be the first time they'd had to suspend their disbelief.

"I'll decide what's necessary and what isn't," the green king said. "That man was a killer and a thug."

"He was also my friend!" Reeves said loudly. "He was friendly to me and he didn't have to be."

"You associate with dogs, you catch fleas, Benjamin Reeves. The kingdoms are a better place without men like David Wilsin."

"You had a message for us. Give it to me and I'll take my friends and begone, with your leave," he said. He couldn't keep the disgust out of his voice. Killing Wilsin just like that rankled. No rhyme or reason, just a tantrum. Respect be damned, he'd made his choice. Get out of here and he'd see the entire place burned.

"Your kingdoms are involved in a civil war," the green king said. "I know this. Mistress Coppinger takes on your leaders and she's winning not just the battles but the hearts and minds of the people one by one."

"Not my leaders," Reeves said. "There's only one man that I answer to."

"You can tell Ruud Baxter as well, in fact I assure you it'll probably be better if you do. The sooner the Vedo accept defeat in all of this, the rest of the kingdoms will as well. We may let you live, though we can't guarantee it. Spellcasters are always to be a cherished asset. We don't have access to the Kjarn for all the fancy tricks you people can do. We'd hate to have to wipe you out."

"Maybe we'd feel the same way," Reeves said. "The way of the Vedo has never been the way of violence…"

"And yet you'll perpetuate it if you have to. That's the way of people like you. That's why the Mistress hated you. All that power and you sat on it, chose to let things swing into a spiralling descent…"

"I was never part of that old order!" Reeves shouted. "I heard about it and we're doing things differently. We're trying to be better. Master Baxter has us doing our part against Coppinger."

"And yet, you're here in Vazara, two hundred miles from the nearest Coppinger in the kingdom. A strange place to be doing your part."

"We all have our places to be. The message, your highness!" Getting a straight answer out of him was like herding wildcats, they each wanted to go their own way and liable to bite and scratch when denied. If he was connected to each of the rustlers via a mind link, no wonder. Hundreds of them were in the clearing alone, it had to be distracting.

"We have Vazara," the green king said. "We're going to take it all, just a case of when we do it, not if. The Mistress is fighting you and not until there's a winner will we make our move."

Reeves' mind raced with the possibilities. That could mean a few things. One, that the green king's position wasn't as solid as he insisted, and he couldn't risk a fight he wasn't sure of winning. Two, he wasn't willing to jump into the ongoing civil war. The last thing he'd want to do is unite two opposing factions against a common threat. Three, if he was telling him his plan to be relayed back, then he had to be convinced that he had a good chance of victory. Too many opposing points of view, not enough time to pick out the right one.

"You will not be able to stop us. You will have torn each other to shreds, those shreds will become swept up and a part of our new world."

"You said you knew Coppinger," Reeves said. He was curious now, considering all the information that the green king had spilled already. "Why not align with her now then?"

"She is beneath me. She clutches for immortality, but she is not there yet, her power is growing but slowly. She will try for the bloods of those born to the Divines but that is a journey harder than she yet realises. Once I worked for her and I doubt that should she see past my identity, she would see us as equals, nor share what she desires." The green king puffed up his chest. "More than that, neither would we. It is not in our nature. Why share when we can take it all."

Reeves said nothing to that, glanced around the surrounding rustlers one more time. "You do realise that your plan is doomed, right? You start to try to take the rest of the kingdoms, everyone will revolt against you? This civil war is splitting people apart, families and friends alike. A common enemy will unite the people of the five kingdoms far better than any other threat effectively could."

"Typical Vedo arrogance. Your belief in people will be your undoing."

A cough from the ground, followed by a wet laugh as David Wilsin rolled onto his back. "You know, that's *cough* about as far from the truth as you get. Reeves is a good man. He's a *cough* useful man. He can't do the showy stuff you expect Vedo to do. But he's exceptional at what he *cough* does do."

Reeves breathed again, the sigh slipping his lungs and flooding his system with relief. It'd worked then. He'd seen Wilsin go down, he'd seen the wound and he'd hoped to all Divines above they'd worked it exactly right or the result would have been catastrophic.

Wilsin had explained exactly what he wanted done to the vest and Reeves hadn't know whether to be impressed or worried. It was the methodological mind of a man who had considered what he wanted carefully. He'd laid it all out and then asked Reeves if he could do it.

Reeves had shrugged. "Only one way to find out. You don't do something by wringing your hands and wondering if you can. You try it."

Wilsin had been right. So many layers of fabric in the vest, it was the simplest thing to start manipulating them. Fabric became lukonium here, diamond there, a gel lining created to cushion the impact. Suffice to say Wilsin hadn't been too keen on the idea of having unbreakable metal plates smashed into his chest without some sort of buffer. They both had seen what force those tendrils could deliver. Wilsin had wanted an edge and Reeves couldn't blame him. Every little helped. It had to be hard going into a fight like this with only wits and weapons to rely on. Reeves had the Kjarn at his back. Wilsin was on his own.

Except he wasn't, was he? He had Reeves doing this. The Kjarn worked in mysterious ways. Master Baxter had insisted he travel to Vazara with Brendan King's team. What if he'd known that his Alchemite skills would be needed here to save a man's life?

This was the problem when your own legend got hyped and twisted beyond any reasonable sort of truth. You started to forget yourself. You started to believe.

Master Baxter had always had a few choice words where belief was concerned, had always said there were a few different types of them. Faith. Blind faith. Self-belief. It wasn't what you believed or what you called it, rather what you did with it. Your actions determined you.

Reeves also knew that Master Baxter wasn't a Cognivite either, so the idea that he could have seen this coming and planned accordingly was ludicrous. Sharing your speciality with an outsider wasn't generally done lightly amongst the Vedo, a long-standing taboo, not unless you and the outsider had developed a special sort of respect. Amongst each other, living as they did, there were few secrets. Master Baxter might be the most powerful Vedo left alive, but it didn't mean that his power was limitless. It worked the same way as every other. His mental abilities might exist but if they were anything beyond rudimentary then he was doing well. There were Cognivites in the group though, he could have consulted any one of them. Ancuta for one. She was a powerful psychic, the tale of how Master Baxter had brought her away from the travelling folk was the stuff of legend. Anne as well, she'd developed her mental powers considerably.

He didn't know. He might be reading into things that weren't entirely there.

"You survived?" The green king sounded bemused as he watched Wilsin struggle to his feet. Reeves could see a shining layer of diamond through a rip in his vest, fabric torn where the tendril had hit him. "You are resourceful, David Wilsin."

"Not really," Wilsin said. "Just try to plan ahead and make use of what I have in my corner. We don't all have an army of weird plant things, do we now?" He picked his blaster rifle back up. "You know what else I have? I know who you are."

The green king leaned forward on his throne, the carved face betraying very little emotion. Those empty eyes grew even more intensely focused on him.

"Do you now?"

"Yep. I wasn't impressed by you in your previous life and I'm not impressed by you now," Wilsin said. "You had a free shot to kill me and you failed. Just like you failed Claudia Coppinger. She's forgotten about you now, doesn't care that you ever existed. She moved on."

"You impudent!"

"Yeah, I'm impudent. You know what else I'm going to do?" Maybe it was the pain in his chest making him bold, maybe the lack of oxygen going through his lungs as he took shallow breaths was affecting his judgement. "I've stopped you before and I'm going to do it again."

"Look around you. The two of you are surrounded. You're a wounded man and an Alchemite with a magic sword. I am legion. I have an army."

"A very flammable army. And you know what I have?" Wilsin held his fingers to his lips and whistled. "I have a dragon."

He'd left Aroon in the trees, a little insurance policy. Now, he didn't regret it one jot. If the green king had killed him, if the tendril had tried to punch through his throat rather than his chest, Aroon would have gone straight for him. And given Nick had failed to kill the green king in his previous life, maybe dragon fire would do the job this time. The beast exploded from the jungle, Wilsin gave the command and fire rained down onto the rustlers. If they'd feared Reeves' minor act of flammable transference the previous night, they were terrified now, incited to panic as flames ripped through them. Above them, he heard the king's voice thundering through the screams and wails.

"Kill them all!"

Wilsin locked another container crystal into his summoner, pushed the button. Running through this battlefield would be suicide. Reeves had activated his kjarnblade, leaped into the crowd coming for them, the glow of his sword bright as it bit through flesh and wood alike. Limbs fell away, bodies dropped but they kept on coming towards him, more than he could possibly ever cut down. He needed help and the spirit materialising onto the battlefield was going to do that job, Scales the veek had already going for the nearest rustler with claws and teeth alike. At close range, few things in the wild could compete with the natural savagery of the veek, a creature embodying the grace of a cat and the vicious nature of a carnivorous lizard, fur and scales creating a mishmash appearance across s slender body.

He needed to get to the rock, needed to get Brendan and the others. He brought his blaster rifle up and started to run, all too aware of what was in front of him. Deep breath, he gave Aroon the mental command. He needed a path. He wouldn't get twenty feet through the mess of bodies ahead before one of them got him. Twenty feet might be optimistic. Too many of them were there, writhing and shaking. The heat had gotten worse, like half the army was aflame, the background humidity rising cruelly. He saw Aroon swoop over out the corner of his eye, fire erupted from his jaws, three explosive blasts raining down on the rustlers, bodies thrown about by sheer force. He fired as he ran, not going for kill shots but aiming for legs and groins, anything to put them down and distract them. If they were trying to get back up, they wouldn't be focused on him. Their attention would be divided. He'd already seen how much it took to bring one down, he couldn't afford to get tangled up in swordplay with them. It'd take too damn long to kill them with the machetes. Hopefully Aroon would sweep up any stragglers on his next pass, charred piles of black sludge the only traces left of ones already dead, grass scorched beyond repair.

Scales! To me!

The veek bounded to his side, crashed to the grass with claws outstretched and took a swipe at the closest rustler with his tail, damn near tore it in half with one swipe. Veek tails were naturally hard, even more so when callers got at them with genetic mods. It was always easier to work with what was already there rather than what wasn't.

Wilsin pointed towards the rock and the veek rushed ahead, snarling furiously as powerful limbs slashed out, tearing apart anything in range. Rustlers went down, limbs torn apart and bodies mangled. Glancing back, he saw Reeves rushing to follow him, clothes torn and his face a smeared mask of blood. He didn't appear unharmed otherwise, blade still aglow. Wilsin fired, dropped another rustler. And another. And another. Up ahead, he could see a narrow path cut into the rock, a way up it. He made the decision in a heartbeat, that was where he'd go for. If he stayed here, he wouldn't last long. If in doubt, go up. Always a sound strategy. Reeves would follow, the Kjarn augmenting his speed and indeed, the Vedo had made it to the path an instant before Wilsin touched rock. Scales bounded ahead, up onto it and Wilsin went next at Reeves' nod. He glanced back, saw the Vedo step onto the path before closing his eyes. Beneath them, the ground started to rumble, gently at first before increasing its ferocity, Reeves' entire body shaking with it as he expelled a harsh breath, a moan. The base of the path was moving, fresh virgin rock slipping up through the stone, rising high. In a matter of seconds, it was waist height. Even sooner, it rose above their heads, the view of the battlefield lost to them.

"That should hold them," Reeves said. "For a while anyway." Behind the wall, rustlers were already starting to pound away, limbs beating the rock, thud after thud after thud. "Way to piss them off, David."

"It's a gift," Wilsin said. "Come on, can't stay here. We have to go." He turned and ran, Scales leading the way up, feline grace making it look so much easier than it truly was. He just followed the veek, trusted in his spirit to guide the way. Scales sprang from rock to rock, not touching the path, tail twitching in the wind.

"Guess you really planned ahead with this, huh?" Reeves said. "I mean, how long can your dragon keep the assault up?"

"Long as we need to, I guess," Wilsin said. "I don't want to think about what happens when the fires burn out."

"That a danger?" Reeves asked. "Can they really burn out?"

"Dragons? Of course," Wilsin said. "It doesn't happen often, especially not in spirit calling bouts. They don't go on long enough. But if you think every fire needs fuel, sooner or later the fuel's going to run out, leaving you with a dragon that can't do much more than cough up smoke. I know they say there's no smoke without fire, they got it wrong here. If your dragon coughs up smoke, he's about to get heartburn."

"You know a lot about that."

"Wade told me," he said thoughtfully. "Wade Wallerington, the spirit…"

"Yeah, I trained with his cousin. The Kjarn is strong in his family."

"Didn't know that."

"I think he wants to keep it a secret. She loves it though. Talented girl. Helped Master Baxter heal her cousin's eyes."

Wilsin remembered that. Felt like too long ago now, mere months but it felt like years to him.

The next corner they turned, they found their friends, Scales stood in a crouch, ears flat against his head as he studied them. Wilsin skidded to a halt, patted the veek on the head.

"Good," he said simply, as he took in the scene. All three of them were still alive, Suchiga looked in the worst shape. His arms had been broken, all three of them bound tight with vines. Brendan's face as he saw them was a picture, flickering from relief to fury and back to relief. "Come on, let's get them out of there."

Reeves coughed. "Are you sure? Brendan looks ready to murder you."

"He's not going to murder me," Wilsin said, drawing one of his machetes. "I mean, we risked life and limb to get up here for them." Behind him, Aroon let rip another blast of fire into the crowd of rustlers beneath them, he could hear the screeches and the chitters singing in outrage.

"I'm not going to murder him," Brendan confirmed. "I may have him disciplined when we get out of here, but that depends if we survive or not."

"Transport is on its way," Wilsin said, pulling the beacon out of his jacket. "We're going to get out of here. I pushed it hours ago, they have to be here soon."

Brendan said nothing, other than to give the beacon a curt glance and then jerk his head towards Suchiga and Tiana. "Get them out first. Mister Reeves, if you can do something to alleviate Mister Suchiga's pain then I'm sure he'd greatly appreciate that."

Wilsin moved to Aubemaya, saw Reeves roll his eyes. Despite all his learnedness, Brendan wasn't as up on the Vedo as he was on other historical matters. Maybe none had confided the information in him. He got the feeling that didn't happen often, it just served to make him feel more special. He hacked at the vines, careful not to hack into her. Her dark skin had several grazes on display, shallow cuts marring smoothness. Reeves had moved to Suchiga, had his eyes closed and his hands gingerly dancing across the ruined limbs.

Several careful cuts and Aubemaya was able to wriggle herself free, massaging feeling back into her arms as she pushed herself up. First thing she did was throw her arms around his neck, not the most unpleasant sensation he'd ever experienced as he felt the contours of her body press against his. "Thank you," she whispered in his ear. "Thank you for coming back for us."

He looked at her, grinned. "Never going to be a chance I wouldn't, my dear." Her eyes were red and blotchy, she looked like she'd been crying. All of this was new to him, had to be new to all of them and different people reacted to different things in different ways.

Suchiga's eyes had closed, he looked at peace, even though his chest still rose and fell with every breath. Reeves coughed, removed his hands and mopped at his brow.

"All I can do," he said. "He needs medical attention, Mister King."

Before Brendan could reply, a crash broke out over the horizon, Wilsin and Reeves looking first at each other and then to the path they'd come up. They'd all heard sounds like that before, rock being smashed, eroded away by hundreds and hundreds of blows, finally worn out by the attrition thrown at it. Already, the sounds of rustling were coming up the trail.

"Think we just ran out of time," Wilsin said. He looked at Scales, jerked his head towards the path and the veek raced away, flung himself across the first rustler that turned the corner, slashing and biting until it couldn't move any longer. The bad news for Scales was he was surrounded very quickly, dozens of the things laying into him and Wilsin heard the yowls of pain, defiant hisses that quickly turned into screams. He pushed the recall button on his summoner, the rustlers suddenly fighting amongst themselves, hitting empty air and each other.

"Someone grab Suchiga!" Wilsin bellowed, startled as Brendan obliged, scooped the dazed doctor over his shoulder and ran. Aubemaya followed him, Reeves brought up his blade hilt again, prepared to hit the button. "No!"

Reeves threw him a sideways glance. "No?!"

"We can't fight them here. Too enclosed. If you can do something to the ground, I'd do it fast. Make it hard for them to follow us as possible. I'll cover you!"

To prove the point, he started to fire again, placing his shots amidst the thronging masses. Too close together, too many to pick out, just hit and hope. It wasn't the most effective way of shooting, but it'd have to do. Any of them got too close, he'd have to prioritise. Too quickly his blaster ran dry, cells clicking empty and he let the pack drop, slammed another one in before resuming. Reeves had dropped to his knees, his hands on the ground, his eyes squeezed shut in deep concentration.

Come on Ben, do your damn thing fast!

The first sign he got things were changing, one of them slipped at the front, losing its footing and sliding back into those behind it, hit them like a skittle ball, the ground beneath its feet looking a lot less solid than moments ago, clawed rustler feet digging into something rapidly losing viscosity. A few more of them stumbled, still coming forward as Reeves jumped up and turned to run.

"Come on!" he shouted. "Don't hang around!"

Wilsin didn't need telling twice, he'd seen the look of emergency on his face, knew it couldn't mean anything good. Even worse, he smelled something familiar in the air, had a feeling that it wasn't water the Vedo had managed to turn the stone into. Several feet back, Reeves stopped, started rubbing his fingers against his thumb furiously, muttering under his breath, "come on, come on, come on." He tore past him, brought the blaster rifle back up and slapped in his last charge pack. This was going to get nasty real fast if something didn't change. He dared himself a glimpse over the side, could see more of them swarming out the trees. Thousands of them covered the clearing below, rustling their way towards the path. Aroon was running on empty, he could feel warning tugging at the back of his mind. All reserves of energy were bottoming out, the fires were waning.

Losing air support now wouldn't be ideal but they'd be dead already if not for what Aroon had done, once again he pushed the recall button and watched the dragon vanish from sight on the horizon.

"Thank you, my friend," Wilsin muttered. He gave another glance over the side, wondered what had happened to the green king. His throne stood abandoned and alone as the bodies swarmed around it. He had to be somewhere out there. Maybe he'd been killed, although he doubted they'd been that lucky.

The green king had shown remarkable perseverance by not being killed by his and Nick's best efforts months ago, he doubted he'd been killed here. He shook his head, jumped back as Reeves let out a screech of triumph, fire billowing from his fingers, roaring towards the slipping rustlers. It hit the liquid beneath their feet, Wilsin grabbed Reeves' arm and they ran as he heard the sucking sound behind them, heat taking the moment to expand and finally the explosion booming out as the ground caught fire beneath their enemies.

It wouldn't hold them for long, but it'd have to do for the time being. He glanced to the side, saw the colour draining from Reeves' sweat-drenched face. He looked done for, shattered beyond recovery. Wilsin wondered how hard he'd had to push himself since this had started. They needed to survive this, they all needed to pull their weight and Reeves' abilities meant he had a lot more weight he needed pull.

At least he could still put one foot in front of another for now. By the time they caught up with Brendan and Aubemaya, Reeves was gasping for breath, his eyes bloodshot and dazed.

"Don't tell me you broke our Vedo, Agent Wilsin," Brendan said, shaking his head.

Wilsin didn't have chance to reply, the smell of smoke and jungle starting to get to him, the stench filtering through every pore in his skin, thick and cloying in his nostrils. He was starting to get sick of this place. A return to civilisation couldn't come fast enough. Behind them, the fires still burned, he just hoped they'd hold out a bit longer. If those things came through, they'd be screwed. Brendan had Suchiga over his shoulder, would have to drop him to fight. Reeves was spent. Wilsin himself had very little power left in his weapons, nowhere near enough to kill one, never mind them all.

This might have gone better had he not believed the green king would have put them all to death anyway. He knew his name, what he'd done back on Carcaradis Island and for all his promises about letting them live, he didn't trust his word one iota. Fighting to survive had felt like the only option and thankfully, it was one he was good at.

He hoped he'd be good enough. He hoped they'd all be good enough. In the distance, he thought he could hear engines. A glance around revealed nothing, the skies empty of anything but the beating sun bathing them in its rays.

Come on! Hurry up! We can't last much longer out here!

Wilsin tried to push it aside, just focus on getting up to the top of the rock, Reeves at his shoulder, Brendan and Suchiga keeping pace with them. Aubemaya, unhindered, lead the way, her slim legs pumping as she ran like a rabbit, not slowing or hesitating. That would be fatal for all of them.

Chapter Twenty-Three. Cradle to the Grave.

"I always thought Cradle Rock was a myth, an allegory. I believed once it was real, but in truth, just because something existed millennia ago does not mean a trace of it might linger today. So much of the old ways have been lost to us, I fear with the advance of technology and our obsession with the future, we risk losing sight of the past."
Jeremiah Blut.

They hit the top of Cradle Rock, nowhere else to go, and Wilsin couldn't help feeling they'd been cornered. At the peak, he could see that there wasn't much to scream about, a flat area about the size of the average spirit calling arena, bare, hard rock underfoot. He wondered idly if this was where Gilgarus had stood all those years ago when he made that proclamation Fazarn had told them about. Felt like a lifetime ago he'd listened to those words.

Brendan moved towards the centre, lowered Suchiga down gently, a look of concern on his face. The injured Burykian's face twitched, a moan slipped his lips. Couldn't be easy for any of them, Wilsin thought. He wouldn't have liked to have done this with two broken arms, possible other unseen injuries.

"Let me go," Reeves said, wriggling in his grasp. "I'm good, I'm okay." He tried to stand up of his own accord, almost fell and caught himself, the flat of his hand smacking against the stone as his legs gave way. "I can do this."

"Ben, you can barely stand up," Wilsin said. "Think about it." He put a hand on his shoulder, gently held him. "You look like you've hit your limits!"

"Vedo have no limits!"

"Everyone has limits," Wilsin said, keeping his voice calm and soothing. "There's no shame in that. You've fought a good fight, you've kept us alive for so far." He glanced back towards the path, then around the area. Resignation tugged at his heart, he didn't know how long they had before the fires burned out and those things started to swarm them. Up here, they'd be surrounded, couldn't hold them off forever.

They had to try though. Another look to the sky. Nothing.
Come on!

He clenched his fist, felt the bite of his nails in his palm. They had to come. They had to. It had been hours now, surely, they couldn't have been delayed for that long.

Please!

He didn't hold much truck with prayer, he was considering it as a viable option. He didn't have much else. He looked at Suchiga, made his choice. "Ben, I need you to keep Suchiga safe. He can't stand at all, let alone fight. We'll try and keep them away from you, but I need to know you'll get them if any get past us."

Reeves looked like he wanted to argue, Wilsin smiled at him. "Please. You might not be able to do what you want, but you need to do what you can. World would be a better place if there was more of that."

Next thing he knew, he felt something being pressed into his hands, he looked down and saw the shining cylinder of Reeves' kjarnblade. "Take it," Reeves said. "You're going to need all the help you can get."

"I can't," Wilsin said. "It's yours, and I don't know…"

"You push and swing," the Vedo said. "Don't hold the button in. Just push it once to activate it, that end's where the blade comes from." He managed a grin. "Don't get that wrong, whatever you do. It'll be painful otherwise. Probably better than those machetes for the job. Real mystic man's weapon, this."

"Don't you need some sort of special connection to the Kjarn?"

Reeves laughed, almost choked on it, the words coming out in bitter spurts. Blood dribbled down around the corners of his lips. "David, we've all got a special connection to the Kjarn. It calls louder in some than in others, but that doesn't mean that it ignores the rest of you. Go. I'll keep Suchiga safe if it kills me."

Wilsin truly hoped it didn't come to that as he hefted the blade's hilt, testing it. Looking at the way Reeves had handled the weapon, he guessed there'd be very little weight to the energy blade and he'd need to compensate. Of course, Reeves could enhance his movements and his reflexes, an ability he lacked.

He just hoped he didn't make a fool of himself as he watched Reeves limp over to sit down next to Suchiga, he turned and walked to stand with Brendan and Aubemaya. Both had spirit summoners out, he had a feeling it might not be enough.

"We fight, or we die," Brendan said. "We've come too far to go down without a fight. We cannot fall here." His right eye twitched as he spoke. Weird. "We kill them before they kill us. Any spirits you have that can defend, summon them and we will mount a defence. None of them get off the path."

"None of them get off the path," Wilsin echoed. It felt as good a sentiment as any. "We stand and fight here."

"Guys," Aubemaya said. "I flunked spirit combat one-oh-one. I'm not sure what I can do here." Yet still she'd clutched it to her chest, crystals already locked in. Wilsin smiled at her, went to put a reassuring hand on her shoulder.

"It's not always about what you can't do," he said. "It's sometimes about what you can do. If you take even one or two out, it's one or two that can't get to us." He glanced back, saw Reeves crouched next to Suchiga, looking like he was about to fall. "Tell you what. Get behind us. Any get past me or Brendan, you take them. Don't let them get to Reeves or Suchiga."

"I heard that!" Reeves shouted, his voice thick with fatigue. "Don't condescend, David, it doesn't suit you."

"Everyone dying because I didn't have a plan doesn't suit me either," Wilsin shot back. "Have a bit of faith, Ben. I'm doing what I can." He looked at Brendan. "Unless you have a…"

Brendan shrugged. "You've done well this far, David. You didn't get captured. You've been calling the shots. You didn't abandon us. You didn't get us all killed yet. Please, keep going. You're on a roll so far."

"Sir, we need to put up an offensive," he said. "You and me up front, spirits out. We need power and durability. I used up most of my dragon getting this far…"

"And it was the right decision for you did get this far," Brendan said. "Don't have regret, David. That's only for the dead."

"Indeed!"

He was there, Wilsin should have guessed he hadn't been killed yet. The green king strode out of the crowd, imperious in his inscrutability, towering high above his subjects. Long legs moved him gracefully towards them, claws tap-tap-tapping against the stone.

"You had your little temper tantrum, David Wilsin. You showed your hand, you proved that you're an angry little man who just wants to fight. And look where it has gotten you." He threw out an arm. "You're surrounded. Your people are dying. You have no way out and you cannot win. This! This is why I was happy to become something other than human. You people will struggle and fight, rush your own destruction forward for something trifling as the urge to be defiant."

"Just because you turned your back on humanity doesn't make you an expert," Wilsin said. "You were smart once, you still don't see it. You can't quantify humanity, can't stick everyone with the same labels. People will always surprise you. I mean, look at this whole damn mission. I never thought it'd come to this. But these people…" He pointed behind him towards the group. "They've fought and scrapped to survive. More than I'd expect from some of them."

"You'll all die together," the green king said. "That survival bond you talk about, that sense of fighting spirit is not going to save them."

"You don't want to kill them," Wilsin said. "You don't want to kill them at all so stop pretending that you do. They're just a bonus. What you really want is to kill me."

"Interesting," the green king said. "What are you proposing?"

"That you let everyone else get out of this jungle unhindered. You and me, we do what we've got to do and everyone's a winner apart from the poor bastard who dies."

"You assume I wish to kill you, David Wilsin."

"I think you already took a shot at me and failed." It was a lot more defiant than he felt. Belligerence had caused all this mess, he'd crushed the green king's ego by not bowing to him and here they were.

"And you assume that if I wished to take another, I would simply not learn from it? Aim for your head? Your throat? Can that vest take another attack? It's a clever piece of Kjarn working but it is no longer as impervious as you might think."

Wilsin held out his arms, exposed his aching chest to the king, couldn't have moved to defend himself even if wanted to. He could feel his heart pounding away in his chest, every beat sending rivulets of pain dancing through his veins. "I'm right here, if you want to take a shot." His words carried a point within them, one directed straight towards his foe. "You can let them go though. Brendan. Tiana. Ben. Suniro. Just let them walk out of here and back to the boat unhindered. You can do that. It's within your power."

"It is. Perhaps I shall and perhaps I shan't. The pleasure of watching you squirm would whip a thousand donkeys. Your desolation would be delicious. Should I?"

It might have been his imagination, but he was sure the curves at the corners of the had twitched upwards, hinting at the mirth of a grin.

"Beg for their live and I will oblige. Beg and I will drag you down with me, watch as that which forged me crushes you beyond recognition. Beg, David Wilsin, beg and watch it all be lost to you."

Well, Wilsin thought. Fuck that!

He'd not begged before. Ever. He wasn't starting now. More than that, he didn't trust the green king not to go back on what he'd offered, wait until they'd all split up and then cut them to pieces.

"Well, it was a nice thought," he said. "But I'm going to have to decline. Sorry, Jeremiah."

The green king reacted like he'd been slapped, turned to focus the full force of his glare on him. "You do know then."

"I didn't try to kill you, Jeremiah," Wilsin said. "I was not the only one down there. Revenge will not solve anything."

"My message still stands," the green king said. "One of you must remain to deliver it."

"Jeremiah?" Brendan finally asked, the acting-director surprisingly silent throughout. He'd missed their previous exchange, perhaps he'd sought only to listen instead.

"Jeremiah Blut," Wilsin said. "I believe you owe Nick an apology, Brendan. Remember that big investigation you did? Harder to kill than we all thought."

"And so much more now."

"You already said," Wilsin said. "Jerry, it's not happening. Do what you will. You might have given up on humanity, but we're not giving up this fight here. You're going to kill us no matter what we do. I know what sort of man you were then, and I doubt you've changed too much."

The summoner trilled in his hand, not just his but Brendan's in accompaniment, and Wilsin's heart leaped as another sound filled his ears, something he'd almost resigned himself to defeat over. Out here in this little slice of the past, untouched by man or beast before today, the present had caught up. The faintest hint of engines in the distance broke through the afternoon sky and Wilsin had to fight to avoid punching the air.

"Agent Wilsin, copy! Chief King, do you read me? If you hear my call, please respond." The voice was garbled and masculine, hard to make out but definitely shouting for them. Wilsin had never been so jubilant to hear someone calling his name.

"What did you say about no way out?" he asked, savage glee in his voice. "Our ride's here."

He didn't know which thought hit him first, the knowledge that it wasn't going to be easy, fear that Blut would move to try and stop them, or that the distance that split them was still great. Blut roared his anger, the sound more animal than human, he guessed something about killing them and the rustlers were moving again.

Brendan's summoner erupted, twin spirits bursting out of their container crystals. Wilsin saw the humanoid figures taking shape, one formed of steel and one of rock. Brendan's golems. They'd even up the battlefield a little. Golems were hard to fight under normal circumstances, Brendan had the talent for building them, even if it wasn't one he employed as much in recent years. Their torsos were stumpy, misshapen but their limbs powerfully built. He wondered about the irony in the situation given the golems also lacked faces like their opponents. Steel and Stone, he was sure Brendan called them. Not very imaginative names he'd thought.

The golems would give them cover, he dropped to his knees, brought the summoner to his mouth. "This is Wilsin, do you copy me? Over."

"Copy Agent Wilsin. This is Commander Little of the Nadine's Grace, homing in on your position. What the hells is that rock? Over."

"Long story," Wilsin said. "We are pinned down against opposition forces, requesting immediate evac and any sort of air support you can provide. Hurry! Over."

Above him, the golems had charged into the crowd of rustlers, powerful limbs tossing them around like ragdolls. Steel hit out with fists the size of plates, a dozen knife-shaped protrusions rising from their end. Stone did the same with arms that ended in smooth domes, large and heavy. Getting hit by one wouldn't be too smart, those reanimated figures exceptionally strong. Everyone who fought a golem tended to remember it for all the wrong reasons. Where they flung out their limbs, rustlers went down. Not being alive in any sort of conventional sense, the golems would fight on and on until they were destroyed. Wilsin could testify that a well-built golem could take a tremendous amount of punishment and still wouldn't fall. The rustlers were getting their blows in, yet they had little to no effect.

"Negative on the air support, Agent Wilsin. Couldn't get it past Vazaran customs. Blew out of Galina Island the first chance we got under civilian guise. We are on our way. ETA three minutes, over."

"Commander, we could be dead in three minutes!" Wilsin shouted. "Hurry the hells up!" His mood hadn't improved, forgetting the protocol at the end of his bellow. He hoped it might convey his sense of urgency. "We have injured down here, over!"

Commander Little didn't reply, Wilsin fought the urge to kick something. He could see the speck in the distance was getting closer, incoming fast. He just hoped it was fast enough. He pushed his own buttons, brought his own spirits into the fray. Chydarm, the tiverian mammoth hit the ground with a thud, not an ideal spirit in weather like this with all that fur but he could damn well cope for the three minutes. If one of them got lucky and killed him, he liked the idea that ten tons of mammoth would bear down on them as a final act of defiance. The other spirit, a Tarrusian bullhound named Zizou skittered across the stone, barked angrily at the rustlers. The hound was heavy, thick with muscle, ears pointing upwards like horns. In one hand, he gripped his Tebbit. In the other, he held Reeves' kjarnblade.

This was it. Their last stand.

Guys! He chided his spirits, felt their attention turn to him in his mind. Don't get fancy. Just kill. Any of them get past the golems, hit them hard and fast. Especially you, Chydarm. You're the first line. Zizou, any stragglers get past, take them down. Limbs and spines. Get them!

The violence had been instant, rustlers giving up trying to fight Steel and Stone, instead choosing to swarm past them. The golems might be brutally powerful, but they could never be called agile, for every two or three that was taken out by the fling of an arm, ten more got to Chydarm who had the same problem. Trunk and tusks swept out, smash and impale, more than once, Wilsin saw the trunk wrap around one wood-covered body, hurl it into the distance. Just too many of them. Ditto Zizou, the hound snarling amongst them but unlike the others, Zizou didn't have size on his side. Like Scales before him, it was too easy for them to surround him. Brendan had his own blaster pistol out, safety off and aiming into the crowd, Wilsin paused him with a shout.

"Aim low! Put them on the ground!"

Their weapons fired in unison, blaster fire ripping through the air and dropping them one and two at a time. It wouldn't be enough, Wilsin realised, firing again and again, the powerful backlash of the Tebbit reverberating through his arms. Too soon it clicked on dry, the weapon stuttering into silence. He allowed himself a glance to the sky, saw the oncoming ship increasing in size. The aeroship was incoming, an older model but no less rapid. He could see twin outlines on either side of it, something flying in formation with them.

Chydarm and the golems still fought, tried to take them out where they could but the holding action had fallen apart, and they were incoming, swarming the plateau in numbers. Blut had vanished, Wilsin noticed, wasn't surprised. He didn't seem like the type who'd risk going down in a blaze of ignominy.

He'd tossed the machetes to Brendan, hefted the kjarnblade and pushed the activation switch down hard, harder than he needed to. The metal felt slick against his sweaty palms. He hadn't expected the kick as it activated, nearly felt it slip through his grasp. No heat came from the blade, found it heavier than he'd expected, still lighter than the machetes. He gave it a few practice swings, felt it buzz in the air.

"Be careful with that thing," Brendan said, irritation in his voice. "You could cut someone in half."

Wilsin looked at him, then at the oncoming rustlers. "That's the plan."

Zizou howled, the rustlers around him recoiled, sounds of pain exploding from them as steam started to hiss from them, limbs contorting, melting into misshapes, twisted and burnt. Zizou's sweat was toxic, almost acidic, and in this heat, he was burning up. His tongue flopped out of his mouth as he leaped up into the air, tackled another rustler.

Behind him, Tiana had released a sandhound, a formidable fighter under the right circumstances. Wilsin had fought them before. Around the kingdoms, the first spirits a lot of callers got were canine-based. Some moved onto wolves and the like, but dogs had a lot of redeeming qualities. They were loyal, a lot had them as pets growing up, they were easy to manipulate and common enough. There'd been a time in the five kingdoms when stray dogs had been a problem. Not any longer. Give enough people summoners and an overabundance of animals became a problem of the past.

He took another look up to the sky, he saw the aeroship coming in closer and closer. Had to be minutes away. The seconds were ticking by and he could already feel them running out. Their time was slipping away.

Nothing to it but to make more. A group of the rustlers had slipped by Zizou, coming towards him and Brendan. They readied their weapons, he took a sideways glance at Brendan and made the choice. He was younger, faster, stronger, he hoped, and he had a better weapon. He rushed them, blade flashing about in his grip, he had to squint through his eyes to avoid the glare. The first swipe cut one in two, pleasant surprise flooded through him at the lack of resistance. They said kjarnblades could hack through most things with ease, to see it proved true was something else. He took another one down, rammed the blade through a third and slashed upwards, cutting the top half of its body into two neat segments. It felt apart like an orange.

Damn, but he could get used to a weapon like this. Though the weight was more than he'd expected, it handled well, the balance exceptional. Wilsin knew weapons and this was a finely crafted implement of death.

He'd seen what it could do in his own hands, he didn't lack for weapons training, but no wonder they were feared. In the hands of a Vedo, almost supernaturally fast and strong, the average opponent would stand no chance. By comparison, his own efforts were clumsy.

"ETA sixty seconds," Commander Little shouted through his summoner. "You have air support coming in in three, two, one… Light 'em up"

His first thought was what the commander had said they had no weapons, not a surprise if he was honest. The Vazarans had become leery as the hells since their secession. They weren't going to let an armed vehicle into their borders unless they really had to. Then he saw the shapes flying in formation and he understood. From a distance, he hadn't been able to tell. He'd thought they were drones at first.

They were fierbirds.

Not the biggest, but massively potent, he'd seen them in action. Some Unisco pilots flew with their spirits, used them in situations like this to defend their craft from enemy fire. It wasn't a conventional situation, but it'd damn well do. Convention had long since gone out the window, seeing them swoop in, beaks screeching open and the fireballs hitting the ground around them was a welcome sight. Fresh heat erupted through the scene, rustlers thrown everywhere by the blasts, bodies blackened and charred.

Damn, but it was good to see. He didn't know how effective it would be at thinning out their numbers, but the effect was reassuring. Fire always was. Between him, Reeves and Brendan and their combined efforts, it felt like dozens that they'd killed and yet they'd taken the hits, weathered the storm. A couple of fierbirds weren't going to make a damn bit of difference.

Not with that attitude!

He ducked the swipe from one, cut it in two with a slash of his own, the blade sweeping through wooden armour and green flesh, emerald blood burning solid as cauterization took place. The two parts hit the plateau, Wilsin turned to see the huge form of Blut barrelling into him like a runaway mag-rail. He lost his feet, might as well have been insignificant against the power and flew several feet through the air until he met the dirt, coming to an undignified landing. The kjarnblade had been lost somewhere, fallen from his grip. Something hot and wet dripped into his eyes, he could see nothing but red out of one of them. He blinked several times, tried to see around the blood.

"You can't stand against us, David Wilsin!" the green king howled. "You are few and we are many. Even now, we spread across your kingdoms and grow stronger while you weaken yourself with strife and war of your own making."

"I didn't start this war," Wilsin groaned. "She did. We're only trying to win it."

"And doing an admirable job. Fault or blame is not my interest, it does not excuse, and it does not justify. Whoever wins, will lose. I give you the message as a sign of the inevitability of that fact. We cannot be stopped. We cannot be reasoned with or bartered or negotiated. We can only be feared."

"You can shut the hells up!" Wilsin said, drawing the Tebbit, squeezed off two shots into Blut's body before the green tore forward like a rampant bull, scooped him up from the ground in one arm and locked fingers around his throat. He could feel his feet dangling off the ground, calling for gravity to lock them down again, could barely breathe with the giant hand around his throat and face. The green king's skin was like leather and moss, smoothly furred against the stubble on his face. Neither shot had fazed him, a chunk blown out of his shoulder, but it didn't appear to be aggrieving him any. If he felt pain, he wasn't showing it. No blood gushed from either wound, the shoulder one or the gaping chasm ripped out of his breast.

"Maybe I should kill you now. You have a part to play in what lies ahead and having you off the board now could be useful. The price of your existence versus the effect you'll have on the future. A choice indeed."

The kjarnblade snapped to life, Ben Reeves flung himself into the corner of Wilsin's vision, weapon in hand. Too late the green king turned and the next thing Wilsin knew, he'd hit the ground, the grip relaxing around his throat as the severed arm bounced off his stomach. Squeamishness didn't come to him easily, he regardless found the urge to hurl it from him, and he scrambled away from the two combatants. Still Blut had shown no pain, no outward show of discomfort and had pulled a sword from somewhere. It looked like it had been fashioned from dead wood, gnarled and knotted, its colour reminiscent of something struck by lightning. What wasn't up for dispute was its sharpness, Wilsin thought it looked like it could split atoms in the air with just a touch.

Worse, it didn't shatter as it touched the kjarnblade, Reeves thrusting in his weapon to test the green king. The Vedo looked like he could barely stand, legs trembling and Wilsin couldn't see this ending well. Even the normally steady blade trembled in his grasp, Reeves' eyes unfocused, he couldn't tell if he was staring at Blut or the landing aeroship.

Holy hells!

His pains forgotten, Wilsin jumped to his feet, Tebbit in his hands. Reeves might not be in any shape to win. He just hoped he lasted a few moments longer.

Wilsin reached Aubemaya first, her and her sandhound barely inches away from Suchiga as they fought against the waves. She'd found a stick from somewhere... His face lit up into a grin as he realised it wasn't a stick... was waving it about, clumping any of the rustlers approaching her. Beating an opponent with one of their own severed limbs took more balls than he'd ever seen, her sandhound looked terrible. It wagged its tail at him as he approached, he scratched the beast's head, saw Aubemaya raise the limb before the comprehension dawned on her face.

"Help me grab him," Wilsin said, grabbing Suchiga's upper body. Above them, the two fierbirds had circled back around, thrown off another barrage of blasts. Their aim had been good, cleared a good chunk of ground between them and the Nadine's Grace. Wilsin's weapon shouted, tore down the last few as he fired one handed at them, the other supporting Suchiga's weight as his muscles screamed under the stress.

Only twenty feet between them and the ship was doable. Between him and Aubemaya, they hit it in record time, the door already sliding open. Commander Little wasn't alone, two other men aboard, already moving to receive Suchiga. In moments, they had him aboard a stretcher, strapping him in for the journey.

"Get aboard!" Wilsin said, looking at her, not removing his gaze until she'd obliged, he put a hand on her back to help her up. "I'll be back in a second."

Brendan was closing in fast, huffing and puffing as a man his age might in this heat. He wasn't the one Wilsin was looking at though as he ran, that honour went to Reeves and Blut, still duelling though it looked as if there'd only be one winner. Blut moved with the grace and dexterity of a practiced swordsman, Reeves had run a long race and he was coming to the end. Every slash looked slow now, almost laboured as his blade cut a lazy arc through the air, bouncing off Blut's blade. Before, it had been a blur. Now, Wilsin could see it against the afternoon sky, just about read the movements.

He didn't know what he was going to do when he got there, he had no weapon and Blut had already shown himself to be stronger than him. All he knew was something trumped nothing. He wouldn't live with himself if Reeves died saving his life. Already the first shoots of recovery were starting to take place, the green king's arm stump starting to repair itself.

Sometimes, it's not about what you can't do. It's about what you can do. Saying those words to Aubemaya felt so long ago, he never thought that they'd feel so apt. He ran, his boots eating up the last few feet and jumped at the same time he saw Reeves stumble, drop to one knee.

Blut let out a triumphant scream, ready to crash his blade onto the Vedo and it was for that one good arm Wilsin aimed, his fingers meeting forearm, his arms locking around it. The green king was still strong, blade still travelling towards Reeves, but his aim had gone and the sword bit into the ground at his side.

His moment of weakness had come and gone, Reeves rose to his feet and buried his kjarnblade into Blut's chest, the bright blade punching through it like it was nothing, Reeves almost falling forwards into him, blade rammed all the way to the hilt. Blut coughed, the single sign of pain Wilsin had seen so far, a single drop of blood falling from the carved jaws and bounced off Reeves' face.

"Intriguing," the green king said. "I imagined that would hurt. I'd forgotten what pain felt like." No emotion in his voice, just cold, stated fact. A moan escaped him as Reeves withdrew the blade, ducked past him to run. Wilsin needed no invitation to follow, as Blut fell to his knees behind them.

He hoped the wound was fatal, yet he doubted they'd be that lucky.

Brendan awaited them as they hit the aeroship, Reeves almost fell through the doors, the two men had to drag him aboard. Wilsin turned to Brendan, ready to tell him to go first had he not been shoved aboard. Across the plateau, Blut rose to his feet, turning to face them. Wilsin could see the anger across his features, the carvings contorting into fury. His hand was full, his blade lost somewhere on the ground, he pitched his solitary arm back, something flying from his grasp.

Wilsin instinctively ducked down behind the stanchion, saw something hit it with a sharp clunk, metal folding inward under the force. A roar of pain broke out, he almost didn't hear it under the sounds of the engines. Instinct took over, he saw another one sail wide of the mark. The one out the door looked like a wooden knife. He didn't want to think about what would have happened if it had hit him, instead focusing on pulling Brendan aboard. The door slammed shut behind them and he heard the roar of the engines kick into life. Within seconds, they were in the air, rising higher and higher, the plateau of Cradle Rock slowly turning into a dot below them.

He couldn't believe it. He knew he was grinning like a lunatic and he just didn't care. They'd really won a small victory, they'd survived an ordeal like that and he couldn't believe they'd all made it. He felt like his grin would hit his ears if he let it get any wider. Behind him, Reeves had collapsed into a seat, eyes closed and his breathing slowing.

"Don'… Don't wake me up," he murmured, his final words before they slipped into snores. There was plenty of room in the hold, Wilsin thought, looking around. Suchiga was getting some medical attention that looked rudimentary at best but had to be better than nothing. Aubemaya had dropped into a seat next to Reeves, her legs folded up under her chin. She let her head rest against his shoulder, her chest still heaving.

Wilsin's hand drifted to his side, he pushed the 'recall' buttons on his summoner, felt the link between Chydarm and Zizou and himself vanish. They'd cease to exist now, until he next called on them.

He wondered if Brendan had done the same, looked across at him. Their eyes met, and the acting-director's expression turned to sorrow. Wilsin saw the dribbles of blood running out his mouth and his eyes, saw that the straps on the ceiling were the only thing holding Brendan up, legs bent awkwardly beneath him. Even now, he could no longer support himself, his wrist slid out the strap and he dropped, fell forward onto his face.

No!

Two of Blut's wooden knives stood proudly out of his back, blood gushing around them, a sticky puddle forming underneath him. Wilsin was next to him in a heartbeat.

"Damnit, Brendan," he said, sounding a lot calmer than he felt. He could feel the life draining out of Brendan King as he lay bleeding out, killed by another foe none of them could ever understand. "You bloody better not die on me here!"

Defiance would take a man far. This was a step too much for it. Even as Brendan raised his head, neck trembling, Wilsin could see the light going out of his eyes. The final breath slipped out of him, rattling through his lungs, slipping out through teeth.

"David," he wheezed, a cough slipped out and crimson sprayed Wilsin's trousers, fine droplets spattering across him. "Don't let them win, never stop fighting."

"I won't," Wilsin said, meaning to keep it as best he could. He didn't know who the 'them' was, he could take a guess. There were quite a few notable threats out there, he could have meant any of them. "Come on Brendan, you can't die! Hold on! We're a fast ship, we can hit a hospital in no time."

"We all have our time to go," he laughed, his voice cracking. "Never give up. Be the best of us all."

Those were his final words, Wilsin realised as the head of iron grey dropped and didn't rise again. The great man was no more, truly lost to the world. Even the knowledge that his golems were probably already trying to tear Jeremiah Blut to pieces didn't give him much solace. His chest felt heavy, like he'd been ripped open and pieces shredded. Feelings he didn't know existed. Across the recent weeks, he'd felt like he'd gotten to know him, all for naught.

"Divines take you with them," Wilsin said as he stood up. "Father Gilgarus, give this man the respect he deserves, Mother Melarius, treat him with the kindness his actions warranted in life.

Enemy Ferros, spare him your wrath. For all that is just and true, let his rest be the one that he earned. Divines hear me."

It had been years since he'd prayed, since he'd felt the need to ask anything of the Divines. Now though, that moment felt apt and he hoped that they'd listen to him on this once.

"Rest in peace, old bastard," he said, more out of affection than enmity. "Give them hells in the next life as well."

Chapter Twenty-Four. Shock Above the Sands.

"Sir, we have a message from Commander Little of the Nadine's Grace... He got them. Strike Team Alpha-Ten have been pulled out of Vazara. He's also promising us we're not going to believe the story he's got to tell us after."
Unisco mission controller to flight command.

The returning flight across the desert untouched by the Green had been a silent one, Wilsin noticed. None of them had felt like talking, Reeves hadn't woken yet and he wondered if he would. He'd never seen so much exhaustion on the face of one individual, he might get through it and he might not. The sleep would come, it clearly was needed and hopefully the Vedo would make a full recovery. He was surprised, now he thought about it, by how good friends the two of them had become, hadn't seen it coming back at the start of the mission. When they got back to civilisation, he might ask that Reeves become his partner full-time. They made quite a good team. Having a Vedo at your back was undoubtedly a great way to stay alive. He trusted Reeves. Couldn't say that for too many people these days.

Aubemaya had woken up at least, they had to have been flying for hours now. No wonder it had taken Little a while to get here, as swift as the Nadine's Grace flew. He'd gone to the cockpit on arrival, introduced himself to the commander and his two assistants, Tim Welsh and Allen Boyle. Neither of them looked shaken at the way they'd pulled off the rescue. Maybe facing plant things was all in a day's work for them. Wilsin hoped so. It'd make things easier if someone out there had experience of what to expect. After all, he wouldn't have believed it if he hadn't seen it. Those things had been everywhere, he was under no illusions that if Little had shown up, they'd be dead by now.

"What are you thinking about?" Aubemaya asked, cutting into his thoughts. He didn't even know how to respond to that. What else could he be thinking about? Their expedition had been wiped out, only the four of them remained from their original number, Brendan lay dead in the back of the cockpit, a shroud covering his body, and they'd just nearly been murdered by things that shouldn't exist by right. What else could he be thinking about at a time like this?

The look he gave her must have said it all, she held her hands up in apology. "Sorry, sorry. My bad. Stupid question."

"What did they do to you?" Wilsin asked. "When they took you?"

She shrugged her shoulders. "Don't really remember too much of it. They dragged us away through the jungle, eventually picked us up because we were resisting. Suniro kept screaming, he was in horrible pain, Brendan kept trying to fight them, even though they beat him." Wilsin glanced back towards the body. "Tough old bastard, no?"

"The toughest," Wilsin said. He didn't look again. The back part of the ship had been made up into a medical area, Brendan laid in state and Suchiga blissfully under the effects of drugs they'd fed into him. They didn't have much aboard, but they'd made do with what they did have. Such was the Unisco way, it was drummed into them early in their career and Divines help them if they complained. "And then what?"

He saw her hesitate, didn't let up on her. "Come on, Tiana. This could be important. Tell me now." Just enough force laced his words to impose the urgency on her. This entire situation felt messy to him, something not right and he wanted to be sure of the details before he started to explain it to anyone outranking him. That was something they always, always, always encouraged in the academy. Any Unisco agent worth their salt stuck by it.

"They took us to... Was that really Cradle Rock? Looked like it in the pictures, right?" she said. He glanced into her eyes, saw her pull away from his gaze. That was suspicious by itself. The only people who didn't like eye contact were liars and people uncomfortable with human interaction and she'd given no indication to him she'd ever suffered from the latter.

"You'd have had to have asked Fazarn," Wilsin said. "He was the one who loved the stories about them." Or Brendan, he wanted to add. Brendan would have known. "Mythology isn't my strong subject."

"They took us there," she said. "Dragged us to the base of the rock, thousands of them surrounding us, all watching us in silence." She gulped. "Total silence. Couldn't even hear the birds or the bugs. Only sounds were when they moved, that horrible damn rustling."

"Uh-huh." That part he could believe. He'd seen them with his own eyes. Thousands more than they'd been able to effectively deal with. Individually, they weren't unstoppable, but he'd found them tough to beat one-on-one, never mind a thousand-on-one. Fire had turned out effective, he knew that much. Not surprising for something that looked like a walking plant.

"And then the big one stepped out of the crowd. The one who said he was their king."

"Blut," Wilsin said softly. Only a small word but he put real feeling into it. That that son of a bitch should still be alive and at the head of an army was a considerable worry. He'd not been a particularly pleasant man when he was human according to the reports he'd read. When he and Roper had confronted Blut on Carcaradis Island, Roper had thrown him into a portal, offered him up as sacrifice if Wilsin remembered rightly and he wasn't likely to bloody forget it. There'd been a big investigation after it, he should remember the details. Brendan had been part of it. He wondered if the Green King had introduced himself as such to the man charged with investigating his murderer. He doubted it.

"Huh?"

"Jeremiah Blut," Wilsin said. "He was…"

"An academic," she said. "I remember Doctor Fazarn talking about him a lot. He was part of that story, remember? The prophecy."

Wilsin blinked. Hadn't there been a line in there about the Green overcoming? He wasn't sure. He'd slept very little over the last few days, he'd been more than tempted to follow Reeves' lead and curl up in one of the seats, he'd spent more adrenaline in recent hours than the rest of his life put together, it felt. He tried to piece it together, couldn't recall. Something sounded familiar.

"That big green guy was Blut," Wilsin said eventually. "Or so he claimed to me. Be it true or not, I can't say. He knew stuff Blut did." Or someone who'd had access to the Unisco investigation files, he wanted to add. Either option was considerably disturbing.

"How is that possible? Wait, you knew Blut?"

"I met him once," Wilsin said. "Shortly before he disappeared." About five minutes before, if memory served. No point breaching ancient history with Tiana. It was a need-to-know thing, and she didn't. If she had her teachers worship of Blut, it might drive her against him, knowing he'd been involved in what they'd all thought was his death until now. "Thought he was crazier than a sack of cats."

"Genius and madness," Tiana said. "Aren't they supposed to be the same impulses?"

"I don't know, you'd have to ask someone smarter or crazier than me," he smiled at her. "I don't know how it's possible either. What did he say to you?"

"Just that…" She screwed up her face in concentration, he didn't think that she was faking it either. Unisco agents were trained to recall things, pick up on every little detail and store it away for further use. Sometimes that unconscious memory took time to throw things up but there it remained beneath the surface of the mind until something dislodged it.

"Come on Tiana, it's important." He smiled at her, looked at her sat filthy and dishevelled on a seat too big for her, hands resting on her lap. She looked like she'd been through the wars, but still she'd survived, determined they wouldn't break her.

"Something about us being there to bear witness to the future in progress. We were the first living mortals to witness the birth of the Green Kingdom and the first to hear the words of their magnificent king." She made a face. "His words, not mine."

Wilsin nodded, he'd already gotten that impression. Blut had been a grandstander, a believer in his own importance. Maybe he wasn't so difference now than he was before.

"We were to carry back word, tell them all of their might and that they'd soon submit to the Green."

"Huh," Wilsin said. "He gave us the same message. Me and Ben. Wonder if he didn't expect all of us to make it out or something."

"Brendan tried to get him," she said, her face twitching with disgust as the memories came back to her. "He lunged at him, they beat him some more, clubbed him down." Her eyes glistened. "I thought they'd turn on the rest of us when they'd killed him, but they didn't. They just kicked the fight out of him and then stepped back, let him carry on with his speech."

"Anything interesting? Or more of the same?"

"Pretty much. Just that he wasn't interested in fighting both the kingdoms and Coppinger at the same time, that he didn't trust Coppinger anymore... Why would a man like Blut know someone like her?" Wilsin said nothing, just looked at her to continue. "When he'd finished, he added that we were bait, more would come to try and save us. I wondered if he meant the rest of you. Keep in mind, we didn't know what had happened to the camp, who'd made it out of there and who hadn't. I saw some bodies fall, wasn't sure who though. Did anyone else make it or just you and Reeves?"

"Just us," Wilsin said. "I think the three of you were lucky. I wonder why they wanted us all though."

"He said bait."

"Yeah but he already had you to try and deliver the message. Why lure us in as well? Me and Reeves."

"Maybe they tried to kill you and failed the first time and thought they stood a better chance with all of them around you like they did. Or maybe he wanted your autograph."

"I doubt that," Wilsin said.

"Mystery then. All that trouble just to lure you in like you said and then try to kill you."

"I did antagonise him," Wilsin admitted. "Maybe in hindsight, not such a smart idea really."

She shook her head in disbelief. "Clearly. What the hells were you thinking?"

"I don't like bullies," Wilsin said. "I don't like being intimidated."

"Do you like the idea of dying even more?" she asked. "Because that's what could have happened." She didn't sound angry, more upset than anything. Wilsin shook his head, tried to clear it. Not easy, as weary as his body was, his mind wouldn't stop running up and down, thinking of all he'd seen.

"All of us die eventually," he said. "Just a case of when, not if."

"I hear that argument way too often!" she said, he could see her eyes were leaking now. "It doesn't mean that you have to rush it forward! Let something happen in its own time, or have you got a complete death wish?!"

"Where's all this coming from?" he asked, holding his hands up. It felt like a surrender, he didn't know why.

"We all could have died down there, nobody would ever have known what happened to us! Do you know what that would have been like for them?! Our families? Our friends! They'd have missed us, we'd have been cleaning the jungle floor all because you decided you were going to sass an eight-foot tree man."

"Some of us did die down there," Wilsin said, his voice deadly serious. He wasn't justifying himself to her. He made the dangerous decisions, so others didn't have to. "Bryce and Fazarn and Nmecha, Ballard, they're all no longer with us. They're gone! Brendan's gone! One of the best damn men I ever knew! Suchiga might not make it!" He hadn't realised he was shouting until he saw her shrink back in terror, her eyes wide. She looked scared, scared of him, scared of the situation she'd found herself unwillingly involved in.

He couldn't blame her, now he could hear his thoughts above the roar of the blood through his veins, the beating of his heart no longer a constant dull drum inside his head. He relaxed, unclenched fists he hadn't realised he'd made.

"It's natural," he said. "You're in shock, Tiana. It's not something you'll ever have experienced before." This time, he tried to be gentle. "At least, I don't think you have given your reaction. Different people deal with different events in different ways, you know?"

She opened her mouth to speak, he raised a hand to silence her. He wanted her to listen for now, hear what he had to say. "You'll think you can deal with an event like this in the aftermath. The adrenaline is pumping through you. Hells, maybe you'll even feel alive. More alive than you ever have before. Natural elation, there's nothing like it and survival makes it kick in like a mule. You made it. You shouldn't have, but you did. Survived against all odds. Whatever it took, you made it, every inch of your being knows that, and it can't help but celebrate."

He knew she'd felt this. Everyone did. Nothing got the nerves firing on all cylinders like a narrow escape from sudden death. He felt it every time he completed a mission like this, the feeling of invincibility. Wilsin wondered if Brendan had felt it in the moments before the missile had penetrated his back, ruptured his organs, killed him in front of his eyes. Had death come like an orgasm, arrived during the moment of jubilation, only for exhilarating joy to be torn away? At least he'd have died happy.

"Then there's the next part," he said. He reached out, took her hand, smiled at her, looked her in the eyes. Eye contact was important. It built trust, developed bonds, made words seem sincerer with their impact. She'd avoided it before. Maybe she didn't trust him. He couldn't blame her. When you see people you know die, being taken hostage, it all added up for the sort of traumatic experience not many shook off without some sort of fight. "What you're feeling now. Survival comes with a price. Guilt. Sorrow. Regret. All of it hits you at once and it's not a fight you can win right away. You have to let them punch you. You have to let them whale on you. That's the price you pay for survival. You get everything in the aftermath you should have got earlier."

He sighed, let his head sink back against his seat. He'd broken eye contact, but he wasn't bothered. He'd made his point, he'd seen it in her face. "It's like acid on your soul, Tiana. You'll feel like things will never be the same again, and you know what, you'll be right. They won't. The experience makes you grow, it empowers you, changes you for the better if you don't weaken under it." Again, he patted her hand, gave her a weak grin. "We are all human, Tiana. Just human. People like him…" He pointed at Reeves. "They make out they're more. Look at him now. He's fucked himself pushing past his limits."

Reeves snorted in his sleep, almost indignant with the noise. If Wilsin hadn't known better, he'd have sworn it could have been deliberate. "We all try to cope however we can," he said eventually. "You might not agree with what I did, but it can't be changed now. You did what you could…" Not a whole lot, he wanted to add, but it felt like he might destroy his own efforts of trying to bring her around if he did. "And I did what I've been trained to do for a very long time."

"And it might not have been enough," she said simply. "You know that, right? One day, everything you know won't be enough."

"You make it sound like prophecy," Wilsin said, gave her a grin. "Don't do that. I like to take each day as it comes, not worry about tomorrow."

"I noticed," she said. "You carry on the way you're going, you won't reach tomorrow." She smiled though as she said it. "Are all you Unisco guys this reckless?"

"I'm probably pretty calm by standards," Wilsin admitted. "Some of our guys are crazy. Real tickled in the head. None of them were like that when they started either. The job twists people up, I've got to say. Some take longer to crack than others."

She gave him a pointed expression as he said it, he cocked his head to the side and looked at her curiously. "What?"

"How long you reckon you've got left before you do?" she asked. She sounded serious as well, nice of her to ask though, he thought. Assuming he hadn't already, he thought with a smile. An expression she frowned at. "I'm not joking. If it fucks you all up that bad, why do you do it?"

"Someone has to, my dear. Someone needs to stand up and be counted. Always there are the battles to be fought…"

The beeping interrupted him, he glanced up to the closest speaker, realised immediately that it was getting louder, had started off tender and worked its way up the noise scale into something almost deafening. "The hells?" he asked, couldn't hear his own voice above the noise. He turned, made a break for the cockpit, Aubemaya on his heels.

Wilsin broke through the door, saw Little fighting with the controls, the aeroship lurched clumsily to the side and he had to grab hold of the nearest doorframe to support himself. "What the hells is going on, Commander?" he asked, would have demanded the answers to the question had the fight not been knocked out of him by the turbulence kicking them about like a randy mule. "Turbulence?"

"I wish!" Little shouted. "Some sod's shooting at us, just launched a Skysweeper at us!"

Wilsin's immediate reaction was to move to the window, try to peer out and see who had the nerve to do this. Vazaran Sun's maybe, even if they'd already waved the Nadine's Grace through onto their airspace, it didn't mean that they were above taking a few pot shots at them in hope of garnering some retaliation.

Skysweepers, he knew about. They were surface to air missiles, usually launched in barrages of four to try and corner a rapidly moved target, making them evade increasingly desperately until eventually they'd run out of tricks. No pilot could jink back and forth forever, either the efforts of their manoeuvres would get to them and they'd hesitate just long enough to be tagged by a missile, or the exertions would make their ship give up on them just long enough for them to give them the sweet kiss into oblivion. Any pilot he'd spoken to about them hated the bastard things.

"Why's someone shooting Skysweepers in the middle of the desert?" he asked, more wondering aloud than expecting a serious answer. Regardless, he heard a snarl of bitter laughter slip from the commander.

"Son get the hells out and let me work," he said. "I've got this. Go. Get yourselves strapped in. Worst case scenario, we hit the desert with a pretty big bang and I don't mean from the impact."

A sobering thought. Wilsin nodded, bowed his head and turned back towards the exit, Welsh and Boyle moving through the ship to check everything was secured. Little was the pilot, Wilsin thought. He knew what he was doing. Best to just leave him be, get on with it and don't worry about any possible consequences. If they died, they died.

Like he'd said to Tiana, they all had to go at some point. That saying might as well be emblazoned on the Unisco logo, he'd always thought. He wasn't the only one who had that idea, the thought wasn't an original one. He didn't want to go now though, didn't want to die in the middle of the desert, his flesh burned away by the explosion of fire and gas, bones picked clean by the birds and the desert creatures. They had to eat too, it didn't bother him. You couldn't change what you couldn't change, and nothing was more appropriate to that than the circle of life.

He moved over to Reeves where he slept, pulled the straps over his body, gave him a pat on the shoulder, moved it into a shake. "Come on, buddy, might need you to wake up!" The Vedo grunted in his sleep, let his head loll to the side limply, not moving, not stirring. Wilsin swore under his breath. Damn, he was in it deep. "Picked a great time to slip into a trance, Reeves," Wilsin muttered. "Damn you." He toyed with slapping him, wondered if it'd really be the best use of his time. Maybe it'd rouse him. Maybe he'd just snap a hand up and stop his blow without even waking up. He was a Vedo, they could probably do that. It wouldn't be any stranger than the rest of the stuff he'd seen from Reeves over the course of this excursion.

"Running out of time here!" Little shouted. "Can't evade them forever. Impact in five, four, three…" Wilsin was already on the move, sliding into a seat, straps clipped into place across his chest. "Two, one!"

That final number was cut out, lost in the roar as the Nadine's Grace lurched to the side, thrown into a tailspin by the impact of the missile, fire racing across the hull, atoms exploding, ripping through the metal, the entire end section of the ship torn away in an instant. Wilsin threw up an arm, grabbed the nearest support and held on, fingers going white from digging into it.

"We're going down!" Little shouted from the cockpit, Wilsin could already hear him screaming instructions into his radio, then at Welsh and Allen. "Mayday, mayday, this is the Nadine's Grace, currently vectoring out of control at coordinates five zero eight four three, Vazara. Taken heavy fire under the banner of aid, we cannot stay in the air. Requesting emergency assistance asap!"

All he could do was hold on, trust in Little not to kill them all with the landing, hope he hadn't used up all his luck in getting on the ship in the first place. He refused to be killed by a ship crash, not after all he'd survived in the build-up. Aubemaya had her eyes screwed shut, she'd strapped herself in, grabbed against the roof and little sounds of fear were slipping her lips, he could see her teeth pressed together so hard, he was surprised they hadn't shattered.

Come on, come on!

When they hit the ground, they hit it hard, didn't even have time to scream before his head snapped back, pain rushing through him and then the blackness came...

He didn't know how much time had passed, only one thing emblazoned in the forefront of his waking mind.

They hadn't died.

He'd hit his head in the crash, felt it bounce off the metal frame of the wall and now his brain threatened to split open on him, but it was better than the alternative. He let out a moan, felt the sound split through chafed lips as he reached to his safety belt with uneasy hands, fiddled with it until the metal gave underneath his touch. Across the ship, Aubemaya was struggling with her own, deft fingers dancing across the unresponsive metal.

"You okay?" he asked, his voice hoarse. Divines alone knew how long they'd been laid here. He sure as hells didn't. Next to him, Reeves still breathed, still asleep through the whole damn thing, the lucky bastard. Wilsin shook his head. Some ships he'd been on, their pilots made a point of bragging about their reinforced holds, especially designed to hold up in crashes in the interest of preserving what lay inside. In this case, it was them, but it could easily have been products. The trick was backfiring on those captains, hijackers had no qualms about shooting them down if they knew what they were after was going to be spared burning up.

Reinforced holds, fireproof lining, all of it had been employed here by the looks of it. The door had bent open on impact, sand spilling at their feet. They'd hit the ground and sunk in by his guess, he struggled up to his feet, the floor at an angle beneath him and crabbed his way to the hatch, pushing it open all the way. Fresh sand gushed down on him like grainy water, he ignored it and stuck his head out into the open air. Hot sun beat down on him, he squeezed his eyes shut, tried to block it out as he looked away, opening them again just a crack.

Nothing for miles around. Not that he could see anyway.

Fuck!

He withdrew, slid back down into the hold and made for the cockpit. He hadn't heard anything from there, his suspicions confirmed as he got the door open beneath him, applying pressure to the handle to make it turn. The cockpit hadn't survived the crash, had folded in on itself like some sort of twisted sculpture. Little hadn't made it, he realised immediately he couldn't have. Even a professional contortionist wouldn't have survived being crushed that way.

Damnit, damnit, damnit!

He didn't blame himself, he couldn't have seen this coming. Whoever had fired the missile was at fault, yet he'd brought Little and his men out here. This was partly his mess, there was no denying that.

"Rest in peace, gentlemen," he said. Allen and Boyle had to have been in there as well, he'd not seen any sign of them in the hold. "May the Divines have mercy upon you."

"They're dead, aren't they?" Aubemaya said as he shut the door. He couldn't meet her eyes, only nodded in agreement. She'd gotten out of her seat, had slid down to squat next to the sleeping Vedo.

"Decidedly," he said. "We have to wake Reeves up, work out a plan. We can't stay here, or we'll die. Best case scenario I think, we'll get on Aroon and fly until we hit civilisation. Need to be careful though, we don't know where that missile came from and..."

He paused, shocked into silence by the sounds of blaster fire outside, he tensed up, swore to himself. Somehow, he got the impression that the question had just been answered. Beyond the shooting, he could hear engines. Speeders if he wasn't mistaken, maybe some speeder bikes.

"Try and wake him up," he said. "I'll go see what's happening out there."

"If you go out there, they'll kill you," she said. "They've already taken shots at you."

He gave her a grin. "Maybe they just want whatever they think's aboard. They might let us go on our way if they see nothing of value." He sounded halfway convincing, he thought, wished convincing himself was as easy. If there were only a few of them, he might get lucky. If there were many, and he could identify at least four different engines, it might be a hopeless task.

He had to try though. "Relax, Tiana. I'll be fine. I took a negotiating class at Unisco. I was deemed acceptable at it." He gave her an even larger grin. "I should have failed the hells out of it though, I convinced them to give me a passing grade. That's how good I am." Not entirely true. Anything to put her mind at ease. "Everyone wants something, it's just a case of finding out what." Time to hope that what they didn't want was everyone aboard dead and looted. There'd be little he could do if that were the case.

Pushing his body through the hatch and landing on the sands, he glanced around the scene in front of him and his heart fell. He'd made an estimate of scenarios and he'd aimed too low. There weren't four. Maybe closer to fourteen, at least, that he could see, bikes whizzing around, speeders armed with cannons coming to a halt less than a dozen feet from the fallen Nadine's Grace. Each of them had a full complement of passengers, at least four to a cab and each of them had blaster rifles. A damn near army right in front of him and not a lot he could do about it.

Oh shit!

"What can I do for you guys?" he asked, giving them a rueful shrug. "We've got nothing valuable aboard. Sorry. You're welcome to come look, but this is a peaceful flight to…"

"Shut up!"

A solitary figure had climbed up onto the hood of the lead speeder, long haired, dark skinned and with a scar across one milky-white eye. Wilsin would have marked him down as their leader in an instant, he wore better clothes than the rest of them, nor did he have a weapon in his hands. He didn't need to, with all the firepower at his back, though a blaster pistol did stick out the waistband of his pants.

"Gauvin LePonq at your service," the one-eyed man said with a grin. "And as of now, you're all the prisoners of the great warlord Alicolici, ruler of the sands and chief defiant of the Vazaran Suns." He pointed his blaster at him, drew it in a flash. "You can run and die, or you can stay and surrender. A choice it is, but one I advise you to make swiftly. What the lost prince doesn't have, he won't miss."

Wilsin stuck his hands up in surrender. No point in a meaningless death. Defiance was all well and good, he'd never got the impression Blut wanted him dead. These guys though, they were a known quantity. He could read them, and he knew fighting would only end badly. They had all the cards here.

Following his lead, Aubemaya stuck her head out the hold and did the same. He hoped that Reeves was up on his feet, and if he was, nothing stupid was going to come out of him. Stupidity would get them killed for sure, if they lived then they could fight another day…

The End
For now.
But the story continues in…

Divine Born.
The Spirit Callers Saga #5

Coming Soon.

A Note from the Author.

Thank you for the time spent reading this book, taking the time to spend your days in this world I created. I hope that you enjoyed reading it just as much as I did when I wrote it. Just a quick note, if you did, please, please, please leave a review on Amazon for me. Even if it's just two words, it can make a lot of difference for an independent author like me.

Eternal thanks in advance. If you enjoyed this one, why not check out other books I've written available at Amazon.

If you wish to be notified about upcoming works, and even get a free short story from the Spirit Callers Saga starring Wade and Ruud some twenty-five years ago, sign up to my mailing list at http://eepurl.com/dDQEDn

Thanks again. Without readers, writers are nothing. You guys are incredible.

OJ.

Just another quick note. Special thanks to everyone involved in helping put this book in front of you from my cover designer to my beta reader for the series, Ethan DeJonge, to the people who tolerate me on Twitter and Facebook.

Also, by the Author.

The Spirit Callers Saga.

Wild Card. – Out Now
Outlaw Complex. – Out Now
Revolution's Fire. – Out Now
Innocence Lost. – Out Now
Divine Born. – Coming Soon
Paradise Shattered. – Coming Soon

Tales of the Spirit Callers Saga.

Appropriate Force. – Out Now.
Kjarn Plague. – Coming 2018

The Novisarium.

God of Lions – Coming soon
Blessed Bullets – Coming soon

About the Author.

Born in 1990 in Wakefield, OJ Lowe always knew that one day he'd want to become a writer. He tried lots of other things, including being a student, being unemployed, being a salesman and working in the fashion industry. None of them really replaced that urge in his heart, so a writer he became and after several false starts, The Great Game was published although it has recently been re-released as three smaller books, Wild Card, Outlaw Complex and Revolution's Fire, now officially the first three books in the Spirit Callers Saga, a planned epic of some sixteen books. He remains to be found typing away at a laptop in Yorkshire, moving closer every day to making childhood dreams a reality.

He can be found on Twitter at @OJLowe_Author.

Printed in Poland
by Amazon Fulfillment
Poland Sp. z o.o., Wrocław